Re
Murder

Remember Murder

Linda Ladd

KENSINGTON
Kensington Publishing Corp.
www.kensingtonbooks.com

KENSINGTON BOOKS are published by

Kensington Publishing Corp.
119 West 40th Street
New York, NY 10018

First electronic edition: June 2013

ISBN-13: 978-1-60183-050-0
ISBN-10: 1-60183-050-5

First print edition: June 2013

ISBN-13: 978-1-60183-211-5
ISBN-10: 1-60183-211-7

Printed in the United States of America

Prologue

Jesse's Girl

The night of the accident

Choking, coughing, gasping for air, all he could hear at first was the blood pounding deep inside his ears. Groggy, he didn't know where he was. Somewhere far away was a raucous wail of screaming sirens. Soaking wet, shivering from cold and shock, he crawled out of the water and laid his cheek on the slick muddy bank, half in and half out of the rushing river, blood streaming down his face and stinging his eyes. Somehow, he knew he had to keep going. He was in bad trouble. One arm felt so numb that he couldn't feel his fingers, felt like it was broken, hurt somehow, but he could move it. He couldn't quite think clearly. He needed to find help. Yeah, that's right, he had to get help.

Oh, God, where was he? All he could see in the dark night were towering trees and thick, impenetrable undergrowth. It was windy, tossing the tops of the trees around and making him shiver uncontrollably. With all his strength, he forced himself to his feet. There had to be a path, a road, a house, something somewhere in these woods. He sank to his knees, legs still shaky, trying to cage his racing mind, to remember what had happened to him, but he was woozy and weak and felt sick to his stomach. The darkness around him was ominous, with wind and sirens and the strident buzz of night insects.

Tired, confused, he just rested there on his hands and knees, struggling to breathe normally. Then he pushed up again and braced both his palms against a giant oak tree, debating which way to go, what to do, and what had happened to him. Finally, the cacophony inside his head slowed to a low, painful roar and he began to remember. There had been a crash, he thought blearily, yes, that was it. His car had plunged into a river; he had barely fought his way back up to the surface and escaped with his life.

Sucking in the humid night air, he forced himself to forge ahead, through the clinging bushes and dead leaves carpeting the ground. The distant sirens suddenly stopped, one after another. The night was dead quiet then, but it was beginning to rain. He could hear the patter of drops striking the leaves above him. Exhausted, he dragged himself along, cradling his injured arm against his chest and pressing his other palm against the bleeding wound on his forehead. When he found a path, he eventually broke out of the clinging vegetation and onto a wide grassy yard. Right there, he went down to the ground again, spent, but relieved he was no longer alone in the deep woods. The lights were on in the old farmhouse up on the hill. Someone was at home, thank God. And now, he was beginning to remember everything that happened. Annie, oh, Annie, where are you? He burst into tears, heaving great, wracking sobs for a few minutes.

Unable to stop crying, he climbed his way up to the house and collapsed wearily at the bottom of the porch steps. He rested there a moment and tried to control his grief over Annie's drowning. Annie was his girl. She'd always been his, and his alone. How could he live without her? Finally, still weeping, he crawled all the way up the steps. The window in the door sent a square of yellow light cascading over him, and he could see the blood on his hands. It was still oozing down his face. Fighting weakness and a woozy mind, he banged one fist on the screen door and then let himself lie there, facedown and filthy, too wrung out to lift his head. A few moments later, the overhead porch light came on. An old woman opened the door and found him prostrate on her doorstep.

"Oh, my word, young man. What's happened to you?"

With effort, he sat up. "I crashed my car into the river, I think. Please help me. Please."

"Why, of course, I will. Here now, can you stand up? Lean on me, you poor thing."

He did that, leaning heavily on her shoulder. Inside the house, it looked like a photograph out of the 1950s or 1960s. Where in the world was he? The small living room's wallpaper was a pattern of big red and purple roses on a yellow background, all faded to dusty pastel hues. He picked up the distinct odor of mothballs and lemon floor wax and maybe the old lady's powdery-scented perfume. He leaned on her frail frame, thinking she was too elderly and vulnerable to let a stranger like him into her house, that she shouldn't open her door to men she didn't know. But thank goodness she was so trusting. She helped him bodily into her small kitchen and lowered him into a red vinyl chair at an old-fashioned dining table with aluminum legs. The top was covered by a red-checkered plastic tablecloth. There was a yellow lazy Susan in the middle with ceramic salt and pepper shakers made like pink pigs and a plastic napkin holder in the shape of a yellow daisy. There was a white apron with a bib and long ties lying over the chair beside him. He felt like he was in Auntie Em's house in *The Wizard of Oz*, and Judy Garland would come downstairs any minute with that little dog of hers. He couldn't remember its name, though.

"Thank you so much for helping me," he managed to get out in a voice that wavered and sounded unfamiliar. Truth was, though, he did feel a little bit stronger.

"Now, now, don't you worry yourself about that, honey. It's not often I get company out this a way. It's real good to hear another voice inside this house."

"You live out here all alone, ma'am?"

"Oh, yes, 'fraid so. Ever since my darlin' Harry died, God rest his precious soul." She walked across the kitchen and retrieved a clean white dish towel from a drawer and wet it at the old avocado-green sink. He glanced around the kitchen. All her appliances were avocado green. She returned with the dishcloth. "Here, child, press this against that gash on your head. It's bleeding all over you." He winced as she fingered the wound. "It really don't look all that bad. I think we can bind it up a mite and not have to run to the emergency room. It costs so much now that it's a wonder anybody goes there."

The towel she handed to him was thin and worn from many years of use. It had little yellow-and-white daisies hand-embroidered along one edge. He mopped some of the blood off his face and then pressed it to his wound. "Do you have a telephone, ma'am? Maybe we could call an ambulance or a taxi to come get me. Maybe I should go to the hospital. I don't feel so good."

"I gave up the phone service nigh ten years past. Had to, livin' on my husband's social security, and whatnot. Don't have nobody to call anyways. Everybody I ever loved has up and died on me. What's your name, hon?" She turned away and opened a high cabinet over the stove. He watched her get out a brown bottle of iodine, debating what he should say. One thing he did remember was that he sure couldn't tell her his real name. Unh-uh. He attempted to come up with a good one, and picked one out of the air.

"Jesse Jordan," he told her, liking the sound of it. "What's yours, ma'am?"

"I'm Mrs. Rosalee Filamount, but my family always called me Miss Rosie. So did Harry, God rest him."

"That sure is a pretty name, Miss Rosie." Jesse looked at the dated stove and fridge and large counter microwave and old-fashioned light fixtures. "Miss Rosie, surely you've got some kind of kin around here that helps you out when you need something. You're not all alone in the world, are you?"

"I do fine here all by myself, thank you very much. Lost my only son in the last war and then lost my little sis two years back. Sissy had colon cancer. She was the last of my family to go on to be with Our Lord. I got her old Caprice out in the barn for when I need to run into town. I can take you in there, once we get you all fixed up and feelin' better. I need to take a grocery run, anyhow." Miss Rosie smiled, revealing a set of ultra-white perfect dentures. Stepping up close in front of him, she refolded the towel and pressed it down on the open wound to stop the bleeding and then applied the medicine. He groaned at the terrible sting when she splashed it on the gash. "Pretty good knock you got there, Jesse, but it'll heal up just fine now that we got it doctored. You hurtin' anywhere else?"

"No, ma'am, I don't think so. My arm's real sore, but I think it's just bruised up pretty bad. I can move it okay now. I guess I'm just pretty shook up." He gave a little laugh that sounded nervous, but his eyes never left her, considering her now, watching. "Sure do owe you a lot, ma'am, Miss Rosie. You've been awful good to me."

"Well, don't mention it, boy. You know, I think every time you help somebody in need, or in trouble, you get a precious jewel in your heavenly crown, don't you, Jesse?"

"Sure do, Miss Rosie. My mama used to tell me that very same thing."

"Well, you listen to your mama. Mamas usually know what they're talkin' 'bout. Is she still livin' amongst us?"

"Oh, no, she's long dead, fell down some stairs and died. But she was really beautiful and kind and took good care of me."

"Oh, my, I'm so sorry. And you still so young, and all. Well, God bless her soul." Miss Rosie rested one palm sympathetically on his shoulder. "You're needin' some aspirin, I reckon. Headache botherin' you?"

"Oh, yes, ma'am, I've got a headache you just wouldn't believe."

Watching her fetch the Bayer aspirin bottle from the same cabinet, he sighed heavily, because now everything was coming back. The hazy confusion inside his brain evaporated and all was clear. He watched Miss Rosie take an old A&W root beer mug off a shelf over the sink. He pressed both hands on the table and stood up. Then he picked up the apron with the long strings and quietly moved up very close behind the old woman where she stood facing the sink. Miss Rosie sensed him and turned quickly. "Oh, dear me, you shouldn't be up on your feet so soon. You might fall."

When he looped the apron tie around her neck and started twisting it tighter and tighter, so tight that her faded blue eyes bulged slightly, she didn't even struggle much at all, just stared up at him patiently, as if she was ready to die and welcomed it. As if Jesse were doing her a favor. Sending her to heaven wearing her heavenly crown with all those jewels in it. It didn't take but a few moments for her face to turn eggplant purple and tiny vessels to start breaking blood red in the whites of her eyes. Strands of her thin snow-white hair straggled out of the tight bun at the nape of her neck and fell down over his hands, longer than he'd figured it was, reaching all the way to her waist.

Her death throes gave Jesse a sort of supreme pleasure, sexually and spiritually, just watching her give up the ghost. Because that's what she really wanted. That's why God had led him straight to her house, why she'd let him in her door, so he could kill her and let her join dear Harry Filamount high up in the heavenly clouds. He began to lick her face as she died. He had a friend in the mental ward at the hospital named Bones Fitch, who taught him how to use his tongue like a dog does. It sharpened the senses, made him able to enjoy all the pain and fear and desperation. Now he always licked people when he got the chance; that's how he got to know them better.

Miss Rosie succumbed to death a lot more quietly than he liked, and more easily than the other people he'd strangled. Poor old lady. She really didn't deserve this kind of ending to such a long and happy life. And he liked old people like her. But he'd make it up to her. He'd take her head along with him when he left. His mama would like that a lot, a new friend to talk to, and he'd introduce them as soon as he dug up Mama's grave and got her head back.

After Miss Rosie went totally limp, Jesse licked the rest of the tears off her face and found she tasted like Cover Girl face powder. He liked the taste of that. His mama had worn face powder before his daddy killed her. He laid Miss Rosie's birdlike little body on the kitchen's yellow and red and blue rag rug and then he checked out all the drawers for a meat cleaver. He was sure Miss Rosie had one. All country people kept sharp, well-honed meat cleavers to cut off chickens' heads, and stuff. Everything was going to be all right now. He was doctored up, free from his troubles, and not hurt badly enough to ruin his plans. But his tears soon welled and rolled down his cheeks again because he'd lost his sweet Annie in the river. All the plans he'd made while in the hospital were gone now. He would never get to take her away, never live happily ever after with her.

But maybe he could find Annie's body. Steal it, like he was gonna steal his mama's. Oh, yes, that would work out really fine. Just when things looked really bad for his future, Mrs. Filamount opened her door and gave him her house and car and a nice quiet place to figure out where Annie's body was. Things were really looking up now. Cleaver in hand, he took hold of the old lady's hair and dragged her down the hall in search of a bathtub. He couldn't bloody up her nice, clean, and tidy house, now could he? Not after she'd been so nice to him.

Chapter One

I wasn't sure where I was. I wasn't sure who I was. I didn't care. It was all misty gray and cool and ephemeral, like drifting inside the loveliest, quietest cloud ever created. I was just floating around, softly, swaying gently, and I liked it. It was peaceful and calm, no noise, no bother, no fear. I realized that I was anchored to the ground, some-where far, far below, at the other end of a shiny silver tether that slipped down through the clouds mounding like giant, fluffy cotton below me. That didn't matter. I didn't want to think about it. I just wanted to be very still and enjoy the soft rocking motions of the gentle breezes. I wanted the clouds to take me higher, up very high, up into the bright white light making the clouds glow above me. It beckoned to me, but I couldn't seem to make myself loosen the silver cord holding me in place so I could float up to that beautiful place.

I shut my eyes and knew nothing more until a man's voice awoke me. It was deep and husky and sounded scared and insistent and determined. I didn't like it, but the voice was familiar somehow, and somehow I knew I had to listen.

"Come on, baby, I know you can hear me. I know you can. You can come back. Just try, try to open your eyes, try to follow my voice back." Then the voice melted away and there was a strangled sound, and I saw a face materialize inside my mind, with blue eyes and black hair, but I didn't really recognize it. I ignored it then and let the rocking lull me to sleep again.

The voice came often and made me weary of listening because

I liked the quiet. And then other voices came, not as often as the blue-eyed face, but enough to disrupt my peace and wake me up.

"It's me, Claire, Bud. C'mon, please don't do this to us. The doctors say you can recover, if you'll just wake up. You're in a coma, that's the problem. You gotta wake up to get well. Charlie's here, too. We're all here."

That voice didn't even sound familiar. Neither did the ones that came after his. I slept again, wishing they would just leave me alone and give me the tranquility I wanted. But they didn't, they wouldn't stop, and the voices seemed to go on night and day and forever.

"It's Black, Claire. Listen to me, listen, damn it. You can do this. Everybody's been here to see you. It's okay to wake up. I've got you back home now, and I'm not going anywhere until you open your eyes. You'll be all right. It's over. I've got the best doctors in the world on your case. You're healing just fine. All you have to do is come back to me. You've got to come back. Just do it. Do it, Claire."

I slept some more. The voice would not stop. Now it was reading to me. Shut up and go away, I thought. Leave me alone. That same face loomed in my mind, and he looked vaguely familiar now, but I still didn't know him. I didn't want to know him.

His voice seemed always to be there, always talking to me. "The sheriff needs you, Claire. You love being a detective, remember? You're good at it. You've put lots of criminals behind bars. You got them, all of them. They're never going to kill anybody again. Charlie needs you back on the job. I need you back."

Then a long time later, another voice came in to wake me, slow and drawling. "Listen here, Claire Morgan, this's Joe McKay. What you tryin' to pull doin' something like this? Scarin' us all to death. You get your pretty little butt back here and outta this bed. Lizzie's here with me. She wants to say hi, too."

The more I heard the voices, the closer they seemed. They were dragging me down through the lovely clouds, down to wherever the silver rope was anchored, and I didn't want to go down there. I wanted them to stop. I wanted to stay here in the soft silence so I resisted and tried to arrest the descent and shut my ears and not listen. Why wouldn't they just leave me alone?

Then I heard the voice of a child, very indistinct and far away. Nothing more than a whisper. "Me and Jules is sad you're sick."

A vision erupted inside me, a little blond boy with chubby cheeks and chubby arms and a fishing pole with a little perch hanging on the hook. I didn't know his name, but I knew he needed me. I haven't seen him in so long. I gotta go back and find him. I left him somewhere, but I don't know where. I've got to find him. He'll be scared without me. I know he will.

Somehow I raised myself from that lovely, dreamy, pearly-white, peaceful bed and took hold of the silver rope. I began to pull myself down, hand over hand, down, down, listening for the little child's voice until the other voices came closer and closer. The one named Black, who pestered me so relentlessly, said, "Oh, thank God, she's coming to. She's trying to wake up."

I stopped there for a while, afraid, because the voices were now so near. Then finally, at long last, when they were quiet, I felt ready to face them. I opened my eyes to darkness, but shut them tight again, terror engulfing me. I tried to climb back up into the clouds, but now the lovely silence was gone, and the most terrible dreams came at me like monsters in the night. Then I heard a different voice, a terrible whispering voice, telling me something about an old warehouse on a river, telling me that we were finally together there, that we'd almost gotten away. And then a vision came in a rush, and I was tied to a chair, in a circle with other people, and someone was making the people shoot each other. Oh, God, please, help me. A man stood up and came toward me. He had a meat cleaver in his hand. He was going to kill me, but instead he turned to the man beside him and swung the cleaver hard. I fought desperately against the tape holding me, cringing back against the chair as he approached me with the bloody meat cleaver.

Panting, terrified, trembling in every nerve and fiber of her body, Claire Morgan opened her eyes. She was fully awake now, instantly cognizant of her surroundings. She was in a hospital bed in a dimly lit room that she'd never seen before. She tried to move, but both her wrists were bound to the bed railings! Oh, God, oh, God. Then she saw the big man sitting in a chair drawn up beside her. He was asleep, reading glasses still perched on his nose, an open manila folder in his lap. She didn't know who he was. Was it the man in her dream, the one with the meat cleaver? Did he have her captive again?

Frantic to flee him and the dark room, she pulled and jerked on the bindings and realized that he'd put all kinds of tubes and wires on her arms and chest, ones that led to IV bags on a rolling stand. What was he doing to her? Drugging her? Horrified, she struggled harder against the cloth bed restraints. When alarms on the heart monitor beside her shattered the quiet with buzzes and bells, the guy in the chair jumped up and leaned over her. Her captor grabbed her shoulders and tried to stop her attempts to get out of the bed.

"Claire, oh, thank God. Listen to me, listen, you're okay. Nobody's going to hurt you. You probably had a bad dream. Calm down, I'm here. I'm right here." Then his arms were around her, and he was holding her up tightly against his chest. He held her there, and she wanted to be free. She didn't know him!

"Let me go, let go!"

Her voice came out hoarse and raspy, her mouth dry and parched. She could barely speak. Where was the meat cleaver? Was he going to kill her? A nurse in blue scrubs suddenly ran into the room and to her bedside. She began to adjust the machines. "Oh, my God, Nick! She's awake!"

The man let go of her, but he kept his face down very close to hers. Cringing and pushing away from him, she felt his hand on her brow, very gentle. She tensed all over. Then she realized that this Nick guy was the man with black hair and pale blue eyes. She could see his eyes shining in the dim light. His voice was deep, very low and soothing when he spoke again. "It's me, Claire. Nicholas Black. Do you remember me?"

"No, no, I don't! Why is it so dark? Why am I tied up?"

"Ssh, baby, don't fight me like this. I'm taking the bed restraints off right now. See, I'm untying them." He continued to talk to her in that same soft, reassuring tone. Now his voice was beginning to sound vaguely familiar, like the one who talked to her so often. Now he was speaking to the nurse. "Monica, quick, turn on the lights, all of them."

The man, Nick, was holding her left hand now between both of his, trying hard to calm her fears. Her heart raced; she didn't understand any of this. "You've been dreaming a lot, sweetheart, having some pretty bad nightmares. You've been thrashing around, fighting against something. I was afraid you'd hurt yourself so I ordered the restraints. See, they're off now. Nobody's going to hurt you or tie you up again."

As soon as the ties came off, she scooted back away from him as far as she could get. Confused, very weak, she pulled a pillow in front of her, a pitiful barrier against him, trying to understand what was going on. She had to calm down, she knew that, but her heart was thudding so hard that her body shook with each beat. Inhaling deep breaths, she managed to calm down a little bit, but it took a while. Her voice came out hoarse and trembling. "Tell me where I am. What is this place? What's wrong with me?"

"You're okay now. You were hurt in a car accident. You've got a serious head injury. You've been lying here in a coma for a long time."

"I don't remember that," she said, and then added with renewed horror, "I don't remember anything."

"You will, I promise. It's going to take time, that's all." The Nick guy smiled down at her. "How do you feel, babe? Do you want anything—a drink of water, anything at all?"

Claire shook her head and tried desperately to remain calm, and didn't quite make it. "Just tell me where I am!"

"We're at Cedar Bend Lodge. That's where we live. Please, Claire, please just lie back and keep calm. Nobody here is going to hurt you, I swear to God."

Staring up at him, she didn't know what to say. She didn't have a clue to who she was; she didn't know if she could trust what he was saying. She'd never seen him before and never heard of any place called Cedar Bend Lodge. She felt sick to her stomach, like she was going to throw up. Bewildered and mind muddled, she tried desperately to relax her rigid muscles and lie still. Her heart still thundered. "Tell me who you are. Tell me why I'm here."

"First things first, Claire. You're completely safe, that's the most important thing for you to remember right now. And you've got to trust me. I'm a doctor, your doctor. I've been taking care of you right here in this room since a few days after the accident. What you're experiencing right now is called retrograde amnesia. It's completely to be expected after a head injury like yours." He stopped then, took his own deep breath, and looked upset. "Just don't worry. Trust me, just for now, and I promise you that your memory will come back. The most important thing at the moment is for you to remain calm and quiet and let me take care of you."

Not sure yet whether she could believe him, she did lie still and listen to what he said. She just felt so weak and queasy inside her stomach. She kept the pillow between her and him as he picked up her hand and took her pulse. Then he asked her to remove the pillow so he could listen to her heart. She did, but she didn't want to. He put a stethoscope inside the neck of her hospital gown and listened to her heartbeat and then wrapped a blood pressure cuff around her arm. Then he nodded at the nurse and they started unhooking all the tubes and wires attached to her body. He smiled the entire time. So did the nurse. Claire frowned.

But she did feel more in control, now that the lights were on. She was inside a normal, regular bedroom, a very nice one, large and spacious with beautiful furnishings, not a hospital room. There were no people tied to chairs and nobody held a gun on anybody. Nicholas Black said he was a doctor and he acted like a doctor, and he wasn't going to chop off anything on her person with a meat cleaver so her first wave of panic receded. She watched him pick up a plastic pitcher and give it to her. Her hands were still trembling so much that she had to hold it between her palms, but she took a little sip through the straw. She didn't look at him again, trying to get her thoughts and emotions in order. She still felt uneasy, as if she was in danger from these people.

When she looked up at Nicholas Black again, he was still standing close beside the bed, smiling as if he was very happy to see her awake. "Do you mind if I ask you some questions, Claire?"

Claire? Yes, that was her name. Or was it? She nodded. Something was off with that name, Claire. It didn't ring the right bells. Panic began to well up inside her again, but she mentally forced it back down. She felt mixed up and ill and afraid. But he was trying to help her remember, she knew that, and she wanted to believe that. "I'm not sure if that's my name, or not, doctor."

The tall, dark-haired doctor smiled. "You don't remember your name?"

Something jabbed through the wall of darkness erected inside her head. "You called me Claire, but I'm not so sure about that." Another glimpse came through, thank God. "A name just came to me. Annie, I remember the name Annie." She grimaced, trying to force up more about it. "No, wait, it is Claire. Claire Morgan, I think. Tell me what happened again. I still don't understand what happened to me."

"Your name is Claire Morgan, and it's a very good sign that you remember that. The car you were in went off a bridge into a river, and on impact, you hit your head on the windshield. You've been lying here in a coma for going on three weeks. Eighteen days, to be exact. Do you remember what state you live in?"

Now her mind seemed to be reacting, more things coming back, fuzzy, fleeting, but they were definitely trying to break out of the dark fog. "California. Los Angeles." She thought hard for a few seconds and recalled something else. "I'm a detective. LAPD."

The doctor and the nurse exchanged a quick but significant look that pretty much told her that she'd screwed up that answer. Somehow that scared her, and she shut her eyes to block the uncertainty out. She didn't want to talk to them anymore, didn't want to listen to the questions he was asking, or anything else he said. She wanted them to leave her alone, and let her figure out things on her own.

His deep voice came back, down close beside her ear, and then to her shock, he kissed her cheek. "That's okay, Claire. You just rest. We'll talk later. And in a little while, when you feel stronger, we'll see if you can eat something, and then we'll get you up and walking."

The unknown doctor named Nicholas Black sat back down in the chair beside her, and the nurse named Monica glided out of the room with the kind of silent footfalls that only nurses commanded. Claire Morgan kept her eyes tightly closed after that, and tried to remember who the hell she was and what kind of life she'd had before she'd gone off that bridge and ended up tied to a bed.

Chapter Two

I felt myself being dragged on the ground by the hood of my parka. I couldn't move my muscles; my arms and legs felt frozen. I heard a latch click and felt somebody rolling me over into a long glass aquarium tank. I tried to see through the glass, but it was too dirty. I couldn't think straight. What was wrong with me? Desperately, I tried to shake myself awake and make sense of what was going on. I shifted my head and realized the side of my face was resting on a soft white padding. Cobwebs. Oh, God.

I struggled as hard as I could to move my limbs, but they felt like deadweights. Above me there were holes in the glass top. I couldn't see anything around me, but I was afraid something was in the case with me. Someone was above me, looking down through the glass. I couldn't reach my weapon. I had to get out. I had to escape, and I saw something come through the hole and bounce on my chest. Oh, my God, what was it? I had to get it off. I had to get it off!

Abruptly, Claire came awake, clawing at the air, trying to fight her way out of that awful glass coffin, yelling, and hysterical, but gentle hands caught hers and held them together. The doctor was there, leaning down close, whispering quiet words.

"It's just a dream, Claire, that's all. A bad dream. Everything's all right. I'm right here. I'm not going to let anybody hurt you."

It took her a while to believe that, and as he dabbed the sweat off her forehead, she kept quivering, trying to recall more, but she couldn't. All she could remember was the fear, the horror, and the realization that something terrible was going to happen to her.

"Ssh, sweetheart. It's just a nightmare. Your mind's protecting you from some bad memories, but your subconscious lets some of them come through. You're safe. I'm going to give you a shot right now that will help you go back to sleep without dreaming." She felt the prick of the needle and welcomed it. "I'll stay right here with you, Claire. Right here. I'm not going anywhere, I promise you."

Claire couldn't stop shaking, and couldn't understand what was going on, but he had been there with her earlier when she first woke up. He wasn't the one in the nightmare; she knew that much. He wasn't going to hurt her, she didn't think, so she clung to his hand and didn't want to let go. After a few minutes, when she was sinking down into that deep and coveted medicated sleep, she felt him stretch out on the bed beside her and pull her bodily against him. Utter shock was her first reaction, disbelief that any doctor would do such a thing. Her primitive instinct was to protest, but she didn't really have the strength or will to do much, only knowing that she felt safer with his arms around her.

More than anything, she didn't want to be left alone with the strange and unknown landscape of her mind. She wanted someone to hold her close and protect her from whatever evil was stalking her. Dr. Black felt big and strong and protective and he held her as if he wouldn't let her go. In time, she stopped worrying about all that, her racing heart slowing down to normal, and she lay comfortably inside the circle of his arms.

At that moment, she didn't care if she knew who he was; all she cared about was being safe. She fought sleep as long as she could, and he spoke softly into her hair, low and soothing words, whispering that everything was going to be all right. In time, he slept, too, still holding her. Then, against her will, the drug took her down into the darkness with it, and she closed her eyes and drifted off into a restless, tortured slumber, but without the dreams of danger that she could not explain.

When Claire next opened her eyes, she jerked upright and found herself alone in the same hospital bed, the doctor gone and no one else in sight. She called out his name, but it was the nurse named Monica who came running. She helped Claire lie back against the pillows. "I'm sorry. I stepped outside for just a second. Don't be afraid. You're fine."

"Where's the doctor?" Claire said, composure slipping a notch. "He was right here with me. Or was he? Did I dream that?"

Monica didn't seem to know the answer to those questions, but she smiled down at Claire, very relaxed and efficient and pleasant. She was a pretty girl, very small and slight. "You're fine. You weren't dreaming. He just left the room a little while ago. He had to shower and check on his other patients out in the bungalows. He'll be back soon."

Kind Nurse Monica's serene demeanor transferred to Claire, and she did relax. She was still fighting confusion, but her mind was clearer now and she was feeling more like herself. She remembered waking up. She remembered how he'd held her and kept her safe from those awful dreams.

"I bet you'd like something to eat, wouldn't you? How about a light breakfast? Just until you feel better?"

The desire for food hadn't occurred to Claire, but she nodded. "Who are you again?" she asked as Monica fluffed her pillows and straightened the sheets and blanket.

"My name's Monica Wheeler. I'm an RN. Dr. Black hired me to be your private nurse. I can't tell you how happy I am to finally see you awake."

Claire considered all that, but she lay still and watched Monica pick up a menu off the bedside table and open it. "How about some orange juice, Claire, or grapefruit juice? Apple juice, maybe. Does that sound good? Or hot chicken broth? You need to start off light, but the sooner you get food in your stomach, the stronger you'll feel."

"I want to get up."

"Okay, you can. But let's wait a little while. After you eat will be a good time to try to walk. Okay?"

"Okay. How about coffee?"

"Of course. I'll call downstairs and have them send a pot right up. You can probably tolerate dry toast, too. Then after that, if the doctor agrees, we'll get you up and I'll help you take a shower."

All that sounded good. She wanted out of that bed. Claire lay back and stared out the windows when the nurse threw back the draperies and flooded the dim room with sunlight. The window was large and unobstructed, and a beautiful and shimmering expanse of lake water and azure blue sky met her gaze. The bright sunshine helped put aside the dark places inside her dreams.

The doctor returned when she was choking down a piece of cardboard toast, and the nurse glided out of the room. He came over and stood at her bedside and beamed down at her. "You look a lot better today."

"Thank you for staying with me last night," she said, right off the bat, and truly meant it.

"I've wanted to hold you like that for weeks."

What the hell? Frowning, Claire said nothing as he poured himself a cup of coffee out of the decanter on her breakfast tray, as if the kitchen knew he'd want some and provided a second cup for him. She found his comment confusing. "Why?"

"Because I love you."

Now that was a shockeroo. Holy crap. "You love me?"

"Yeah, and you love me, too."

"I don't know you."

"You will soon enough. We've been lovers for a long time now."

Wow, he believed in putting it out on the line. But that was more information than she wanted to handle at the moment. She wasn't so sure she believed it, either. She shut her eyes and pretended to sleep until he went away. But she did feel stronger, now that she'd eaten a bite, and she was bound and determined to get up and out of that bed before the day was done.

Lunch consisted of Melba toast, cream of chicken soup, lime Jell-O, and apple juice. Yeah, a real appetizing spread after eighteen days of fasting. It was gross, and she didn't eat much of it. By that time, her ragged nerves were knitting together and well under control, and she began to feel more like herself. But she wasn't sure who herself was, so go figure. Her confusion was letting up a tad, and she found it strange, almost interesting, that she couldn't remember much about her past. A few things clicked in place, of course, regular day-to-day mundane routines. But she couldn't recall any accident or much else that had gone down since she'd left Los Angeles. Even some things before and during her sojourn in L.A. were crouched down and hiding in great wide chasms inside her brain.

By force of will, she mustered enough strength to get up and let Monica walk her into the bathroom. She showered and washed her hair by hanging on to the bar on the shower wall, with the ever-solicitous Teensy Monica standing close, waiting with a big fluffy black towel. Claire watched the bathroom door, half afraid that Dr. Black a.k.a. *the-man-who-claimed-to-be-her-lover-but-that-she'd-never-seen-before-in-her-life* was going to barge in himself and lather up some serious bubbly suds on her person. No way. She would jerk the brake on that idea fast enough.

Maybe he held her last night and she appreciated that about as much as was humanly possible, that's for damn sure. You betcha, after that horrific scary dream. Maybe they were hot to trot before her accident—she sure didn't have a clue if they were or not. Not that he would be a bad guy to trot with. But even if they were lovers, he was the only one out of the two of them who knew it. Thus her reticence to share her bathtub and naked body with him was to be understood.

Already craving more substantial fare, for instance, a Quarter Pounder with cheese or a Big Mac, or both, and supersized fries with a Cherry Coke would hit the spot. To no avail. With vocal protestations that she could walk just fine now, thank you very much, she was taken via wheelchair by the aforementioned Monica down a long and über-luxurious black marble hallway to Dr. Black's private office. He wasn't there. Some bedside manner that, huh? Especially if he was her honey and true love, and all that rot, as he had so professed, and earnestly, too.

Monica got her settled in front of the doc's giant and expensive teak desk and put the brakes on her wheelchair, and did a few other nurselike busy things. Jeez, where were her lap blanket and hearing aids? She was beginning to feel like an eighty-year-old invalid with two broken legs. Truth was, though, she felt a whole hell of a lot better after her ultra-delicious lunch. All she had to do was keep it down, and maybe somebody would sneak in some decent fast food. But so far, so good. Funny how no meat cleavers made life seem grand. All in all, though, she was feeling exceptionally well, considering the fact that she'd been deeply comatose around this time yesterday with demonic creatures chasing her around with sharp weapons.

Fifteen seconds after Monica left the room, Claire stood up without any nursemaid's help and did feel a bit woozy for a second or two, but hey, that was understandable enough. The dizzy spell passed quickly. But she wasn't deranged, just forgetful, so she needed to take things slowly and carefully, unless she wanted to end up tied to that bed again. She had thoroughly inspected her face and physique in the bathroom mirror after she took her shower. Her arms and legs were quite muscular and lean, and nothing seemed particularly out of whack or broken or distressing to her sensibilities. There were a few massively gigantic and hideous scars on her person that she couldn't explain the origin of, and that Monica didn't seem capable of explaining, either. But on all other accounts, she seemed to be a healthy enough specimen of law officer, after surviving that pesky coma thing.

Claire found she could walk fine, just as she told Monica earlier. She was just a little wobbly and uncoordinated, but she could stumble her way from point A to B well enough. She wouldn't be running any charity 5K race anytime soon, but she wasn't particularly wild and impetuous, either, so she braced one hand on the shiny desktop as she moved alongside it. A moment later, she stopped her exhausting trek to the other end of the desk and stared out the vast set of floor-to-ceiling windows overlooking the water and one sweet view. The good Dr. Black's practice was going like a house on fire, she figured. Great, even, if he could afford digs like this. Well, good deal, maybe that meant he had the expertise to make her remember nearly everything about herself, which at the moment made a blank blackboard look chatty. The idea sobered her some, depressed her, even.

She'd been struggling to recall things ever since she woke up all freaked out and crybaby scared, but she had yet to get past the large dark hole sucking everything out of her brain. She kept getting quick flashes, cute little film clips, in fact, of faces, of places, of people, and lots of them, but didn't know who or what or why. Yes, aforementioned snuggle-happy doctor had assured her that all would be well and normal as the day was long, but could she believe him? Yep, she had landed in the proverbial pits, believe it.

On the other hand, good Doc Black had to be super savvy with head examining. Just one look at that Picasso hanging on the wall behind his desk proved it. The painting looked to her like a woman's face with one large and rather bulbous almond-shaped eye, a pig's snout kind of nose sticking out the side, all of which were sliding down her neck. Jeez, she'd seen better stuff in a preschool class. But hey, she did recognize the artist. Good sign, right? If she could remember Pablo Picasso, maybe she could eventually remember where she lived.

Claire hobbled around the desk and checked the artist's signature, just to make sure she wasn't dreaming again. Yes, indeedy, it was a legit Picasso, for God's sake. And with its own special little spotlight pouring down on it. Yikes, that prize had to cost said doc a pretty penny. She usually hated rich guys with a passion, and their arrogant, entitled behavior even more, so maybe Claire didn't love Dr. Nick as much as he thought she did.

And where was her supposed lover slash doting doctor, anyway? The guy was supposed to be in love with her, right? So where was he and what was he doing? Taking a snooze down the hall? Probably, if indeed, he'd really spent all those nights hovering over her bed and wanting to get in it with her. But she did appreciate him jumping in last night so she wasn't going to notify the A.M.A. Wow, she remembered the big M.D. association. Yep, all the important things were flooding back willy-nilly now. Nick Black wasn't forced to hug her to sleep last night. Nobody had a gun trained on him. And where was her weapon, anyway? She was a law enforcement officer. She wanted her gun back.

But back to Mr. M.D.: He probably had other equally messed-up and ex-comatose patients to see to. She wondered if he'd do that bed-hopping thing for them, just up and climb right on in and make himself comfortable. He probably even stole the covers off her last night after she went to sleep. Maybe he was in bed with some Sad Sick Sue somewhere right now, pulling off her sheets every time he turned over. Claire then envisioned the big handsome doctor getting in and out of bed with a whole ward of patients as he went down the line. The idea struck her funny, and she laughed softly to herself. Good, at least she still had a sense of humor.

There were half a dozen photographs sitting around on Nick Black's desk, all held in pricey silver frames, except one smaller gold one, and all polished to a shiny gleam, to boot. These rich-as-Onassis folks, what's a gal to do? Claire picked up the biggest one, trying not to leave a smudge mark, for fear that the doc might get all bent out of shape and have to buff it off. Heaven forbid. The picture portrayed the doctor and her, and yes, they were getting mighty cozy in that hot tub by the looks of things. She knew it was her because she had studied her face in the bathroom mirror after examining her scarred-up body. Her face at present was not a pretty sight, nope, not even close. Especially in that shaved-off spot where they'd stitched the wound on her right temple. The hair was growing back, though, in a sort of blond fuzz like a newborn Daisy Duck's. Monica insisted the head wounds were healing quite nicely, her words, and that they'd taken out the stitches days ago. With the one on her forehead, too, and that Claire was almost as good as new. All she needed now was to get her strength back. And her memory. And her life. And it wouldn't hurt to figure out how the hell to find her house and go home, either.

Still waiting for the smokin' hot doctor to show up, Claire stood there and stared for a long time at a second photograph of the two of them, laughing, all happy and lovey-dovey with each other. Hell, they looked downright ecstatic. Claire sure as hell didn't remember being ecstatic with anybody. And she looked a heck of a lot better in that photo than she did now. This one had been taken on some beach somewhere with a fantastic view of crashing waves and a turquoise sea that faded into cobalt on the far horizon. She had on a little, itty-bitty, yellow string bikini, and her blond hair was shorter and wet and combed straight back. She was deeply tanned, which made her eyes look awfully blue, but still not as pure azure as his did. He was tanned then, too, and more deeply than he was now. In the picture, he wore white swim trunks and no shirt and looked damn good without it, too. Her new and not on time doctor lifted mucho weights and worked out a lot. Probably out on a beach somewhere, yep, no doubt about it.

Picking up his other photographs one at a time, Claire realized they were all of her or the two of them. So maybe that nailed down the romantic duo thing. Multiple examples of photographic evidence were hard to argue with. She was drawn to one photo in particular and leaned a hip against the desk while she studied it up close and personal. It was of the doctor and her, too. He was holding her on his lap with some long white taper candles sitting on the table beside them. He was wearing a white pleated tuxedo shirt with a black silk cummerbund around his waist, and a black bow tie pulled loose around his neck. She had on his tuxedo jacket, as if she had gotten cold. She couldn't see what she had on. Obviously taken after whatever they were celebrating was over. A fish-slippery memory slid its way down a hidden slope inside her stunted brain cells, and she almost caught hold of its tail, but then it was gone way too quickly for her to figure out the feelings it evoked. Oh, well, better luck next time.

Jesse's Girl

The day after the accident

Jesse awoke with a start. Instantly afraid, he sat up quickly and peered around in the pearly-gray light of dawn and let out a relieved breath. He was still in Miss Rosie's bedroom, still fully dressed in his muddy clothes and soggy shoes. He had been so exhausted after he made Miss Rosie his new friend that he barely managed to drag himself up the stairs and collapse on her white wrought-iron feather bed with the squeaky springs. Uh-oh, he'd gotten mud and water and lots of her blood all over her pink-and-blue striped sheets and pretty pink chenille bedspread.

Miss Rosie was going to be so, so mad at him. He'd have to do something special for her to make up for the dirty bedclothes, something like he used to do for his own mother. Tears came to his eyes when he thought of his sweet mother with her long blond hair that he'd liked so much to plait into a long tail down her back. May she rest in peace, wherever they'd buried her when they took her head away from him and locked him up in that hospital for the criminally insane. That was a laugh. Him, insane? No way, and far from it. Anyway, now he was free again and had a brand-new old lady to live with, now that he'd lost his beloved Annie in the dark depths of the river.

What he needed to do right now was take a hot shower and go in to town for supplies. There was lots of stuff he liked that Miss Rosie probably didn't have on hand. Standing up, he carefully straightened the bedspread and pillows like his mother had taught him, trying to hide a lot of the dirt so Miss Rosie wouldn't be too upset. Then he walked down the hall to the small green-tiled upstairs bathroom. The rest of Miss Rosie was still in the downstairs tub where he'd left it the night before, so he'd have to use the upstairs bathroom to clean up.

Jesse stopped off in the second bedroom and found some old clothes, probably her husband's, that Harry guy who she loved so much. The red-and-blue checkered shirt and faded Levi dungarees were pretty old-fashioned, but he put them on anyway. They were a little big, but he could make them do with a belt. After that, he methodically searched the house until he finally found a coffee can in the kitchen cabinet just chock-ful of cash. It would be plenty, more money than he expected the nice old lady to have on hand. She must've saved every cent of her husband's social security checks.

Opening the door of the fridge, he stared down at Miss Rosie's head where he'd put it last night. He had chosen a really cool blue-and-white flowered platter to put her on. He'd found it displayed on a little stand on the mantel in her living room. So it must have been one of her favorites or she wouldn't have given it such a special place of honor. Now it was in another even more important place of honor. Last night, he had gently combed Miss Rosie's lovely white hair back into the bun at the back of her head as she had worn it when they'd met. He so wanted to please her, to show her how grateful he was, and how much he loved her.

"Good morning, Miss Rosie. And how are you feeling today?"

Jesse listened to her answer, but didn't like it much. "Well, I'm sorry you're so cold. I guess I should've put a hat on you, or covered you up, or something. But I have to keep you in there where you'll be safe. Please understand and don't be mad at me."

Again, he listened to her angry complaints. "I'll be right out here, but there's no room in there for me, too. Right now, I'm going to check and see what you've got for me to eat."

Carefully, he picked her up on her pretty plate and held her in one arm while he checked out the contents of her fridge. "Well, I can see right off that you need milk and eggs, and I like strawberry preserves so I'll get some of those. I love to cook, Miss Rosie. You'll see what good care I take of you. I'll fix you anything you want. I promise."

Now she was smiling and wanted a kiss so he did that on her mouth because he did love her so much. Then he carefully placed her back on the top shelf and shut the door. When he went outside, the morning was warm and sunny and the honeysuckle smelled heavenly. The barn was out back, but the door was closed. It opened easily, however, and the old metallic blue 1971 Chevy Caprice stored inside fired up pretty fast. It smelled musty and ancient, kinda like mildew, but he took it into town, weeping inconsolably when he thought of his beautiful Annie, now dead and gone and drowned and getting eaten by the fishes, and how they'd never get to live happily ever after as he had always dreamed. He knew the small Missouri town pretty well, so he wiped his tears away and drove straight to the nearest Walmart Supercenter to buy groceries. He pulled into the lot and parked. Outside the store, on the busy sidewalk, he spied a stack of the *Springfield News Leader* in a newspaper vending machine. Shocked, he stopped in his tracks and stared down at Annie's photograph. The headline read: MURDER/ATTEMPTED MURDER IN OZARK.

Fumbling in his pocket for the right change, shaking all over, he finally got it out and into the coin slot. He grabbed out the top newspaper and leaned his shoulder against the wall to read the article.

Ozark, Missouri—The abduction and attempted murder of two women by an escaped mental patient left three prominent psychiatrists dead and a sheriff's detective in critical condition. Ozark police officers arriving at the scene said the mental patient escaped and possibly drowned when his truck plunged off a bridge on the Finley River.

A female victim related to officers a terrifying ordeal that began when both she and Canton County Sheriff's Detective

Claire Morgan were taken captive with several other victims inside a deserted warehouse two miles upriver from the well-known Riverside Inn Restaurant in Ozark.

Jesse skimmed some more of the article, eager to find news of Annie's fate. He had assumed she had drowned because she was still in the car when he fought himself free of the wreckage. He couldn't get back to save her because the flooded river current was too swift and swept him away from her and downstream against his will. Then he saw what he was looking for, and his heartbeat went wild and soared with joy.

According to a witness at the scene, the perpetrator, Thomas Landers, was attempting to abduct Morgan when their truck went into the river. Morgan suffered severe head injuries and is at the Cox Medical Center in Springfield where she remains in critical condition. The other victim and an unidentified teenager were also admitted for observation.

Jesse could not believe it! Now he and Annie could be together after all! All he had to do was find her and take her away with him and Miss Rosie. Thrilled beyond belief, he went into the store and bought a bunch of groceries because now he would have to cook for three. Maybe he could even get Annie while she was still asleep at that hospital, which would be ideal. She'd probably be mad at first because he'd driven her into the river, but she'd forgive him. He'd make everything so wonderful for her that she couldn't help but smile and kiss him and Miss Rosie and want to live with them forever.

Heart happy, a new and hopeful smile on his face, he drove straight home and told Miss Rosie the wonderful news. Then he fixed them both a bacon and tomato sandwich with mayonnaise and lettuce, and a pear salad with cheese and a dollop of mayonnaise on top, and freshly brewed ice tea with lemon slices. Just before bed, he wrapped Miss Rosie and her pretty platter in an old red USA sweatshirt he'd found in her husband's closet, because he thought it would make her feel safe and she loved to cuddle up with her husband. He kissed her good night and placed her on the pillow next to him. Now she'd be nice and warm and very pleased with him. He fell fast asleep. His last thought was that everything was going to be all right now. His beautiful Annie was alive, and they'd be together soon. Life was good. Everything would be all right now.

Chapter Three

Nicholas Black strode swiftly across the vast black-and-gold and crystal-chandeliered lobby of Cedar Bend Lodge, eager to get up to Claire's room again. Although he had been neglecting his patients to some extent, they had been willing to wait at times and understood that he was preoccupied with Claire Morgan. Stepping onto his private elevator, he nodded at Isaac Ward, the former Marine security guard who kept people out of the penthouse, and rode without a sound up to the top level. He was so eager to see her again. It had taken way too long and was much too awful an ordeal waiting for her to come out of the coma.

When he didn't find her in the bedroom, he walked down the hall-way to his office. He'd told Monica to take her there after lunch. He hoped she hadn't been waiting very long. He stopped in the thresh-old. Claire was standing at his desk, a very good sign. A runner and exercise fanatic, she had been in superb physical condition before the accident and that would help her get back on her feet more than anything. She was studying a photograph of them taken at his villa in Bermuda, not long after they'd met. He wondered if it was jogging loose some memories. God, he hoped so.

"You gave that photo to me," he told her, walking into the room and making his presence known.

Whipping around, the gold-framed picture still in her hand, she stared at him but didn't say anything. He felt something inside almost tremble at the sight of her standing there before him, alive and well. There was a visceral catch in his gut, to be sure, as beautiful as she looked to him, even now after the worst ordeal imaginable. He hoped to God that she would remember him soon.

Smiling, he moved toward her, and she didn't back away, just stood there and gazed up at him.

"So, how tall are you, anyway?" she asked.

Thinking it an odd question, he said, "Six-four. Why?"

"Just wondered. I can't remember a damn thing, remember?"

That was just so Claire that his hopes ignited again. "Do you recall the place in that picture, Claire?"

"Nope."

"You gave it to me for Christmas."

"Is that so? And exactly how long have we been together?"

"Just over a year."

"We're not married, though? And please say no, this is already weird enough. Not that you're a bad catch, or anything."

Black had to smile. "No, we're not married. Yet."

"Engaged then?"

"No. But we're seriously committed."

"Do we live together?"

"You live here with me unless I have to fly somewhere on business. Then you usually go home to your own house until I get back."

"So I have my own house, huh? Now that sounds more like it."

"Yes, you've got a cabin on the lake. You love it, so we spend a lot of time out there together. It's on a nice quiet cove off the main branch of the lake."

One corner of Claire's mouth turned up, just a little. "Then I can go back home as soon as you tell me where it is."

He laughed, but he sobered almost at once. She didn't laugh. She was serious. She was ready to take off.

"You are home, Claire."

His eyes held her big blue skeptical ones, but she did not turn away. She was looking him over as if she'd never laid eyes on him before. That dashed his hopes that she'd recovered recollections of their time together. What was more, he wasn't sure she wanted to. Her next words proved it.

"Isn't that for me to decide?"

"Yes, of course. Once you remember things, no problem. Right now, I suspect it'll be difficult for you to make good decisions, suffering from retrograde amnesia and perhaps some kind of dissociative recall."

"Wow, lookee here, psychology mumbo jumbo. That's what you are, right? A damn shrink."

At that point, Black realized, with concern, that not only could she not remember their life together, but that she had regressed to the person she had been when they first met. All the defense mechanisms he'd worked so hard to pull down inside her psyche, so damaged from her miserable childhood, were back in place and impenetrable again. God help him, that was the very worst-case scenario that could've come out of her awakening from such a deep coma. She had disliked him intensely and unreasonably when they first met, and it had taken him a long time to figure out why. As it turned out, she distrusted the psychiatrists she'd seen in her youth, especially wealthy ones, and nearly everybody else in her life. So here they were again, back to square one, and square one was not a good place. He tried to hide his disappointment. She was observing him closely, with those cop's analyzing eyes of hers, as she had been trained to do so well in the L.A. police academy. She would brook no nonsense. She would not take to his therapies lying down or cooperatively. And that was a major setback.

"So, why so glum, doc?"

"Claire, why don't you come over here and sit down so we can talk about all these things."

Claire eyed him suspiciously and then started a painful wobble toward the couch. Finally, he took pity and supported her arm the rest of the way, not a little surprised she let him.

"So, tell me, you're quite the moneybags, aren't you? What do you charge, anyway, a thousand dollars a minute?" Her voice had that old contemptuous tone that he hadn't heard in a very long time, and his heart fell at the thought of going back over all those old and terrible issues again. But she was worth it. She was worth everything he had, or would ever have.

Actually, he did get a lot of money for his services, but he wasn't going to tell her that. "Not quite that much. But I've done well enough, I guess."

"So you *are* one of those dastardly shrink types, huh?"

"I'm a forensic and clinical psychiatrist, yes."

"Well, is this my lucky day, or what? Just don't expect me to pay you a boatload of money for sitting there and staring at me like I'm some kind of time bomb."

Black had to chuckle at her attitude. Okay, he found her amusing, and had from the beginning, then and now. She had a quick wit, a strong intuitive intellect, and something else ingrained that drew him to her like a moth to a bonfire. Maybe that's why he fell in love with her. Now, all the time they'd spent together, all the progress they'd made was for naught. She was the old prickly Claire and didn't mind showing him that his money or his degrees or anything else about him did not impress her in the least. He watched her sink down onto one of his long white couches, and he sat down very close beside her. Really close, couldn't help himself. He put his arm around her, resting it on the back of the plush cushion. He wanted to grab her up and hold her like he did last night, but first and foremost, she had to remember him. He had to be patient. Claire did not like to be pushed around, and that was putting it mildly.

"Think you can get any closer to me, doc?" she said, scooting away from him with exaggerated annoyance. "You're a hot guy, and all, but come on now, give me a break here. I let you help me out last night in bed, but enough's enough. You smell good, though."

"So, tell me, babe, how do you feel today?" he asked, changing the subject and deciding to treat her the same way he had before her accident. He'd thought about that all day, which way he should go with her. He'd decided to act like nothing had happened, that things were exactly the same as before. They were together; and they were damn well going to stay together, so she better get used to it. His eyes lingered on her mouth. God, it had been so long since he'd kissed her and made love to her. And now this had to happen. Claire was not going to let him touch her that way unless she wanted to, not in a million years.

"Better," she said, scooting over some more, putting most of the sofa between them. "Don't take this wrong, but I don't like the feeling of being smothered, and you're invading my personal space.

So please lay off. It's not you, you understand. It's just a thing with me that I do remember."

"Sorry. So you don't feel desperate or like you're going to pass out? Any dizziness or nausea?"

"Some, but it's not going to keep me in that bed anymore."

"Good for you," he said, fighting the urge to move closer again. If she didn't remember him quickly, this was going to be like trudging through a field of sucking mud. "I'm really glad to see you're feeling better. Sorry to make you wait, but I had to see about a patient that I've been neglecting."

She nodded, carelessly hitched a shoulder, and stood up. Restless, she started moving around the room, so stiff and slow that he had to conquer the urge to get up and help her. She was looking at his personal objects and mementos where they were displayed on bookshelves and reading his framed medical degrees and certificates hanging on the walls. "Don't get me wrong, doctor, I appreciate the way you comforted me after I had that nightmare, and all. I wasn't myself or I wouldn't have acted like a big baby, trust me."

"I was looking for any excuse to get into that bed with you, trust *me*. It's been a long time since we made love." He smiled, but he was careful that his words were light and didn't come off like some kind of sleazy come-on. He was pleased and happy she let him hold her at all. What he wanted was to do it again, and sooner rather than later. He changed the subject before she could say it wasn't going to happen again. "Does your head hurt, Claire?"

"Not really. I'm just grossed out by all this crazy stuff."

"It's going to take you some time. Have you remembered anything else?"

"Not much." She lifted one shoulder again, the same disinterested little shrug, but then she turned and gestured at his desk. "I do know that's a Picasso hanging on the wall over there. Pretty weird, I think. But to each his own. You might like some kind of Cyclops' eye staring at your back when you work, but it would freak me out."

He smiled again, couldn't help it. God, he was glad she was back and up on her feet.

She was looking at him again. "You've got dimples."

"Yeah. So?"

She didn't say anything for a moment. Then she said, "Look, Dr. Black, I think I'm a pretty honest person. You seem to be pretty special, I guess, sexy and rich, and all that good stuff. But I happen to have bigger problems than a forgotten love life with a real hunk like you. So, I guess we oughta just keep things platonic, at least for now." She paused, apparently waiting for his reaction. Since she brought it up again, he deduced the subject was worrying her. He didn't give her a reaction, his own training kicking in, but she was right on target. She had regressed big-time to the woman he'd first met when he topped her murder suspect list. She had rebuffed him then, as well.

Claire was impatient by nature, he knew that well, and she didn't give him time to consider the best way to reply. "Okay, doc, then you also ought to know this. I'm just not one of those come-and-get-me-honey-on-the-first-date kinda gals. Therefore, any kind of seduction and all that kinda thing is gonna have to come post–memory recovery, and not before."

"Is that right?"

"Oh, yes, sir, it sure is. I'm not gonna pussyfoot around with you, doctor. As far as I know, we're strangers in the night. Don't think about rushing me into something I'm not ready for."

"Well, I'm afraid everything you just said is just not going to work for me."

"What? The rich doctor doesn't get his way so he's going to push the issue?"

"I'm not going to push the issue. I'm just going to try to help you remember sooner rather than later so all this will be a moot point."

A deep frown creased Claire's forehead. She rubbed her temples with her forefingers. She was getting a headache, all right. She'd get a lot more of those before she got well.

"All right, Dr. Black, I can see your point. I'm not blind, and I'm not insensitive. If all you say is true, then it's probably gonna be hard for you to back off, I take it? That's what you're talking about?"

"Oh, yeah. It's just not going to happen."

Openly annoyed, she contemplated him a moment. "Okay, I can see where you're coming from. It's gonna be harder for you than for me, if we were a couple. But here's the deal, as I see it, doctor. I want you to tell me about myself. It's obvious that we spent time together, I saw those pictures over there, so why don't I remember you? Why don't I remember that beautiful lake out there and whatever it was that put me in that coma?"

Black remained calm, and held her gaze. She was extremely grave now. She was reacting to just about every single thing the way she would have done early in their relationship. She would rebel against almost anything he said as she had in the beginning. It would be best to go along with her for the time being, just like he did then. "You don't recall anything yet because you are experiencing a short-term memory loss, which, actually, is a good thing. It could've been a lot worse with two hard, concussive blows to the head as serious as yours were. It's also good that you can remember some things, including details about your law enforcement career and that you lived in Los Angeles, for example. You'll remember everything else in time. Sometimes it comes back in a sudden rush when someone or something triggers it. Sometimes it's in piecemeal fashion, one experience at a time. You need to quit worrying about remembering and about our past relationship, and try to relax, recuperate, and let it happen as it will."

"Well, that's easy enough for you to say, now isn't it?"

"No, it's not easy for me to say. It's taking every goddamn ounce of my willpower not to throw you down on this couch and make love to you."

That caught Claire by surprise. Her face went red, and she turned away from him. He didn't know if that was caused by anger or embarrassment. Her next words told him.

"Well, now. Wow. You don't believe in mincing words, do you? That sounds awfully sexy, I declare. Extremely titillating, doctor. If I knew you from Adam."

"And there lies the problem," he said, remaining composed, but it was getting harder for him to remain unruffled. She got under his skin, always had, always would, and in more ways than one. "But that doesn't keep me from wanting the woman I love."

Claire looked away from his challenging stare. "Okay, I get the picture. But I guarantee I'm not ready to jump in bed with you, if that's what you're getting at."

"Oh, I'm hoping for that, all right. But I do understand how you feel. So don't worry, Claire, I'm going to give you all the time you need. But know this, too: It's going to kill me to keep my hands off you. And that's the truth. It's as simple as that."

"Hey, I know, let's change the subject. Tell me about the accident. What exactly happened? Where and when and why, everything."

"Do you recall anything about it?"

"Nothing, nada, zip."

"That's normal, too. Trauma often causes this kind of memory loss. Some people never recall the traumatic event. The accident, in your case."

After that, Claire watched him so long that he grew uncomfortable under her steady gaze. She was extremely perceptive and could read people's feelings and emotions like the crack detective she was. "You're hedging. You don't want to tell me what happened. Why not? Just tell me and get it over with. In complete detail, please."

"This is not a police interview, Claire. Don't try to sweat it out of me. It's complicated."

"Okay. I'll pay close attention. That suit you better?"

Black didn't volunteer anything else. So she prodded him some more, just like he knew she would. But he did not want to tell her just how terrible it all had been, couldn't, wouldn't, not yet.

"I'm not at LAPD anymore?" she asked suddenly.

"No." Again, she made a long, suspicious, narrow-eyed scrutiny of his face. Lord have mercy, he was glad to have her back. He had missed this—her, his life with her.

"You're very reluctant to tell me about this, aren't you? You are definitely hiding something. Why? Was my life that bad?"

"You've always been observant." Black sighed and formulated what he could and could not say. "I'm afraid that you've had a lot of trauma and heartbreak in your life."

"Oh, great, that's just dandy news. Exactly what I wanted to hear. Maybe I shouldn't try to remember anymore. Stay right here in this land of the I-Forgot-Everything-But-Oh-Well." But he was watching her jaw, the way it was working under her skin, the way she'd grown tense as if she knew but her mind couldn't let go of the details. She frowned, licking her dry lips.

"Are you thirsty?" he inquired. "Would you like a Cherry Coke, something like that?"

"No. I guess it's all right if you wanna hit me with a sudden and traumatic thumbnail sketch of my horrible life. That ought to be a barrel of laughs, but I can take it."

"I think it's better to wait a bit. You're just now getting used to being up and on your feet."

She said, "Let's talk about L.A. later. Start with the accident."

Black's eyes dropped to her mouth again. She saw it and turned away. It was going to be another long hellish night, damn it.

"I think it's too soon to get into every detail, but I'll give you the basic facts. You were on a case. You got caught up with a serial killer. He abducted you and drove his car off a bridge into a river to evade capture. I happened to be there and was able to pull you out before you drowned."

Claire swiveled around. "You just happened to be there? That sounds rather convenient, don't you think? How did that happen?"

"I was concerned about your safety and followed you."

"I'm a police officer here in this town, I take it?"

"You're a Canton County homicide detective, yes."

"And you were following me to keep me safe? That doesn't sound like L.A. police procedure. In fact, that sounds slightly bizarre and like I'm some kind of wimp."

"You're not a wimp, believe me. Like I just told you, I have some expertise in forensic psychiatry. Your sheriff sometimes lets me help out in your investigations. His name is Charles Ramsay."

"What about the killer?"

"He is presumed dead, drowned in the river. They never found his body and think it washed downstream into the James River and maybe on farther, out into Table Rock Lake, perhaps."

"And this happened several weeks ago?"

"Yeah. Three long, endless weeks ago."

"Tell me about the case I was on, Dr. Black."

Black shook his head at her formal address. It seemed so odd coming out of her mouth. She shot him another frown.

"You never call me that."

"What?"

"'Dr. Black.'"

"What then? Nicholas? Or Nick, I guess?"

"No, actually, you call me Black."

"Black? Really? Just your last name?"

"Yes. Now anything else just doesn't sound right."

She obviously decided to get back on point. "Okay, Black, tell me about the victim."

Black was not thrilled to get into that, but he obliged. She could take a little dose of the horror, he guessed, but just a little. "A man was found hanging under a bridge not far from here. When you went back to search his apartment, you found a dead woman inside his house."

Now that appeared to set Claire back a bit. "So it was a murder-suicide?"

"A serial killer murdered both of them. Unfortunately, you seem to have a tendency to get tangled up with every psychopath that wanders through the lake area. It was a terrible thing."

"And you're sure this perp's dead?"

"Yeah, the guy, the one who abducted you and had the accident? He killed him."

"What was my assailant's name?"

"His name was Thomas Landers." He paused, and looked directly at her. "He's psychotic, Claire, and he has a fixation on you."

"Oh, more fantastic news. This sounds suspiciously like we're playing parts in an episode of *Grimm*. Hey, I remembered that show."

Black couldn't summon up a smile this time. They were approaching no-man's-land, some very dark, unpleasant business, and she wasn't ready for it.

"You're suddenly Dr. Serious, all of a sudden."

"This is serious. Everything about this is serious. We both need to take it that way."

"Well, I'd be glad to, if I could remember. You'd think I would, since it's so awful."

"You have blocked out all the terrible things, including him. He was a sick man, like I said, a murderous psychopath."

"Jeez, this just keeps getting better. And we're not a hundred percent certain that he's dead?"

"No, but he's presumed so. They searched downstream for his body for days and didn't find a trace of him. The river was high and running fast the night you went in. Bud searched awhile with the Ozark P.D. He thinks the guy's dead."

"So who's Bud?"

"Bud Davis. He's your partner. And a good friend. For five years or so, I think, maybe more."

"Oh, my God. I don't remember the last five years or more! I can't believe I don't remember my own partner." Claire shut her eyes, and kept them closed. "I can't really remember his face, but he's kind of tall, isn't he? And he got this book that we laughed about. He's from the South somewhere, I think."

Smiling in triumph, she looked at Black for verification. "I'm beginning to get it back, right? That's an encouraging sign, don't you think, doctor? I mean, Black."

"Interesting, yes. Do you know what made you remember those things about him?"

"I don't know. Glimpses and thoughts just dart in and out of nowhere. Little flashes. You know, like minnows in the shallows. Kinda like film clips but fuzzier."

He gazed at her, smiling, definitely encouraged. "We'll talk. I've put together some pictures for you to look at after you get used to what's happening, and then some friends of yours want to come by and see you. They've all been up here to visit you while you were sleeping. A lot of people care about you, Claire."

Black watched her, frowning, because her eyes were closed and all sorts of naked emotions were flitting across her face. "Was there a little child that came in to see me? I heard a child's voice in my dreams, I know I did."

Okay, now he was really worried, fearing she could be remembering Zach, and that was one thing he did not want her to have to deal with yet. He hid his consternation quickly and chose his words very carefully. She was looking at him in dread, as if knowing it was going to be terrible, whatever it was.

"The voice you heard was a little girl named Lizzie. Her father's name is Joe McKay, another friend of yours. They came to see you often." He hesitated, half afraid to say what came next, and she looked afraid to hear it.

"I think this is enough for today. We'll have another session tomorrow and see if we can pull out more memory. Your brain is protecting you, giving you time to recover before you have to face everything. There's no need to force it. It will come back."

Her back was to him now as she sauntered casually around the room, getting her sea legs back. She trailed her fingers across the gleaming surface of the grand piano that was sitting in front of the windows. "Nice piano," she commented.

"That was my mother's. She played beautifully."

Claire picked up the old violin case on the top, opened it, and took out the fine-tuned instrument. "And I suppose this is mine?"

He was startled, as that was a question he hadn't expected. "No. That was hers, too. She could play both."

"So can I."

Now that was an interesting development and news to him.

"You didn't know?"

"You never mentioned it before." He couldn't hide his surprise. He thought he knew practically everything about her past, but she'd certainly never mentioned musical talents.

"Maybe I have lots of secrets you don't know about."

"Maybe," he said carefully.

"Do you think I'm lying? Do you want me to prove it?"

"I don't think you're lying. But I'd love to hear you play."

Expertly, she put the violin against her chin, brought up the bow, and began to play. Black sat transfixed as she played the most beautiful, concert-worthy rendition of a haunting song he couldn't name, a Chopin sonata, maybe. In the middle, she stopped abruptly with a discordant squeak and quickly repacked the instrument and bow inside the case.

"Why did you stop? It was beautiful."

"It brought back some bad memories. Foster parents from hell, and all that sort of thing. Funny how I remember them, and not you."

Black said nothing; his gut told him she didn't want to talk about it. He wasn't going to question her. But bad or not, one more memory was back in place.

Claire surprised him by coming back and sitting down on the couch, closer to him than before. They stared at each other, and he picked up her hand, kissed the back of it, and then let it go before she could snatch it away. If she thought he wasn't going to touch her until she recalled everything, she had another think coming. "Let's order up dinner. What do you say? Whatever you want, just name it."

Claire must have decided that he was not such a threat, after all. "Okay. I've got a feeling that whatever you were going to tell me was pretty bad, and I'm not so sure I want to hear anything else like that right now. My dreams are terrible enough."

"Good girl. Now what are you hungry for?"

"A Big Mac and fries. That's what I want. I'm craving it, in fact."

Black laughed, relieved but seriously worried, too. Not so much that she didn't remember him but that her regression was going to make it a lot harder to get her back to the same level as before. And that it'd take longer. "Fine, that's what we'll have."

Claire sat there watching him, and he picked up the phone and asked the desk clerk if he would find somebody to make a run to the nearest McDonald's. Then he turned back around to find Claire pinching her arm.

She answered his question without him having to ask. "Just making sure I'm not dreaming again. My dreams are that vivid."

"Oh, yes, this is the real thing. Look at it this way, Claire. Tomorrow at this time, you may have already remembered everything, including me."

"We can only hope," she said.

But they both knew it was unlikely, and they'd both do well not to get their hopes up for that quick of a recovery. This was going to be a long haul.

Chapter Four

I was locked up in a cold dark place. I could smell hay, the odors of a barn. I heard someone coming, but I didn't know who it was. When I saw the man's face in the dim glow of a flashlight, I was terrified. He dragged me out and held a gun to my temple. Then we were inside a house, and he was threatening to kill me. Again, there were others there, tied up, helpless, and I knew he was evil, so very evil. He had a large pair of scissors in his hand, and he was going to use them on one of us. Oh, God, I had to get loose. I had to stop him. . . .

Claire jerked upright in the bed, shivering, clammy with sweat, heart thumping. Then an instant later, Nicholas Black was there beside her, and she was inside his arms. She clung to him, trembling, terrified. This was day three of her just hunky-dory new life, and her dreams were still so real, so frightening that she lost all control of her nerves, and Black had to come in and take charge. She felt like a fool every single time, but not enough to push him away, not at first, anyway. He felt solid and real and safe, and he always ended up saying that he loved her and that everything was all right. Oh, yeah, everything was just fine now. *Not.* In fact, that's why she was still clinging with both fists to the front of his white T-shirt, like she was drowning and he was the life preserver. She swallowed hard and forcibly tamped down the overwhelming panic attack that always came at her so fast and hard, while Black tried to soothe her.

"How long is this going to go on?" she got out against his shoulder.

"Probably until you remember it all," he whispered, stroking her hair, his mouth moving against her temple. "You want a sedative?"

Claire considered that, but she knew she had to get over these night terrors, and do it quickly. Sedatives weren't the answer. She had to face them and get over it, already. "No, I'm okay. Are these things I'm dreaming about real?"

"I suspect they probably are. You've dealt with some really bad people in your cases, serial killers. Once you remember everything that happened, in context, you'll be able to handle it. You were dealing with it well enough before you got hurt this last time."

Claire couldn't bring herself to ask about the gory details. Instead, she disentangled herself from his arms, sat up, and looked at the windows. Daylight was graying the edges of the drapes. "What time is it?"

"Six-thirty. I've got a conference call with my London clinic in forty-five minutes. I'm going to take a shower and go over my notes before it begins. Do you want to get up? We can have a late breakfast together later, if you want."

"No, go ahead. I'm okay now. I am. I want to look through those pictures you gave me. See if anything clicks."

"Good idea, Claire." Black held her tightly for a moment, kissed her on the cheek, and smoothed her hair away from her face. Then he got up and walked into the giant black marble and white subway-tiled adjoining bathroom.

Claire sat there and watched him go. At that moment, she realized that she had better learn to steel herself against this guy's overabundant sex appeal, which absolutely dripped off him like wax off a half-burnt candle. Or maybe she'd be the burning candle. Whatever, she wanted to get to know him before she said, "Yes, take me now and hurry it up already." Yes, indeedy, Nicholas Black had enough masculine come-hither-and-let-me-wow-you to fill up two Ryan Goslings and three Liam Hemsworths.

Glancing through the open bathroom door, she could see him vaguely inside the shower in all his glory, although the glass walls were steamy and pretty well blocked her view. Jeez. And yes, she was attracted to him, so she could very easily believe she had been so before her accident, too. Hell's bells, she was getting a headache, he was so charming and too good to be true. But she did not know him, did not know if he was for real or putting on an act. Why he'd do that was yet another question that didn't make much sense. Maybe she was just an interesting case that he was intrigued with. Maybe he was writing a book about cops with amnesia. Yes, she was a suspicious woman; she couldn't help it. Claire rubbed her temples, suddenly feeling trapped in a strange Bizarro world with no fire exits.

Claire looked around the room. She was sleeping in Black's master bedroom at his request, but he wasn't forcing himself on her. In fact, he was sleeping in another room next door. When she told him she wasn't ready to get friendly, he had backed off big-time and didn't mention it again. But he was growing on her, to be sure, and she now was pretty sure that she used to love him back. She was trying to jam everything together, and the puzzle pieces just didn't quite fit.

Swinging her legs off the bed, she stood up and walked down the hall barefoot to one of the guest baths. Quickly showering, she dressed in a black T-shirt with CANTON COUNTY SHERIFF in fluorescent yellow letters on the front, and black sweatpants that Black said belonged to her. They were a little loose, but Black told her she'd lost a lot of weight, so she made do. He was certainly trying to force-feed her enough, now that she was awake and hungry. The Big Mac had been a bust; she'd barely been able to eat half of it.

Once she got over the shattering effect of the scissors dream, however, she felt better, stronger, rather good, actually. So good, in fact, that she wanted to meet this Bud Davis fellow and get back to work. She figured being on the job would help her more than anything. Besides that, she didn't like feeling so cooped up, and she was ready to escape the constant eagle-eyed protectiveness of tiny Monica Wheeler and big buff Nicholas Black. She also decided without a lot of encouragement that Black was one nice guy. He was very caring and attentive, and certainly not hard on the eyes, and sexy to boot, with the added advantage that he could barely keep his hands off her.

If he was her own special love interest, as he had repeatedly told her, then she was one lucky gal. She was also getting some vague notions once in a while, in short, jerky film-clip versions, about them together, blurry images that didn't tell her much. Just that they were somewhere doing something at some time together. Real precise, that. Unfortunately, none of it concerned the lovely, lovey-dovey stuff that no doubt went on between them. She didn't feel anything much about him, one way or another, other than the admitted admiration for his many manly attributes. One thing, for sure, he was paying her a lot of highly enamored attention that was hard to miss, or resist.

She was walking more now and tiring less. The exercise in his private lap pool downstairs on the grounds of the resort was helping, of course, and making her feel better about her sorry state of affairs. At loose ends, as usual, she walked outside on a nice shady balcony off the living room that faced a gorgeous view of the lake. A whole flotilla of sailboats dotted the glittering blue water, gliding here and there while motorboats zipped around pulling water-skiers. Black told her it was Lake of the Ozarks, but she didn't remember it, or the town or county, either. He had to tell her just about everything. She was gradually recalling something here and there, but according to Black, all of it was pulled out of her past life from a good while back. The short-term memory loss had blocked out nearly all of the last few years living on this nifty lake somewhere in the middle of Missouri.

Nicholas Black had been rather medically dictatorial to date, to say the least, and refused to let Claire have any visitors yet, not that she'd know any of them. Said she wasn't strong enough, had to go slowly and carefully into that morass of nothing. But he had allowed in a small and brainy herd of friendly neurologists, world-famous ones, at that, who came around to examine her head and diagnose if she had any modicum of sense left, she supposed. But they all agreed on the primary diagnosis, i.e., she couldn't remember, but eventually would, so not to worry. Yeah, easy for them to say with all their degrees and fancy certificates on the wall. She could have told them that without any kind of medical degree or paying them the pretty penny they were probably earning.

Today, however, some of her unknown friends were coming to see her and try their dead-level best to jog her recalcitrant memory back into a complicated but slickly designed and finished life journey. Actually, she was really nervous, but trying hard not to show it. She was nervous about everything and everybody, in fact. Not knowing anything was highly annoying. Kind of like a six-month-old baby in a high chair trying to pick up diced peas and carrots. She now was convinced that she had indeed moved in with the handsome doctor some time back. They weren't married. Problem was, the good Dr. Black seemed to think they were in every sense of the word. Or should've been. Or soon would be.

"Here you go, Claire. Time for your meds."

Claire's trusty private nurse, Miss Monica Wheeler, sashayed in without a sound on the shiny walnut hardwood floors, with her usual brilliant smile and chipper, you're-gonna-be-fine-little-sweetie attitude, carrying a white-towel-covered tray. The meds were in a little white cup alongside a Cedar Bend monogrammed glass full of water. Pretty sick of meds by now, yes, she was, but nevertheless, she obediently took them. Too bad they didn't have a magic pill to give her total recall, but that's for the movies, she guessed. Now that would a pill really worth taking.

Monica Wheeler was young, in her early thirties probably, extremely good at her job, and nice enough, sweet even. Always chatty and smiley, she was just a little bitty thing, not much over five foot. Pretty and petite and energetic as all get out, and yes, she made Claire feel, at her greater height, like some kind of Teutonic female warrior clomping around, shield in hand. Yes, one could usually hear Claire coming, no doubt about it. Monica's long dark brown hair was pulled back into a bun, encased in a silver metallic kind of net or something, a hair accessory that Monica called a snood. Never heard of that, but Claire had never heard of a lot of things lately. Monica was built rather well up top and had a quick and pleasant smile and that knack for making no noise, literally or figuratively. Claire figured Monica's memory was considerably better than hers, at least at the moment.

"Hey, Monica, the good doc tells me that he and I were quite an item before I hit that river. That true? Or is he just trying to take advantage of me now that I'm all sick and weak and can't remember my own name?" Claire smiled, just so Monica would know she was kidding. The nurse got it and smiled back.

"I'm afraid I didn't know you at all until I came here to take care of you."

"Okeydoke. How long have you known Dr. Black?"

"He had a patient in cardiac intensive care at Barnes Jewish Hospital in St. Louis. That's where I work. Guess that was about five years ago." Monica picked up the glass of water and handed it to Claire. "He wanted somebody here that he could trust when he had to work. I took vacation time to come here. He's an excellent physician, you know."

Actually, Claire didn't know, but thought that was certainly worth a hearty double thumbs-up. "Well, thank you for coming and taking care of me."

Monica looked down at her and surprised Claire by momentarily dropping her usual highly professional nurse to patient demeanor. "I can tell you for a fact, Claire, that Nick was absolutely distraught when you were in that coma. He stayed by your side every single moment that he could and only left when he had to. I felt so sorry for him during all those long days and nights. He did everything he could for you. He himself did the physical therapy every single day to keep your muscles agile. He said you'd want to get up as soon as you woke up. I know you can't remember him, but please don't have any doubts about the two of you. He loves you deeply, I can promise you that."

All that made Claire feel rather warm and kitten-soft fuzzy, true. "It's just been so strange, all this stuff. Living in a kind of dark night, where I don't really know anybody."

Monica squeezed her arm. "I know we keep saying this, Claire, but you will get better. You will remember everything; just give it a week or two."

"Thanks. I needed that." Claire decided to inquire further into Monica. How else was she going to get to know people? "What about you? You miss your friends back home?"

"Yes, some of them. There are a few that I can do without."

They both laughed at the truth in that.

"I wish I had some friends to talk to."

"You do. They'll come to see you. You wouldn't believe how many people came up here and sat with you and talked to you. They all tried very hard to bring you back."

"I know, but I don't know them anymore. You're the only person I feel like I know, Monica. Except Black, a little, I guess."

"Well, I've enjoyed getting to know you, too." Uncharacteristically, Monica sat down on the couch across from her. She didn't do that very often. Never, actually. It pleased Claire that she did so now. Yes, she was lonely, she realized with some surprise.

"I met a guy here," Monica offered with a shy smile. "I really like him."

"Well, that's great. Who is he?"

"His name is Jesse. He works downstairs in the restaurant. That's how we met, when I ate lunch down there or brought Nick up a tray from the restaurant."

"Is it serious?"

"I am, already. I think he likes me a lot, too. We've been talking about getting married someday."

Claire clapped her hands, genuinely happy for Monica. "That's great. Does that mean you're gonna stay here at the lake?"

"I'm looking for a house right now. I love it down here. People are just so friendly. Nick says he can get me a job at the Canton County Medical Center, if I want it."

"He's a good guy, huh?"

"Oh, yes, he is. You're lucky to have him."

"Yeah, I guess so." Claire knew that, in a way. But in a different way, she still wasn't so sure. "What does Jesse do?"

"He's a busboy and waiter down in Two Cedars."

"Maybe Black and I can have dinner with you and Jesse one of these days."

"When I get my own place, I'll cook dinner for the four of us," Monica offered, seeming very pleased. "I'm a really good cook, if I say so myself."

"It's a date. I think that's exactly what I need, to get out and have some fun. I'm feeling pretty cooped up and stir crazy."

"Hey, you know what, Claire? I do have a girlfriend here at the lake. She's only here for the summer, though. She works at the sheriff's office, too. She assists the medical examiner. Her name's Nancy Gill. I know you'd like her. She's a lot of fun."

Claire frowned, frustrated. "I don't remember her, Monica."

"You wouldn't. She just got here at the beginning of the summer. Some kind of exchange program, or something. She said she never met you. We've been going out to her uncle's place a couple of times a week. It's called Jeepers and it's a cool restaurant/bar at one of the marinas. She bartends there, when she's off duty. We're going out there next Friday night, if you'd like to come along. You know, a girls' night out. I think you'd like it."

"Well, I'll have to ask Black," Claire started out, and then she realized that she didn't like the sound of that. Not even the least little bit. She shouldn't have to ask him to do anything. She felt good, and Monica apparently thought she was well enough, too. "Okay, I'm game."

"How about we get together right after I get off work? We can take my car."

"I'll look forward to it."

"Great. I can't wait for you to meet Nancy."

Monica picked up the tray, and then paused again at the arched entranceway. "Oh, yes, I almost forgot. Nick asked me to tell you he's finishing his rounds down at the bungalows and will be back soon."

Monica glided away in her nifty nurse shoes and left Claire alone. Maybe she should learn to walk like that. She was a detective. She snuck up on people. Maybe it would come in handy.

Jesse's Girl

Two days after the accident

Once Jesse arrived at the hospital and found out his darling Annie had been flown back home to Lake of the Ozarks, he packed Miss Rosie's Chevy Caprice with all they'd need. He swaddled her head inside a soft, pink baby blanket and belted her snugly into the old infant car seat he'd found in her basement, and then headed north to pick up Annie. At first, he was furious because her false lover had gotten to her first and whisked her away. That despicable

Nicholas Black always did that. He hated him, and wished he'd just up and die. Annie was Jesse's girl, and she always would be.

But then he remembered the very nice little house that Jesse had lived in at Lake of the Ozarks before they caught him and carted him off to the hospital. Maybe it was still there. Maybe he could live there with Miss Rosie. He'd love to see it again. Miss Rosie would love it there, he knew she would. And so would his mother, when he found out where she was buried. But that would have to wait awhile. Annie was his only concern at the moment.

The road trip was uneventful, but Miss Rosie didn't like being covered up where she couldn't admire the passing scenery. Finally, she quit complaining and dozed off to sleep. His old homestead was out on a remote arm of the lake. Very few houses were built around there. He hoped it was still empty and they could move right in. He turned on the overgrown gravel road and followed it about two miles up a hill overlooking the water. Wow, it felt just like the good old days.

When he came out from under the tree canopy, there it was sitting in the same clearing. The old house stood there, nice and friendly, just how he'd left it. It looked a bit more rundown now and was in serious need of a paint job. The windows were boarded up, and a no-trespassing poster was tacked on the front screen door.

"I'll be right back, Miss Rosie," he said, lifting off the blanket for a moment so she could hear him. "Now be patient. We're almost home now. I've got to make sure nobody's here before we can go in."

Just in case anyone came snooping, he covered up Miss Rosie again, and then he ran up the steps and tried to pry the boards off the front door. Dark clouds were moving in, and it looked like rain. He wanted to get Miss Rosie in the house before the storm hit so she wouldn't get wet. Luckily, the boards came off fairly easily, and he jerked the last one loose, and tried the handle. It was locked. He turned to fetch his hammer out of the trunk, but whirled back around when the front door suddenly opened.

"Yes? What're you doing here?"

A young woman was standing there, frowning at him. Her dark red hair was coiled up in curls that fell over her shoulders, and she had on a white silk blouse and short black skirt and red shoes with very high heels. He thought she was real pretty. Unfortunately, she held a stun gun in one hand and a cell phone in the other.

"Oh, ma'am, I'm so sorry. I didn't think nobody was home."

"Obviously. Since you were trying to break in. You better get out of here, or I'm calling the police."

Jesse looked at the stun gun she was holding in her hand. It looked a lot like the one he used to have. "No, no, please, don't hit me with that thing. You got this all wrong. It's not like that 't'all. This here's my grandma's house when I was a little kid, and I just wanted to take a look inside. She died, see, but I got a lot of fond memories about living out here. I just wanted to see her stuff, just for a second."

The pretty woman looked out past Jesse to the old Caprice. "My mom and dad had a car like that when they first got married. But it was white."

"It was Grandma's. It still runs real well, though," he said, smiling his best smile. He was lucky that he was born with such an innocent, nonthreatening look about him. It worked nearly every time. "Hey, ma'am, like I said, I'm really sorry to bother you. I'll leave now. Sorry, if I scared you, too. I'm goin'. I'm outta here right this minute, I promise."

The woman hesitated, looking sympathetic, like she thought: poor little guy missin' his grandma. Yeah, he had her, hook, line, and sinker.

"Oh, well, I guess you can come inside and take a quick look around. I'm Miriam Long. I'm a real estate agent, and I'm helping a friend who's handling probate on this place."

"Oh, okay, I really didn't mean to bother nobody. I never woulda taken anything, or nothin'. I just wanna look at the house and think about Grandma and me." He glanced around. "And I didn't see no car so I didn't think nobody was here."

"That's because I came out here by boat. It's tied up down the hill at the dock. The back door's got a lockbox on it. It's just so much closer by water. I've got to keep an eye on it. Judge's orders. The last owner was murdered here, and she left no kin. So we're waiting for the case to wind its way through the courts."

"Oh, no! Somebody got murdered in Grandma's house!"

"Yes, the whole thing was quite terrible, really. Some crazy maniac killed her. C'mon in, I guess, but I can't stay long. I have a flight to catch."

"You're really nice to let me come in, ma'am." He gave Miriam an earnest look, but inside he smoldered at the maniac crack. He wasn't a maniac, and he wasn't crazy. How dare her say that about him? "I won't take but a few minutes, I promise."

Miriam stood back and allowed him to pass her and walk into the small foyer. He watched her put the stun gun in her handbag on the hall table, and then he looked around, nearly overcome by all the good memories. All his and Suze's furniture was still there, just like he'd left it. My goodness, it was so good to be back home again.

"I'm going down to check the basement for leaks. There was a terrible storm just a few nights ago. Go ahead, look around all you want." Miriam Long walked to the basement door and hesitated there for a second when she heard the roll of thunder out over the lake, and then she gave him another one of her warm smiles. She was really cute. "Hey, I guess you wouldn't want to put a bid on this house, would you? It's going to go cheap after we finally get a judgment."

"Not if it's got a leak in the basement." He laughed a bit, just to put her at ease. This was going to be so easy. Easier than any of his kills in a long, long time. He could hear the rain now, beating on the roof.

She laughed, too. "Well, let's just check it out then. I'd love to keep this place in your family."

The door under the steps was closed, and she opened it, switched on the light, and then carefully started down the steep and narrow steps, sort of sideways in her high-heeled shoes. He went after her, and two steps down from the top, she turned around and looked at him as if to say something. Her eyes went up at once to the brand-new, shiny, ten-inch Walmart-brand meat cleaver where he held it high over his head. He brought it down hard on top of her chest, and she screamed in agony and went flying backwards down the steps, head over heels, just from the extreme force of the blow. She hit the floor, hard and headfirst, and lay there groaning and gasping with pain. His blade still dripping with her blood, he carefully descended toward her, looking around the familiar reaches of the unfinished basement. Just the same. Everything. Even the old refrigerator was there. Great! It was so good to be home.

Miriam Long was still moaning and her fingers were twitching on her right hand. He stood over her for a moment, enjoying the seeping blood slowly staining the front of her white blouse scarlet and pooling underneath her. Then he found his old aluminum baseball bat, still in the spot where he'd hidden it under the bottom step so long ago. He raised it in the air and bludgeoned her in the face until she was dead. The real estate agent wouldn't bother them anymore, now would she? Miss Rosie liked her privacy, and so did he. He'd put Miss Rosie in the freezer. Then after it got dark and quit raining, he'd take his new friend, Miriam, far out into the middle of the lake and dispose of her body from her very own boat. That's what he'd do. Man, he hoped she had a good-looking boat. He always had loved to speed around out on the lake and enjoy the cool wind in his face.

Chapter Five

Nicholas Black did show up, just a few minutes after Monica took her leave, alongside a white-coated young waiter pushing a cart with several silver domes on top and acting honored to be accompanied by the big boss man himself. Black was dressed to the absolute nines in a tailor-made black pinstripe suit, yellow tie over a crisp white shirt, and yes, it did have his initials on the cuff, all three in a sweet little line. Just to the side of his solid gold cufflinks. Poor guy, must have to shop at K-Mart, and all.

"Hope you're hungry," Black said, shedding his jacket, draping it on the back of his chair, and sitting down across from her.

"Actually, I am. I only had three pounds of the food you ordered up for breakfast." He was piling the calories up on her, yes, sir, he sure was. "What's for lunch?"

"Chicken salad on croissants and home-made potato chips. Baked beans and slaw. Strawberry shortcake and vanilla ice cream for dessert. A bowl of frozen Snickers bars on the side."

"Oh, my God, frozen Snickers. I knew I had to like you for a reason."

At that, he looked inordinately satisfied, which was sort of endearing, actually. So they sat there, all pleasant like and domestic, with smiles and everything, while the efficient but nervous waiter served them. Then Claire watched Black open his large white linen napkin and settle it atop his lap.

She did the same. "So, Black, Monica just told me that you're absolutely crazy about me."

He looked up quickly. "And that's news to you? But just for the record, yes, I am crazy about you, and we are a very happy couple."

Claire decided to tease him a bit, check out his sense of humor. She hadn't seen much of that, yet. And she liked guys with senses of humor. He was Dr. Serious as Sin, and most of the time. "Were we just happy, or really, really happy?"

Stirring a big spoonful of sugar into his iced tea, no Equal for him, unh-uh, he focused those bluer than blue eyes on her face. "We are really, really happy together. Maybe even a couple of more reallys. Deliriously, even."

"That's present tense."

"You bet it is."

"What if I never remember you again? That's not going to make us all those reallys very happy, I suspect."

"You will remember."

"That sounds more like wishful thinking, doctor."

Claire decided that she was insecure about remembering, she had to admit it.

But it just wasn't happening, and it had been a while. She watched him squeeze a slice of lemon into his tea. She was highly curious about him. Not just his surface good looks, either. What was he all about? What did he believe in? What had he done in his life? Although she was fairly self-confident about her own feminine appeal, and all, this guy was the real catch of the year. She wasn't bad, or nasty looking, or anything, but she highly doubted if she, a lowly and poor detective, and he, a famous psychiatrist, had schmoozed around in the same circles, unless she was arresting one of them. "So tell me about yourself, doctor. All your deep, dark secrets. You look like the kind of man who's had a boatload of women, if not a Carnival Cruise liner. Am I just the last one you happened to be sleeping with?"

That was another attempt at ha-ha, sort of. But she did wonder if he was a bit of a womanizer. After all, he was wealthy and super hot and charming and super hot and muscular and super, super hot.

His stare was dead-on and unblinking, enough so to make her want to squirm, and everything.

"You're the only woman in my life and have been since the day we met."

She had the distinct impression that she had offended him big-time. He was not smiling and that really, really happy thing they supposedly had wasn't going on at the moment, either. Truth was, though, she was rather pleased as punch to hear him avow his fidelity. That is, if he didn't speak with forked tongue. Time to make nice, summon that smile to come hither.

"Well, doctor, I do like to see how you smile when you see me coming. Makes me feel all warm and fuzzy."

That did the trick. He did grin, all white teeth, dark tan, and arctic-blue eyes. "Well, Claire, maybe that's because I like to see you coming."

Wow, what a guy to have panting after her. Sure wished she knew more than his name. "Well, then, how did we meet, Mr. True Blue and Faithful to the End?"

Claire could actually see him relax. He took a leisurely sip of tea, and then put down his glass and picked up his fork. "Well, I can see you haven't lost any of your spunk, Claire. That's a good sign that you're definitely still you somewhere inside there." His next words, however, shocked the hell out of her. "Truthfully, Claire? We met because you thought I had murdered a woman. You went after me hard, bound and determined to bring me down, lock me up, and throw away the key, come hell or high water."

Absorbing all that, Claire took a moment and unwrapped the first Snickers of the ten or so that she planned to enjoy. "And that turned you on, I take it?"

"Damn right. Especially when you frisked me and slapped me in cuffs."

Claire felt the beginning of a smile. "Did I really?"

"Yes."

"Damn, wish I could remember it. That must've been fun."

"We could do it again, if you want."

She laughed at that thought. "Well, I frisked and cuffed plenty of guys when I worked at LAPD. I do remember that. It didn't turn me on all that much. Them, either."

After that exchange, they ate lunch and stared at each other some more, and she could see in his eyes that he was about to get all sappy and sentimental. Finally, he came out with it. "It's been a long time,

Claire. If I don't get to kiss you soon, I'm going to lose all control. I'm not sure what might happen if it comes to that."

So he did have a sense of humor, after all. She considered all the ramifications of doing what he wanted. No, she did not remember him. Would letting him kiss her be a nasty and grotesque thing to endure? She thought not. "I don't remember you. It would be like kissing a stranger."

"So?"

"So I'd feel awkward."

"That won't last long; I'll make sure it doesn't."

"I'm not sure, but I don't think I make a habit out of going around and kissing strangers."

"I hope not."

"I doubt very much if you'd do it, either, if you were in my boots. Or would you?"

"If it was you, I would, damn right."

Tempted was she, oh, yeah. Then again, she was still a little shaky on all cylinders. Kissing somebody like him might throw her off and make her do something stupid and needy. "I'm sorry, but I'm just not ready for playing kissy face with you. Not yet."

"Then I guess we'll have to start all over. Get acquainted, go out, fall in love again. I'll just have to make you want me as much as I want you right now."

That wouldn't take a ton of persuasion, not the way her pulse was reacting to this highly titillating conversation. "You mean you want to woo me, take me out on dates, and all that crap?"

"No, but if I have to, I will. Just so we eventually end up together. I love you, Claire. I need you back, I really do. Watching you lie in that bed, near death, was not exactly easy."

Feeling absurdly silly about the whole conversation, she was somehow pleased, too. Claire wasn't sure what she should say. She had told him the truth already. She wasn't ready to go to bed with him, a complete stranger. It just wasn't in her. "I'm sure I probably love you to pieces, too. It'll be interesting to find out. Someday."

He was calm, observing her, all relaxed and loose-limbed again, and waiting. Yep, he was a psychiatrist, all right. She was pretty sure that she hated psychiatrists. "Yes, very interesting indeed," he agreed. "Someday."

They chuckled together, both realizing the utter absurdity of the whole situation, and that mutual amusement relieved the building sexual tension. But then he grew serious again. "The people we discussed, your friends? They're planning to come see you. You know all of them well. I'm hoping talking to them will help you come back."

"And they are?"

"Your partner here in Canton County, for one. Bud Davis. Your boss wants to come, too, Sheriff Charlie Ramsay. Harve Lester is coming later."

Claire perked up at that name. "Harve's my partner at LAPD. I remember him. I can't believe he's living out here, too."

Nicholas Black smiled at her, his eyes all warm. When he picked up her hand and kissed her palm, as was his wont, it seemed, her breath caught just a little bit, as was her wont. Wonts going on helter-skelter, it seemed. Something tugged at her then, way, way, far back in the foggiest reaches of her paralyzed mind. The two of them together in Nicholas Black's big bed. Not platonically, not comforting her after a nightmare, unh-uh, but making love, enjoying each other. It was a mere glimpse that faded quickly, but it was the first time she had any clear recollection of him in a carnal way. They had been lovers, all right.

"You just now remembered something, didn't you?"

"Sure did. The two of us together. In bed. Rolling around and having a big time. We were having sex."

"No, we were making love. There's a big difference."

Their gazes locked for a long moment, and then Claire said, "You were kissing me, and it seemed that I was liking it well enough."

"Maybe we ought to go into the bedroom, have a reenactment, of sorts. Let me kiss you for several hours and see if it jogs some memories."

"Oh, it's gonna jog something, all right." But a single kiss wasn't going to burn down the house, as they say. That's what he wanted, and what if it did bring back their love affair? "Okay, go ahead and kiss me, and we'll see if we've still got a spark. Or if that bonfire's burned out and is done for."

Nicholas Black looked at her, and yes, he looked knowing and pleased and extremely self-confident. He stood up and pulled her up, too. He put one arm around her waist and jerked her tight against his chest. Then his mouth was attacking hers, no namby-pamby little peck on the cheek that, not even close. She liked it enough to open her lips under his mouth and slide her arms up around his neck. They enjoyed themselves awhile, getting all hot and bothered and breathless. At least, until she pulled away. They were breathing hard, not exactly unaffected by their little carnal experiment.

Claire worked to keep her voice steady. "Well, now, I do believe the part about us getting along really, really well."

"That's just the tip of the iceberg."

"It still feels strange."

Black was not ready to go back to his afternoon of shrinking head cases. "The more we do it, the less strange it's going to feel."

"You're pretty good at this kissing thing, Black. Makes me wonder."

"Wonder what?"

"Wonder about other women."

"There aren't any other women. And you haven't been seeing other men."

"Just let me get back to normal. You said it wouldn't take long."

"Okay. I told you we'd go along at your pace, and we will." He stepped back, hands on hips, and sighed. "By the way, I've got to fly to Miami for the weekend. I'm leaving Friday morning. I thought you might want to come along with me. Enjoy the sun and surf."

"Thanks, but I just made plans to go out with the girls."

That obviously threw him for a loop. "What girls?"

"Monica and a friend of hers named Nancy Gill."

Black looked less than pleased now. "Where are you going? Somewhere here on the Cedar Bend property, I gather?"

"You gather wrong. Monica says Nancy's uncle has a new restaurant called Jeepers. We're going to check it out."

"I'll stay home and go with you."

That made Claire want to laugh. "So now you want to go out with me and the girls? Oh, puh-lease. Black, give me a break already."

"You just came out of a coma, Claire. You've bounced back better than I ever would've expected, but going out partying is pushing it."

"It's not partying. It's just dinner and a little fun. And your very own, handpicked nurse is going to be there with me. That ought to make you feel better."

"It doesn't."

Suddenly, Claire felt a rush of her own annoyance. He'd done a lot for her, true, but Sir Black didn't have any right to keep her locked up inside his castle. "I don't like being controlled. I don't know much about myself, but I do know that."

"I don't want to control you."

"You just enjoy girls' nights out. That it?"

For the first time since she regained consciousness, Nicholas Black looked highly perturbed. He glared down at her, but he got over it pretty quick, too. The psychiatric composure came sliding down over his flash of anger like a theater curtain on the last act.

"Okay, go ahead, have a good time. Like you said, Monica's going to be there if anything goes wrong. Just remember to be aware of your surroundings. Lots of crimes happen around this lake and lots of crimes happen around you."

"I'll take my brass knuckles and pepper spray."

"Very funny."

Okay, they were having their very first fight in Claire's Brand-New Alternate Universe Adventure. She didn't like it. He didn't, either, judging by his massive black frown.

"Don't think I'm not glad you're doing this well. I just want it to continue."

"And you think I don't?"

"Then I'll back off and give you some space to breathe, if that's what you want."

"I'm not trying to offend you. You've been very good to me."

Black just stared down at her, not a happy camper, not a happy anything. "I've got a meeting in a few minutes. I'll see you later. Call my private number if you need me."

Black left quickly to take care of business down the hall in his office wing and to cool off about her snarky little independent streak, too, she suspected. After he left, Claire sat alone and finished eating Snickers bars, feeling better now that she finally remembered something about him, a very personal something that verified his story of their love life. She could see now how she could have fallen for him, oh, yeah, she sure could. And yes, she was a bit irritated, too, that he was being so damn overprotective. So she unwrapped another frozen Snickers and took a bite. Then she ate two more as fast as she could get them in her mouth. Comfort food. And Nicholas Black provided her with all the frozen Snickers she wanted, too. Gee, what a guy. That almost made up for their first little tiff.

Chapter Six

"So, you finally decided to wake up and quit lazing around, huh, Morgan?"

Claire spun around from where she was standing and staring out the big glass windows at the gloriously sun-spangled lake and thinking about the more than impressive way Nicholas Black had kissed her and the way she'd gone a little weak in the knees. A nice-looking guy with thick auburn hair cut to perfection was striding toward her. She'd never seen him before. Then when he gave her a big grin, she got some fluttery images of him that rushed up out of those dark and murky depths inside her head. They were laughing together, shooting service weapons on a firing range. The guy with the book. And his name came easily.

"So you're Bud, my partner. Right?"

"Well, hell, Morgan, I'm downright hurt you don't remember me. You spent a helluva lot more time with me than you ever did with Nick."

Tall and lean, tanned, he kept up with that slow grin, a very pleasant one at that, as he stopped in front of her. He was wearing a sharp gray suit with a light blue shirt and red paisley silk tie. His shoes were shined to a black gloss and his hair was well-cut and gelled up a bit on top. He looked as neat and stylish as any male model in *GQ*. He said, "You look pretty good, too, Morgan, 'cept for that little bald spot on your head. Tryin' for the Bruce Willis look?"

"Thanks, I really needed somebody to make fun of that."

Truth be known, she'd been a mite edgy and fearful about meeting her law enforcement buddies, especially her own mystery partner. However, this guy seemed pretty cool and easy to get along with. He just had this little wicked gleam in his eye that worried her but tickled her, too. "I do remember one thing about you, Bud. Some kind of book I got you—don't know what kind, and that's about as far as it goes."

Bud threw back his head and gave a deep, pleasant laugh. "Is that the only thing you 'member about me? That book you gave me about phrase origins? Well, now, maybe that's a good thing."

"Why? We butt heads a lot on the job?" That query came out a bit on the wary side. She sure hoped that wasn't the case.

"What you sayin'? Nope, never. We're like two peas in a pod, only better looking." His smile faded and his face waxed serious. "Actually, you're my best friend, Claire. I missed you like hell."

They stood there then, facing off. He was staring hopefully at her, and she was just staring at him. Uncomfortable? You bet your life. She felt like the new kid at school, all awkward and embarrassed and scuffing her toe in the dirt when somebody tried to make friends.

"You really can't remember me, can you?"

Claire shook her head. "A little bit. Dr. Black said I would get everything back soon. Maybe it'll happen now while we're talking. Who knows?"

"Dr. Black? Wow, that's pretty damn formal, Morgan. He rub you the wrong way again?"

"Actually, he hasn't rubbed me at all," Claire told him quickly, feeling a little guilty about that kiss. But he had rubbed her the other night, but certainly not the wrong way. It was when he'd massaged her shoulders and back after she'd awakened from one of those awful nightmares. Yes, they'd both gotten a little worked up before it was over, but it had stopped there. She felt her face grow hot and hoped she wasn't blushing. "I don't remember much about him, either. He's been working with me, though. What I want is to get back to work. I feel fine. I'm bored stiff sitting around here."

"Well, you got my vote on that one. I've been doin' all your paperwork way too long. You owe me, big-time, Morgan. Don't think I'm not gonna collect."

They laughed and the tension eased. One thing she did remember was how much she hated doing paperwork. Most cops did. She felt more at ease with this guy than she did with Black. Bud didn't seem to want anything from her except for her to come back to work. On the other hand, Black wanted everything from her, and she couldn't bring herself to give it to him yet. Sometimes she'd look into those eyes and almost melt. Other times, she just felt smothered. "Are you working a case now?"

"We got a missin' person out of Camdenton. White female. Vanished a few weeks ago."

"Any leads?"

"Nada. We got officers out lookin'. No dice."

"Okay, Bud, why don't we just sit down and you can tell me everything we ever did together. What'd you say?"

"Might take some time. We've been through some pretty hairy things."

"Yeah, that's what I hear. But we're both here, alive and well, so we must be good at our jobs." She smiled hopefully.

"Trust me, Morgan, you might wanna take advantage of this amnesia thing while you can. Sometimes I wish I had it." Bud was super sober now; his eyes were large and the color of ashes. They searched her face. "You still havin' those nightmares?"

"Yeah. Just about every time I shut my eyes. Black thinks that's what brought me out of the coma. Something frightened me so much I woke up to get away from it."

"Join the club. You remember the dream?"

Claire shook her head. "Not everything. The dreams are different. Just a man with a gun. People killing each other."

"Yeah. I've had that one." They shared a commiserating look, but then Bud grimaced. "I'm gonna warn you, Morgan, you're probably gonna remember a lot of really, really bad things. That's a given in this job." He sprawled down on the white couch and grabbed a handful of the miniature Snickers bars off her dinner tray. "Mind if I eat the rest of these?" he asked, already poking one into his mouth.

"Sure, help yourself. They were frozen but they're good melted, too. So how about answering some of my questions?"

Claire sat down across from him and watched him unwrap a

second miniature candy bar and pop the whole thing into his mouth. Nobody who liked Snickers could be all bad, that was her motto.

"Go ahead, shoot," he said, chewing slowly. "What d'ya wanna know?"

"So we're partners, been together a long time, that right?"

"Yep. Like I said, I spend more time with you than Nick does. Bugs the hell out of him, too. He likes to keep you all to himself." He picked up another candy bar, and she watched comprehension dawn across his face.

"You really don't remember him? You kiddin' me? The high and mighty Black?"

"High and mighty? Don't you like him?"

"Oh, yeah, he's a great guy. I'm just kiddin'. I meant because he's so rich and famous, and all that."

"He's famous?"

"Yep, pretty famous. He's a big-time shrink, you know, been on Fox News and CBS and all over the place. Larry King, too, when he was on. Writes self-help books, lots of stuff. Owns a bunch of hotels all over the place. Hasn't he told you all that?"

"No. He says it's best for me to remember things on my own."

"Well, he's loaded. He owns this hotel and some others, too. But don't get the wrong idea. He's a nice guy, really. He's done a lot for me and some of our other friends, too. He's not like some of those billionaires that you hear about."

"He's a billionaire?"

"I don't know, probably not. But he's got a lot, I can tell you that." He stopped. "I still cannot believe that you don't remember him, of all people. He's your guy."

"I don't remember much of anything, Bud. Some things, but they're just little bits. I don't remember the depth of our relationship, you know, the personal part. But I'm trying hard. So is he."

"Yeah, I bet he is. He's nuts about you. I bet he's not handling this all too well, is he?'

Claire shook her head.

Bud leaned back in the chair and propped a foot on his opposite knee. "Know what you need about now, Morgan? You need to get the hell outta here and take a look-see around our little neck of the woods. That's what's gonna help you remember stuff. Hell, I'll take you out seein' the sights myself. Get your guns and let's go."

Claire laughed. "Amen, twice over. Dr. Black's not sure I'm ready to be out and about. Thinks I'm still too shaky."

"You don't look shaky to me. A hell of a lot better than when you were laid up in that bed like some kind of white-faced zombie. Maybe skinnier than usual, but I reckon you could still beat me in the mile. I bet Nick hates you calling him that. It's always Black, from the very beginning."

"Why?"

"Beats me. That's just you, Morgan, matter-of-fact as hell."

"Well, you're right. But whatever. I think I'm getting better. I remember how to be a cop. I've just blocked out a couple of years."

"Retrograde amnesia. He told me."

"I still know how to do my job. I haven't forgotten that."

"Crazy weird. But also good."

"It's just that he hovers all the time. I appreciate it, I do. How strange is it that we were together and I can't remember much about it?"

"Ya'll are über into each other, count on it. He's probably just frustrated as hell. I would be."

That pretty well summed it up. Claire didn't need a full memory to recognize the desire in Black's eyes. But enough about that, already. She didn't say anything.

Bud eyed her for a second. "Well, c'mon, then, let's get outta here. Fly the coop. Leave him a note and check yourself out. I'll bring you back in one piece."

She really, really wanted to take Bud up on that offer, but Nicholas Black had been pretty awesome to her. She hated to just up and take off without a word. But she was definitely feeling all caged up and antsy and yes, trapped. She just wanted to get out from under Black's thumb for a while, meet other people, and see what her life outside the luxurious halls of Cedar Bend Lodge had been all about.

"Give the guy a call. Tell him I'll take good care of you."

Bud's grin was absolutely charming and so was his deep Southern drawl. She bet girls fell in his wake like downed oaks.

"Where're you from, Bud? Somewhere down South, I reckon."

"Atlanta, Georgia, and proud of it. Go Bull Dogs."

Bud Davis was a really cute guy. She wondered if she'd ever had a thing with him. "What about us, Bud? We ever, you know, have a fling?"

He looked quickly at her. "I wish. You always said you were too neat for me."

"I'm neat?"

He laughed another genuine, heartfelt one. "No, I'm kiddin', you're pretty sloppy, to be honest. I'm the neat one. Just take a look at me. Sharp, huh?"

"Well, you dress well, judging by the you I see at the moment."

"Wait until you remember me in my dress uniform. Or all dolled up for a weddin'."

Claire liked this guy, Bud. She suspected she liked him a lot before her accident, too. He was going to be easy to get along with.

"Look, Morgan, pick up that phone and see what Nick says. I don't wanna do anything that'll put you back in that bed. Me, I don't see the harm in takin' you outta here, maybe down to the office for a nice little show-and-tell, then around the lake."

"Me, either."

"But if Nick thinks it's a bad idea, I'll back off. He's the shrink and a helluva good doctor, too. Charlie'll be glad to see you up and walkin' around. You didn't look so hot lyin' there, hooked up to all those monitors, bandaged up, and half dead. You scared everybody to death when nobody could get you to wake up."

"You know what, Bud? I think an outing with you is the best medicine I could have. You're not exactly boring, Bud. What's your last name again?"

Bud laughed. "Davis. Budweiser Davis."

"Your name's Budweiser? No way."

"Yeah, my daddy had a funny sense of humor. His favorite beer, get it?"

Smiling, she picked up the phone and punched in Black's private cell number. He answered on the first ring. "Yeah, Claire. Everything okay?"

"Sure. I'm fine. Bud's here. We've been having a nice chat."

"You remember him?"

"Not much, but I like him."

Bud grinned and gave her two thumbs up. Guiltily, she realized that she already felt more comfortable around Bud than with Nicholas Black. Maybe that was because she and Bud weren't romantically involved.

Black said, "That's good. You're getting better."

For some reason, Claire hesitated, and then realized she didn't want to offend him. On the other hand, she was bound and determined to go out with Bud and maybe get right back to work. "Listen, Black." The name still didn't roll easily off her tongue. "I'm going down to the sheriff's office with Bud. See if that helps me."

"I can't go with you right now. I'm in the middle of a session."

"That's okay. I'll be fine. Bud says he'll be with me."

A rather long hesitation followed. Claire waited him out. "I'm not sure you're ready. I'd like to be around if you remember anything upsetting. You haven't had enough time to get your strength back."

"I'm going, Black."

An audible sigh sounded at the other end. "Now that sounds more like the Claire I know and love."

"Hey, Nick, don't worry. I'll take care of her," Bud yelled. "I can show her around the jail and give her pictures of all the homicidal maniacs she's locked up."

Claire laughed softly.

Black said, "If you do go, don't forget to take your cell phone. Let me talk to Bud a minute."

She handed over the phone.

Bud listened carefully, but he winked at Claire. "Yeah, doc. Don't worry about a thing. I'll keep her in my sight at all times." He listened some more. "I know. I'll take her by her house, too. You can pick her up there later."

"It's a go," Bud said, handing her the phone. "You're sprung. But don't try to get away. I'm armed."

The remark brought on a flood of disjointed visual images that streaked like shooting stars through her head: cleaning her weapon at the kitchen table. Two guns. She could see them clearly. "I own a Glock 9mm automatic and a .38 snub nose. I wear the Glock here"—

she touched just under her left arm——"in a leather shoulder holster, right? And the .38 pistol goes on my right ankle."

"Woo-hoo, Morgan, now we are cookin'. See what a good influence I am on you?"

"Where are my weapons? I want them back."

"I forgot. You don't got 'em, do you? Charlie took 'em. We retrieved them at the crime scene. He's waitin' for you to come in before he gives them back. He's gonna be happy to lay eyes on you, I can tell you that."

"Well, that settles it. Let's get out of here."

Outside, it was sunny and hot with a vivid blue sky and a slight breeze tossing the trees. It felt so good to have the sun on her face again. As it turned out, Bud drove a white Ford Bronco. She climbed into the passenger seat and looked around at all the bells and whistles and über luxuriousness going on outside Nicholas Black's resort hotel. The grounds were as beautiful and immaculate as the inside was. There were well-tended landscaped gardens and grounds, verdant golf courses, and huge hanging baskets of petunias and salvia and other flowers that Claire did not remember the names of.

There was a large marina behind the hotel, several pools, the whole works. It was a miniature Disneyland. In Claire's mind, she saw a big boat, and Black steering it, his black hair blowing back off his forehead, dark aviator sunglasses covering his eyes. As she and Bud drove away from the hotel proper, she recalled going down a road that led off to their left. There was a wood-sided cottage down that way, sitting right over the water. It was not one of the quick flashing images she usually got, but very clear and precise. A chill of reaction shot through her.

"Where's the wood cottage on the water, Bud? The one down that way with a big deck and potted geranium plants. Something bad happened there, I'm sure of it."

Bud glanced at her, nodding. "Yeah, we worked a particularly gruesome crime scene down there."

"Oh, God," she said, as a second disturbing image flashed like lightning. "There was a body under the water, a girl with blond hair. Sitting at a table."

"Right on. You're gettin' close to gettin' it all back now, Morgan.

Hang in there. You're gonna to remember me soon. Then you'll love me even more."

"Yeah, I'll bet. Run some of our old cases for me."

Listening to him give her the particulars on a couple of cases, Claire was a little shocked at the extreme grisly factor. "I thought this was supposed to be a quiet little backwoods hamlet on an equally calm lake."

"Wrong. This place hops. Murderers seem to like our sunshine and beautiful views."

The rest of the drive was pretty much light in mood, with Bud pointing out various points of interest and teasing her. When he pulled into the back parking lot of the sheriff's office, a whole bunch of work-related stuff started flooding back.

"I'm remembering things right and left now, Bud. I do believe it is going to come back." She suddenly felt elated.

"Good deal. Now let's go see the boss. He's quite a guy, has a vocabulary you won't believe. Won't like, either. Used to use the F-bomb every other word until his wife and preacher heard him and got all bent outta shape. Now he's a bit more sedate. But not much more. Charlie's one of a kind."

Claire followed her very likeable partner into the sheriff's office, more than wary as to what she would find inside, but very excited, too.

Jesse's Girl

Three days after the accident

Jesse hated, loathed, despised, and detested Nicholas Black. He quivered all over whenever that name intruded into his mind. He actually shook physically with rage. His fingers clenched with overwhelming jealousy and the urge to get his hands around that man's neck and strangle him until his eyes bulged and he died a terrible, slow, agonizing death. He burned with the desire to make him suffer for taking Annie away. She thought she loved Black now. But he had made her think that, and she didn't. How could she? And now, according to the news reports, she was held captive in his lair, that big, fancy, ostentatious hotel called Cedar Bend Lodge.

The newspapers in Springfield and Camdenton both said she lay there in a deep coma, but he didn't believe it. She was fine. Black was just holding her there against her will. But not for long. Jesse was already planning how he could rescue her. He had a home base now and had already settled Miss Rosie in her own bedroom. She was much more comfortable in the freezer, so he kept her there at night while he was sleeping. But he was preparing himself for his move. He'd dyed his hair brown and combed it forward like that Justin Bieber kid used to wear his hair and purchased dark brown contacts and large wire-rimmed glasses in the town of Osage Beach. Then he started growing a mustache and goatee. Despite all the publicity about the accident, nobody knew him; nobody even came close to recognizing him. According to the news accounts, the authorities thought him dead and washed away into the lake. Stupid fools. All so trusting; all so easy to dupe. He'd been able to pull the wool over people's eyes all his life. Only difference was, he was extremely good at it now, better than ever.

The Cedar Bend Lodge was a busy place, lots of tourists, lots of staff members, many of them college kids only working for the summer. He could walk around freely; nobody noticed him, nobody bothered him. He watched, listened, ate in the sidewalk café and poolside snack bars and in Two Cedars, Black's fancy five-star restaurant just off the giant black-and-gold lobby. It didn't take him long to find out that Annie was upstairs in Nicholas Black's spacious penthouse apartment. Black was taking care of her himself, with the help of a shy and pretty young nurse named Monica Wheeler.

When he saw the help-wanted flyer for the Two Cedars Restaurant, he knew he'd hit the jackpot. The busy season was in full swing with several conventions ongoing. With all the young kids quitting and heading off to college, Cedar Bend needed all sorts of help. Jesse went after the one that would get access to upstairs and into Annie's room. Busboy or waiter, either would do the trick. He charmed the human resources manager to high heaven. The guy couldn't wait to hire him on, didn't even ask for references. After all, what credentials did a busboy need? Anybody could clean off tables and carry dishes to the kitchen sink. When he told the guy he could cook, too, the H.R. guy told him a promotion was possible if he proved himself in his entry position. Now all he had to do was find an opportunity to take Annie's meals up to her. Surely, Black would order up some of their meals. Then he'd see what the truth was. Then he'd find a way to take her away with him just like he did the last time. She'd be so grateful. She loved him as much as he loved her. But he had to stay out of Nicholas Black's sight. Despite his disguise, which was very good, Black might recognize him and so could some of Annie's other friends. He would have to keep a sharp lookout and stay under their radar.

No one had found the real estate agent's body, either. Yes, things were certainly meant to be. Step by step, he was getting closer. Then, to his delight, a real stroke of luck went down. Annie's nurse, the lady named Monica, asked him if he'd like to sit down and have a cup of coffee with her. He'd been extra friendly to her from the get-go, every time he saw her eating in the restaurant. Smiling shyly at her, offering to get her more Coke or tea, giving her the idea that he was interested. She was ripe for the picking, and that's exactly what he'd do.

"My name's Monica Wheeler. I hope you don't think I'm being too forward," she'd said, lowering her lashes in an endearing and rather bashful manner. She was a pretty girl, tiny, barely five feet tall, with lovely skin and big doelike, innocent brown eyes. She thought he was handsome, and she wasn't trying to hide her attraction, not in the least. She wanted to be with him. And she was right. Her head would look lovely sitting on a platter like Miss Rosie's. He needed a friend at home to talk to. Miss Rosie went to bed way too early. But she was an old lady, after all. So he never snapped at her or reprimanded her to make her feel bad. Yes, he'd take Monica's head home with him, right after she outlived her usefulness.

"No, ma'am, not at all," he'd answered her. "I'm new here. I just started a few days ago. I'm Jesse Jordan."

"Well, I'm new here, too. Dr. Black hired me to take care of one of his patients. She's in a coma."

Wow, was this ever going to be easy. God was with him. "Maybe we can hang out. I don't know about you, but I'd like that. We can go exploring together."

"I'd like that, too."

"Where're you from, Monica?"

"St. Louis. I worked at Barnes Jewish Hospital, but they said I could take vacation leave and come help Nick Black take care of Claire. He's very well thought of there."

"That was kind of you."

"Yes. Nick's paying me generously, of course, and it's such a shame about his girlfriend."

"A shame? What do you mean?"

"Haven't you heard about her accident? It's all over the news. She was in a car crash with an escaped mental patient. He was completely crazy and drove the car off a bridge down near Ozark. She would've drowned if Nick hadn't gotten to her in time."

"How awful. What about the crazy guy? Did they catch him?"

She shrugged. "They didn't find him, but they don't think he survived the crash."

The idiots, but he rather resented the crazy part. He was not crazy. Maybe he wouldn't take Monica home and make her part of his family, after all. She was being hateful. "How's that woman now?"

"She's still in the coma. Poor Nick. I feel terrible for him. He's at her side night and day. The only time he ever leaves is to clean up or see to his other patients. That's when I watch over her for him."

"You mean she's never even opened up her eyes, or said anything?"

"No, she's in a very deep sleep. She appears to have terrible dreams and thrashes around sometimes, and we think she's coming to, but she hasn't yet. But who wouldn't have nightmares? It's tragic what that psycho put her through."

Jesse went tense. Psycho, was it? He looked at the steak knife lying on the table. All he had to do was snatch it up and stab it into her eye. She deserved it for saying all those bad things about him. She didn't know him. She didn't have the right to treat him this way. But there were other people in the restaurant. In time, he'd get her eye, all right. He'd take it out and keep it. But that would come later. Right now, he needed to charm her.

"Hey, how about us going to a movie or something?" he asked.

When she hesitated, he said, "Oh, never mind. I bet you don't date the kitchen help, do you?"

That got to her. "Oh, of course, I would. It's not that. I just don't have much time off. Just a few hours through the day. I've got a room up in the penthouse. The doctor sits with her all night. He is just worried to death about her. I don't know what he'll do if she doesn't wake up soon."

It won't matter, Jesse thought, because Annie was going to be long gone very soon. So far away, in fact, that Black would never, ever find her. It would be easy enough, if she was still unconscious. All he needed to figure out was how to get her out of the penthouse without anybody seeing him. That shouldn't be much of a problem. He'd done a lot worse. And he was patient, very patient, and very clever. He would get Annie soon, and Monica would be his ticket upstairs.

Chapter Seven

Once they were inside the cool white halls of the sheriff's department, Bud and Claire walked together to the detective bureau, where she was greeted with a quick and impromptu standing ovation. Startled, to say the least, Claire nodded to the men and women applauding from their desks, but she was glad they didn't gather around and slap her on the back and say stuff like good job, glad you're awake, cool beans, etc. It was touching, to be sure, but also bewildering. She didn't know them, didn't even know exactly why they were so glad to see her. Grinning like a proud papa, Bud led the way back to the sheriff's private office.

The brass plaque on the wall was engraved with the name Sheriff Charles Ramsay. A tiny little munchkinlike secretary was on her feet and around her desk in nothing flat, hugging Claire before she could get out a word. The older woman reached to about Claire's shoulder, despite her five-inch heels. She was even smaller than the diminutive Monica, and that was saying something. She wore a lobster-red business suit and a black blouse with a red-and-white striped scarf knotted around her throat. She looked to be in her sixties, or maybe early seventies, and she had a nice smile and black rectangular reading glasses hanging on a chain. She hugged Claire as if she'd never let go.

"Hi, Madge, how's it goin'?" Bud said.

Madge ignored him. "Claire, Claire, thank God you're all right. I was so, so, so worried about you. My Red Hats have prayed for you at all of our meetings."

What the hell were Red Hats? "Thank you. I'm feeling pretty good now, as you can see. Up and walking around, ready to go back to work."

"Wonderful, wonderful, you poor little thing. But you look good, and pretty as ever, even after all that terrible stuff that happened to you."

As far as Claire could remember, which wasn't all that far back, a couple of days, in fact, nobody had ever called her a "poor little thing." Maybe it was because she still wasn't armed like all the other deputies and had that ugly bald spot with some noticeable ex-stitch marks on her scalp.

"Hi, Bud," Madge said to him. "Charlie said for you to go right in. Welcome back, Claire. Everyone's missed you so much."

So right in they went, and Claire got more little shivers of déjà vu as a man stood up from where he'd been sitting behind his large oak desk. He was smiling, too. Everybody was extraordinarily glad to see her. She must've been a good person. Well, that was an encouraging sign. They could've all booed her when she walked in and made her feel like crap. Sheriff Ramsay came around his desk to meet her, too, but he just grabbed her hand and shook it vigorously. He was not much taller than she was and had some serious bulldog jowls going on and some rather bloodshot blue eyes, too. But his smile was big and genuine and pleased. Despite that pleasant expression, he looked strong and capable and tough, certainly not one to be trifled with.

"You look great, Claire, just great, absolutely as good as new. Can't tell you how glad I am to see you up on your feet and already back here at the office. I was planning to come see you again after work today, but you beat me to the punch." The sheriff took a deep breath while he held her by both arms and gazed at her. "I wasn't so sure there for a while, but Nick always said you were going to make it."

"Thank you, Sheriff. I'm very glad to be here, believe me."

"You remember much yet?"

"Some things. It's coming back, bit by bit."

"Well, good, good. Sit down, sit down, both of you."

They sat down, and silence reigned until Sheriff Ramsay said, "I've got to say I'm surprised you're up and about so soon. Nick has released you to go to work, I take it."

"I have released myself, sir. I feel fine, and I'm ready to do my job. I don't remember everything that happened during the last couple of years, but I remember how to work a case. I can do my job, Sheriff. My memory loss doesn't affect that."

Charlie Ramsay considered her as he picked up his pipe, tamped the tobacco down with his right thumb, and struck a match. He sucked on the pipe for a moment, making it glow slightly. Bud and Claire sat patiently, breathing in the gray smoke curling around his head and waiting for his lighting-up enjoyment to wane. Luckily, the pipe smoke didn't smell all that bad. Not real good, either, but not stomach turning. Finally, he said, "It feels a little soon to me. I'd feel better if Nick writes you a clean bill of health."

"With all due respect, sir, Dr. Black is not in charge of my life. I'm not in the hospital, and I'm not his patient anymore. I'm just staying at his place for the time being."

Charlie couldn't hide his shock. Lowering his pipe to an octagonal glass ashtray on his desk, he said, "Dr. Black? You mean to tell me that you don't even remember Nick?"

"I remember some things about him, but I've got a ways to go. It won't interfere with my job performance."

Bud said, "She seems just fine to me, Sheriff. I'm swamped with work. I sure could use her help."

"So you remember your job training, but not a lot of your past interactions with people? That what you're sayin'?"

"Yes, sir. Dr. Black says that's normal for some people who've suffered head traumas."

Charlie looked at Bud, apparently still thrown off by her Dr. Black references. She better lay off that from now on, and just call the guy, Black. "Very curious. You look good, though, Claire, considering."

"I am fine, sir. But I feel naked without my guns and badge. Bud says you have them here. I'd like to get them back now, if that's all right with you."

More hesitation. What did he think? That she was going to grab them and shoot up the place if somebody yelled boo?

"You went through an awful lot, detective. Are you absolutely certain you want to put this added stress on yourself this soon?"

"I don't remember the accident, or the aftermath. Black is going to continue to work with me and, as my partner, Bud will be with me when I'm on duty. In case I need him."

Chagrined, Claire picked up the hint of desperation in her own voice, but she couldn't help it. She felt anxious, all right. "I'll go crazy if I have to sit around much longer doing nothing, Sheriff. If I feel overwhelmed, I'll back off, I swear. If I think it's too much for me and might put Bud in danger, or any other fellow officer, I'll hand over my badge and take more medical leave. I won't be a risk to your other deputies, sir."

Sighing, Charlie puffed some more. They watched some more. The smoke was making intricate swirling designs in the air, like oil in water. "I just hate to see you get hurt again. This wasn't the first time, you know."

"I'll be fine, sir. You've got to believe me. I'm not going to do anything stupid or reckless. As I understand it, the perpetrator who was after me is dead. So that doesn't matter anymore."

"Yes, that's true." Charlie swiveled his gaze to Bud. "Davis, you agree to stay close to her for the next few weeks, help her along the way, if she needs it?"

"Yes, sir. No problem."

"Well, okay, but for just half a day at first, and by that, Claire, I mean half a day. Don't abuse it. You need to ease back into work. I know that, Nick knows that, and I think you know that. Can you abide by that directive, Detective Morgan?"

Claire didn't like that directive, not one little bit. She ought to be the one who decided how much she could take now, or in the future, or any other time. However, she could also see the writing on the wall, and since she could be pragmatic when she had zero other options, she said, "Yes, sir. Half a day. In the beginning."

Charlie's face had *skeptical* written all over it. He turned to Bud. "Davis, I'm going to hold you to that."

Glancing at Bud, Claire read his expression to be: *What? Me? She's the one with the amnesia.*

"Okay, Claire, your badge and your weapons are right here. I kept them close because I knew you were going to beat this thing. Not this soon, maybe, but I knew you'd be back."

Pulling open the bottom drawer of his desk, he fished out her

Glock 9mm and .38 snub nose. Claire was so glad to see her guns that tears almost welled; it was like seeing two long-lost, protective friends. Both weapons were snug inside their holsters, the belts wrapped around them. Charlie's phone rang just as he was sliding them across the desk. He picked up the receiver and swiveled his chair around to face the windows. Claire quickly grabbed the weapons, handled them with some reverence and loving care, and then shoved a clip in the Glock and shrugged her shoulder holster into place. Just as she was fastening the Velcro holster on her ankle, Charlie swung back around and looked at her.

"We got a body out on the lake, hung up in a duck blind. Our jurisdiction. You two want it?"

"Yes, sir," Claire said, before Bud could open his mouth. She was eager and rarin' to go. She felt happier already, ecstatic, even. This is what she wanted, more than anything.

"You're absolutely certain you're up to taking on a homicide this soon?"

"Yes, sir. In fact, I think this is the best I've felt since I woke up."

"You up to it, too, Bud?"

"Yes, sir. Investigating the crime scene won't be too dangerous for her. The guy's already dead." Bud and Claire smiled. Sheriff Ramsay didn't. He handed Claire her badge, still hanging on the chain, and gave them the location of the body. She looped it over her head and felt truly whole again.

"Don't make me regret this, Claire. Half a day, no more."

"Yes, sir. You won't be sorry."

The two of them got out of there in a hurry before he thought better of the idea. But he'd made the right decision. She was all healed up, bored stiff, ready to go to work. Her hunch was that she'd remember a lot more of the last two or three years hard at work on a case, instead of sitting around Black's luxury digs staring out the window and feeling sorry for herself.

Luckily, this late in the day, a lot of the other detectives had gone home and their desks were empty and she wouldn't have to face another embarrassing round of applause. They walked outside and climbed back into Bud's Bronco and were on their way within minutes. Claire had no idea which way to go. "Do you know where we're headed, Bud?"

"Yeah, Buckeye and I fish out that way. I've done some duck hunting with Harve out around there, too. The boat's at the department's marina."

"How is Harve?"

"You remember him?"

"I remember that we were partners in L.A. I don't recall being here with him."

Bud took a right onto a busy highway and signaled over into the inside lane. "He's doin' okay. He's worried about you. He'll be glad to see you. Maybe we can drop by there when I take you to your place."

"He lives close to me?"

"Just down the road."

Bud wasn't babying her, not tiptoeing around on eggshells, and Claire appreciated that. She concentrated on remembering where she lived on the lake and did remember a house. An A-frame sitting right on the beach. She loved it there. She knew that. Black had said so, too, but she felt it. The idea of going home made her feel happy and eager to get there and check it out. Already, she was feeling more confident about things working out okay. Coming back to work was turning out just fine.

As they drove along a highway that skirted the lake and wound its way up and down the spines of high forested hills, Claire could see shining glimpses of the lake and welcomed the awesome views. She remembered driving this road, remembered kidding around with Bud. She asked him a few questions along the way and continued to be grateful that he wasn't saying much, just sitting back and letting her sort things out in her own mind. Yep, she liked him better all the time. They must've been good friends. The idea brought another picture blooming up inside her mind. "You were bitten by a snake."

Bud glanced over at her. "You got that right. A timber rattler. Wasn't much fun, either."

"On a case."

"Yeah, a real nasty one. Lots of snakes and creepy crawly things."

More memories flooded back, of a dim cave, of the smell of

sulfur, and the disconcerting sense of extreme anxiety. The images vanished as soon as they came, and she let them go. Black said not to force the traumatic things, that they'd come back in time and that was soon enough. Fine by her.

Bud turned left and drove down a steep, winding road to the lake. "The water patrol's got a departmental boat at the marina below here. We can ride it out to the scene."

A guy that Bud introduced as Al Pennington was waiting, already inside the speedboat and manning the controls. He had on his brown patrol uniform; his blond hair was cropped short in a military cut, and there was a big grin spreading across his sunburned face. He had biceps about the size of small Christmas hams, straining the seams on his short sleeves. "Welcome back, Morgan. I heard you were gonna make it."

"Thanks."

Claire's colleagues weren't pushing her and asking her a lot of nosy questions, and that was a giant relief. She didn't have any answers, anyway. They climbed aboard, and Pennington maneuvered the craft out of the marina and didn't open it up until they hit the floating markers on the main channel. After that, they seemed to fly over the choppy water, bumping atop waves caused by the wakes of speedboats. Claire pulled down the brown departmental cap that Pennington tossed to her, snugged it tighter on her head, held it with one hand, and was jolted by another tidal wave of the past. Black had a boat, a blue-and-white one, larger and more powerful than this one. He came to her house in it. She got a mere inkling that she had a physical fight aboard it, but she didn't see whom she fought with. Probably not Black, though. Guess her protective little mind was in action again, shielding her from the evil things still crouching in their dark hidey-holes.

It was a beautiful place, she decided, this unknown lake she lived on. She already liked it a lot better than L.A. The roar of the boat's motor drowned out any conversation. She was glad about that, too. She watched the horizon, until a ring of identical police boats came into sight, moored around a duck hunter's blind built up out of the water on wood pilings. As they neared, she got a glimpse of the body. It was propped up against the stand in a sitting position. It looked like a female, but the victim's head was down, the chin resting on the chest, so she couldn't tell yet. Minutes later, Pennington shut off the motor and the boat's wake washed them up closer to the crime scene. They immediately picked up the sickly sweet and awful odor of the decomposition of human flesh. Bud tossed a line to the water patrol officer standing on the deck of the rather large duck blind.

"What can you tell us about the victim?" Claire asked the officer, as soon as the boat was secured. The patch on his breast pocket said Lt. Steve Clemons.

"Not much yet, detective. We got a white female. My guess is maybe mid-thirties. No visible ID, no sign of sexual assault, but the M.E.'s gonna have to determine that. The call's in to him. Buckeye should be here with his team any minute now."

Claire got a picture in her head of the man, Buckeye. She almost smiled because memories were coming back, one at a time, maybe, but they were coming back. It couldn't be soon enough, either. She was ready to roll, ready for the needle to point right at normal. Today, right that moment, she felt like a million dollars.

"Any identifiers that you can see? Tattoos, jewelry?"

"Can't say yet. We haven't moved the body. She's fully clothed. Sitting up, head down. We might get lucky and find something when we move her."

"She's out of rigor?"

"She's been dead a while. She's in decomp. Some flesh is sloughing off."

Bud was looking at Claire. "I do believe you're back in the game, Morgan."

"I told you I didn't forget how to do my job."

"Well, I, for one, am glad you're here."

Bud had that cheesy grin back in place. His perfectly styled hair and silk tie were now fluttering about in the wind. Almost without thinking, Claire said, "How's Brianna?"

Bud's smile faded instantly. A look of chagrin overtook his face. That made her nervous. What had she said wrong?

"You remember Bri, Claire?"

"I remember that she's your girlfriend, right?"

"She used to be. She moved away, but we keep in touch. I'll tell you all about it someday."

But not today, Claire thought. Bud was extremely hesitant to discuss the woman named Brianna, and she could take a hint. "Okay, let's take a closer look at the victim."

They moved into the bow, where they could get a better look at the position of the corpse. The dead woman was wearing a long-sleeved white silk blouse and a short black cotton skirt. The bottom of the blouse and top of the skirt were stiff with a dried brown substance, probably blood from a wound hidden by the long matted hair flowing down over her bowed head. She had been posed, hands clasped, legs demurely crossed. The soft breeze was picking up some of her hair and blowing it around. Her legs and feet were bare and darkly tanned. Both her shoes were gone.

Claire said, "I guess she could be a victim of a boating accident and somehow managed to crawl up here to die. Any reports of collisions?"

Al Pennington shook his head. "Nope. Nothing like that around this area."

Claire looked back down at the body. "She's not dressed like a woman out fishing or boating."

Bud said, "Could be she's an office worker, or lawyer, a professional woman. That's my guess."

Claire turned to Steve, the water patrol officer. "Have you guys checked out the inside of the duck blind? Maybe the assault took place right here."

"Yeah, we looked inside. Didn't see much. A couple of beer bottles, some fast food wrappers. Her shoes aren't in there. Forensics can tell us for sure."

"Do you know who owns this blind?"

"Not yet, but we're on it. She's been here a while—you can see that by the level of decay. That's all I can tell you so far."

The sun was incredibly hot, beating down on their heads and making them perspire. It had to be ninety degrees or more, probably closer to a hundred. And she wasn't used to the heat. Sweat rolled down her forehead, and she wiped it off with the back of her hand as she turned and looked at the pleasure boats speeding around the lake, many of them pulling skiers. A handful of boaters were anchored nearby, including a party barge, the passengers sitting around and watching them go about their grisly work.

"Somebody needs to get those people out of here," she told Steve Clemons.

"No problem. We'll take care of it."

"You're back to yourself, all right," Bud said to her. "Nick's gonna be pleased."

Claire wasn't so sure about that. All she knew was that this was what she lived for. This was the best medicine she could take. Past happenings were being triggered right and left, lots of them disjointed, true, but she was remembering. One thing she was sure of, though: She knew her job. She enjoyed her work. And she was very glad to be back to it.

Chapter Eight

It didn't take long for the Canton County forensics team to show up. Claire didn't recognize any of them, not a face, not a voice, nothing. Disappointing to say the least, but hey, she did know Bud had that book, was bitten by a rattler, and dated somebody named Brianna. However, they must've been fairly close friends of hers, because they all erupted with whooping and hollering and yelling out hellos and glad you're backs before they even got out of their boat.

The first one to her said his name was Buckeye Boyd, who she knew to be the chief medical examiner. He looked a lot like that guy, Bob Keeshan, on the old reruns of *Captain Kangeroo*. White hair, black beard and mustache, looked to be in his late fifties, sixties. Jeez, how could she remember old reruns and not her best friends? This was as freaky as all get out, but she smiled and tried not to show how upsetting it was.

"I know you don't remember me yet, but man, am I ever glad to see you working again. I was beginning to think that you were never gonna wake up."

Returning his engaging smile, Claire wracked her brain for any tiny, inconsequential tidbit about him, but to no avail. She was totally blank on him. "I'm sorry, Mr. Boyd. I just don't remember you yet."

"Mr. Boyd? Wow, you are out in stranger territory. Nick said you were struggling with some memory issues. Wish I could help."

Buckeye Boyd meant that, there was no doubt in Claire's mind. His dark eyes were full of kindness and understanding and encouragement. "Yeah, he says I'll remember everything. So I guess we'll all have to be patient and wait it out. It's not easy, though."

"That's my gal. Well, under the circumstances, I guess I'd better introduce you around. Like I said, I'm Buckeye, but you usually call me Buck. I'm the M.E. here. We've been friends ever since you moved out here from Los Angeles." He glanced around. "And by the way, we go bass fishin' together whenever I can get you out of Black's clutches." He grinned. "Which isn't very often, unfortunately."

Claire laughed uncertainly. So she spent all her downtime with the good doc. It also seemed that her friends liked him. Good enough, she supposed. It appeared they were all one big happy forgotten family.

"This here crazy guy is Shaggy. He's our criminalist and does one hell of a good job. I think it's safe to say that he's missed you like crazy."

Claire looked at the young man who had just walked up. He was giving her a huge goofy smile, and before she could blink, he had her in a bear hug and was squeezing her and talking at the same time. "God, Claire, this is weird shit. You really can't remember me, nuthin' 'bout me? That's so not cool."

When he let her go, Claire stared hard at his face, trying to get past the black bolted door blocking out her life. Again, frustration hit her hard. It was utterly demoralizing, because the memories were right there, in her reach, but too foggy, like trying to remember how to spell a word or recall who won Best Actress last year. It made her want to scream in sheer helplessness. She finally said, "You look really familiar, Shaggy."

That much was true. Shaggy Becker had some serious dreadlocks going on, reddish-blond, lots of earrings, eight or nine maybe, and he was dressed in long biker shorts and a garish green-and-red-and-white Hawaiian shirt. He was his own man, all right, and eccentric, no doubt about it. But he had to be good for the M.E. to allow him such leniency in office dress. Everyone else had on polo shirts with the M.E.'s logo on the pocket.

"This here's Vicky, our office photographer." An older woman stepped forward, nodded and smiled shyly. She was about five-six and curvaceous, with a dark complexion and brown hair caught in a bun. She got right to work and snapped pictures of the victim's body.

"And here's our new colleague. Name's Nancy Gill. She hails from way down yonder in New Orleans. She's been assisting me this summer, and I'm going down there next fall to work at her office for a time. Sort of a medical examiner exchange program I've gotten into."

Nancy Gill was the girlfriend that Monica had mentioned. The girl whose uncle owned the place called Jeepers. She came straight up to Claire and held out her hand. Claire took it, and they shook hands. Nancy was a very pretty girl, as tall as Claire was, maybe an inch or two taller, with the most beautiful chestnut brown hair and cinnamon-colored eyes almost the exact same color as her hair. The woman's smile was friendly, and somehow understanding, as if she knew what Claire was going through. Claire took to her immediately. Maybe it was because Nancy hadn't known her before, and she hadn't known Nancy before, either. They were starting out on equal footing. Both were surrounded by virtual strangers.

"It's a real treat to meet you, detective. I've heard an awful lot about you, all good, too, even way down yonder in bayou country as Buck likes to say. You're a famous lady, I guess you know, for takin' down all those serial killers. Or maybe you don't know, not quite yet."

"No, not yet. We have a mutual friend, I believe. Monica Wheeler? In fact, I'm going out with the two of you next Friday night."

"Yeah, she told me she was gonna ask you. Well, that's great. We have lots of fun out at Jeepers."

Everybody went to work, and Nancy immediately joined Buck beside the body. But Claire did like her. Maybe the two of them could be friends. Maybe they would have fun, would laugh, and Claire wouldn't have to remember anything about her.

Buck called back to Claire and told her the names of the newly arriving water patrol officers. None looked even remotely like anybody she'd ever seen before. She did like all these people, but she was beginning to feel more and more isolated and alone, like she'd landed on Mars. *I will remember*, she told herself sternly, *I will.*

But would she really? And what if she never did? Then what? Start over? Make a new life?

"So what do we have here, Claire?"

Grateful that Buck was now back to business, Claire jumped right in, pleased she remembered how to investigate a murder. That was one thing she could pour her full concentration on without getting depressed or distressed.

Claire told them what they knew so far. "A Caucasian female. I estimate she's probably early or mid-thirties. A group of kids out skiing noticed the body while circling back to pick up a skier. They called it in, and water patrol made it to the scene in less than ten minutes. No means of ID that we can see. No purse or other personal items. Nobody's touched the body. A report of a missing person came in few weeks back. What was the name on that, Bud?"

"Miriam Long. Real estate agent out of Camdenton. Fits the basic description so far."

"I reckon nobody can say you've forgotten your stuff, Claire," Buckeye noted, but his eyes were now focused on the corpse. "Maybe we got your missing gal, right here. Okay, let's get started and get this poor woman out of here."

Relieved the attention was off her and onto the victim, Claire moved back into the stern of the boat and watched Vicky snap pictures of the body from every possible angle with the departmental digital camera. Then she picked up her video cam and filmed the duck blind, inside and out, and moved carefully around the corpse, including a shot of the law enforcement officers observing the retrieval from their secured boats. Finished, Vicky moved to one side. "Okay, Buck, she's all yours."

Buck and Nancy Gill donned protective gear and climbed down closer to the waterline and took a moment with their initial examination of the deceased.

Buck said, "Well, she wasn't killed here. Somebody took a lot of time to pose her just so. Probably for some fetish known only to the killer. He had to be fairly confident that nobody was around to see him lift her out of a boat and carry her up here. Any witnesses yet?"

Seems Claire was designated to do the talking. Bud stood back and watched, no doubt letting her get her feet wet. She liked him better for it. He was all right.

"No, but there are lots of ski boats around here. Somebody might have seen something. Nothing reported yet that we've been told."

A minute later, Bud did venture his opinion. "Probably dumped her here late at night when it was nice and dark and nobody was around."

Nancy Gill spoke up. "At least a couple of weeks ago, I'd say. Her legs are discolored and bloated. The skin's degrading fast, sloughing off on the exposed surfaces. She's been out here in the sun and heat a good long time, you're right about that. We get this kind of thing in the bayous. Heat accelerates the decomp."

Buck unclasped the woman's left hand and examined her fingernails. Then he turned the hand over and examined the fingertips. "I might be able to get some prints off her, but it's iffy. Maybe we'll get lucky, though." Shaking his head, he stood up and looked at Claire. "We had another case similar to this, a couple of years back. Remember any of it, Claire?"

"Not a lot." She felt sure he was talking about the girl she'd remembered, the one sitting at an underwater table, but she kept that to herself. "So you think it might be the same perpetrator?"

Everybody looked at her, then at each other, but nobody answered for a moment. Now that kind of behavior can rattle an amnesiac's nerves. Shaggy finally spoke up, without the wide grin, serious for the first time. "That dude's dead. Killed in that car crash, the one that knocked out your memory."

Well, that was news to Claire. The guy obsessed with her had struck before. She started to demand details, but wasn't sure this was the time or the place. Apparently, Buck was reluctant to get into that, too.

"Let's finish this and get her bagged," Buck ordered, and then turned to his photographer. "Vicky, be sure you get a clear view of the retrieval on video. We don't want any sloppy procedures for some slick defense lawyer to pick apart."

Claire stepped closer. "Doesn't look like she was raped. The clothes are all tucked in place. The pose has got to mean something."

Buck took hold of the corpse's hair and lifted the head. He

grimaced and blew out a quick breath. "Looks like that's the only break this poor lady got."

When he moved aside, they all got a view of her face, or what little was left of it.

Bud groaned. "Oh, God. He beat the hell out of her face."

Buck knelt and gave them his initial appraisal. "She's unrecognizable, so I hope I get those prints. There's a deep laceration at the center of her chest. Coupla inches deep, it looks like. Maybe three or four inches, actually. Could be she was stabbed first, and then beaten up once she fell down. God, this is brutal. Lord, the killer sure didn't show her any mercy. These lacerations on the face go down to the bone. The blade wound is severe, but this victim died from the beating, I'm pretty sure. I'll know for certain after we get her downtown. God, this never gets easy." He shook his head. "I'm not sure I've ever seen a beating this severe. If I had to guess, I'd say the murder weapon was a hammer or an iron bar, or maybe a bat, something like that."

Claire said, "Looks personal to me. Rage against a wife, maybe. Or a girlfriend. Somebody he knew very well."

Buck nodded, looking up at her. "Yeah, Claire. Somebody lost control, all right. It took a while to do this much damage to the facial bones and skull. Most of the blows landed on the face and side of her head. The body looks relatively untouched. Except for that one deep gash at chest level."

Glancing around the lake, Claire tried to determine what had happened. He had to have used a boat, but where did he put in? It could've been a hundred different places, private and commercial. When she caught sight of a large, sleek motor yacht anchored in the far distance, she pointed to it. "Anybody know who owns that boat over there? See it?"

The guy named Shaggy laughed out loud, then sobered instantly when his boss gave him a severe glare. Shaggy looked hangdog. "Sorry, Claire. It just surprised me that you didn't know. I forget that you don't remember much."

Bud spoke up. "That's Black's boat, Claire. You used to spend some time aboard with him. You know, before all this happened."

Claire felt idiotic and stupid and at a loss for what to say. But hey, she had a double knock on her head. What did everybody expect?

"You'll remember all this stuff one of these days." That was Bud again. Being sweet.

The whole interchange was downright embarrassing, so Claire changed the subject. "Maybe somebody onboard saw or heard something. Is it always anchored way out here in the middle of the lake? Has Black been out here onboard?"

Bud shrugged. "I doubt it. He's probably been staying at home with you."

"So it just sits out here waiting for him? Nobody uses it?"

"Pretty much. It's a mini getaway, I think."

"Wow, must be nice to have something like that to fish off of." That came from Nancy Gill.

Claire said, "Well, let's go check it out, Bud. See what the crew has to say. Call me, Buck, if you get anything else off her."

They took off, but said little to each other over the roar of the water patrol boat's motor. Thank God, she had something worthwhile to do with her days. Even if it turned out to be a horrendous and brutal murder to start off her shiny, spanking-new life. Unfortunately, she had a feeling it was pretty much par for the course in her past life, too.

Jesse's Girl

One week after the accident

Sweet little Monica Wheeler was just so unbelievably easy to move in on. She was starved for attention, and affection, too, no doubt about it. But he liked women like that. It was very difficult for him on their first few dates, however, because all she talked about was Nicholas Black. How wonderful he was, how dedicated to Claire Morgan, how he sat beside her bed all night, talking to her, trying to get her to wake up, totally dedicated, totally in love with her. That's what Jesse needed to do. Let Annie hear his voice. That would bring her awake. Annie loved him as much as Jesse loved her. She just wouldn't admit it.

Jesse waited until the security guard was peering out the door at some rowdy teenagers, then pressed his body against Monica's, pinning her up against the wall beside Nicholas Black's private penthouse elevator door. Not that he was worried about getting busted by the guard. Jesse was hotel staff and had hotel credentials, and best of all, he was usually with Monica, who was a good friend of Nicholas Black's. Jesse kissed her mouth until she was breathless and wanted more. He felt nothing, of course, but convincing her that he cared was necessary to his plan to rescue Annie. When she finally pulled away, she murmured softly, her breathing hard and turned on, "I don't want to, but I've got to get upstairs. The doctor's in a meeting, and he doesn't want Claire left alone longer than a few minutes."

"Hey, let me go up with you. I've never seen anybody in a coma. C'mon, Monica, he's in a meeting. He'll never know."

"No, no, he'll fire me on the spot!"

Monica jerked loose from his grip just as the elevator doors slid open. She ducked inside and waved. "Tonight. I'll see you at six when I get off."

Just as the doors started to slide together, Jesse quickly slipped in sideways and grabbed her back into an embrace.

"Stop, Jesse, I mean it. There's a camera in here," she cried, but her resistance was halfhearted, and he silenced her complaints with his mouth. She'd started calling him that name, and he liked it. And whoever manned the cameras would think it was just two kids making out. Monica had the run of the place; nobody would cause her grief.

Monica seemed weak-kneed and deliriously happy when he pulled back. "He's in a meeting, like you said. C'mon, he'll never know."

On the top floor, when the elevator opened, he could hardly contain his excitement. Annie was somewhere nearby, and he was going to find her. He followed Monica out into a wide black marble hall. Lots of floor-to-ceiling windows looked out over a view of the hotel grounds and the lake. The apartment was totally silent; everything was clean, expensive, and shiny. No wonder that jerk doctor could make Annie think she loved him. He had everything she could ever possibly want. It made him want to vomit.

"Where is she?"

Monica clutched his arm and put her fingertips over his mouth. "Ssh, keep your voice down! Dr. Black's office is right down there around that corner." Poor Monica was a nervous wreck.

"C'mon, show me where she is. Let's get out of the hallway before he hears us."

Monica grabbed his hand and pulled him to a large bedroom, heavily draped and dark. The drapes were closed, making everything dim except for a white lamp sitting on a table beside the bed. And there was his Annie, eyes shut, lying so very still and pale. It did seem like she was just asleep. All kinds of monitors blinked with red lights and flashing digital numbers, and IV tubes were taped to her arms. And they'd tied her arms to the bed with white cotton restraints. He had tied her up once so she couldn't leave. But this, this was so wrong. She was Black's captive. *Oh, Annie, my poor little angel. What has that monster done to you?*

"I've got to go get a new IV bag. You need to get out of here. Now!"

Jesse shook his head. "No, just let me stay here and watch her for you. I won't get caught, I promise."

Monica hesitated, looked quickly at the door and back to him. "Well, okay, but don't touch anything, promise me."

"What am I gonna touch, huh? You better hurry up before he finds me in here."

Still standing near the door, he watched the stupid little nurse rush down the hall and wave as she turned down another corridor. Then he smiled to himself, cold chills rising on his skin, as he walked to Annie's bedside. He stared at her, so happy, and then he leaned close and put his mouth close beside her ear.

"Oh, Annie, Annie, sweetie, I'm here. I'm right here," he whispered softly. "I've found you at last. I'm going to save you, and this time, we'll be together forever."

Annie had no reaction to his whisper, the heart monitor beeping with the same very slow, very steady beats. He ran his fingertips down her soft cheek to her lips. He leaned down and put his mouth on hers. He kissed her deeply, holding her face with both his palms, forcing her mouth open with his tongue, the way he'd always dreamed of doing. He ran his tongue over her mouth and her cheeks and her forehead, savoring the taste of her, the essence of her. Glancing back at the door, he lifted the neck of her hospital gown, slid his hand down the front of her body, and cupped her right breast in his hand. He squeezed it hard, shut his eyes, and felt pure pleasure flood through him. In that moment, she was his, his alone. He loved her. Oh, God, please, he had to get her out of there. Away from Nicholas Black. He had to get her. He had to get rid of the evil man who kept her a prisoner in her bed.

Annie's beautiful blond hair had been cut shorter on one temple where she'd hurt herself, and he stroked the bandage covering the wound. He whispered in her ear again. "I'm so sorry, Annie, that I couldn't get you out of the car. I tried to dive down and save you, but I almost drowned trying to get to you because the water was pushing me so hard. It took me downstream so fast I couldn't fight it." A sudden sob escaped him; tears burning his eyes. "But I got here as soon as I could, I swear. And I'm gonna get you out of here. I'm gonna save you from him, I swear."

"What're you doing?"

Monica was back. Frowning, looking suspicious and ugly.

He explained himself quickly, hurrying back to her. "Nothing. She moved a little, and I wanted to make sure she hadn't pulled out the IV, that's all."

Monica looked at her patient. "We think she has bad dreams sometimes. That's why we put on the restraints. But that's good if you saw her move. That means the coma's not as deep as we thought or she's coming out of it. Most of the time, she doesn't move at all." Her whispers got more strident. "Now you get out of here, Jesse, before we both get fired."

"Oh, all right. But don't forget. Six o'clock. How about I stop and get a movie to watch after dinner?"

"Whatever. Now go on! Sometimes he comes in unexpectedly just to look at her. I've never seen anybody so devoted. He's so much in love with her that it's sweet to watch."

"Yeah, I'll bet."

He also bet that dear Dr. Black better enjoy it while he could, because he wouldn't have Annie much longer. Jesse and Annie belonged together, and together they would be. Soon.

Chapter Nine

Nicholas Black's yacht had been christened the *Maltese Falcon*. Claire figured that out because the name was spelled out on the side in big black letters. And it was one helluva impressive boat, oh, yes, you bet it was. All sleek and handsome and shiny and rich. Sort of like its owner. All it needed was a pair of piercing light blue eyes to stare at her mouth. The more she explored the lake and its surroundings, the wealthier she was finding her doctor/purported soul mate to be. A girl could do worse, she decided. Looked like she had grabbed hold of the proverbial gold ring and didn't let go. Too bad she didn't remember all the perks their association probably gave her, not that perks were the most important thing, of course. But they didn't hurt once in a while. And Black didn't appear the typical stuck-up, look-at-me-you-little-peons sort, either. Which was highly surprising, considering.

A tall and smiling crew member in a uniform made of crisp and spotless white fabric and shiny brass buttons appeared on the deck as they approached the big boat. Very tanned, which seemed to be a summer prerequisite in these environs, and very sharp and attractive to boot, the sailor man met them at the landing platform at the side of the yacht. He saluted them sharply as Pennington killed the motor, and then he expertly caught the rope Bud flung to him. He secured them in three seconds flat, and then came forth and greeted Claire, all smiles and official courtesy.

"Welcome back aboard, detective. We're all so pleased to hear you're feeling better. You don't look like anything bad ever happened to you."

Ah, that was because her cap was still pulled down over the embarrassing bald spot, Claire decided. She was never going to take it off again. Not that she was vain, or anything, but the surgically shaved hairdo did make her look a bit like a mental patient who'd undergone a recent lobotomy.

"Thank you," she said, climbing the ladder without his help, just to show her companions that she was as right as rain. Bud swung up behind her with his lithe, athletic grace, and all that, despite his glossy Italian shoes. This boat was probably used to expensive shoes, though, not high-top, black-and-orange Nikes like she was wearing.

"In case you don't recall," Black's erect and polite *capitano* said, "my name is Geoffrey. I'm the captain of the *Falcon*."

"Hello, Geoffrey. You got a last name?"

"Yes, ma'am. It's Geoffrey Lancaster."

"We do have a few questions for you, sir. Is there a place where we can talk privately?"

"Of course. We can use the Grand Salon."

Grand Salon, was it? Wow. Well, that sounded awfully *la-di-da*, but Geoffrey seemed like an okay, down-to-earth captain of an awesome and impressive yacht kind of guy. So she just followed his lead and trailed him down a shiny, scrubbed to a gloss, teak deck and into a large air-conditioned living area with more couches and tables than you could shake a stick at, and a fully stocked bar, to boot. A myriad of crystal goblets and tumblers and short glasses sparkled in the mirrored magnificence behind the bar, and she wondered why the hell she couldn't remember anything so awesome.

"Would you like your regular, Miss Claire?"

Miss Claire? Wow, he was quite the guy. A little old South and Rhett Butler rolled up together, but still über courteous. "And my regular is?"

"Plain water in a bottle."

"Sounds pretty plain."

Bud laughed softly. Geoffrey smiled as if he meant it. "You aren't much of a drinker, we've found."

"That's the good news. I don't need any liquor fogging up my mind. It's already fogged up enough." She was the easygoing, unworried detective pretending she wasn't in misery about barely remembering her own face.

Geoffrey smiled. "I'm really sorry you're not yourself quite yet. But knowing you, it won't take you long to recover. You're quite a go-getter, if I may say so."

Claire liked this guy, too, almost as much as she liked Bud. And she was pretty sure by now that she was going to absolutely love her newfound reality when, and if, it ever paid her a return call.

They all sat down, and a rather spectacular-looking lady bartender or waitress or some kind of a female nautical officer dressed all in white glided out of nowhere and gave the two men fancy goblets of deliciously icy water on top of little white lacy-paper doilies. She put a bottle of Ozarko water in front of Claire. But she got a doily, too. Claire took a drink and had to admit it tasted great, even though they were still in eyesight of the ongoing removal of a beaten-to-death corpse right outside the magnificent Grand Salon tinted windows that faced them.

Claire watched the pretty girl give Bud an interested look, and he looked at said nautical female like he'd rather have a long drink of her instead of the water. She countered with a come-into-my-parlor-you-good-lookin'-thang look. Claire waited a second for them to get their lustful ganders in check. That didn't happen until Bud was finished watching the girl twist herself out of sight.

"So, how may I assist you, detectives?"

Claire put down the bottle on the tan marble-topped coffee table in front of them. "How long have you been anchored here, captain?"

"Since a few days before your accident. Nick didn't get out here much after he flew you back to Cedar Bend from the hospital."

"Does he come aboard often?"

"Not since he met you."

Surprised, she looked up from her trusty notepad. "What? I don't like magnificent yachts?"

He smiled, and somewhat knowingly, too. "No. I think he just kept himself very busy with you."

Yes, and that sounds rather provocative, she decided. When she glanced at Bud, he thought so, too, judging by his smirk and the way he was nodding agreement. But the guy, Geoffrey, probably didn't mean it that way. She hoped he didn't, or maybe, she did. How would she know? Maybe she and Black were hot and heavy and crazy into each other every single minute of every single day. Stranger things have happened. Probably threw some wrenches in their day-to-day job descriptions, though.

"Have you noticed any unusual activity around here?" she asked Lancaster.

Geoffrey shook his head. "What kind of activity do you mean? Boats throwing wakes on us? Coming in too close? Yelling obscenities at the crew?"

Claire really hadn't thought of any of that, but she nodded.

"All the time. The *Falcon*'s a bit of a rarity around here. Dr. Black had it reconstructed into a motor yacht when he bought Cedar Bend. It's the only one on Lake of the Ozarks."

No kidding, Claire thought. *Donald Trump better get a move on.*

Bud said, "Any of these reckless boats do anything suspicious? Make threats?"

Geoffrey frowned. "I'm not sure what you mean by that, but nothing untoward has gone on lately, not that was reported to me, anyway. What did happen over there?" He gestured at the flotilla of police boats surrounding the distant crime scene. "Was there a boating accident?"

"No." Claire looked at Bud. He picked up on his cue.

"We found a body not far from here. Propped up against the wall of that duck blind out there."

"Oh, my lord, that's awful."

Claire said, "We believe the victim was murdered and posed out there."

"Oh, my God. Why would anybody do that?"

"We don't know yet. Did you notice any boats hanging around near that spot?"

"No, but a couple of weeks ago, I guess, I did wake up to the sound of a motor pretty close to us. It turned off for a time, but then it started up again a short time later. I got up and looked around with our spotlights, but it was raining that night and the visibility was bad. I stood there until the sound of the motor faded away into the distance."

"Which direction did the boat go?"

"Back toward Cedar Bend."

"Do you remember what day that was?"

"Not offhand, but I noted it in my daily report. I also thought it peculiar enough to call Dr. Black and ask if it was him, by any chance. Sometimes he comes out here in the launch at night."

"In the rain?"

"Sometimes."

"Why?"

"He says he likes being out under the night sky. You know, stargazing and such as that."

"How often does he do this stargazing business?"

"Not much since he met you."

Sounded like Black didn't do much at all since he met her. She was beginning to wonder if he got any work done since she came into the picture. Truth be told, it did make her curious as to exactly what he did do before he met her, and whom he did it with. She hadn't really thought much about his former life before, so obsessed was she with her own dilemma. Maybe she should look into that a bit further. Might just turn up some interesting tidbits to mull over.

"But you're saying it wasn't him that night?" Bud prodded.

"I don't know. I left him a phone message on his staff line, but he never got back to me. I just assumed he was still sitting vigil at your bedside."

"True, he rarely left her," agreed Bud.

Claire wondered if everybody within a hundred miles was that interested in Black and her. Their little love-life scenarios seemed popular topics of conversation to most people who knew them. What were they, anyway? The Brangelina of Lake of the Ozarks sans the six kids?

Bewildered how she could remember two movie stars and their brood and not her own lover, she said, "Do you have any outside video surveillance cameras trained on the water?"

"No. We've never had the need. We have licensed firearms aboard in case anybody tries to board us. You know, rob or hijack us. Dr. Black gave us permission to use force in any situation where we might feel in imminent personal danger."

"Are there valuables kept here?"

"Dr. Black's got a safe in his office. I have no idea what he keeps in it."

Probably huge stacks of banded hundred-dollar bills, she thought, but didn't comment on that speculation.

"That night when you heard the nearby boat? Did you hear anything else? Screaming? Cries for help?"

"Not that I recall. You can ask Sadie and Jack. They both live aboard the *Falcon*, too, down in the crew's quarters." He stopped, and his brows knitted together as he thought about it. "Actually, though, I believe Sadie was on vacation around that time. Dr. Black gives all of us a month-long paid vacation every year."

Generous vacation benefits, indeed, but she was finding that Nicholas Black was not a stingy man. But that's not the reason Bud and Claire glanced at each other. Sadie just might be their victim. So she said, "When was the last time you saw Sadie?"

Geoffrey grinned. "Five minutes ago. She's the one who brought us the water."

Bud looked inordinately relieved, obviously already planning his future assignation with the lovely and enticing Sadie. "Mind if we take a look around?"

"Not at all. If you're looking for your personal belongings, they're stowed in the master bedroom."

But of course they are, Claire thought. But then again, she was a bit curious. While Bud nosed around in the galley and crew's quarters, no doubt looking for Sadie and/or chocolate Ding Dongs and Cokes, which she also remembered that he liked. When she heard him laughing, she suspected it was Sadie that he'd found. Down the hallway, she did a quick look-see in Black's floating office/boudoir. She found lots of her departmental T-shirts and jeans in the closet and a toothbrush that might be hers in a holder next to Black's, all cozy and loverlike, for sure.

Claire went through the dresser drawers and found stacks of neatly folded shirts and pants and khaki shorts belonging to Black, but didn't see any makeup, hair products, not even a tube of lipstick in yet another big black-and-tan marble bathroom. She did locate a gun-cleaning kit and oily cloth alongside a box of .38 shells by the sink, though. She pocketed the shells. Okay, now she was pretty sure she wasn't vain or girly-girly, at least not when spending time on Black's giant fancy boat. Not anywhere else, either. Except for that damn bald spot. That Friar Tuck look did bite into her ego a tiny bit. Thank goodness for ball caps.

Back in the Grand Salon, Bud was leaning on the bar chatting up the beauteous bartender, and Geoffrey was coming toward Claire with a honey of a smart phone in his hand. "Dr. Black would like to talk to you. He said you aren't answering your cell."

Claire felt around in her pockets and realized she'd left it in Bud's Bronco. Not good. Okay, she was still rusty and unused to being fresh out of a coma. Still, she needed to keep it at hand. It was dangerous not to.

"Hello," she said, trying not to sound guilty for forgetting the damn phone.

"I've been trying to call you, Claire."

"Sorry, I left my phone in the car."

Short silence. An annoyed one, she suspected. Then he said, "How're you feeling by now?"

Okay, now that was a question she could do a nosedive into. "I am doing great, Black. I feel better than I've felt in a long, long time. We got a homicide today, by the way."

"Yeah, Charlie told me."

For some reason, that irked her. Her tone intimated as much. "Do you have every single person in this town calling you and filling you in on where I am and what I'm doing? Is that it?"

Another pregnant silence followed. "No, of course not. I called him when I couldn't catch up with you. I was just checking to make sure you didn't have a headache or any weakness from being on your feet so long."

This time it was Claire's silence that stretched out longer than necessary. Okay, she did feel a tad guilty for jumping on the guy. He had done a lot for her, true. And she appreciated it. He was worried and for good cause, and she knew that, too. "Well, I appreciate your concern. But I really do feel fine. Good, in fact. No headache. No weakness. The sun glare bothered me at first, but Bud lent me some sunglasses. I know you're worried about me, but there's no reason to be, really."

Except the truth was, she was getting tired. Closing in fast on exhausted. Since she awoke from the coma, she'd spent the first few days swimming a few laps in the pool, and walking for short bursts on the treadmill, very short ones. But this working half a day was different and she wasn't self-destructive enough to keep going until she collapsed and ruined all the progress she'd made. On the other hand, Black didn't need to know all those tiresome details. He was upset enough with her. "Besides I'm getting ready to wrap things up for today and come home."

"Good. I'm just concerned about you, Claire. You've been in a coma. You need to take it easy. Get back into things slowly. You don't think working a case like this will be too much for you?"

"No, definitely not. Truthfully, Black? It makes me feel alive again and like I've got a purpose, you know, a reason to get up in the morning. You told me yourself that was important."

"It is important. Any leads yet?"

"Not many. We've got no identifying credentials. We're hoping for fingerprints."

"I take it that you found the body near the *Falcon*."

"Yes. We were hoping your crew would've seen or heard something."

"Geoff says he heard a boat one night, but nothing else. I do remember getting his message about that."

"We're bound to find something soon."

"You always do."

Claire liked that. Blatant encouragement, just what she needed. It was turning out that she liked a lot about Black, too. A good indicator, under the freaky circumstances they found themselves in. She certainly didn't want to dislike her own true love. That just wouldn't get it done, now would it?

"So you're coming back here right now?"

"Bud's taking me to my house so I can nose around. Maybe it'll help me remember some more stuff."

"Does that mean you've remembered something today?"

"Yes, quite a few things, but not the whole picture yet."

"It's going to come to you, Claire. Why don't I meet you at your place in an hour or so? I'll bring dinner from Two Cedars."

Claire looked at the giant pendulum clock positioned over one of the black leather couches. It looked like a French antique. So how did she know that? she wondered, but couldn't answer her own question. "Make that two hours, and it's a date."

"Okay." A beat of silence, then he said, "I miss you."

Claire hesitated, but the truth was that she had thought of him a lot throughout the day, as exciting as getting back to work had been. She glanced at Bud, but he was still flirting with Sadie while she wiped down the spotless and shiny marble bar. "I miss you, too."

"Now that's what I'm talkin' about."

His pleased tone made her smile, but she sobered when she saw Bud looking at her with a knowing grin. "Okay, gotta go, Black. See you later."

Bud swiveled back and forth on the bar stool. "Looks like you're startin' to remember old Nick better all the time, huh, Claire?"

"Yeah, maybe," she said. But what she wanted was for everything to come back crystal clear and detailed. Maybe she wouldn't ever love him again. Or maybe they'd just fall in love again, just like before, and all would be well. Lightning could strike twice in the same place, and all that rot. Or not, her good sense added. And therein lay the problem, a very big problem indeed.

Chapter Ten

The closer they got to Harve Lester's house, the more excited Claire became. The road back home was not familiar, of course, but Bud was still pointing out this and that, and telling her what she needed to know. Her mind was whirling hard, trying to sledgehammer down that damnable dam and let her past roar forth. Turning off the highway onto a narrow gravel road, Bud stopped at a security gate blocking the entrance, slid down his window, and punched in some numbers.

"Do you remember Harve's gate code, Claire?"

"Nope."

"I'll write it down for you, or Harve can. He put this gate up because a bunch of vulture reporters were out here doggin' you and Black a few years back."

"Tell me about that case."

"That's the one where we found the soap actress under the water out at that bungalow at Cedar Bend. Down that road you said you remembered." He turned his head and looked at her. "That trigger anything?"

"I recall the house, a few other things, nothing that ties together. Did we solve it?"

"Oh, yeah. We solve all our cases." His broad grin was back. "We don't know any other way."

"How'd it go down?"

"Black told me that it's better for you to remember the bad stuff on your own."

Oh, great, more bad stuff to remember. It seemed that's all there was in her past. Sure didn't make her feel all jolly and confident and on top of the world. Dread and unease suddenly seemed to be the new flavor of the day. "Oh, yeah, Bud, he told me. My mind's protecting me, let it do its thing, and all that shrink verbiage."

"Well, he knows his stuff." Bud waited for the barrier to lift and allow them passage. "It's beginning to come back anyway, right? You know Harve, right? Maybe talking to him will help."

"Yes. We were partners in Los Angeles. It'll be great to see him again. You know, to sit down with somebody I actually know."

Bud drove up to a neat little property about a quarter of a mile down the road that ran along the edge of the lake. The house sat lower than the road, the back very close to the water. There was a small, front, screened porch with an American flag flapping in the wind beside the screen door. Bud shoved the gearshift into park and turned in his seat and looked at her. She sensed reluctance on his part. Oh, God, what now?

"Claire, you remember what happened to Harve?"

Uh-oh. "What d'you mean?"

More hesitation. He did not want to tell her this, whatever it was. "He's paralyzed from the waist down now. Got a bullet in the line of duty. He's in a wheelchair. But he gets along just fine, does just about anything he wants to."

"Oh, my God, Bud, no, I don't remember any of that."

"Well, I'm sorry, but I didn't want you to walk in there blind."

"No, no, you did the right thing," she said quickly, but inside, her heart ached and she couldn't really believe her strong, vital mentor at LAPD had been felled by a bullet.

For a moment, she and Bud coordinated their investigative plans for the next day, and then Harve came out on his porch in a motorized wheelchair and called out a hello to her. Claire was so glad to see him that she bid Bud a quick good-bye and ran across the yard to her old friend. Leaning down, she gave the guy a big hug and didn't want to let him go.

"Bud just told me, Harve, about you getting hit. I'm so sorry."

"No dice on remembering that, either, huh?"

Claire shook her head. Harve looked good, still strong and

muscular from the regimen of weight lifting he used to do and apparently still did. Hair was a little more steel gray, maybe, but those sharp, see-through-the-bull blue eyes were the same. He was the best detective she'd ever met, and a partner who always had her back, always—on the job and in private life. He was in his late fifties now, but nobody had ever looked so good to her. "Oh, God, Harve, I'm so glad to see you. The last few days have been pretty damn awful."

"Well, c'mon in. Joe brought me an apple pie yesterday, and I was gonna take it over to Cedar Bend for you and Nick when I visited. It's still sitting on the kitchen table, just waiting for me to dip out the ice cream."

Claire realized in that moment how good it felt to actually recognize somebody and know everything about them, or almost everything. How often had the two of them sat down at a diner or an all-night restaurant together and had a piece of pie and a cup of coffee? More times than she could count. Following him inside the house, she looked around for anything else familiar but nothing clicked. "Let's sit and talk in the kitchen, Claire. It's so good to see you back here, whole and in one piece. You were in really bad shape last time I saw you. Have to be honest: You had me worried this time."

Claire sat down at the table, her heart wrenching at the sight of Harve in the wheelchair, but he got around fine and seemed to have adapted extremely well. Harve Lester wasn't the kind to complain about anything, especially his own challenges. She watched him fetch some plates and forks from a low cabinet and bring them back to the table.

"If you'll get the ice cream out of the freezer, I'll cut the pie."

"You got it."

Harve cut them both absolutely huge pieces. She pried open the ice cream carton and scooped out equally generous portions of ice cream. She'd lost weight. Now was the time to put some meat back on her bones. Vanilla ice cream ought to do the trick.

"So you don't remember much of anything, huh?" he asked Claire, handing her a fork.

"I remember you and some of our work in Los Angeles, but that's just about it."

Harve took a big bite and wiped his mouth with a paper napkin. "What about Nick and Bud?"

"Apparently, my memory took a hike on them. But thank God, not you. You came before the move here, I guess." She took her first bite, and her stomach nearly purred with true love. "This's really good. So who's Joe?"

"Joe says it's his mom's recipe. You don't remember him, either?"

"No, and I haven't met him again yet. I'm slowly getting to meet everybody else. I'm beginning to recall bits and pieces. A lot came back today at work."

"Nick told me this might happen. He also said that it wouldn't last long."

"Well, that's the good news. If you believe it."

"Too bad you don't know Black."

"Well, what can I say? The guy treats me like a queen. I'm attracted to him, but I don't know him well enough to feel anything more than that."

"You two are good together." He pointed with his fork toward his dock. "He gave me that boat sitting down there. Free of charge. It's handicapped equipped so I can go fishing. I've spent many an hour out on the lake in it."

Peering out the kitchen windows, Claire realized that he was talking about a big, sleek Cobalt 360 cruiser, very similar to other boats she'd seen at Cedar Bend.

"You're gonna be all right, Claire. You do realize that, don't you?"

Inhaling deeply, she said, "Why'd I change my name, Harve? It used to be Annie, didn't it? Nobody's telling me enough. There are so many blanks in the story I've been told."

For the first time, Harve didn't seem to want to look at her. She waited, wishing someone would just tell her everything that she'd been through, get it all over with and let her deal with it, no matter how awful it was.

Harve didn't speak as he finished his pie and leaned back in his wheelchair. "Nick will tell you if you don't remember soon." Serious now, he took hold of her hand. "You've gone through some tough times down here in Missouri. I think he's afraid it's too much for you to absorb all at once."

"It's gonna have to happen."

Harve's eyes were kind, and she could read the familiar understanding inside them. "Hell, Claire, maybe he'll change his mind. Ask him. Demand it. I wouldn't like being kept in the dark like this, either."

"I think I will. Tonight. He's supposed to meet me down at my house, which will be interesting, too. Surely my own place will seem familiar."

Feeling more and more helpless to figure things out on her own, she felt locked up inside her own personal dark closet while all her friends held keys but refused to let her out. She was beginning to feel sorry for herself, which was a feeling she wasn't used to and did not like.

At that moment, Claire decided to quit worrying about it, quit thinking about it, and get on with her new life. At least she had a life, after a very serious car wreck. "I remember some things about us, about L.A., but there's a lot missing. Tell me a little bit, and I'll stop boring you with my problems."

"You were young and eager and gung-ho when you came out of the academy. Let's see, you were, are, a great cop. You were decorated for valor at LAPD multiple times. You love police work. The best detective I've ever known, and I've seen plenty, young and old."

"I was just thinking the same thing about you. But thanks, Harve." Claire tried to digest things. "I remember the work, the procedures. I remember all that, but little about my personal stuff. You know, relationships, emotions."

"Maybe later today, maybe tomorrow. You're back at work. Concentrate on that and let things be."

"I guess I'm just frustrated."

"Well, give yourself a break. You've been through a helluva lot the last few years."

"You're probably gonna be seeing a lot of me, hear a lot of my angst."

"I'll be right here if you ever need a thing, day or night."

Claire nodded, squeezed her old friend's hand, and felt much better. Apparently, she had lots of friends to turn to. She needed to be glad about that. "Bud said I lived just down the road from here. I'm going to walk it, get some fresh air and exercise. Black's meeting me there."

"About another quarter of a mile down from here. Nice, snug, little A-frame with a dock like mine out front. I signed it over to you for Christmas."

That surprised Claire. "That's one fabulous Christmas present."

"You're my best friend."

"I can't wait to get down there. If anyplace rings a bell, it's got to be there."

"It's full of your stuff. Your Explorer's parked in the garage."

"I don't know if I'll stay out here. Black doesn't want me to." Claire glanced at her watch. "He's probably there now. Pacing the floor."

"Ah, he's not going anywhere without you, believe me."

"I guess I owe him. He saved my life, and all." They shared a smile. "I'll come back soon, Harve, okay?"

"You're welcome to stay here for a while, if you need a safe place to crash. I've got two empty guest rooms, and I like your company."

Claire nodded, wondering if that wasn't such a bad idea. "We got a new case today. A homicide."

Harve perked up. "Want to tell me about it?"

"I suspect I've confided in you before."

He nodded. "I help you whenever I can. I'm pretty good on that computer in there."

"We found a dead woman out on a duck blind near Nicholas Black's yacht. Bud says the two of you have hunted out of it."

"Yeah, I've fished out there, too."

"Whose blind is it?"

"Mine. Dad built it years ago when I was a little kid. Guess I was around ten. I keep it in good shape."

"Do you let anybody else use it?"

"Most of my friends. Was the body hidden inside?"

"No. She was outside, propped against the wall."

"How'd she die?"

"Not sure yet. The perpetrator bludgeoned her with some kind of weapon. It was overkill, to be sure."

"You'll get him."

"I hope so. This guy's got a screw loose."

A worried expression flitted across Harve's face, and Claire picked up on it. "Yeah, I hear I've met crazies before, more than once."

"You're a homicide detective. Goes with the territory."

"Good point." Nodding, she sighed again, and stood up. She was doing a lot of sighing lately. "Guess I better get going. Black's going to think the worst. He's more worked up about all this than I am."

"Come back soon, and I'll fry up some crappie for us. You do remember my famous fried fish dinners, don't you?"

"Oh, yeah, and I'm getting hungry again, just thinking about it."

Harve reached out his arms for a hug, and she leaned down and gave him a long and heartfelt one. If nothing else, she'd always have Harve, and that made her feel better than she had in quite a while.

Outside in the fresh air, Claire started down the road that led to her very own piece of the world. It was still hot out, but the road was partially overhung with oak trees and their leafy boughs, making the walk fairly shady. And it was a pretty place, too, with the lake lapping against the narrow rocky beach. The water was serene and smooth and glassy and green. She was wearier than she wanted to admit, for fear of getting her half day jerked out from under her, and the ire of the handsome doctor awaiting her. She needed to get out more, work up to a jog, get her tight muscles lean and agile again. No pain, no gain, as they say.

But she was tired and so glad to see the house when she rounded the next curve of the cove. A strange sense of peace rolled down through her. Not exactly recognition but a good feeling, a good vibe. She hadn't had much of that of late, so she welcomed it whole-heartedly.

The place appeared deserted, until she glimpsed another big Cobalt 360 moored alongside the small dock. The house looked as if it had been added on to recently, sort of modernized, it looked like. Then she heard a shrill and happy little yap.

"Hey, Claire! Down here!"

Then Claire saw him. Black was out in the water, about twenty yards off the end of the dock. A dog's head was bobbing around, too, closer in. She broke into a smile. A big strapping man and his sissy, but adorable, little dog relaxing together after a long day at work. At least, the good doc wasn't going to get on her back for being late. Which she did appreciate. Strolling down the small incline from the road, she walked out onto the dock. "You're making yourself at home, I see."

"The water's great," he called out, doing a breaststroke in closer. "C'mon in."

"No can do. I don't happen to have a swimsuit on me." But she was big-time tempted. It was still at least ninety and the water looked cool and inviting. So did the doctor.

"Your swimsuit's in the boat. Top drawer of the bedroom dresser. Go get it on. It'll be good for you to do some swimming. Relax your muscles. Cool you off."

"So I know how to swim? Just checking."

He laughed at her joke. She hadn't been making many of late. He seemed rather pleased. "Yes, you do. You've made it over to the far shore and back plenty of times."

Claire glanced at the other side of the cove. "Then I am pretty good, aren't I?" Actually, she knew she could swim. She had visited the hotel pool since she woke up. She was just teasing with him a little. After all, they were lovers, and everybody on the lake knew it but her.

"So, tell me, what is that? A dog or a white rat?"

"Hey, quit insulting the dog. He's your biggest fan. He's a French poodle. I gave him to you for Christmas."

"Really? So where's he been?"

"He's been around, downstairs with various staff people. He missed you so much at first that he wouldn't come out from under your bed. When his whining and crying got so bad that I wanted to get under there with him, I decided to give him a little vacation from the stress. You adore him, by the way."

Claire looked at the little poodle paddling around just below her. He was looking up at her and yapping his head off. "What's his name?"

"Jules Verne. I got him on a trip to Paris, that's why you named him that. Quit wasting time and get on your suit."

So, what the hell? It would feel good, and she was all sweaty from the walk. She climbed aboard the big, luxurious craft, made her way below and found quite a setup, a kitchen with all the works, luxury sitting area, small bedroom, and tiny adjoining bath. The swimsuit he mentioned was there, all right, what there was of it. She held up the tiny, little, itty-bitty, yellow string bikini, which gave her pause, to say the least. But she'd seen herself wearing the self-same suit in one of his photographs, and they'd been intimate, or so she'd been told. He'd seen her naked before, if they were normal into-each-other folk. And no telling what he'd seen when she was unconscious.

She slipped it on, which took two seconds. She couldn't have been very modest if she'd worn this thing around in public. Black's eyes fixed on her when she stepped outside, and didn't waver, like a laser beam on a bombing target. Slightly embarrassed and resisting the urge to cover herself with crossed arms, she was pretty sure she didn't pick these two little scraps off a bathing suit rack.

"Well now, you are a sight for sore eyes, detective."

"I didn't buy this thing, did I?"

"Nope, but you wear it well, believe me. C'mon, get in."

Claire considered dipping one toe in and testing the water, and then easing in all ladylike, but hey, she was burning up. She dove in and hoped the pressure didn't rip apart the strings holding the suit together. The water felt cool and wonderful against her hot skin. She swam underwater and then surfaced, somehow feeling much more comfortable with Nicholas Black today. Yes, she did like this easy, laid-back banter they were throwing back and forth a lot better than his psychoanalyzing. He seemed much more approachable out here. He looked different, too, now that he had shed his perfectly tailored suits and expensive silk ties. Okay, she did like him in his black swim trunks and sunglasses, with his black hair all slicked back off his forehead. That's all he wore, too, which gave her a good, measuring look at his ridged six-pack and muscular shoulders. He would do just fine in the hunk category, oh, yes, he would. Besides, he seemed all loose and relaxed, and the perpetual frown of worry was nowhere to be found.

Black and the dog were already right beside her. When Jules Verne started paddling in excited circles, Black treaded water and laughed. His teeth looked very white against his dark tan. God help her, but he was just so damn sexy. She needed to get a grip.

"Told you it felt good," he said.

"It feels great. And the dog's cute. Wish I remembered him."

"So, tell me, how did your day go? Make any Sherlock discoveries? Lock anybody up? Throw away the key?"

Claire smiled, but he was so close and she was so aware of his masculinity that she felt unsettled. She had better be careful, right here, right now, or she wasn't going to use her head at all. "I discovered I've got some pretty cool friends. Makes me feel like a lucky woman." Having him so attentive wasn't bad, either, but she didn't tell him that. Not yet.

"You are lucky. In lots of ways." His gaze was so intimate, so hot and hungry, that she felt her heart flutter like some virginal girl's. She felt so mixed up. Truth was, though, his charisma was beginning to reel her in like some helpless and gullible little guppy caught on his hook. Why in the world could she not remember him? And hey, why not, maybe she should just go with her gut feeling. Maybe that would send her down the road to recovery quicker than anything else. But there came the conundrum. What if she never remembered? Wouldn't that be worse for both of them?

Luckily, Jules Verne dog-paddled in closer, and she grabbed him as a diversion and let him lick her face and kick his little legs. He was such a cute little thing; it was hard not to like him. Same went for Black, of course, but the ramifications of cuddling with him were a lot more dangerous. So instead of grabbing him and saying *take me, please, and do hurry it up*, she swam around a little, keeping her distance and pretending that Jules Verne was her primary concern and avoiding Black and any kind of skin-on-slick-skin contact.

Her doctor/lover was being a good sport and playing with Jules Verne, too, but he was keeping close enough to make her breathless. It didn't take him long to give in to the temptation she read so easily in his eyes. He came up close, and she couldn't look away from his face as he pulled her in against his naked chest. The angel on Claire's right shoulder said: whoa now, baby, pull away, stomp on those titillated brakes, but then her little devil only laughed, and she knew they were in on this together. She believed without a doubt that they'd been in love before the accident, if only by the way he looked at her, touched her, and by the way she reacted to his touch. She also knew it was killing him not to touch her the way he was obviously used to. He'd told her as much. But it was just so strange. It was like making love within minutes to a guy you'd just met. That wasn't her bag, never had been.

"God, you feel good," he whispered against her hair.

Sexual desire worked both ways, even with a complete stranger, she found. He felt very warm and wet, with bulging muscles in all the right places, and he was undeniably glad to see her. Okay, so her body remembered him, even if her brain couldn't compute.

"I've missed holding you like this." His voice sounded gruff, his lips were soft on the side of her neck until they actually started singeing a brand on her flesh. He knew her tender spots, oh, yeah, that was a given. She enjoyed it for a while, too, sliding her arms around his neck and letting him hold her up in the water. The embrace tightened, then shot like a bottle rocket to a dangerous level, erupting almost as fast as her boiling hormones did.

Claire placed both palms against his bare chest. "Wait, wait," she got out somehow, not sure why, and not sure she really wanted to stop him. To her mingled relief and disappointment, he immediately dropped his hold and moved back away from her. He turned and swam a few yards away from her. Then she called out to him, "I'm sorry. It's just too soon. Don't be mad."

A minute later, he was back beside her and apparently no worse for the wear. That was more than she could say. "I'm not going to force you, Claire. You've been through enough. Things will get back to normal soon, so I can wait. Your mind needs to heal. I won't do this to you again."

Every nerve inside Claire's body urged her to swim back into his arms, and she felt very alone all of a sudden. The emotions shivering through her were neither pleasant, nor relaxing, nor anything else but upsetting. Oh, God, when was she ever going to remember him?

Jesse's Girl

Eighteen days after the accident

After that first time alone with Annie, Jesse sneaked up to the penthouse as often as he could get away with it. Monica finally quit objecting because she thought that he couldn't wait to make out with her, the stupid bitch. Nobody else ever visited Annie when Nicholas Black was working. They came only in the evening when he sat with her. Jesse was ultra careful about Black, though, because Monica was right, he'd often come into her room at unexpected times and sit beside Annie's bed. Once he almost caught Jesse there, but Jesse moved quickly into the adjoining bath and listened to everything he said.

Nicholas Black stayed with her for a long time, just chatting about things they'd done together as if she were awake and able to hear him. It was weird to watch. Black's very proximity to her and some of the things that he revealed in the conversation were almost too much for Jesse to bear. Annie had sex with Black. Oh, God, Jesse couldn't bear to hear that. The image of them together sent the explosive red cloud of rage boiling up into his head and setting his brain on fire. His fists clenched hard, his teeth nearly broke off as he ground them so violently. How he hated Nicholas Black, hated him so much. He could barely stop himself from sneaking up behind him where he sat by the bed and clubbing him and then lopping off his head for a souvenir and burning his body to bits.

And he would. Someday, he would do it exactly that way. But right now, he couldn't risk it. Black was on his own turf with lots of security everywhere. And Black was a lot bigger and stronger than Jesse and was well able to take care of himself. But Annie was helpless— in Black's clutches, tied to her bed, and now Jesse had to think of a way to rescue her, to get her away from that devil holding her hostage.

Once, when he was waiting for Monica to get off work and come downstairs to the restaurant, he pressed the security code on the elevator, carrying a tray to fool the security guard, and went upstairs by himself. He caught sight of Monica carrying Annie's dirty linens down the hallway. She didn't hear the elevator open, so he tiptoed down the hallway to Annie's door and pushed it ajar. Annie lay very still in the bed, very small and lifeless, no different than the last time he crept into her room. Nicholas Black was in the room, too. But he was lying on an upholstered chaise on the other side of the room, his long legs hanging off the end. He had one arm flung over his eyes. He was asleep. Jesse listened and could hear his even breathing in the quiet room.

Jesse waited a few minutes, hesitant to approach the bed, watching the man's chest rising and falling with an even cadence. Then he just couldn't help himself. He had to get closer; he had to touch Annie again. Moving silently across the floor, he crouched just below Annie's bed, out of the sight of Nicholas Black. He waited some more, but nothing happened. He wanted to talk to her. Talk to her the way Black did. Black was brainwashing her, telling her things she would absorb in her subconscious mind that would make her love him. But it wasn't going to work. Two could play that game.

Jesse raised himself up closer to Annie and took Annie's hand. He licked it. Then he slid his hand into the neck of her gown and squeezed her breast. It was so soft and made him feel wonderful and happy. He put his mouth on hers, licking his tongue along her lips and down her cheek to under her chin. He was so affected by her closeness that he couldn't suppress the moan that came from deep inside his throat. Still, nothing happened. Black slept on. Annie slept on. So Jesse put his mouth close to Annie's ear. He licked it inside and outside for a while, liking the taste of her skin, the taste of soap and water. Then he began to whisper to her, telling her about the last time they were together.

When she suddenly moved, just a tiny jerk, he was so shocked that he backed away, looking quickly at Black to see if he had awoken. But then she settled down to absolute stillness again, and he licked her forehead and eyebrows. Then all of a sudden, she let out a little muffled cry and began to struggle weakly against the cloth ropes binding her to the bed. He jumped back and hid himself behind the long drapes closed against the sun as Nicholas Black leapt up and ran to the bed.

Jesse's heart thundered in his ears. If Black found him now, he would recognize him, despite the disguise Jesse had adopted. And if he did, he would beat him up again, just like he did the last time he'd seen him. So Jesse stood where he was, frozen with fear, because Black didn't go back to the couch. Instead, he sat down in the recliner beside the bed and picked up a file and began to read it. Jesse didn't move a muscle, didn't dare. In time, though, thank God, Black dozed off again, his reading glasses still on his nose.

Finally, Jesse could get out safely. He backed away toward the hall door, but then Annie suddenly opened her eyes. Oh, my God, she was awake at last! And it was because of him. His voice had brought her back, he knew it. Not Black's, his. That proved he was Annie's one true love.

Then she started struggling, pulling on her bindings, and Jesse moved into the shadows against the wall. Black awoke and came to his feet. He called her name, tried to soothe her fear, but she was yelling, crying out for him to let her go. Black yelled for Monica and started untying the restraints. Jesse didn't dare to stay longer. When Monica ran into the room, he edged along in the shadows and quickly melted outside into the hall, but he waited there, listening to what they were saying.

Inside his heart, though, he was ecstatic. Oh, Annie, his darling Annie, she was back. She had come back to him, because she loved him. That's when he vowed to himself, vowed on his very life, that Black would not get to keep her. Never. Black would have to die, or she'd never be free of him. That was the exact moment when he started planning Nicholas Black's early demise. And he couldn't wait. Couldn't wait to take his meat cleaver and separate Black's head from his body. And he'd keep it on a spike like they did in the good old days in England so Annie would never have to be afraid of Nicholas Black again.

Chapter Eleven

The frisky cavorting in the lake off Claire's dock didn't last long after their intimate embrace. A few minutes later, Claire pulled herself up onto the boat's swimming platform and grabbed one of the black beach towels Black had left there. She wrapped herself in it, sat down and dried her hair and watched Black heft his Adonis-perfect body out of the water and rub himself down. She averted her eyes. He wasn't going to make any more sexual advances, so she better not want him to, either.

All dried off now, Black turned to her, one of his big black towels looped around his neck. He worked out, all right, no doubt about it. He had enough sun-browned muscles to make a San Diego lifeguard jealous. Claire looked away again, weakening, and feeling incredibly silly. She was attracted now, too, just like she obviously had been attracted the first time she fell for him. *So, give me a break here, hormones.* "I remembered a lot of stuff today," she told him, changing the subject from her stupid thoughts.

"Yeah? Well, that's good. Just what we wanted to happen." He looked down at her as if truly happy to hear it and then let it drop. Maybe he wasn't in the shrink mood at the moment. Maybe he quit at five o'clock and didn't examine any heads after that. "You ready to go home and get something to eat?"

Or maybe he was just hungry. "I think I'd like to go inside my house first and look around. See if that does the trick."

Black stooped over and fished Jules Verne out of the water and wrapped the wriggling dog in a towel. "Okay, let me get this mutt dry and we'll do it."

Hesitating, Claire really hated to say what was coming next. "I think I ought to go in alone, this first time. You mind?"

Watching for any sign of hurt or disapproval, she waited, but he merely turned his head and gave her a killer smile. "That's not a bad idea. The door's already unlocked and the security system's off. I'll stay here with the dog. Call me, if you need me."

Well, Black was going to back off, just like he'd said. She liked that. She didn't like that. But she left him as he dove back into the water and started a very measured and practiced crawl stroke away from the dock. Maybe that's how he got all those toned abs.

As it turned out, Jules Verne preferred Claire's company, and he trotted behind her down the dock, up the slight incline, and onto the front porch. Jules jumped up and wagged his tail and propped his front paws on the front door as if thrilled to be home. Claire took one cleansing breath and reached for the knob.

The door opened easily. Jules nearly knocked her down beating a path inside. She let him go and then walked in and stared around the home that she didn't know she had. Well, okay, now, she had quite a comfy little nest for herself. Beige sofas, big-screen plasma TV hanging on the wall, and last, but not least, a large hot tub in a window alcove with half-burnt vanilla candles on the windowsill. She could still smell them. Now that was one heck of an added perk. Something told her that she and the good doc out there might've spent some enjoyable interludes in that big bubbly hot tub, probably some on the couch, too. She was beginning to crave a passionate reenactment, true, but first things first. Better get to know the guy beforehand. Just in case all this was a big hoax and conspiracy to get her into his bed. Yeah, right. *As if Nicholas Black needed any help getting women in bed*, she thought. Or maybe all this was an episode in some stupid reality show like *Big Brother* or *Survivor* or *The Truman Show.* Yes, she did recall reality shows and movies, but nothing personally significant, and that was getting on her nerves big-time.

But, for the first time since Claire opened her eyes and found herself tied to that damn hospital bed, she felt distinctly at home, completely, comfortably at home in her own house. It was very quiet, with no sound, no people, no demands. She felt as if she was exactly where she belonged. The most soothing sensation of serenity, safety, happiness, inner peace, all those things, gradually settled down inside her frazzled, ever-searching-for-truth mind. This is where she belonged, not at Black's huge and richly appointed penthouse. Nicholas Black wasn't going to like that, but it's the way she felt.

Claire snooped around a bit, searching for the key that would unlock her recalcitrant memory banks and/or anything that even looked vaguely familiar. It appeared as if she had just left this place a moment before. She'd gone off to work, perhaps, like on any other day on the job, with no fear or inkling that she would end up blacking out for the next three weeks of her life. *How awful*, she thought, *but law enforcement officers face that kind of danger every single day.* In time, all the reasons why, all the circumstances would be revealed, and she would understand. She just had to trust Black's treatment method of letting nature take its course. But she was an impatient sort, and she was already tired of waiting.

Nicholas Black waited for a while, swimming a few circles in front of the dock, but he was anxious to get inside and see how Claire was reacting to the sight of her own place, one that she loved so much. He had pushed her too hard earlier, and as badly as he wanted to touch her, he wasn't going to make that mistake again. She was right. She needed time to heal. He had been thinking of himself and not of her. He couldn't do that and expect her to respond to him.

Despite his good intentions, after about half an hour, he got out again, dried off, and headed up to the house, the black towel still hanging around his neck. He opened the screen door and found her standing alone in the living room, just staring into the kitchen.

"Any good news?" he asked her, startling her more than he intended to.

"I feel good in here. This is home. This is where I belong."

Now that reaction he did not particularly care for. However, he was careful to keep his expression neutral. "That's good. It's your home. You take turns living here and out at Cedar Bend with me."

A brand-new and great big problem was looming up between

them now, almost tangible in its importance. So tangible, in fact, Black felt he could reach out and grab the tension. She heaved in a deep breath and appeared reluctant to throw his hospitality back in his face, but she did, anyway. "I think I want to stay out here from now on."

More ideas to dislike, but he was careful not to show concern. His training helped with that, a knack he had developed years ago. But separate living quarters was not a good or a safe idea right now. "Fine. We can live here, if it helps you."

Claire hesitated and looked annoyed. He knew her so well, her expressions, her desires, her feelings. What she meant was that she wanted to live there alone, but she didn't have the heart to just haul off and boot him out the door. So she said nothing. They would have to hash that out, because he sure as hell wasn't going to let her live in such an isolated area alone. Not yet.

"How long have I lived in this place?" she suddenly asked him.

"Ever since you moved here from Los Angeles. At least, that's what Harve told me."

"It's very peaceful, isn't it, Black? No people around. No boats or commotion going on around the clock. Just the sound of the water lapping the bank and the birds singing in the trees."

"That's exactly why you chose to live way out here in the woods. Along with the fact that your best friend lives just down the road."

Claire stared at him, at the towel around his neck, not saying anything, but he needed to know what she was thinking and feeling. She was doing extremely well. He never would have dreamed that she would be back to work so soon. But she had always been strong of body, and even stronger of mind and will.

"What?" he asked when she kept staring at him. She was so watchful, so distrustful, just like she'd been in the beginning. It was going to be a long, arduous road to get her back, but he would do it.

"You're a crack psychiatrist, aren't you, Black?"

"I do okay."

"You do know that I admire that and appreciate what you've done for me, right?"

Oh, God, that sounded like the beginning of a Dear John letter, if he'd ever heard one. "Yeah. And?"

"Nothing. I just think you're a good guy to help me out like this, spend all this time taking care of me, you know, all that. So, thank you."

Well, that pleased him, but he still was worried that she was in the process of letting him down easy all the way to the curb. "You're pretty special yourself, Claire. And I'm in love with you. That ought to explain a lot."

They stared at each other some more, dancing around the great big elephant in the room. But Black stayed true to his word. He didn't try to touch her; he got down to business. "I think you're strong enough now to start some therapy sessions. See if I can't ease you back into letting go of some of the memories that your mind is apparently blocking out."

Her face lit up, and she nodded. "It's getting back to work, I think. It takes my mind off other things. Relaxes me."

"Apparently. But then again, you've always loved your job." But he was wondering how much he should reveal to her. What might throw her back into a terrified state, her mind unable to accept all the terrible tragedies experienced in her past? He was beginning now to think that she was exhibiting a selective memory loss. She was disassociating herself from anything that her brain knew she couldn't handle yet. He had to think long and hard which way to go, without making her worse and/or causing her to take off on her own and hide out somewhere safe. She had done that once. Gone into hiding and left everything behind for an entire year. She might do it again. He did not want that to happen. He was tiptoeing around inside her head, making decisions, and that made him nervous as hell.

"So it's okay to stay here tonight?" she finally asked him.

"Sure. I love it out here."

Black watched her glance upstairs at the bedroom in the loft. He knew what she was thinking, but she only said, "Don't you need to go home and pack a few things?"

Black tried not to smile. "I keep some clothes and shaving gear here, just in case. Like I told you, we move back and forth a lot. Whichever place is more convenient at the moment. I've wanted you to move in with me full-time for a long time now, but you don't want to give up this house. Can't say I blame you. It's a great place."

"Now that I've seen it, I can understand why I didn't want to let it go."

"Everything's going to fall back in place soon, Claire." And God, he hoped to hell it did. And when it did, all hell could break loose and he had to prepare her for that eventuality. Her life had been anything but easy, from childhood on, and there were lots of other bad things that she had apparently not told him. The fact that she could play the violin like a concert violinist, for one. He had to start somewhere with her, so he decided to use questions to delve into her subconscious.

"Tell me about the place where you learned to play the violin like that, Claire."

Surprise, then a quick frown followed by another slight shoulder jerk. "Here and there, I guess. I got passed around to a lot of foster homes when I was a kid." She looked him straight in the eyes. "You didn't know about that, I take it."

"I knew about foster homes, but I didn't know any specifics. You never mentioned particular ones." And neither did John Booker, his private investigator, when Black had him dig up her past right after he first met her. He got plenty of scary stuff at that time, but nothing about the violin.

"It's no big deal. That's probably why I didn't mention it."

"Were you fond of any of your foster parents?"

"I didn't like that one. They used to slap a flyswatter down on top of my head when I missed a note. That's why I play so well, I guess."

Black frowned. He couldn't help it. "So you play the piano equally well?"

"Yeah, I guess."

"Where were these people who mistreated you?"

"In Louisiana. Some lived around Baton Rouge. Some closer to New Orleans. I finally ran away from the last one. I found a family who took me in, and that's where I stayed until Family Services found me again. The LeFevres were cool, but the state took me away from them and put me in a home up in Lafayette."

Shocked at her casual revelations, ones that he'd never heard before, Black sat down on the couch. He was from New Orleans, and he and Claire once had been there together. At the time, she had acted as if she knew nothing about the area. Why? "Sit down, Claire. You'll be more comfortable."

She didn't take his advice. She paced around, touching things, looking at things, as she had done in his office that first day. She was uncomfortable or nervous. Or both. Probably both.

"Did any of your foster parents live in the bayous?"

"Yeah, that's where the LeFevres lived. Not the ones who forced me to take music lessons."

"So you play both piano and violin?" He just could not believe she was an accomplished musician.

"I'm better on the fiddle."

Black thought about it for a moment. She was definitely comfortable now revealing background that he'd never heard before, and he'd made it a point since they'd met to know as much about her as he could. Had she been keeping this back for some reason? Or had her mind blocked out some unpleasant things that her head injury had brought out again?

"You know, I liked it down there in the bayous. They lived in a big white house and they had a neat houseboat, too." She frowned. "The best thing about it was that they had a couple of kids for me to play with. The boy, Gabe, he was really cool. I was a big tomboy back then. So it wasn't so bad living there."

"So you hated leaving the LeFevres?"

Claire frowned. "Yeah, they had to drag me out of there, with Gabe hanging on to the back of my T-shirt. It was pretty brutal."

Black watched her closely. Claire had acted uneasy in the bayou when they'd been there together, afraid of it, in fact. Something very strange was going on. He watched as she sat down and rubbed her temples with her fingertips. "I'm getting a headache," she said. "But you know what? I think I'm just going to forget how strange all this is and accept it for what it is. You know? Embrace the unknown. Stop fighting it and trying to force things. Just veg out and let it be."

Well, Black could embrace that. Her problems went deeper than even he knew, and he thought he knew everything about her. God, he knew enough about her tortured childhood. She said she liked that set of foster parents. Perhaps her mind was just letting out mostly good things and not much else. Even some experiences that she hadn't discussed with him in the past. Right now, she was tired and had a headache, time to let her rest.

"You hungry?" he asked her. Food seemed to be a safe subject between them, and she needed to eat. She was rail thin.

"I happen to be starving."

"That probably has something to do with your headache." He looked around. "I brought fried chicken and biscuits, if that sounds good to you. It's down in the boat. My guess is that you don't have much here to eat. You usually don't. You hate to cook."

"I know."

"You do?"

"Just now came to me. But I can do it in a pinch and it tastes just fine. I just don't like anything about doing it, is all."

"How about us just relaxing tonight? Watch a movie, maybe. We've got some DVDs we haven't seen over there in that drawer. We can just lay back and enjoy each other's company. No more questions, no demands from me, no trying to remember. Just a nice quiet night together, doing nothing. You and Jules Verne and me."

To his surprise, tears welled up in Claire's eyes. Claire Morgan was not a crier, not even close. But now she had raw emotions and sharp edges. "Sorry, that just sounds so good, so regular, so normal, and I haven't felt normal lately."

"Okay, we will sit here tonight, and not do a damn thing. Look, I'm going down and get the food. After that, we'll just sit around and do anything we want to do. No pressure. No worries. No pushing at you."

And that's exactly what they did. And it did work out very nicely. They ate, watched a movie called *The Blind Side*, which made her laugh a couple of times, and then Black offered against every nerve and desire in his body to sleep on the downstairs couch instead of upstairs with her. Claire climbed to the loft with Jules on her heels to the giant king-sized bed that he'd bought her not long after they met. He lay there awake and miserable and listened to her cuddle and stroke the dog, and wished it were him. He tossed and turned and muttered a few choice curses to himself, but he didn't go upstairs. Hell no, he didn't go upstairs, goddamn it, but he wanted to, about as much as he'd ever wanted anything in his entire life.

Chapter Twelve

Upstairs in the loft, Claire tried to concentrate on her case, which was what she should be doing, instead of badgering her erased mind into submission. It just might be a nice break from the mental crowbar she'd been wedging on her cerebrum. Let things rest, lay fallow, get comfortable, and feel all safe and relaxed, and then some memories would spring up and enlighten her like a message from Buddha.

Try as she might, Claire could not come up with anything helpful or eye-opening about their bludgeoned victim, and probably wouldn't until they nailed down the woman's identity and interviewed her family and friends. She and Bud were going to start on that first thing tomorrow morning. Around midnight, she got up and peeked over the balcony railing and saw where Black was sprawled out on the sofa, looking too big and very uncomfortable. Next time, she would take the sofa and he could have the bed.

She finally fell into a sleep as restless as Black's, and when she awoke next, it was daylight, and Black was in the shower off the bedroom. She sat up and picked up the alarm clock on the bedside table. It said six o'clock. When he walked out of the bathroom, he had on a pair of khaki shorts and a black T-shirt with a gold foil New Orleans Saints logo on the front.

"I've got to get back. One of my patients is freaking out about a bad dream. I've got to go in right now and calm him down."

"Okay."

Then she waited for him to order her to get up and go with him and was mentally rebelling and formulating reasons not to, but as it turned out, she didn't need them.

"I guess you're going in to work again today, right?"

Relieved, she nodded. "Bud's coming by and we're gonna check out the missing woman and talk to the deputy who investigated the call. See if anybody can identify the clothing the victim was wearing."

"Well, be careful. Duck and weave, you know the drill."

Black smiled as if she would react to the boxing analogy. "Ooo-kay," she said. "You, too. You never know what your other head cases like me are going to do."

"It's just a thing we used to say." Black grinned. "You're more yourself, every day. The old Claire is making herself known, slowly but surely. If you need anything, just call me. I'm minutes away. I'm gonna call for a Cobalt to pick me up, so I can leave the one at the dock out here for you, in case you want to come over to Cedar Bend for the night."

So he was letting her go, giving her freedom to spread her wings, but now she wasn't so sure that's what she wanted him to do. "Would you want to come back here tonight?"

Black gave her a quick smile and looked pretty pleased. "If you want me to, wild horses couldn't drag me away. Just let me know what time you'll be home. I'll meet you here."

While he made the call, Claire pulled on a robe, went downstairs, and fixed them both a cup of coffee. She knew where everything was, knew exactly what to do. They sat across from each other at the bar while they waited for his ride and talked about what a beautiful morning it was, how hot it was going to get. In other words, it was meaningless small talk. Neither of them mentioned the sexual tension still crackling like a white-hot wire between them, nor what they were going to do about it. They just pretended it wasn't there, shooting off all those glowing red sparks and titillating possibilities.

In time, they heard the roar of a powerful boat and one of the Cedar Bend Cobalt 360s flew across the calm water of the cove throwing chevron wakes onto both shores. As it maneuvered in at her little dock, Black got up and gave Claire a quick peck on the cheek.

"Take care of yourself. Call me if you get a breakthrough."

"Don't worry. I'll be fine."

Black stopped at the door, his hand on the doorknob. "Sweetheart, this is the best I've felt about you since I pulled you out of that damn river. Just stick close to Bud, that's all I ask. See you tonight."

Claire picked up Jules Verne and stroked his fur while she watched Black until he was out of sight, the boat disappearing out of the cove. Then she showered and dressed, anxious for Bud to come by so they could get to work. She was feeling better about her personal problems, but they still had an unknown corpse lying beaten and lifeless on one of Buckeye Boyd's stainless-steel tables inside the medical examiner's office.

Around eight o'clock, Bud's Bronco pulled up into her driveway. Claire gave the little poodle a hug and then ran out and got inside. As they backed out and headed up the road, she turned to look at him.

"So, Bud, what's the missing woman's name again?"

"Miriam Long. The deputy who got the call is meeting us at her house."

They drove for a while, fighting morning traffic as everybody went off to work or to have some fun out on the lake or at one of the many shopping malls and arcades they passed along the way. About fifteen minutes later, they reached Bagnell Dam.

"Our turn is across the dam and on the left," Bud told her.

They drove the length of the dam, and Bud hung a left on a lake road that led down a steep hill to a faded blacktop street where several houses sat on flat, shady lakefront properties. A Canton County deputy's car was sitting in the driveway of a low and sprawling, flat-roofed yellow house. They pulled up beside their colleague's car underneath a huge pecan tree with low-slung and spreading branches. A lush grassy lawn surrounded Miriam Long's house, and a deputy in Canton County departmental brown stood beside his driver's door. He didn't look familiar.

"That's Ben Welch," Bud told her, turning off the engine and shoving the gearshift into park. "He's been with us for a couple of months now. You didn't know him all that well. He's a good cop, though."

Bud had gotten into the habit of a running commentary that inserted missing pieces into her life's half-finished puzzle. But surprise,

surprise, Claire liked that. Gave her a heads-up on what she was facing. Since she already seemed to be a primo topic of some amazement and curiosity around the department, Bud made it easy for her to act like she knew who she didn't know.

"Howdy, Bud." Welch looked to be in his early twenties, right out of the academy, in fact. He was clean shaven, his hair shaved over the ears but longer on top with gel holding it in place. His eyes were big and brown and watchful. Sharp and inquisitive. At about five ten, he stood just a little bit taller than Claire. He looked at her, as if tiptoeing his way across a carpet of eggshells. "Hi, Claire. How you doin'?"

"Hi, Ben. I'm doing fine. Thanks for asking," Claire said in return, which seemed to put him into a quick, relieved relaxation mode around the office's most disconcerting amnesiac detective.

Claire moved on quickly. "So, Ben, I understand that you took the call when Ms. Long went missing."

"Yes, ma'am. I immediately drove to this location, checked the doors and windows, found the front door key where it was hidden under that flowerpot over there, and then took a quick look around inside. Nothing appeared unusual, nothing out of place that I could tell, and no sign of foul play."

"Your report indicated that her office called and reported that she wasn't answering her phone and hadn't checked in at work. The sheriff put out a BOLO on her, but didn't get any credible responses. Is that correct?"

"Yes, ma'am, exactly."

Bud said, "Who was the last person to see her?"

"My understanding is that she last saw her real estate partner the afternoon she disappeared. The partner told me that Miriam Long was getting ready to go abroad for several weeks, so she didn't miss her for quite some time."

"So you've interviewed the partner?" Claire asked.

"Yeah. Name's Kay Kramer. Her statement says this behavior is not like Miriam Long at all. That she always calls in, but she was excited about going to Italy so Kay thought she forgot. Kramer didn't think anything was wrong until Long's husband called and said he couldn't get in touch with her."

"We'll go downtown and reinterview Kay Kramer. The description you have on the BOLO is a pretty close match to our homicide victim. We need fingerprint analysis to ID the body before we go see Ms. Kramer."

"Yeah, I heard the perp did a real job on her face."

Claire nodded, remembering and wishing she didn't. She couldn't recall much, true, but that poor woman's face was forever imprinted on her mind.

"We need to gather some items inside the house for fingerprinting and DNA analysis."

"Okay. I didn't touch anything when I went inside. Just the front doorknob and a couple of closet doors. The place is small."

They snapped on white latex gloves and stretched paper footies over their shoes while Welch opened the screen and unlocked the front door. He stood back and remained on the porch while they proceeded into the house. Inside, it was very cool, frigid even. Felt nice after standing outside in the morning's sweltering heat. She was finding that Lake of the Ozarks did not have the temperate climate of southern California. But more important, Miriam had left her air conditioner on full blast. Nobody would do that right before a transcontinental flight and lengthy holiday. No way did this look like a house that a professional woman would leave behind when going away.

The living room was decorated professionally, very neat and orderly, but in a homey, comfortable way. The color scheme was muted blues and beiges and dark browns. The accent color of burnt orange made its appearance in the sofa pillows and a large picture depicting a pitcher full of sunflowers and daisies that hung over the mantel on a dated redbrick fireplace with black soot marks on the bricks.

There were enough masculine touches to indicate a man lived there, too, meaning the worn brown leather recliner and locked mahogany gun case on the wall against the kitchen. Claire walked over and inspected several long hunting rifles and the Remington shotgun that were displayed behind the glass panes. Miriam could be a gun enthusiast, of course. Lots of women were, including Claire, but somehow she doubted it. Obviously, they belonged to Miriam's husband.

"Where is Long's husband? Didn't Welch say the partner said he couldn't get in touch with his wife?"

Bud said, "I think he's deployed in the Gulf."

"Oh, God, I hope our victim isn't this woman."

"I think she is." Bud was not optimistic. It was just too much of a coincidence. Chances were that the victim and missing person were indeed one and the same.

When they pushed through the swinging door that led to a separate kitchen, they found a Bose radio playing very softly on the kitchen counter. It was tuned to a country station. The kitchen was old, but looked recently updated with new stainless-steel appliances, a brown granite countertop, and white cabinets. There was a dark mahogany table built up taller than usual, with four high bar stools around it. The window over the sink was cracked about an inch to let in fresh air. This woman had been planning to come back before she left the country, no doubt about it.

"Oh, man, that's 'Kissed You Tonight' by Gloriana. Have you seen their video, Claire? I'm telling you, man alive, that girl who sings with them is smokin'."

"Nope. This amnesia thing crimps my video watching of late. But I did remember Picasso the other day." Bud didn't reply, too busy singing along and thinking about the man alive, smokin' hot singer, no doubt. Even after this short time, she'd figured out that Bud Davis liked women big-time and they more than liked him back. He had the charm and looks, to be sure. He'd told her they hadn't been an item, and she believed him. Office romances were never a good idea, especially in police departments.

After they finished a tandem and thorough search of the living room and kitchen, they moved down a short hallway to an open bedroom door. Inside, things were fairly messy, more so than anywhere else in Miriam Long's house. It was painted a colonial blue, and Miriam Long had a white bedspread on a mahogany sleigh bed with lots of matching white pillows. The one centered in the middle had a large blue "L" on it. There was a matching dresser with little drawers under the mirror.

A blue-and-white porcelain lamp sat on one side, switched off. A large crystal frame sat on the other side, and the photograph inside depicted a nice-looking man standing in front of a couple of palm trees and a large white outdoor fountain. He was tall and tough looking and wearing desert camouflage fatigues.

"She's married to military, all right, Bud. Take a look at this picture. My bet is Iraq."

Bud walked over and took it out of her hands. "Poor guy. My gut tells me that he is now a widower and doesn't even know it."

Claire put the frame back where she'd found it and focused her attention on a complete set of matching white leather luggage spread out over the bed, all open and unzipped and half packed.

"It's pretty obvious she wasn't ready to leave yet."

Bud glanced at the bed, too. "Well, she went somewhere. I don't see a purse. A woman doesn't leave the house without their purse, do they?"

"I don't know, Bud. I doubt it." Claire frowned. "I didn't see one at my house. In fact, I better check and see if I've got a driver's license somewhere. I hadn't even thought about my having a purse."

"Sorry, I keep forgetting. It's probably on the bottom of the Finley River. Don't worry 'bout the license. I won't arrest you." He grinned.

"Thanks a lot. But about that purse, most women I know carry them. I did, too," she said, after thinking for a moment. "A big brown leather one." Right now her memories weren't flashing like film clips; they were more like ingrained thoughts she just dug up from deep inside her brain's gray matter.

Bud said, "Yet her car's sitting outside under the carport. She didn't drive herself away from here."

"Could be somebody picked her up. Took her someplace for a last-minute bon voyage lunch, something like that."

"Maybe. Ben Welch canvassed the houses around here on the day she was reported missing. Nobody remembered seeing her that day, but the next-door neighbor said she had a motorboat that's gone now."

Claire pulled back the sheer white curtains covering the bedroom window. A little dock lay at the bottom of the flat backyard, one that looked a lot like Claire's. No boat. "Nothing's turned up. But I bet she took it out on the lake for some reason."

Bud stared at her, palms planted on his hips. He'd already taken off his suit coat because of the heat outside and rolled the creased sleeves of his dress shirt up to his elbows. He still looked nice and unwrinkled and unsweaty. Unlike her. How the hell did he do that? Everybody had to perspire sometimes, didn't they? He said, "If I was off to Italy, you can bet I wouldn't be out sightseeing on Lake of the Ozarks before I finished packing my bags."

"Me, either. Maybe she had a good reason to go off with somebody."

Inside the missing woman's daffodil-yellow-and-white-tiled bathroom, Claire found an empty yellow-and-navy plaid cosmetics bag with an "M" and "L" embroidered on the front. All the contents were already emptied onto the white marble double sink. Brushes, mascara, lipstick, Roc night cream, Clinique overnight eye repair, and a small bottle of perfume, Obsession. She could smell the fragrance lingering faintly in the room and somehow remembered it from somewhere, but couldn't place where. Miriam Long's toothbrush was still sticking out of a hammered nickel holder. With gloved hands, Claire carefully picked up the toothbrush between thumb and forefinger and slipped it into a plastic evidence bag. She did the same thing with the hairbrush and lipstick. All three should have Miriam's fingerprints and her DNA on them. She gathered up the evidence and carried the bags out of the bathroom.

Bud was standing at the kitchen counter, bagging a laptop computer in a large brown paper evidence bag. "This has gotta have her fingerprints on it. Maybe even the murderer's, if she is our victim. And God, I hope she's not."

"It's also got her e-mails, I bet. That might give us a clue as to who wanted her dead. Maybe she had a boyfriend, too. A jealous one."

They poked around some more. In the bedside table, Claire found a whole pack of photos lying loose in the drawer. Most all of them portrayed the same man that was in the large crystal frame, but this time he always had his arms around a woman who she assumed was their missing person. Miriam Long had long dark red hair, just like the woman at the duck blind. Claire bagged all of them. What a shame. Miriam looked to be around twenty-six or twenty-seven, a really pretty girl. Apparently doing fairly well in real estate, considering the new model black Cadillac out in the driveway. She was hugging an older woman in one of the photos. Who? Her mother, probably. Or her sister?

Claire stood there, staring at the picture and wondering a moment about her own mother, her father, her life, if she'd ever remember her family. She did remember those foster parents that she'd mentioned to Black, but not her real parents. Why would that happen? Maybe she didn't have any kin. None of them had come to see her when she was in the coma, or if they had, nobody had thought to mention it. Then she shut down those maudlin thoughts. Black said she would remember things the way she was supposed to, and if she didn't, he'd tell her about the blanks in her childhood and adolescence. She could wait it out. Meanwhile, she'd just do her job as well as she could and try not to think about her past. Let go of the stress of wracking her overwrought brain night and day. Relax. Get mellow. Yeah, sure. She didn't think so.

Thirty minutes later, they locked up the house and took the items they'd collected down to the criminalists at the Medical Examiner's office. Inside that cool and silent building, Claire's old/new friends, Nancy and Buck, were working on the victim's body, wearing full protective gear and breathing masks. Bud and Claire donned theirs at once. Buck had removed and bagged the woman's torn and bloody clothing, swept her body for evidence, and then washed her flesh clean. Claire wasn't hoping for much trace evidence left on the abused corpse. This woman had been in the summer sun for days and was in full decomposition. She just hoped to God they could match the prints and get a positive ID so next of kin could be notified. Claire's gut already told her, though, that the body in front of them indeed belonged to Miriam Long.

"You got that missing woman's prints for me?" Shaggy Becker asked them, rushing in through the swinging door that led out to the hallway. "I already got a scan of the deceased's prints. Hey, you 'member me, yet, Claire?"

"Yes, about the prints. No, about you. But that's okay, I like you already, anyway. I don't need to remember anything else."

"Cool. You always said I was awesome. Which is true. I'm all fun and games. You used to like comin' over and watchin' Bruce Willis flicks with me. Wanna do that sometime?"

"Sure. I remember liking him, too. *Die Hard*, right?"

"Well, you still got the important things goin' on up there." He tapped his forefinger to the fuzzy dreadlocks at his temple. Claire handed over the evidence bags, and he took off with them toward his own lab next door. Apparently, he did everything at a run. "Be back in a sec," he yelled over his shoulder.

Through a glass wall separating the cold autopsy room from his lab, Claire watched him sit down in front of a laptop, with all sorts of computer equipment, complicated-looking instruments, TV screens, and lots of other criminalist goodies lining the counters and walls. He had to be good, with all that apparatus.

Looking back down at the victim, she wondered how anyone could hack, or pummel another human being in the face like that. The victim must have been terrified when she realized what was about to happen, if she'd been conscious and aware. Buckeye could tell them how she died soon enough.

Buckeye was staring at the picture of Miriam Long that they'd brought in. "She was a pretty lady. Hope this isn't her. Too bad, this poor girl had to die at the hands of some deranged murderer. And that's what he has to be."

Bud said, "All we need is another psycho running around the lake killin' people. When's it gonna stop?"

Both men looked at her, then at each other, as if they'd let something awful slip and felt terrible about it. People seemed to be doing a lot of that lately. Claire said, "Well, don't look at me. I didn't do it. I was in a coma."

Both men appeared startled, but then they laughed. The tension in the room went away, and she stared down at the beaten body lying on the table and shivered. The whole day seemed surreal verging on bizarre. The deep sleep of her coma was looking better all the time. Maybe Black was right. Maybe she'd come back to work too soon.

Nancy Gill hadn't said much, but she put her hand on Claire's arm. "You know what, Claire? You oughta come down to my neck of the woods when Buckeye does his stint down there. You could do the same exchange thing in the detective bureau. Sheriff Friedewald would be happy to get your services for a little while. Russ is great to work for. You'd like him."

It was funny how the state of Louisiana, and New Orleans in particular, kept coming up. Maybe God was trying to tell her something. "Maybe. We'll see. I lived down there for a while when I was a kid. Don't remember a lot about it, though."

"It's an interesting place. You'd like it. You can live with me if you do come down. I have plenty of room at my house on the bayou."

"You live on the bayou?"

"Yeah, in LaFourche Parish."

"Got it," Shaggy yelled, bursting through the doors again and heading quickly toward them. "Perfect match. Our victim is Miriam Long. One hundred percent. Without a doubt. You can notify next of kin."

"We got the impression she's got a husband overseas, but we don't know how to contact him. Her partner ought to know. Bud, you ready to go pay a call on Kay Kramer?"

"Yeah, now we're getting somewhere."

Yes, they were, but not the place they really wanted to be. In that better world, Miriam Long would not be lying on that cold stainless-steel table beaten to a pulp. She would still have her pretty face intact and would now be in Italy, smiling at her handsome husband and holding his hand.

Jesse's Girl

Twenty-four days after the accident

The next few weeks felt as if all Jesse's dreams were coming true. He got to see his Annie nearly every day. She didn't recognize him, of course; she didn't recognize anybody. But it still broke his heart not to touch her and smell her and lick her soft skin and tell her how much he loved her. He thought it would be different for them, that she would remember him because they were soul mates and always had been. But she didn't recognize Nicholas Black, either, and that was good. That made Jesse so very happy. She had amnesia, but Monica said it wouldn't last forever, that it was temporary, and that she would soon come back to reality and recollect everybody and everything that had ever happened to her.

Jesse just hoped that her memory loss lasted long enough for him to put the rest of his plan in action. First and foremost, he had to get rid of Nicholas Black, but he felt anxious, because right now would be the best time to steal Annie away with him. He feared she might still be angry about what he'd done in the past, about crashing them into the river and injuring her, and all that sort of thing. But her anger wouldn't last long, not really. She had told him before that she loved him. She did love him, and he loved her.

During the last few days, he'd convinced Monica to let him walk Annie's little poodle. Monica said Annie adored the dog. Monica had been walking him on her breaks, but Jesse took over that job for her and let her sit longer over her lunch while he and Jules Verne, that was the dog's name, got to know each other. He fed Jules bits of steak and bacon on the sly so the dog would love him. He'd take Jules, too, when he took Annie away. They'd all be happy together then, with Miss Rosie. Everything was working out beautifully, and Monica didn't have a clue as to who Jesse really was.

One time, he had even passed Nicholas Black in the resort's busy lobby and had quickly turned his face away for fear Black would recognize him, despite his changed looks. But the big man barely glanced at him. He looked extremely distracted and hurried. If Nicholas Black only knew Jesse was right there in the hotel and getting a paycheck, to boot. Nicholas Black was footing the bill for Jesse to steal Annie away from him. Jesse laughed inside. And now Monica had asked him to take Jules upstairs to Annie because she had to accompany Nicholas Black on his rounds. Oh, God, Annie was awake, and he was going to get to talk to her.

His nerves were so jittery, so ragged, and he was breathing so hard when he left the penthouse elevator that he could barely catch his breath. Holding the sweet little dog, he fed him a piece of fried bacon and then stood there and listened for Annie's voice. He was supposed to just put Jules Verne outside the elevator and go back downstairs, but he didn't. Nicholas Black was already halfway out to the patient bungalows on the point. Monica was with him. Neither one could stop him. Annie didn't need Monica much anymore since she had regained consciousness and was walking and getting along so well on her own, even working half a day. In fact, Monica was looking for a house to buy now, which wouldn't help Jesse's plan one bit.

Okay, he had to just do it. She wouldn't recognize him, no way. He glanced inside Annie's bedroom, but the bed was empty, the covers properly made, the pillows fluffed. It was late in the afternoon so Annie was probably somewhere nearby. Oh, God, what if she did recognize him? What if she remembered all they'd meant to each other? But no, no, she hadn't. Monica told him only this morning that Nicholas Black was disappointed she hadn't recalled more than she had. Jesse wasn't disappointed. He was thrilled to hear that.

Walking slowly down the silent hallway, holding the wriggling poodle and glancing into one beautiful room after the other, he felt inferior to Nicholas Black as to what he could give Annie. The views of the lake were gorgeous up so high. He'd have to find a home for Annie and him up high on a hill or she might be upset that she couldn't see the lake. He wished he hadn't killed the real estate agent right off the bat like that. She might've come in handy at some point. When he reached the huge living area at the end of the hall, he saw her. She was sitting down on a couch, alone, silent, just staring out the window.

Then Jules saw her, too, and began to go crazy in Jesse's arms, barking and twisting and trying to get down. Annie turned quickly and saw them behind her. Then she stood up, smiling, and called the dog. Jules ran straight to her, jumped up on the couch, and then the rest of the way into her arms.

"Hi," Annie said to him, with her angel's smile. "I guess you've been walking Jules Verne for me."

Jesse felt his throat clog up, his heart thudding inside his chest with love and the terrible need to touch her and tie her up. He nodded, all he could do for a moment, and then he stammered when he tried to speak. "Yes, me and Monica both walk him."

"Well, thank you so much. I love this little squirt. He's so cute."

Annie hugged the dog and let him lick her face. Laughing, she said, "Has he been a good boy?"

Jesse could only stare at the poodle's little pink tongue lapping against her beautiful face. He wanted to tear the poodle out of her hands and lick her himself, tie her up and lick every inch of her body. He tried to control his heaving breaths.

"Are you okay?" Annie said then, looking curiously at him.

Jesse nodded, trying to get hold of his rampaging need to have her under his control, but he felt a little safer now. She didn't recognize him with his long hair and facial hair and contact lenses, and it wouldn't hurt for her to know him as a different person. That would make it easier to take her away, if she was used to him and trusted him. And she was so concerned about him. She did love him, even now, and sensed that he was her true soul mate. "Oh, yes, I'm just a little tired. I've been workin' all day long. That little Jules is a good dog. He doesn't give me any trouble. I love animals."

"I do, too. Do you have a dog at home?"

"Not right now. But I had a squirrel once. I called him Mr. Twitchy Tail."

Annie looked at him for a moment, and he was afraid she did remember the pet squirrel they'd played with when they were little kids, but she only laughed and said, "Well, that's a really good name for a squirrel."

Oh, how he loved Annie. She looked better, too. Her hair was washed and combed, and she had on a baggy sweat suit, a black one with CEDAR BEND LODGE spelled out across the chest and down the side of the pants' leg. But her feet were bare. How he wanted to go over and grab her and lick her toes and make her see how much he adored her. But he couldn't, not yet. But soon, soon, he'd have her for his own.

"You're Monica's Jesse, I bet, aren't you? She told me about you, how you've been helping her out. But hey, let me tell you myself how much I appreciate all you've done for me. You've been very kind and helpful. Jules sure likes you."

Annie loved him. She did. "You're welcome. I'm just awful glad to see you up and awake and gettin' better."

Nodding, Annie stroked the dog's fur. He resented the dog, and the attention she was giving it. "You know, truth is, I feel good now. Don't remember much yet, but it's coming back gradually. At least, that's what the doctor tells me."

"I hope so."

Then, there followed a moment of silence when he couldn't think of what to say. So he just stood there, staring at her, wanting to run over, get her down on the floor and run his hands up under the sweatshirt and down the pants and all over her. So Annie finally said, "I'm looking forward to my night out with Monica."

"She didn't tell me about any night out. Where're you goin'?" He wondered if Monica was trying to move in on Annie and take her away from him. That would not be good, no, it would not. He would have to deal with Monica if she ever tried anything like that.

"She wants to go out to that new restaurant on the lake called Jeepers. This Friday night, in fact. Girls' night out, you know, should be fun."

"Oh, yeah, I almost forgot. She did tell me that. That'll be fun," he answered with a false grin. Well, he'd just have to join the girls there. Wouldn't that be great, to spend time with Annie outside this hotel without Nicholas Black sniffing around and keeping Annie to himself. Maybe he could even steal her away right then and there. That is, if he could find a good way to ditch Monica at the restaurant. And he could, no problem.

Down the hall, he heard the faint pinging sound of the elevator doors opening. Fearing it was Nicholas Black coming home early, he said quickly, "Well, I better get goin'. I don't want to get in trouble with the boss."

"Okay, it was very nice to meet you, Jesse. And thank you again so much. Maybe I'll get a chance to return the favor someday."

"Oh, no need. I wanted to do it."

Annie nodded and said good-bye, and Jesse fled quickly. But it was Monica walking down the hall, not Black, and she got a big frown on her face when she saw him. "You're not supposed to be up here alone and you know it. Where's Jules Verne?"

"I took him down the hall to the lady. I didn't mean anything by it."

Monica was not happy. Her face looked ugly when she was bent out of shape. Her voice was low and furious. "I told you that you couldn't just hang around up here any time you want. Not now that Claire's awake. You're gonna have to stop it, right now, or you'll get fired. And so will I."

Jesse felt a familiar tide of rage rising up fast inside him, like a big rolling flame. Monica wasn't so nice anymore, and she'd sure pay the price for her meanness, and sooner rather than later. But she was an integral part of the plan he had devised to get rid of Nicholas Black, so he had to play it cool. He forced up a smile.

"I'm sorry, babe. I won't come up here anymore, if you don't want me to. I promise. I was just hoping to get a minute with you."

Her face softened, and then the idiot fool of a woman literally beamed up at him. "Maybe we can get together tonight, at my place. I'm off tomorrow so you can stay as long as you want."

"Great," he said, hugging her, but inside he was already planning how he would kill her. Yes, things were going to move faster now. But that was good. He was ready to have Annie all to himself now, and it was finally going to happen.

Chapter Thirteen

The Kramer/Long Real Estate office was located in Camdenton. Situated in a remodeled cream-colored Victorian house just off Highway 64, it didn't look particularly busy as Bud and Claire turned into its paved parking lot. There was one car, a white BMW, all shiny and new and sparkling, sitting under a portico attached to the house. Business must be booming, or the proprietor leased her vehicle to wow her clients.

Inside, the air-conditioning was once again a welcome reprieve against the harsh and hot noonday sun. The high temperature was sapping Claire faster than it should have, but she had been under the weather, to say the least. All the running around was giving her some strength back, and it felt good to be out in the sunshine and doing something productive.

Nobody was sitting at the receptionist's desk. In fact, nobody was in sight. No sounds, no tapping of computer keys, not even a tinkling bell on the door to announce their arrival. The small, white French provincial desk with cabriole legs was sitting beside a lovely old staircase that rose to a landing, then went on again at a right angle to the second story. The floors were dark oak hardwood, and a fancy chandelier made of iron and crystal droplets hung above the desk. There were rooms off to their right and left. One was a sitting area with blue-and-white floral couches around a white fireplace and a white, glass-topped wicker cocktail table. The other room looked like a conference room with a large, round, shiny table surrounded by eight armless white leather chairs. Kay Kramer's office was an upscale, swanky-looking professional place of business. Some big bucks contracts were signed on that polished conference table, count on it.

"Somebody's got to be here. I smell French vanilla cappuccino." Bud was apparently a coffee connoisseur, too. But something did smell really good. Claire guessed she liked French vanilla coffee. She'd have to buy some at Kroger's and find out.

"Hey, anybody here?" Claire called out, not patient, and not shy about raising up missing receptionists.

"Hello," called a distant voice filtering down faintly through the white upstairs banisters. Claire looked up and found a woman with short, stylishly cut hair that was layered and highlighted in a nice wheat shade. She was peeking over the balcony at them. She looked to be middle-aged, but still quite pretty and young looking, tanned to perfection, and anorexic thin.

"Yes, may I help you?" she inquired, with a very pleasant, let-me-sell-you-a-seven-figure-house greeting.

"Hello, I'm Detective Claire Morgan"—boy, did that not roll easily off her lips, hadn't said it in a while—"and this is my partner, Detective Bud Davis. We're with the Canton County Sheriff's Department."

"Oh, my God, you've found Miriam! You have, haven't you?"

Oh, my God was right, which she'd find out soon enough. "Are you her partner, ma'am? Kay Kramer?"

"Yes, I am. Please come on up. We can talk in my office. My receptionist is out to lunch, so I'm here by myself through the noon hour."

They climbed the steps, and Claire admired the old home with all the intricately carved woodwork and the magnificent round, stained-glass window on the staircase landing. She realized that she liked old places and was pleased that she knew it. Kay Kramer met them at the top of the steps, right hand extended, impressive big smile plastered on her face, in full Realtor mode now. Guess she thought Bud might want to buy a four-bedroom brick house in a good school district. Kay Kramer was tall, made to look more so by incredibly uncomfortable-looking, black-and-white, six-inch heels with lots of Roman-sandal-style straps around her ankles. But she wore them well, and she also wore the black suit and beige silk shell well, too.

A large, diamond-studded fleur-de-lis was pinned to her left lapel, and it glittered in the ambient light from the chandelier's crystal prisms.

"I've been so worried about Miriam. She's never done anything like this. I've left so many voice mails, but I still haven't heard a word."

They followed her into another big room that overlooked the street out front. It had probably been the former master bedroom in the old days, since converted into a large, beautiful, and feminine-appointed office. The walls were covered in white bead board, from floor to ceiling. More blue floral couches, similar to the ones downstairs, flanked another white fireplace, and she gestured at the two white chairs with blue cushions as she rounded the big white desk to her own rolling blue suede chair. A nice bouquet of fresh yellow daisies sat on her desk. "Please sit down, detectives."

They sat down. They looked at her, neither of them wanting to make this one of the worst days of her life. Claire finally took the plunge, and said, "Ms. Kramer, I'm afraid we've got some very bad news."

"Oh, my God, she's not dead, is she? Is she? Don't tell me that." Her voice faded in a half-squeal sort of moan.

"Yes, ma'am, I'm sorry to say that she is deceased."

Her attractive face blanched, her jaw dropped a bit, and she stared at them, blue-gray eyes wide and stunned. "How? Where? Where is she? Why?"

Kay Kramer hit all the essential questions, and all in one breath, too. "Her body was discovered out on the lake. We got a positive identification less than an hour ago."

"But I gave the young officer a picture of her to use for the missing person flyers." She studied their faces for answers, but then the awful truth dawned on her; the exact moment was easy for them to see. "Oh, my God, what happened to her?"

"I'm sorry, Ms. Kramer, but we think she was murdered," Bud said, making his voice gentle.

Kay stared at him, then at Claire, back at him, and then at her desk blotter. Then her shock dissolved into incredulous horror. She burst into tears, legitimate ones, which flooded down her cheeks and made her nose run. Nobody could fake that kind of grief, nobody.

Not even Meryl Streep—another inexplicable celebrity reminiscence out of Claire's amnesia darkness. Her brain had to be a movie fan.

Kay was trying to speak through her sobs. "Oh, no, no, please don't tell me that. Miriam was so young, like a daughter to me. Why? Why?"

Claire said, "We don't know that yet, Ms. Kramer, but we're going to find out."

Swiveling around, Kay grabbed a tissue from a blue Puffs Plus box on the white credenza behind her. She mopped her face and wiped her eyes, but the tears kept on rolling. She couldn't seem to talk anymore and just sat there and wept as if brokenhearted.

They waited for her to regain control of her emotions, but she never did. It was hard to watch. Finally, Claire tried again. "I know this is a shock to you, Ms. Kramer. I know this is a terrible time to have to talk about this, but we have questions that need to be answered. Do you think you're up to it?"

Kay kept crying. Her chair was turned away from them and facing the curving bow window. But she finally nodded and tried to snuffle away the tears.

"Do you know anybody who might've wanted to hurt her?"

She quickly swiveled the chair back to face them. "Oh, God, no. Nobody. Everybody loved her."

"What about her husband? Or a relative?"

"Her husband's deployed to the Middle East. She's been counting the days until he got back. That's why she was going to Italy. She was going early to rent a house for them so they could spend some time alone in Tuscany before they came back here. They never got to have a honeymoon. They eloped right before he left."

"How long has he been gone?"

She dabbed at her watering eyes, but she was becoming calmer. "Eighteen months. He left the day after the wedding. That's why they wanted to have time alone. He called me when she wasn't in Rome to meet him, worried to death about her. That's the first I knew she was missing. He called me today, too, after he landed at the Kansas City airport. He rented a car and is driving home. He's probably already here."

The weeping intensified. Bud looked miserable. Claire felt her pain, too. She hated breaking the news to a murder victim's loved ones worse than poison. Another lovely thing that she hadn't forgotten.

"Does she have any other family?"

"No, that's why we're so close, especially since my divorce."

"Is there anything that you can tell us that might help us find her killer?"

Kay pulled herself together a bit, or at least kept trying to. "I don't know a single person who didn't think the world of her. Oh, Oliver's going to be so devastated. I can't bear to think about it."

"When was the last time you talked to her?"

"When she left work around noon Friday before last. She was leaving for Rome the next morning."

"Did she say anything unusual that day, tell you she was having problems with anyone? Anybody following her? Harassing her?"

"No, just that she was going to check out a couple of vacant properties and make sure they were secure before she left the country. Said she had to stop the mail and the newspaper. Pick up some book she wanted to read on the plane. Stuff like that. She was really excited about the trip."

"A neighbor said she has a boat. We noticed the small dock at the rear of her house."

"Yes, a small runabout. She likes to fish. It should still be there. She never takes it in for storage when she's gone. Except during the winter months."

"The boat's not there."

"Well, it should be. Maybe she lent it to someone."

Or maybe her killer took her out in it, dumped her body on the duck blind in the dead of the night, and kept the boat as a souvenir, Claire thought.

At that point, Bud picked up the interview. "Was she working on any property that was involved in a nasty divorce settlement, or some kind of contested will? Anything on that order?"

"Not that I know of. I think she would've told me if there was anything too litigious going on. We were so close, like family. Really we were."

"Is it possible for us to get a copy of all the properties she was handling?"

"Yes, I'll get Mandy to get them for you. I heard her come in a minute ago. She'll run copies of anything you need."

It was clear to see that they weren't going to get much else out of her until she came to terms with her friend's death. Claire stood up and handed Kay one of her cards. "Please call us, if you think of a single thing that might help us find her killer, no matter how insignificant it might seem. Will you do that, Ms. Kramer?"

She nodded and took the card.

"Again, we're very sorry for your loss. If there's anything we can do to help you, please feel free to contact us."

Sobbing again, she got out, "Thank you. You're very kind."

Bud and Claire left, both even more depressed than they'd been before. Sometimes being a homicide detective sucked. This was definitely one of those times.

Chapter Fourteen

Before they even reached the car, Claire's cell phone rang. It was Charlie, so she picked up in a hurry. Charlie didn't waste any time getting to the point. "Claire? Miriam Long's husband just got in from Iraq and paid me a visit about half an hour ago. I had to tell him that his wife was dead, and that was no fuckin' picnic, let me tell you. He left here about ten minutes ago, said he was going home. I want you and Bud back over there. See what he can tell you. He wasn't ready to be interviewed when I saw him—shocked out of his mind, in fact, but he probably can talk about it now. Appears to be a good man. Did you get to talk to the partner?"

"Yes, sir, but she was pretty upset, too. Didn't help us much."

"Well, let's just hope Captain Long can give us some kind of take on who might've done this to his wife."

The little yellow house on the lake looked the same except for the dark blue Camry sitting out front. She and Bud got out in the driveway, but when Claire looked down at the lake, she saw a man standing beside the water. He wore a Marine uniform, the formal one with the white belt. He'd taken off his white hat and laid it on a nearby metal chair. He was just standing there, very erect and straight, hands hanging at his sides, staring across the lake at the distant shore.

"There he is," Claire told Bud. "His name's Oliver Long, right? Captain Oliver Long."

Bud nodded. "Okay, let's get this over with. Can't say I'm looking forward to it much."

This arm of the lake was extremely crowded at the moment. Lots of boats and pontoon party barges zipped around the choppy waves, leaving creamy white wakes in their paths. This was the kind of day when Black and Claire used to go out in his Cobalt 360 for the afternoon. The water used to feel so cool and silky when they jumped in and swam around the boat. Claire smiled, couldn't help it.

"I remembered something just now, Bud. Nothing important or life-shattering but I did remember it. Maybe this nightmare's almost over."

Bud looked quickly at her. "Great, Morgan. What'd you remember? Something about me?"

"Nope, boating on the lake with Black."

"Well, I'm hurt."

"No, really, it just came into my mind. I didn't even try. That's got to be a good sign, don't you think?"

"Oh, yeah." Bud grinned. "Hey, I'll be glad when you get it all nailed down. You owe me five bucks for that last pizza I got us, you know."

Both of them became dead serious as they started down the backyard. When they were almost upon him, Oliver Long turned and saw them.

"You guys are the detectives, I take it?"

Claire held up the badge on the chain hanging around her neck. "That's right. We're both homicide detectives at the Canton County Sheriff's Office. I'm Claire Morgan. This's Bud Davis."

"Did you get the bastard who butchered my wife?"

Although his voice remained low, almost a growl, his graphic terminology put them on alert. Claire matched his calm tone. "Not yet, but we're working on it. We hope you can help us get him."

"Oh, I can help you, all right. I'm gonna kill that bastard with my bare hands as soon as I find him."

"I'm sorry, man," said Bud, placing his hand on the captain's back. "I know how you feel right now. From experience. Trust me, it's like hell on earth."

And he did. Claire had seen him in a similar situation when his girlfriend, Brianna, was the victim, and it hadn't been pretty. It hit her again that yet a second recollection in just the space of a few minutes had come like lightning out of the blue. Reeling with excitement and expectation, she nevertheless told herself to get real. This was not the time to rejoice, not standing alongside a grieving widower. But everything was on the verge of coming back; she felt it in her bones.

When the two men stared at each other and nodded in silent commiseration, Claire knew she better take the lead on the interview before they turned the investigation into a posse. She motioned to four metal chairs sitting on the dock. "Mind if we sit down and talk to you for a few minutes, Captain Long? We know you just got home from Iraq, just found out about your wife, but it's important that we know anything that might help find Miriam's killer."

Oliver Long hesitated, looked at her, and then at Bud. Then he just waved his arm toward the chairs. They sat down, but he remained standing, in that terribly rigid military stance. He was a striking man, not particularly tall but impressive. But what man wasn't damn impressive in a crisp Marine uniform? Claire wondered what he did in the service. He'd been in Iraq and probably now blamed himself for not being home when somebody took a club to his new bride. Oh, God, Miriam Long had been so brutalized. Claire hoped her husband didn't see her before the mortician worked his magic on her body, if he even could repair her shattered face.

Oliver Long's dark eyes were bloodshot and tired and jet-lagged. He looked ready to collapse. He needed to go to bed and get a long night of deep healing sleep. But he probably couldn't and wouldn't.

"Do you have family who could be here with you, captain?"

"My mom and dad are on their way. Miriam has no family. Just me."

"Is there anything we can do to make things easier for you?"

"Just catch him and make sure he fries in the electric chair."

"We will get him." That was Bud, making promises he might not able to keep. But they usually did catch the bad guys, or at least that's what she'd been told. She and Harve definitely had in Los Angeles.

"We won't stop until we find him," she told Oliver Long, almost as confidently as Bud.

"Thank you. That's what I needed to hear."

For the first time, he relaxed, albeit slightly, and sat down across from them, but still holding the ramrod posture of a Marine just home from war. "What do you have so far, detectives?"

Not much, Claire thought, but she said, "We know that she was last seen that day by her partner, that she was packed and ready to meet you in Rome. Kay Kramer said your wife was going out to check on some of her listings before she caught her flight, just to make sure everything was in order. We don't know which ones, but we're going to check them out, one at a time."

Bud said, "We should get through most of them today and tomorrow."

"Did she ever mention to you that she was going to do that, captain? Visit her listings, I mean."

"No. The last time we talked, she"——he stopped there, his voice getting thick, and they waited silently for him to regain control——"No, she just talked about wrapping things up here so we could be together. She's never been to Italy. We were going to meet in Rome, spend a few days there, and then drive up to Florence."

Claire took a deep breath, wanting to give this guy a break, but unable to. "Does she have any enemies that you know about?"

"Miriam? No way. She's an angel." He stopped again, his jaw tightening up. "She was small and delicate. Gentle as a lamb. She wouldn't hurt anybody or anything. She used to take moths in the house outside in a paper cup so she wouldn't have to smash them."

That was pretty cool, actually. Claire usually smashed any bug that got in her house. But she hated bugs, all of them, especially spiders. Not a new memory. She'd been killing mosquitoes ever since she woke up. "What about old boyfriends?"

"She didn't date much before we met. She was engaged once to a high school sweetheart, but he died in a car wreck just before they went off to college. She didn't go out much after that, just worked on building up her career, until she met me."

"Where did you meet?" Bud asked.

"She sold me this house when we lived in Springfield. She finally moved up here with me two years ago."

Springfield was a city about an hour southwest of the lake. "Did she have enemies in Springfield?"

"No. She was too nice. Nobody could not like her."

His eyes got all wet and wide, and the muscles under his cheek worked as he ground his teeth. Bud and she glanced away as he mastered his emotions. Miriam was really an angel now, but she sounded like a woman the world might've needed. The captain sure did.

Claire gave him a few minutes to regain his composure as she stared out over the lake and wondered what Black was doing. Probably worrying about her.

"Captain, again, forgive us for bothering you now so soon after your wife's death. I know this is not easy for you. I just have a few more questions. We noticed that your boat is gone. Did your wife put in it in storage, by any chance?"

Captain Long glanced at the end of his dock, as if it were the first time he noticed the boat was gone. He verified that in his next remark. "I didn't know it wasn't here. I had it checked out and examined before I deployed, so Miriam wouldn't have any trouble with it. She loves to go out on the lake. Fishing. Waterskiing. All that." He looked at them quickly. "Do you think it could have been a boating accident? That the damage was done by a motor blade?"

Claire noticed his present tense, but let him have that much. The blade reference only brought back to her the condition of that poor woman's face. Charlie must have told him the extent of the injuries. "I don't think so, sir. First thing we need to do is find your boat. Can you give us its description and license number?"

"Of course. It's a fairly new runabout, red and white, sixteen footer. The serial number and sales info is in the house with our other papers."

"Good. We'll put out a BOLO with the water patrol today."

They questioned him a bit longer, but with no obvious break-through in regard to suspects. But the boat could be the key. If they could find it, it could give them a heads-up on the killer's identity. Meanwhile, they would keep checking out Miriam's listings and in-terview all her clients. With luck, something helpful would eventually rise to the surface. They left Captain Long just sitting there alone on his dock, his eyes on the far shore, and his head full of memories of his dead wife.

Chapter Fifteen

Around four o'clock that afternoon, Bud dropped off Claire at her place. Black wasn't there yet, but her cell phone went into the "Mexican Hat Dance" about ten seconds after she stepped foot on her driveway. Good grief, Bud wasn't even out of sight. She looked around for a flash of binoculars to see if somebody was tailing her and reporting back to Black. Nope. Jeez. Did he have ESP, or what?

"So, how's your day going?" Black asked her. He sounded out of breath, as if he'd been hurrying or that around-the-clock shrinking was more strenuous than people thought.

"Good. I just got home, and I tell you one thing, this half-day stuff sucks. It's not fair that Bud has to do my work, too."

"I'm sure Bud doesn't mind. Enjoy it while you can. You're getting stronger, so you'll be full-time soon enough. Was the missing person your victim?"

"Yeah, positive ID. We got a perfect fingerprint off her hairbrush. Miriam Long's her name. Lives on a lake road near Bagnell Dam. Her realty company's name is Kramer and Long. Heard of them?"

"No. The ID ought to make the investigation go easier."

"Yeah, Bud's trying to run down some of her clients this afternoon. Tomorrow, we're gonna check out locations on her properties. We're trying to locate her boat that's missing. Her husband was deployed, but he's back here now. He's been notified."

"Good God, that poor guy, to have to come home to this. How do you feel, Claire? Your energy still up?"

"Good. Already bored, now that I'm home with nothing to do."

Claire hesitated, not wanting to sound needy or ridiculous or worst of all, clinging. But truth be told, she was beginning to like having this guy around. And she did remember today that they used to go boating together, one more piece of proof that he was her true honey bun. She went with it. "Are you coming back over here tonight?"

"Yes, but I've got some business to take care of first. A couple of meetings I've been putting off for weeks now. Would you want to bring the boat over and stay here tonight? I don't know how long all this is going to take."

She considered what he asked her to do, and that big boat sitting down at her dock did look awfully fast and dangerous. She'd been dying to drive it. "Okay. If you think you can trust me with that fancy Cobalt of yours."

"It's yours, too, remember. Think you can find your way over here?"

"Since you have that sweet GPS tracking set up on it with Cedar Bend as the destination point, I'd say yes."

He laughed softly. "Why don't you come now? Get some rest here in the penthouse where it's nice and quiet. Actually, it's a little too quiet with you and Jules gone."

"Not as quiet as it is out here." She glanced up at the front porch of her very own home and was very pleased with what she saw. "Besides, I want to hang around and sort through my stuff. See if any of it trips my memory back full force."

Silence reigned briefly, as if he wasn't sure that kind of tripping met his super-psychiatrist approval. "Okay. Call me when you start across the lake so I'll know when to expect you."

"C'mon, Black, you're acting like my puppet master again. I better check my arms to make sure there aren't any strings attached."

Yet another short pause followed. Enough to make Claire feel a tad guilty about the tone she'd used. He was trying to let go of her leash, give her some slack. He'd shown that today. She was out of line.

"Yeah, you're right. I do sound that way. Sorry. Can't help it. I worry about you."

Claire's heart shivered. He was pretty good to her, she had to admit. "Sorry, I snapped at you. I guess I'm more tired than I thought. I just didn't want to stop working. It's so good to be back on the job."

"Well, don't overdo it." Claire heard a voice in the background. It sounded like Miki Tudor, his executive assistant. Always dressed immaculately in expensive yet feminine business suits and wearing strings of real pearls, that girl liked to crack the whip on Black's obligations. Talk about a marionette manipulator. "Okay, gotta go, babe. I'm swamped here. The next meeting's getting started."

They hung up, and she looked down at her dock, considering a nice long dip in that calm and glass-smooth green water, but then she saw Jules Verne's little white face peering out the front window. He had to be standing on the hassock near the window, and she could see his tail beating back and forth like crazy. He was giving Claire a thank-God-you-came-home-I've-been-waiting-all-day doggie smile. He was just the sweetest little thing. And he never asked her any questions. Or told her what she should do. One thing she knew for sure, Black loved that dog. They were like Timmy and Lassie, for God's sake. But so did she.

When Claire poked in the security code and stepped inside, Jules was right there, almost as glad to see her in one piece as Black usually was. He jumped around, like a canine pogo stick, yapping and showing her how much he liked her. Then he sort of just collapsed on the floor as if joyously exhausted. She went to the kitchen and brought him out a moist and meaty dog treat, compliments of Black, and in appreciation of Jules Verne's highly dramatic show of affection. Then she sat down, too, and propped up her feet, tired but feeling pretty good about things, as she observed how she'd chosen to decorate her home before she went into that river and landed in no-man's-land. She still liked everything she saw, so she guessed her tastes hadn't changed all that much. She still liked Black, too, but what the hell was there not to like?

Strange, peculiar, and mind-boggling state of affairs, yes, it certainly was. Her whole life was upended and staying that way, at least for the moment. After a few minutes of sprawling out in complete relaxation, feet up, eyes closed, she rose and moved into the kitchen. She spent some time going through the kitchen cabinets, familiarizing herself with what she had and didn't have. She looked through the desk drawer for anything even slightly interesting or exciting or mind-opening, but only found some paid electric bills and a supply of extra checkbooks. Nada. Yep, no letter that explained her life in two paragraphs, although that would be peachy keen.

After a while and at complete loose ends, Claire clicked on the giant television built into the wall and watched the news. On KY3 out of the nearby city of Springfield, they gave a brief thumbnail sketch about the case, just a news flash with a short and terse interview with Sheriff Ramsay. He told them absolutely nothing at all, but in a very politically savvy fashion. And nary a single, solitary cuss word. Not even his favorite and rather odd one: dadgummit.

There wasn't much in the fridge, nothing edible, to be exact, so Claire wrote herself a mental note to shop for groceries ASAP. Or maybe she should just take the Explorer out of the garage right now and go get them. She couldn't remain a watched-like-a-hawk invalid forever, even if her nursemaid looked like a Greek god. Yep, everybody meant well, of course, but if she wanted to be a master of her own destiny, and all that crap, she better get her ducks in a row.

The extra set of car keys was in a bowl on the counter. She had no clue where the other set was. Probably on the river bottom enjoying a mud bath alongside her driver's license. She fished the keys out of the bowl and headed for the garage. Her hand was on the doorknob when a knock on the front door startled her big-time. Nerves up and fluttering like newborn robins, she immediately drew out her Glock, as a ridiculous tingle of dread raised goose bumps on both her arms. She hadn't been alone much since she woke up. And she just found out that she wasn't as secure of her safety as she'd thought. Nope, the idea of opening that door without knowing who was standing outside did not appeal to her. And she wouldn't, unless it was Black or Bud or the other handful of people she'd met lately. This amnesia stuff was getting very old, very fast.

Edging down the wall beside the door, she was able to see through the window that a man and a little girl stood on her porch. The guy was tall and lean with rather long dark blond hair. He looked sort of scruffy, a five o'clock shadow darkening the angles of his jaw. He was a rather dangerous looking individual, in fact, until she glimpsed the Disney picnic basket in his left hand. The little girl was kneeling in front of the window, where Jules was scratching on the glass with both front paws and whining with pleasure. Well, Claire's dog seemed to know them. She, however, had never seen either one of them before. They didn't look particularly threatening and had never made an appearance in any of her night terrors, so she decided she could probably handle them. And she was armed with two serious you're-dead-if-you-touch-me weapons, which was also a major plus in said scenario.

Claire sheathed the Glock and opened the door. "Yes?" she said to the man.

"Yes?" the guy repeated, and yes, it sounded a bit sarcastic, but then he laughed out loud. "C'mon, Claire, I know you lost some brain cells to that dunk in the river and whatnot, but it's me. Nobody forgets me. I'm too awesome."

He smiled again, a very nice smile. He was cute, all right, not as scruffy as first deemed, but with some sexy dark whiskers and that blond hair long enough to tuck behind his ears. He wore a white, V-necked T-shirt and tight Levis and white sneakers. He had a *Semper Fi* tattoo on his forearm. A Marine, like Oliver Long. The little girl was beautiful and blond and tiny and was staring up at Claire out of huge cornflower blue eyes.

"And your awesome self is . . . ?" But Claire determined somehow that she did know him. And she knew right off that he had meant something to her. She just didn't know what. Maybe he could tell her.

"Joe McKay, ma'am, at your service. This here's my perfect little Lizzie baby girl, who's quite in love with your little hyperactive pooch. She wants to know if Jules is at home and can he go swimmin' with her?"

Jules answered that by barreling past Claire and out the door and jumping with one bound into the child's arms. That staggered Lizzie backwards and engendered laughs from all of them. Lizzie ran inside with the poodle, but put him down quickly and attached herself to Claire's knees in the sweetest and tightest leg hug. Claire knelt down and held the child close for a minute, and all kinds of memories started tugging and jerking emotions alive inside her heart. So this was the child who Black said she heard while she slept in that coma.

"Thanks for that big hug, Lizzie. I'm glad you came to see me." Lizzie smiled then, but didn't say a word, just took off with Jules to the couch. She threw herself up and onto it, and Jules followed and settled himself on her lap.

"Don't worry, you know us. In fact, you love us." Joe McKay was still giving Claire what could definitely be called an intensely charming, devil-may-care grin. "Actually, I almost forgot, we're married. Sneaked off last year to Las Vegas and did the deed. We've been keeping it secret. That's why nobody's told you about it. So we better get up to the bed quick; it's been a long time." His eyes raked downward over Claire's body in the most lascivious manner imaginable. "You are lookin' hot as hell, indeed, detective."

"Yeah, right, Mr. Awesome. I might have amnesia, but I'm not stupid enough to fall for these lame come-ons."

"Well, it's always worth a try. So, may I come in and make your day?"

Claire couldn't help but smile. This Joe McKay guy was just oh-so-sure of himself. He oozed sex appeal, almost as much as Black. But then again, nobody oozed more sex appeal than Black. From what she'd heard from women in the know, like Monica and Miki, and Bud, too, women fell in Nicholas Black's wake like swooning, panting maidens all in a row. That is, they'd always added, until he met Claire. But Claire could relate to such panting maidens, too, oh, yeah. She said, "I guess you can come in, but just so you know, I've never seen you before. Guess I'll have to take your word that I know you."

"Can't you give out one small hug to a guy who is absolutely starved for your affection? Lizzie got one. I bet Jules got one, too."

Joe McKay caught her up in his arms before she could object, and gave her a tight, quick, I-mean-it-like-crazy hug. "God, I'm glad you're okay," he said, very low. "I missed you like you would not believe." He held her a little too long after that for her comfort level. But then he let her go, and smiling, pushed past her into the living room.

"Hey, you hungry, Claire? I got some delectable food, right here in this basket."

"You brought me food? Why?"

"Because I've missed you, and so you'd let me and Lizzie swim and fish off your dock. Made these goodies all myself. Baked honey ham sandwiches and potato salad. Beer for us and apple juice for

Lizzie. I made some chocolate chip and raisin cookies that'll melt inside that luscious mouth of yours."

Claire could only stare at him as he made himself very much at home in her kitchen. "I don't know you from a hole in the wall."

"Well, now, guess we'll take care of that today."

"Who exactly are you?"

Joe McKay threw back his head and laughed, an infectious sound, indeed. He shook his head. "This's gonna be fun, yes, ma'am. Mind if I turn on some cartoons for Lizzie?"

"Be my guest."

Standing back, Claire wasn't really all that alarmed. The guy seemed harmless enough, silly, even, and he wasn't armed. She'd checked that out when he hugged her. A little quirky, maybe, but this guy was using a whole different approach than any of her other friends. That would be the ones who considered retrograde amnesiacs and dissociative disorders to be serious things. Little Lizzie settled down to watch *Team Umizoomi,* with Jules Verne still sitting on her lap and trying to lick her face.

"Sit down. Don't look so upset. You still keep your paper plates over the refrigerator?"

She shrugged. "Who knows?" Then she remembered that she'd just seen them there. "Yes, I do."

"See, you're remembering our shared paper-plate memories already."

"I just looked through the cabinets five minutes ago."

"You ready to eat? I bet you skipped lunch, didn't you? Probably breakfast, too?"

Actually, she had. All but a piece of toast with butter and black-berry jelly. And she was hungry, but her cupboard was bare. "Didn't have time. Didn't have any food, either."

"Just a tidbit for your on-empty memory banks: you never do."

Funnyman Joe unpacked his picnic basket. Claire should have felt ultra-uncomfortable at the way he'd barged into her house like he owned the place, but she didn't. She felt something for this man, she knew that, but she couldn't get any specific kind of vibes about him. He was interesting, though, she'd give him that much.

"How do we know each other?" she asked him, sitting down at

the bar and watching him grab some plates out of the cabinet and slap one down in front of her.

"I helped you on a case once. Charlie brought me in. You see, I'm really something special, got psychic abilities, and everything. Don't laugh."

"Why would I laugh?"

"Let's just say you don't have a high regard for ESP, and don't trust it as far as you can throw it. Anyway, after that, we became friends. Sort of."

"Sort of?"

"Yeah. Sort of romantic for me. Sort of not romantic for you."

Claire observed him, and considered that remark. "But you were special to me, weren't you?"

Apparently surprised, McKay stopped taking the foil-covered bowls of food out of the basket and stared at her. "God, I hope so."

Trying to sort out her feelings, and finding that was a lot like feeling her way out of a pitch-black room, she said, "I feel like there was something between us. I can tell by the way you look at me."

They stared at each other, silent, measuring each other. He grew serious. "Well, I try to hide it."

Claire frowned, confused.

"Okay, I had it pretty bad for you once upon a time."

I cannot tell you how weird my life is, she thought. *All these people who care about me, and I have to ask them who and what and why.* "What about me? Did I have it bad for you?"

"You had it bad for Nick Black. You still do."

She thought about that for a moment. "So we broke up because of Black?"

"We were never together, not that I didn't try like hell. I'd try now, if I thought I had a chance."

That came off as a question, almost. "You have feelings for me now?"

"Oh, yeah. But like I just said, you only have eyes for Nick. You met him first, damn it." McKay laughed, but the humor didn't quite reach his eyes. "The story of my life. A day late. A dollar short. The girl of my dreams lost to a rich shrink."

"I don't remember much about anybody. Not him. Not you."

"You will. And don't get me wrong. Nick's a great guy. He loves you, and you love him. It's just a matter of time before you know that. It's all gonna come back. Give it time. It hasn't been all that long."

He was being honest, but Claire still had a nagging sensation going on about the two of them. "I do remember feeling something for you. I'm just not sure what it was. I don't remember exactly how I felt about him, either, but I do know that we were together before the accident. And I like him."

"Like I said, you will remember sooner or later. It's been hands off for me for quite a while now. And trust me, I'm not masochistic enough to put myself through that kind of rejection again."

"If I loved him as much as everybody says, why can't I remember what I felt for him?"

This time he was completely sober, dropping that knowing smirk like a hot pan handle. "I don't know, Claire. Brain injuries are hard to figure. Nick says you'll be good as new soon, and I believe him. He knows what he's talking about."

"Can you use your ESP to help me remember?"

Joe grinned then, all loose and jokey again, just like that. Turn it on, turn it off, and she decided he was really pretty attractive in a bad-boy, goofy kind of way. She envisioned him in a black leather jacket on a giant Harley, flirting with every chick that wandered by. "What's so funny?" she asked him.

"You used to mock me and my 'so-called' powers, as you put it. When I first met you, you called me a quack, charlatan, con man, and you kept going with the insults."

"That sounds like I was pretty rude."

"You were, and alas, you are. Not all the time. Just when you need to be."

Well, he was the first of her friends to point out one of her faults. Guess he was either ruder or more honest, take your pick. She watched him fix Lizzie a plate and take it over to her.

"It's okay if she eats on the couch, isn't it? She's pretty neat for her age. And the sippy cup's not going to spill."

"Sure."

McKay came back, took the stool beside her, picked up a ham sandwich, and took a big bite.

"Show me how it works. This psychic thing of yours. Can you tell me if I'm ever going to remember? And when? Preferably time, date, and year."

"Now that sounds like your old self. Sassy as hell."

"Please, I'm serious."

Eyeing her solemnly, McKay finished chewing, swallowed, popped the tab on his Bud Lite, and took a swig. "Okay, if you want. We can give it a try. I need to touch you. Mind?"

"No, unless you try to take advantage."

"Usually, I do try to take advantage and every chance I get. But since you're recovering, and all, I'll tamp down my desire and won't jump your bones, but it's gonna be hard."

They stared at each other. She rather liked this guy, believe it or not. Then he took her hand and held it flat between both his palms. He shut his eyes. She studied his face while he concentrated, but when he opened his eyes again, he didn't look like he was ready to throw out any good news. In fact, he looked like he was sorry he did it.

"You're in danger. Good God, Claire, I see that same thing every damn time I touch you. Somebody's after you again, trust me. I don't know who, but I can sense it. You're headed for more trouble. You've got to be careful and watch your back."

Well, that made her sorry she'd asked. Maybe he was a fraud. "Are you any good at this, or did you just make all that up?"

"I'm good sometimes. Sometimes it just doesn't come at all. I hope to God I'm wrong this time. You've been through hell and back already. It'll probably be better if you don't remember all the shit you've gone through. Trust me on that, too."

"Can you at least tell me who's after me?"

"I don't know. I didn't see a face. I felt like he's close to you, that he watches you. You need to be very careful who you associate with until you know who's who. You shouldn't have let me in, either. I could've been him. I could've been dangerous."

"That sounds awfully sketchy and more than foreboding. And you know what, I think you are dangerous."

"Good. I am. Just not to you. You need to take care, I'm just sayin'. Don't go off alone and get your pretty little butt in trouble."

After that, they ate and dropped the subject of her imminent danger. He told her that he was refurbishing an old Victorian house in Springfield and on his way to opening a bed-and-breakfast inn, where he was eventually going to give psychic readings in the evenings. He told her about his little girl, and it was absolutely crystal clear that he adored her. Claire wondered about the case they worked together.

"What kind of case were we working on?"

"Murder. Multiple murders, if you want the truth."

"Tell me about it."

"I'm not supposed to. Black told me the last time I came to see you that if this happened, you needed to figure things out on your own. Suits me."

"So I take it, the case was pretty gruesome?"

"Oh, yeah. Wish I didn't remember it."

As they finished eating, the roar of a boat's motor out on the lake filtered in to them. Claire walked to the window and looked outside. "That's Black. I wasn't really expecting him. I was supposed to go over to his place tonight."

"That's cool. We'll get outta here. We just came over to fish and take a swim, anyway. Didn't we, Lizzie?"

McKay and Claire stared at each other. She was trying to read something into his words, in his actions, trying hard to recall what he meant to her, if anything at all.

A few minutes later, Black tapped on the front door, and then walked inside without waiting.

"Thought I was coming over to Cedar Bend tonight," Claire said.

"I decided to wrap up the meetings early and get over here," he said, but he was looking at Joe McKay. "Hi, Joe. It's good to see you again."

McKay came forward and they shook hands, and Claire watched to see if there was any hint of animosity or discord. None that she could detect.

"Yeah, same here. Lizzie and I just dropped by to get some fishin' in."

Black looked at the little girl who sat rapt in front of the cartoon show. "Hi, Lizzie."

To Claire's surprise, Lizzie ran over to Black and hugged his legs. He picked her up and held her in one arm, and the child hugged his neck. So the three of them appeared to be good friends, too, all hunky-dory as could be. Claire felt a bit like a fifth wheel, a stranger butting in on three good friends, but she shook off that feeling as self-defeating.

"We came out to fish and decided to share our picnic basket with the detective here," Joe was saying to Black. "We got some ham sandwiches left, if you want some."

"Thanks, but I brought dinner over from Two Cedars. Picked up some groceries for you, too, Claire. For this week when I'm gone. I'm still hoping you'll change your mind and fly down to Miami with me."

"I would, but I really don't want to miss going to Jeepers with the girls. I want to get to know Monica and Nancy better. And Bud and I have work to do on this new case."

Black didn't look thrilled and didn't say anything, yea or nay. So Joe McKay filled the silence, "That's a great place. Jeepers, I mean. A great band, lots of karaoke, and good food to boot. Especially the meat lover's pizza."

"Does it have security?" Black asked him.

"Oh, yeah. Claire's gonna be safe as can be. They have big guys at both doors."

"Good."

They were talking around her, like she was Lizzie's age, for God's sake. She did not like that, almost disliked it enough to fire up her Explorer and let them discuss her in private. Who did these guys think they were, her mothers? She was an armed officer of the law. And what the hell had gone on among the three of them? Some kind of perverse romantic triangle? Did she love them both? Or neither one? She sincerely doubted either of those conclusions. If she had been stringing one of them along, which would probably be McKay, it was certainly over now. She vowed to find all that out posthaste because she was damn sick and tired of being kept in the dark. Black needed to answer all her questions. Because, truth was, she wasn't remembering anything much and it didn't look to her like she was going to. So, it was time to fill her in, and fill her in he would, or she would find somebody who'd do it for him.

Chapter Sixteen

On Friday night, Monica Wheeler picked up Claire at seven o'clock sharp at Black's privately guarded outdoor entrance at Cedar Bend. As it turned out, Black had bid Claire good-bye earlier that afternoon and summoned his own personal, sleek, and fancy Learjet and was probably winging his way somewhere over Tennessee or Georgia, well on his way to south Florida. He hadn't said much about Joe McKay showing up at her house or her Friday night out with the girls. He had been pleasant enough about her desire to strike out on her own without him riding along on her coattails.

On the other hand, Claire now knew him well enough to know that he didn't like it one little bit. In fact, he didn't like her being anywhere without dragging him along to stand guard. Especially if Joe McKay was involved. Black, however, was displaying his usual unruffled, calm, and composed self. Sangfroid, you bet; in spades, even. Which somehow made her feel guilty, which also made her feel annoyed with him, and which alerted her also that Nicholas Black knew her only too well and how to handle her. After all, he was purported to be the sainted shrink of all shrinks.

So, Claire decided to push the doctor completely out of her mind as she rode down the elevator and got into Monica Wheeler's waiting red Sebring convertible. Monica was smiling and happy, and looked really cute in a white denim skirt and black tank top and black suede sandals. Claire had on her usual T-shirt, white this time, and black jeans, and one of Black's fancy white dress shirts, super baggy enough to hide her shoulder holster. Yes, she had both her sweet little weapons tucked in their sweet little beds, ready to go if any bogeyman jumped out at her.

Okay, truth? Everybody's ever-ballooning paranoia about her safety was getting under her skin. Yep, one hundred percent on guard, she was. The Glock was handy; the .38 was secure on her ankle. Her badge was on a chain tucked inside the neck of her T-shirt to flash at the big and burly bouncers hired to protect the rowdy customers of Jeepers. Claire didn't feel nearly so smiley and Disney-World-happy as Monica. Truth be told, she was feeling edgy, angry, and ready to get on with her life. She was tired of only getting half a day to work the Long investigation and the feeling that everybody was in cahoots to keep pertinent facts hidden in a deep dark well and far away from her retrieving bucket. Maybe these new girlfriends of hers would give her a chance to vent her wrath, since neither of them knew her before the accident. People who were very much in the dark about her as she was about them. Did that ever sound good.

Jeepers was located in a big marina that housed at least a hundred boats and was in walking distance of a perpetually busy, outdoor tourist trap and shopping mall. The place was accessible by boat or car, and it appeared to be a jumping hot spot to hang out, judging by the packed parking lot and the loud music blaring out into the early evening with a giant, orange setting sun as a backdrop.

There were two security guards, both of them big and bad and bald, dressed all in black like hefty and overdeveloped ninja assassins. Nope, they wouldn't be dancing around in the treetops like in those cool Chinese movies. *Hey, I remembered Chinese movies. Great, that's sure to come in handy solving homicides in rural mid-Missouri.* The larger door guard, about the size of New Jersey, and the little one more like Rhode Island, waved them in without checking Claire's badge. Guess he didn't see all her loaded guns.

Inside the rowdy restaurant and bar, all the tables were full of people having a raucous and loud but good-natured, helluva fun time. The band was called Handshakes and was on tour out of Los Angeles. It was really good, and they had one hell of a good drummer named Todd Ramsey. They were winding down one of their songs named "Vacation" right before they took a break. The amateur karaoke began at once with "Friends in Low Places" by

Garth Brooks. Yes, she remembered that, too. Totally insignificant things seemed to carry great importance in the frozen depths of her mind, while she didn't remember squat about herself, so go figure. Temporary amnesia was maddening, and she was highly maddened. Claire hid that inner turmoil from her new girlfriends, though.

"There's Nancy," Monica yelled over the deafening roar of music and boisterous laughter. "She's got to tend bar until eight, and then she can join us at the table. Look, two spots just opened up at the bar. C'mon, let's get them before somebody else does."

"Hey," Nancy said, coming up to them as they sat down on the tall bar stools. "I've been looking out for you guys. What can I get you? It's on the house. My treat."

"I'll take a strawberry daiquiri," Monica said without one second's hesitation.

"Me, too." Hell, Claire didn't know what she liked, except for bottled water. Tonight, probably anything alcoholic would do. She had some serious sorrows to drown.

For about the next thirty minutes, they sipped on their icy drinks and watched the wild and crazy customers make fools of themselves. By that time, however, Claire's law enforcement training was kicking in, and she was listening to the loud laughter and watching for drunken altercations. Maybe she just wasn't the barfly type, girls' night out, or any other kind of night out. Handshakes was still off stage, and the karaoke was still bringing screams of delight. Monica and Nancy were trying to talk over the incredible din in the restaurant about how Monica had just moved out of Cedar Bend and into her new house. Claire already knew that, because she helped Monica carry stuff out of her room in Black's apartment. Black made no secret that he was relieved to get Monica into her own place so he and Claire could have more privacy, but Claire already missed her big friendly smile and lovesick chatter about her "darlin' Jesse." Those were Monica's moonstruck words, not Claire's.

There was some freak up on the stage now, dressed like Darth Vader, big black helmet, and all. Why, she did not know. It certainly wasn't Halloween or Hollywood Boulevard. He started singing a real shaky rendition of "Tiptoe Through the Tulips" in the Vader voice, which was bizarre onto itself. But he got a smattering of enthusiastic applause, which told Claire then and there that a goat's bleating would be cheered on in the environs of Jeepers.

Nancy grabbed her hand. "C'mon, Claire, get up there and sing us a song."

Claire shook her head. "Unh-uh, no way, that's not my thing."

Sitting beside Claire, Monica was more than interested in climbing posthaste onto that stage. She was thumbing through the song list printout with great eagerness. "Oh, look, here's some Whitney Houston. I love her voice."

"Yeah," said Nancy, leaning one arm against the bar in her best bartender pose. All she needed was some shot glasses to polish. "Maybe when I get off, the three of us could do some Supremes. How about 'Stop, in the Name of Love'?"

Hey, Claire remembered that song, too, and Diana Ross. She was turning into a regular pop music aficionado. Why didn't she remember the important things? She wished Black could explain that to her. She shook her head at Nancy's offer and politely refused to partake of the microphone hell playing out in front of them. For some reason, Claire was slightly wary of trilling golden-oldie ditties in front of drunk-as-skunks, wolf-whistling, horny guys. As her two brave new friends discussed the duet they would sing, she wished Black was home at Cedar Bend, and that she was there with him.

As Claire looked out over the young crowd, all having such a great time, she wondered if any of them might have beaten Miriam Long to death and were now celebrating it with a pitcher full of foaming draft beer. A couple of said patrons looked capable of such crimes, judging by their tacky swastika tattoos and dirty beards and greasy ponytails. But there were more patriotic tats, too, to be fair, pictorializing American flags and pretty red roses, and various girls' names and "Mom" surrounded by a heart, so that was the good thing.

"I'm up next," Monica informed them a few minutes later. "I'm gonna sing 'Somewhere over the Rainbow.' Wish me luck."

Inwardly, Claire bowed to Monica's gutsy choice and hoped the strawberry daiquiri hadn't given her false hope. Nancy and Claire watched their petite friend wend her way up to the small raised platform at the front of the room. She got applause and catcalls from several guys. Just for her good looks, Claire suspected. Nope, Claire would not be caught dead up there with that microphone clutched in her sweaty hands.

"She's pretty good," Nancy was telling her. "She and her boyfriend came in the other night and did some songs together."

"Jesse, you mean? He seems like a nice enough guy."

Nancy leaned closer. "I really hate to say this, Claire, but if you want to know the truth, I think he's a little strange."

"Really? How so?"

"Oh, yeah, and speak of the devil, here he comes now."

To Claire's surprise, she turned and found Monica's "Darlin' Jesse" heading straight for them. He climbed up on Monica's stool beside Claire. "Hey, I thought I'd come by and see ya'll and find out what's up. Hi, Nancy, get me a beer, will ya?"

Nancy went to fetch it for him, and Jesse smiled at Claire, but behind it, his dark brown eyes looked serious, intense even. "Why aren't you singing?" he asked her, scratching his goatee.

"I'm shy and retiring."

"Me, too."

Claire did get that same peculiar feeling about him. He was nice enough, okay, but there was just something about him that she couldn't quite put her finger on. He bothered her somehow. Maybe he was the one McKay had been warning her about, who knows? He turned and watched Monica when she started singing, and Claire was surprised at how good Monica's voice was.

Halfway through the song, Jesse sidled up closer. She could smell the sweet scent of his cologne, almost like roses. "You like this place?"

"It's pretty wild."

"Wait until midnight when everybody's drunk outta their minds. That's when this place goes bonkers."

Claire nodded and clapped when Monica finished her song to rousing applause and shrill whistles. On the verge of one of what she lovingly referred to as her "coma headaches," Claire glanced around, again wishing she was home with Black, when who should appear in the door but the charming and psychic Joe McKay himself. He, too, headed straight for them and the bar, grinning that cocky and highly arrogant grin of his.

"Fancy meetin' you here, detective."

"Yeah, fancy that."

"When I heard you were goin' out partyin', I just couldn't resist taggin' along. You aren't exactly a party animal, so I had to see it in person. Where's Nick?"

"In Miami at the A.M.A. giving the keynote address. Where's Lizzie?"

"I got us a live-in nanny now, real nice older lady named Carol. Lizzie loves that woman, thinks she's her grandma."

Jesse was leaning close and eavesdropping on their conversation. Not particularly trying to hide it, either. So she moved closer to Joe and away from Jesse's cloying cologne and made the introductions.

"Joe, this is Jesse. Jesse, Joe. Jesse's Monica's boyfriend."

"Monica, your nurse?"

"That's the one."

The two men gave an acknowledging nod, and all pithy repartee died like a cold motor. Luckily, Nancy came out from behind the bar and ushered them to a table near the bandstand. They all sat down together and the others started chatting about the band. They were off their break now and rocking out again. Nancy seemed to know Joe McKay, and he talked to her with the same easy masculine charm with which he flirted with Claire, and probably every other female human being, too. Monica was talking animatedly over the din, too, but Jesse just sat there and said next to nothing.

Claire made a valiant attempt to include him. "Monica's got a great voice, don't you think so, Jesse?"

"Yeah, she's real good."

Jesse drained his beer mug and then got up and headed for the bar, their empty pitcher in his hand. What was it about him that bugged her?

"Where'd Monica find that odd duck?" That was Joe McKay, speaking close into Claire's ear. "He looks like a girl in that wife-beater undershirt."

"You're pretty rude, aren't you?" Claire pointed out, just to rile his extreme masculine self-confidence, but actually, his observation was pretty much on the mark. Jesse did appear a bit effeminate at times.

"You call that rude?"

"Yes, I do."

"You haven't heard rude yet. Here's rude: I think he's creepy as hell, and looks more like a woman than a man."

"Yep, that's ruder, all right. In fact, it verges on insulting. Hey, I know what, McKay, why don't you hold his hand and tell me all his inner thoughts? That oughta be interesting."

"Don't think so. Number one: I don't want to touch him. Number two: No telling what's going inside the head of a guy like that."

"Better not let Monica hear you say that kind of stuff. They're planning to move in together. She's crushing on him big-time."

"Well, I know how that feels, oh, yes, sir, I surely do." His eyes scorched their way across her person, just so she knew he was talking about her.

Tired of his sexual innuendo, Claire swiveled to face him squarely. She used her expression to tell him he was barking up the wrong female body. His expression dissolved into *the* bad boy grin.

She said, "Okay, I get it. You like me. So tell me this, McKay, what's the deal between you and me and Black?"

McKay dropped his playful flirtatiousness like a fumbled football. "No deal, Claire. It's no threesome, if that's what you're thinkin'. We're friends. Both of us love you, if that's what you're gettin' at. But he got you fair and square. Wanna dance?"

Frowning, Claire ignored his grin and clumsy attempt to distract her from the serious subject. Talk about cavalier. She stared at him. "Well, I remember him better than you, but I don't remember loving either one of you all that well."

"Well, you do."

Sighing in frustration, Claire decided she was more than ready to call it a night. However, the night was early and she was trying to make new friends. Since Nancy was off work now, McKay asked her to dance. Claire watched them enjoying themselves on the dance floor. She watched Jesse and Monica, too, who were also dancing, and then felt an overwhelming need to hightail it outta there.

The evening wore on, really wore on, dragged as slowly as an ant pulling an anchor, but as they all talked together and laughed at McKay's jokes, she ended up having a pretty good time. She got tired of the fun fairly fast, but not to worry, her phone vibrated inside her pocket and Black's name popped up on caller ID. Now having an excuse to leave the table, she moved out into the hallway leading to the bathrooms in back, where it was, maybe, one iota quieter. By the way her heart reacted to the sound of Black's deep voice at the other end, the romantic spark had been ignited, if it had ever gone out at all. He was growing on her, oh, to be sure.

"So how's your night with the girls going?"

"Okay, I guess. How was your flight?"

"Uneventful. By the sound of the music and laughter, it's going more than okay."

"I'm too tired for all this fun."

"The noise giving you a headache?"

Black knew his stuff. "It's trying to get started, and it's almost to the finish line."

"Take two of those pills I gave you. Unless you've been drinking a lot. Have you?"

Claire ignored that, because she really missed him, a lot more than she thought she would. "Just one strawberry daiquiri. I'm finding that I'm not the bar type."

"I know. I'm not, either. You can take the pills, if that's all you've had."

"So where are you, Black? Sitting out on some balmy beach on the lookout for a woman in a bikini who remembers you?"

At the other end, Black gave a little laugh. "Oh, yeah, that's the first thing I did when I got here. Actually, I'm having a late dinner at a friend's house in Coconut Grove."

Inside her mind, some twisty snake of an idea started writhing around and wanting to lunge out and bite her. She caught hold of it long enough to see a face, an older man with white hair and white beard and white linen clothing. She frowned, trying to force more of it out of the dense gray fog. It happened in Miami, she knew that, and he was Black's friend. What was the name? It was so close, but she couldn't get it, dammit.

"Claire? You still there?"

"Yeah. I just remembered that I went down there with you and met your friend, I think."

Silence. She got the feeling he was stalling. "Yes, you did."

Black didn't offer anything else so she pushed the point. Any time he was reticent, she pounced. It was just the way she was, that's all there was to it. "I met a man, white hair, white clothes. Hispanic, maybe. We went to his house. What was his name?"

"That's right. That's where I am right now. He said to say hello."

Claire wasn't going to be put off. "What's his name?"

More hesitation. Claire sensed he did not want to answer, not in any form or fashion. "His name is Jose Rangos," he told her finally, and then made one of his skillful U-turns in subject matter. "Who's with you?"

It was her turn to drag her feet. "Monica and Nancy. And Monica's boyfriend came in."

"I didn't know she had a boyfriend. Who is it?"

"Jesse Somebody. And Joe McKay showed up a bit ago."

There was a longer silence. Unhappy silence? "I guess you forgot to tell me that Joe was invited. Is he one of the girls now?"

"C'mon, Black, you sound almost jealous. He wasn't invited. He just showed up out of the clear blue sky."

"How'd he know you were there?"

"We talked about it right in front of him. Remember? But that doesn't matter. I miss you."

"Well, that takes the sting out of being down here all alone while you're with McKay."

"What'd you think? I'd forget all about you?"

"It's beautiful here. Full moon. Soft warm breezes. Whispering waves. It all could've been yours. I've got the same penthouse suite at the hotel we stayed in when we were here last time. It's ours now. I bought it the week after we left."

"But of course, you did," she said, but she did wish she was there. What he was describing beat honky-tonk karaoke and vulgar tattoos all over the place.

"I miss you, too. Next time I'll drag you along."

"Next time you won't have to."

"I want to make love to you. Every night. All night long."

Believe it or not, that turned her on. Maybe it was the gruff and longing desire in his voice. Maybe it was the mental picture she was getting of him in his swimsuit that day at her dock and all those hard ridges making up his six-pack. She decided not to mention any of that. "You must be Superman then, if you can do that."

"If you only knew how you affect me." There was a wry sound to that remark.

Claire smiled, had to. "Maybe we can do that when you get back."

"Please tell me you're serious."

"I'm serious. I told you I miss you."

"I can be in the air in under an hour."

She laughed at that idea, but was secretly pleased. "Do your thing, Black, and I'll do mine. I'll see you on Tuesday. Then we'll see how super in bed you really are. I suspect I can outlast you, just out of a coma, and everything."

"If I'd known you were going to react to my absence this way, I would've come down here days ago."

"Just concentrate on giving your speech and quit worrying about me. I'm fine."

It was at that point that Claire saw a couple of familiar faces at a table in the far corner near the swinging kitchen doors. "Oh, my God, Black, guess who's here?"

"Who?" He sounded alarmed.

"Captain Oliver Long and Kay Kramer. And they look pretty darn cozy. I can't believe they're out together this soon."

"Who?"

"You know the victim out by the *Falcon*? The real estate agent. It's Miriam Long's husband, and he's with her partner. Looks like a real heavy date to me. Think I'll go have a little chat with them."

"Are you armed?"

"Of course, don't be silly. What do you take me for?"

"If you think it's going to get nasty, call Bud for backup."

"Give me some credit. I'm not going to slap them in cuffs on the karaoke stage. I'm just going to see how they explain this little night out on the town. They haven't even released her body yet, for God's sake."

"If you need help right now, get Joe to help you. He's a Marine. God, I wish I was there."

"Don't worry. I'm just going to talk to them. I gotta go, Black."

"Well, call me back and let me know what happened. I'm invested now in your being in good shape when I get home. You know, lots of stamina. You're going to need it."

Laughing at him, Claire hung up and headed straight for her two new suspects. She still couldn't believe they were out together in public so soon. Especially in a place like Jeepers.

By the time she reached their cozy little table and got a load of Captain Long's face, however, her suspicions dwindled to dust. He looked sick and ashen and tears were running down his face. Kay Kramer was weeping, too, quietly and heartbrokenly. They saw her before she could reverse her engines, do a sheepish sort of back pedal, and leave them alone to console each other's grief.

But the captain was immediately up on his feet, wiping his tears away with the back of his hand. "Have you got that bastard yet?" were the first words out of his mouth.

"No, sir. I'm sorry to intrude. I'm here with some friends, and I just wanted to tell you again how sorry I am about your wife." *Do I feel like a rotten, dirty dog, you bet your life, I do.*

Kay Kramer took hold of Claire's hand and pulled her down into the chair beside her. "Please, tell us, have you made any progress? Anything at all?"

Okay, this is why she didn't like this half a day crap. How could she explain that little problem to them, huh? *So sorry, but I've been in this coma, see, so I'm only working half-time on finding your wife's brutal murderer.* It made her sick to her stomach. Charlie was going to have to reverse that decision and let her get back to work, that's all there was to it. Black would okay her working full-time now; she knew he would.

"We've been checking out all her listings, trying to find something suspicious. Where she might have gone that day, who might've seen her, talked to her. So far, we're not getting many leads."

The captain leaned toward her. "I did come up with something, detective. I was too out of it the day you interviewed me to remember much of anything. I'm not sure whether it's gonna help you or not, but Miriam did tell me that she had a listing in the name of her former employer, a guy named Larry Carter over in Springfield. I think she said it's a probate property, a real creepy place, she said, but I can't be sure about that. Some kind of crime happened there a while back, I think. She was in a huge hurry that day when she mentioned it. She goes a mile a minute all the time." His voice went dead with renewed shock and horror about his wife's murder, and he shut his eyes. Claire took a mental pencil and x'ed him off her suspect list as having anything to do with the crime. Nobody was that good of an actor.

"That's right, I'd forgotten about that place," Kay said, half shouting over the din. "It's not our listing, and it's way out in the woods somewhere. I really don't know much about it."

"Can you tell me where this house is? The address?"

"No, I didn't have anything to do with it. It was a favor she was doing for Larry. You'll have to ask him about it."

"We will. Thanks for the tip."

Captain Long said, "I want you to catch this guy, detective."

"So do I, captain, so do I."

Claire asked them a few more questions, but they couldn't think of anything else that might be pertinent to the investigation.

"I had to get out of that house," Oliver Long was telling Claire now. "Everything I see, everything I touch reminds me of Miriam. I was going to lose it if I didn't get out of there." He looked at Kay Kramer, who was still crying. "Kay thought coming out here might get my mind off things. She doesn't want me to be alone. She doesn't want to be alone, either. But it's not working. Let's get outta here, Kay."

"I'm sorry," Claire said. "I know this has to be terrible."

Kay said, "I'm ready, Oliver. You're right, this wasn't such a good idea."

They both stood up, in a big hurry now, and she shook hands with them and promised to give keep them posted on any developments.

Back at Claire's table, Nancy was ready to go, too. Monica wanted to stay awhile with Jesse. Joe just watched and grinned.

"Okay, we'll see you later," Claire said to the table in general.

"I tell you, Claire, if I didn't have to be down at Buckeye's office so early in the morning, I'd hang around awhile. That McKay guy really rings my bells, he really does. What a hottie. He looks sort of dangerous, too. You know, like Jason Bourne, or Colin Ferrell."

They both looked back at the object of Nancy's lust as Burly Ninja One opened the door for them. McKay was watching them leave. He gave a little farewell salute with two fingers. He was pretty cool, she did have to admit.

"My God, he is so damn sexy," said Nancy as they got into her big white Tahoe.

"Yeah, he's got a certain charm, I guess."

"Almost as sexy as Nick Black," Nancy added. "But he's taken, to say the least. Monica says he's nuts about you, that nobody else has a chance with him."

"Black's got a certain charm, too."

Nancy laughed knowingly and pulled out of the driveway.

Truth was, Claire was never so ready to leave a place in her life. Maybe hanging around with Black in his spacious penthouse 24/7 wasn't so bad after all. Maybe she was beginning to feel about him the way he said she did. Maybe they were going see where this thing was going as soon as he got home. Until then, she was going to throw herself back into the Miriam Long case. She had to catch this guy for Captain Long, and this half-a-day stuff was going down like a load of bricks.

Jesse's Girl

Present day

A few days after Jesse had spent time with Annie at Jeepers, he was on pins and needles, wanting to get the deed done. Everything was in place now. Annie had not regained her memory, didn't recognize him even when they were only inches apart. Thank God for that. But she was back at work and spending a lot of time at her own house. And Black had gone to Florida, out of the picture for a while. Everything was perfect. At long last, the moment was at hand.

And Annie trusted Jesse now, so she'd let him come inside her house without blinking. That would make things so much easier for him to grab her. He was very familiar with her little A-frame cabin, too, had been out there several times to case things out. It would be quite easy to sneak up on her there, through the woods or off the lake. Either way, he could surprise her. Jules was friendly, too, and probably wouldn't bark but just wag his tail. No, the dog wouldn't put out an alarm. But if he did, it would be easy enough to wring that stupid poodle's neck. He could always get Annie another dog, if she cried or was upset about it. Maybe she'd just be satisfied with Jules's head on a saucer.

Jesse had been working out his plan for weeks now. As a Cedar Bend Lodge employee, he had access to all employee break rooms and the basement work areas, where the resort's laundry was located. That's where they washed and bleached the expensive sheets Black provided for his guests. Better yet, that's where they washed and ironed Black's personal belongings. He had gotten into Nicholas Black's own dirty laundry bag and stolen a couple of his pricey monogrammed shirts. He had already filched an expensive black leather belt that Black left lying around in Annie's bedroom when she was still in the coma. Jesse had taken goblets off the room service trays that Black had used, all covered with his fingerprints. He had accumulated all sorts of incriminating evidence against Black. And now, at long last, the time had come to put the second stage of his plan into action.

Jesse was supposed to move into Monica's new house tonight. He was there already, having wiped the house clean of his own fingerprints. He was just waiting for Monica to show up. When her Sebring finally pulled up outside, he picked up a hammer so she'd think he'd been working and not wonder why he had on work gloves. He walked to the front door to meet her. He was so filled to the brim with eagerness, excitement, that he could barely draw his breath. Monica had been more than helpful; true, he had been lucky as all get out to find her. He had to admit that, but it was time for her to die. Stuffing Nicholas Black's belt in the back of his pants, he opened the front door with a big welcoming grin.

"Hi, sweetie," Monica said brightly. He'd never seen her look so happy, so pretty. She was carrying two bags of groceries in her arms. "I'm so glad to be home at last. Just think, we'll get to be together all the time now. I just can't believe how fast all this happened."

"I've been dreaming of this moment, too," he said with his most gentle smile. "Every single night."

Hurrying to the dining room table, Monica put down the grocery bags and pulled a small gift-wrapped box out of the top of one. "I got a little housewarming present for you," she gushed, so very happy. "Just because I love you so much."

"Baby, you shouldn't of done that. I really do love you so much, too."

"Oh, Jesse. I'm glad that Nick got me that job at Canton County Medical Center. I didn't want to go back to St. Louis without you."

"We'll be together forever. I want you to meet Miss Rosie soon. She can't wait to get to know you."

"I can't wait to meet all your family."

Jesse opened the box and found it contained a beautiful silver band with one big diamond. "Wow, Monica, this is really awesome."

"It's a promise ring. I had to guess at your size. I'm going to wear one just like it."

"That's so neat. You are just the sweetest little thing," Jesse told her, truly admiring the glittering ring. He was pleased. He would take Monica's matching ring and give it to Annie. It would make the perfect homecoming gift for her.

They embraced, and then he kissed Monica one last time, a good-bye-forever kind of kiss that she'd never forget. Then he pulled the belt out from behind his back as she clung to him. Then very quickly, he pushed her away from him and looped the leather belt around her neck. He jerked it tight and twisted it and kept twisting it, harder and harder. Monica looked shocked in that first instant, and then she started struggling, desperately clawing at the belt cutting off her air and feebly trying to hit him in the face.

Leaning back away from her blows, he smiled the whole time so she'd feel better about giving up her life for him. She was stronger than she looked, but she was way too little and too weak for him. It would take him a while to strangle her unconscious, at least ten or twelve minutes, he bet. His arms would get tired—

Suddenly she dropped to her knees and threw his death grip off balance. The belt loosened a notch as she fought like crazy and tried to scramble free. She got to the table and knocked off the grocery bags, spilling everything all over the place.

Jumping on top of her, Jesse used his body to hold her down and control her. He forgot the belt then and put both his thumbs on the base of her throat and pressed down with all his strength. Monica fought him a few more minutes, her eyes wild and bulging, and she seemed to take forever to die. Tears wet her cheeks, and Jesse put his face next to hers and licked them off. They tasted salty and really good. He backed away a little, watching her face as he choked her. Then he glanced at the clock on the wall when she finally went limp, and then looked back down at her. She had lasted a full twelve minutes before the light in her eyes died away and turned black, and she lay still and dead underneath him, still looking up at him. Panting with exertion himself, he got off her body and sat there on his heels a few seconds, catching his breath.

Standing up, he glanced around, ready to stage the crime scene. Their struggle had overturned a side table beside an easy chair and broken a lamp. Groceries were scattered all over the floor. Oranges and apples and cans were everywhere. But that was okay. That would go along nicely with his scenario to frame Nicholas Black for her murder. Black was due back sometime today. Monica had told him that much, and he was probably coming in later that night. And Annie was staying at her own house. Everything was going according to Jesse's plan.

Staring down at Monica's body, he watched to make sure she didn't start breathing again. Sometimes people fooled him after he strangled them. But she wasn't, and then he got up and walked into the kitchen. He found some leftover homemade pizza in the fridge, and he took it out and stuck it in the microwave. He picked up an apple off the floor, washed it thoroughly in the sink, and ate it while he waited. Man, Monica had been a good cook; he was going to miss that about her. He switched on the TV to Cardinals baseball and ate at the dining room table where he could keep an eye on Monica, in case she moved and he had to finish her off again.

After that, he went out to his car, picked up the box of evidence incriminating Black, and then he placed it all around her house in the appropriate places. Oh, yes, Nicholas Black's fingerprints and DNA were going to be all over Monica Wheeler's crime scene. If that didn't work, the personal diary he'd typed into Monica's laptop would certainly do the trick. Nicholas Black was gonna be out of the picture for good. And then, and only then, would Annie be all Jesse's. Then she would no longer be able to be with Nicholas Black. The bastard would either be in prison or executed for Monica's murder. Either way, he'd be out of the picture forever. Even if Black had a good alibi in Florida, it would still take his lawyers a long time to explain how all his stuff got inside Monica's house. Long enough for Jesse to grab Annie and cross into Mexico, and that was the important thing. Once they were out of the country, then everything would be all right. Then she and Jesse would live happily ever after.

Chapter Seventeen

Just after noon on the day Black was scheduled to get back, Claire got into Bud's white Bronco at her house, and off they went toward the listing on the lake that Captain Long had told her about at Jeepers. She had spent the last few days at her own place, because Black didn't know what time he was getting in and there was a possibility that he'd have to stay an extra day. She had enjoyed getting used to her personal property and had spent some time down the road at Harve's. Truth be told, though, she really missed Black and couldn't wait to see him, for more reasons than one.

Claire smiled to herself, thinking about it, until her phone started up with "The Mexican Hat Dance." She grabbed it out of her bag, thinking it would be Black giving her his ETA, but caller ID said "Charles Ramsay," so she picked up in a big hurry.

"Yes, sir, Sheriff."

"Where are you?"

"Bud and I are heading out to check out one of Miriam Long's property listings. Her husband gave me a lead on it the other night. Said a crime was committed there a while back. But nobody here knows where it is. We called her former boss in Springfield to get a bead on it, a guy named Larry Carter, but he's been on vacation, but should be there today. We decided to go down and interview him and his staff in person, so we can get the key and permission to enter the property, and see if anything appears suspicious about this guy. Carter could be a viable suspect."

"Well, turn around. We got another murder, and I want you two on it." He paused. "You know that girl who helped Black when you were sick? The nurse? Name of Monica Wheeler?"

"Yes, sir. What about her? She okay?"

"She's dead, Claire."

That shocked Claire enough to force out an audible gasp. "Monica Wheeler's dead?" She choked it out, hoping she'd misheard him.

Hearing that, Bud hit the brakes, swerved over onto the shoulder, and slammed to a stop, every bit as shocked as she was.

"That's right. We got an anonymous call. I sent a coupla patrol officers down there to check it out. They saw the body through the front window. They kicked in the front door in case she was still alive, but she was already long dead."

"Your nurse's dead?" Bud was saying to me. "Are you shittin' me?"

Claire ignored him and tried to get out her words. "Oh, my God, Charlie. That's awful. I was just out with her the other night."

"How quick can you get over there?"

After he told her the address and she repeated it to Bud, Bud said, "Tell Charlie we'll be there in ten minutes."

Claire did so, and then she hung up and stared at Bud's profile as he did a screeching U-turn and put the blue flashing light atop the roof. She could not wrap her mind around perky, sweet little Monica being murdered in her own house. How? Who would do such a thing?

Bud pretty much floored the accelerator because there weren't many cars out in the boondocks, not this early. Not ever, she guessed, by the looks of the thickly wooded tracts on both sides of the road.

"How did she die, Claire?"

"He didn't say. Buck and the team are on their way, too."

After that, Claire just sat there and rode in stunned silence. Monica Wheeler was dead? It just didn't seem possible, but it was true. And she was going to have to look at her new friend's corpse, and the idea made her sick to her stomach. She spent the rest of the drive steeling herself for what was to come. Nancy would be there, too. Oh, God, what had happened to Monica? Who had done this? And where was Jesse? They'd have to tell him, too. Or was Jesse involved? He was so peculiar that she pegged him as a top candidate first off. Then again, he seemed to care so much for Monica.

When they reached the crime scene, way far out on a rural road but not too far from Cedar Bend Lodge by water, there were two patrol cars and Charlie's vehicle was double-parked out front. Bud and Claire jumped out and headed to the front door, where they were still stringing crime scene tape.

"You got a positive ID that it's Monica Wheeler?" Claire asked the officer at the door.

"That's the name on the mailbox out on the road. Buck can tell soon enough."

Good, maybe it wasn't Monica. God, she hoped it wasn't her. She'd been a good friend to Claire when she had so desperately needed one. How could she be dead?

Hurriedly donning their protective booties and snapping on gloves, they stepped through the front door. The first thing she noticed was the temperature. It was so cold inside that she could almost see her breath. And the victim was Monica. No doubt about it. She was lying on the floor not far from the front door, her feet almost under the dining room table, faceup, a black belt cinched so tightly around her neck that her face had turned purple and her lips were black and bloated. But it was Monica.

Unlike the woman at the duck blind, Claire knew this woman. Monica had watched over her, helped her get well, fed her meds, and laughed with her. She swallowed down bile and tried not to think about any of that, tried to disassociate herself from those thoughts. Black was going to be really upset. He had been delayed, and there was a storm building somewhere in the middle of his flight plan. She was glad he was gone. He wouldn't take this well. Claire wasn't taking it well.

"Has anything been touched?" she asked the young blond patrol officer. She didn't know him, and Bud didn't introduce them. Bud was freaked out, too.

"Not a thing. I kicked open the door, checked her pulse, and then called it in. I stood outside and waited for you."

"Good work."

Bud said, "It's pretty obvious she was coming in the door and was surprised by the killer."

Claire looked around. "There are two place settings still on the table. Maybe he left fingerprints. It looks like he tore out of here in a hurry."

"Nope, he didn't take time to clean up, all right. This place is a mess," Bud said, stepping carefully over broken glass and the cans and fresh fruit scattered all over the floor.

When Claire looked closely at the dinner table, she recognized the silverware and plates. "This stuff came from Cedar Bend's restaurant. Two Cedars. Even the goblets are from there."

"Maybe she stole herself a whole set to get started with."

"Maybe, but Monica wasn't a thief. Black paid her a lot of money for dropping everything and coming down here. She told me that herself and talked about how grateful she was to him. They were old friends."

"Nick brought her in special, just to help him take care of you, right?"

"Yeah. They met when they worked together at Barnes Jewish Hospital in St. Louis. She worked some for a Dr. Brunt and a Dr. Margenthaler, but mainly in the Cardiac I.C.U."

Bud said, "I never really got to know her. I just saw her when I went up to visit you. What was she like? A party girl?"

"Not that I know of. We went out the other night, and she got up on the stage and sang karaoke. She was drinking, but she never was drunk." Claire stared down at her friend's lifeless body. "She was just a regular girl, a good nurse. Took good care of me. She was going to stay here. Black said she didn't want to go back to St. Louis. Black will know all this stuff. We need to interview him and look at her employee record at Cedar Bend. And Jesse will know, of course."

"Who the hell is Jesse?" Charlie asked.

"That's her boyfriend. He was gonna move in here with her. He was with us Friday night, too."

"What's his last name?"

"Nancy said his last name is Jordan. Monica always called him Jesse. He works at Cedar Bend in the restaurant. Human Resources over there ought to know. Where is Nancy, anyway?"

"She got a call to get back down to New Orleans. A workplace shooting came up and they're shorthanded. She's packing up as we speak."

Bud said, "We'll get Monica's next of kin at Cedar Bend, too."

"I guess we better take a quick look around," Claire told them. "I'm not sure, but I think she just moved in here. It had to be within the last few days. She stayed in the penthouse while I was in the coma and then for a while longer, until she bought this place."

"Yeah, there're a lot of empty boxes out in the carport."

Monica Wheeler's house was very small, only two bedrooms. One was completely empty. The other had a double bed and not much else. She hadn't even bought furniture yet. Only the living room and dining room were furnished. They checked out the closets, the single bathroom, which had brand-new white towels on the towel racks and new cosmetics inside the medicine cabinet. She lifted the lid on the wicker dirty clothes hamper. There were clothes inside: a man's shirt. Somebody had lived there with Monica.

Claire dropped the lid back into place and turned when she heard Buckeye Boyd's voice in the living room. She walked back and found Shaggy and Vicky there, dressed in their white lab jumpsuits. Vicky was already snapping pictures of the victim. She moved around the room, taking her crime scene photographs, while Bud and Claire joined Buckeye beside the body.

Buck said, "Okay, Claire, Bud. What've we got here?"

"Female victim. Her name is Monica Wheeler."

"What?" That was Shaggy's outburst. Heartfelt, too. "That's your nurse's name, man. What a bummer, Claire. She used to bring me up ice-cold Mountain Dews from downstairs when I sat with you. She was awesome."

"Yeah, I met her once up in your room, too. Nice girl." Buck frowned. "God, she must've fought like a son of a gun. Just look at this place."

"Hope that means the perpetrator left us something to nail him with," Claire said slowly, but something about all of it didn't pass the smell test. Not with her. She had a bad feeling, but then again, who wouldn't?

"He must've surprised her. She's such a small woman; she couldn't fight him off."

Buck went down on one knee beside the body. "She's been dead a while. Looks like cause of death is strangulation. See the petechial hemorrhages in her eyes? Lack of oxygen ruptured the capillaries.

I'll have to do the autopsy to be sure, but it's fairly apparent somebody used that belt as a ligature and asphyxiated her."

Claire watched Buck turn Monica's body over and empty the pockets of her black shorts. She was wearing a simple white cotton peasant blouse and sandals with silver studs on the straps. Her toenails were painted coral pink.

"She was just coming home," she said. "I think he was already here waiting for her. Or she could've let him in, or he might have broken in."

"No sign of any break-in," said the officer.

"Then she knew him. Monica was friendly. Helpful. Maybe somebody came to the door and said his car broke down, that he was lost. Once he was inside, he killed her, and then took off."

"She's been here a while. Air conditioner kept down the rate of decomp, and the smell."

Not enough. The smell was faint, not like at Miriam Long's crime scene, but it was familiar and awful and crept into Claire's very pores. She knelt down and picked up Monica's hand. "Her fingernails are broken off. Maybe she got some DNA off him."

"I'll get on that as soon as I can get her downtown."

After the initial examination, they loaded the body on a gurney and rolled it out the front door. Shaggy began his work, serious now, dusting the plates and glasses for fingerprints, while Vicky videotaped everything throughout the house.

Shaggy looked at Claire, nodding in triumph. "We got lucky here. These latents are pristine."

"Good."

Claire moved to the coffee table after Vicky finished dusting. She opened Monica's small red purse and dumped out its contents: billfold, lipstick, chewing gum, comb, compact. No key chain, no personal notes, nothing that would help them. There was about seventy dollars in her wallet. "He wasn't after her money," she said.

"Claire, c'mere. I got her laptop, and it's open to her personal calendar. She's got it set up as a diary."

Claire hurried to join Bud in the kitchen and caught sight of the kitchen towel set and oven gloves that she'd given Monica as housewarming presents. Bud was sitting on a kitchen chair, intent on the

Dell laptop open atop the kitchen table. She looked over Bud's shoulder as he started scrolling through the pages of the diary.

"Daily entries. Starting way back in August, right after she got here. Whoa, I do believe we just got lucky."

Claire frowned. "Hit control and home and go back to the beginning."

Bud did so, and read the first line on the page. *"Got to Cedar Bend Lodge today around noon. Saw Nick. I still can't believe he likes me enough to bring me all the way down here. He's as good-looking and charming as the first day we met."* Bud stopped and looked up at her.

"Let me see that," Claire said, pushing him out of the chair and sitting down. Bud handed it over, but bent low so he could read it with her.

Silently they skimmed the following entries and found:

I hope there's more than one reason that Nick brought me here. My heart goes wild every time he walks into the room. I'm still crazy about him, and he's interested in me this time, too. He told me that he thought about me a lot when we were apart. The patient I'm to tend is a young woman named Claire Morgan. She's in a deep coma and has been since a car accident about a week ago. He's extremely concerned, but not so much that he didn't invite me to have dinner upstairs with him in his own kitchen. Oh, God, help me, I really do think now that he might love me. Why else would he choose me to come here and live in his apartment with him? I can only pray that's true. I've loved him for so long.

"Oh, my God, Bud. She was in love with Black. She says he's in love with her."

"No way. Let me see that."

They read more of the diary together while Claire scrolled down through the days that Monica spent at the lake. The nurse talked about the private time she and Black spent together, that he seduced her and took her to bed while Claire still lay unconscious in the next room.

When Claire looked at Bud, the expression in his eyes told her the whole story.

"I don't believe it, Claire. Are you kidding me? Black messin' around while you were right there, sick and maybe dying? No way, no freakin' way! I don't know why she wrote down this kinda stuff, but I don't believe one word of it. And you shouldn't, either."

Claire stared mutely at him. Shocked by some of the more intimate details that the nurse alleged went on during all those days Claire was unconscious and unaware, she wanted to know it all. So she sat right there and read every single word, while Bud paced around the kitchen and muttered cuss words and tried to convince her that none of it was true. Oh, God, Monica wrote down that they had sex in Black's bed while Claire slept in her room a couple of doors down the hall. No, no, it could not be true. Black wouldn't do that to her. Or would he? How well did she really know him? All she knew was what he told her. And he was rich and handsome and controlling. She'd seen for herself how women reacted to him. He could have anyone he wanted. Maybe he did have a fling with Monica. Maybe he killed her to cover it up.

"Black wouldn't do this. It's just not in him," Bud said softly, squatting down beside Claire again. Earnestly, he searched her eyes. "Don't think it. This has got to be pack of lies, some kind of setup."

Claire held up the laptop. "No? Then how do you explain this? That it's Monica's big fantasy, that she made up all these details, just for the hell of it?"

Bud met Claire's angry stare. "It's not like it's in her handwriting, Claire. Anybody coulda typed this stuff in. We'll ask Nick and see what he says. It's not true, and you oughta know that."

"Yeah, I ought to know that. But I don't."

Charlie walked into the kitchen and listened intently while Bud ran the case so far, including the part about the incriminating diary. Claire just sat there and said nothing.

"Where's Nick?" Charlie asked her.

"As far as I know, he's either in Miami waiting for the weather to clear, or he's in the air on his way back. At least, that's what he told me. He might've been right here in this house all weekend, for all I know."

"So you can't alibi him for the last few days."

"No, he's been in Florida at an A.M.A. meeting. That's what he said."

"I don't believe he's capable of doing anything this heinous," Charlie said quietly. "Do you, Claire? Really?"

She jumped up, paced around some herself. "I don't know. I don't know him. I don't even know you very well. All I know is that this diary, right there on that table, puts him as number one on our suspect list. And I think everybody here has got to agree with me."

Buck, and Shaggy, and even Vicky stopped what they were doing and looked at her. What they said then was that they couldn't believe Nicholas Black could possibly be involved. On the other hand, not a one of them could explain the incriminating words in Monica's diary, and so they worked the rest of the scene without much conversation. Not even when they emptied the clothes hamper and found that the shirt she'd seen earlier was one of Black's expensive, tailor-made white dress shirts wadded up in the bottom of the hamper. She hadn't recognized it until she saw his initials monogrammed on the cuff.

This was indeed looking pretty grim for the man who said he loved her so much. Worse than grim, if you really got down to it. He was probably going to turn out to be this young woman's killer, unless he could find a way to prove otherwise. One thing Claire did know for a fact: She wasn't going back to his place at Cedar Bend Lodge, not now, maybe not ever. For sure, she was keeping her distance from him until he was ruled out as Monica's killer. If he was ruled out, and she was no longer sure that was going to happen.

Bud and Claire worked the crime scene until almost seven o'clock, and then returned to the sheriff's office. Now they sat in Charlie's office, watching him where he sat behind his desk, carefully reading a printout copy of Monica Wheeler's computer diary, his bifocal reading glasses perched atop his nose. Claire tried not to fidget as the minutes lengthened. She felt about as bad as any human being could feel. The thought of the two of them, her doctor and her nurse, her self-avowed lover and her friend having sex while she lay next door struggling to wake up from a coma, was so awful to consider that she tried desperately to clear it out of her mind, but not with a lot of luck. So there they all sat, waiting. Solemn. Sick at heart.

When Charlie finished, he looked straight at her. "How do you feel about this?"

Ha, what a question. "Terrible. Betrayed. How do you think I feel?"

"So you believe this crock of shit?"

"It was her private diary, written on her personal laptop. Why in God's name would Monica make up these kinds of lies?"

Charlie shook his head. "Well, I don't know, but I don't believe a damn word of it. I've seen how Black is about you, how anxious he was when you were lying in that hospital bed. He was distraught with worry. He couldn't fake something like that. He wouldn't look at another woman during that time. It's simply impossible, to my mind."

"I don't remember him as well as you do, Sheriff. You've been friends with him for a long time. I don't know if he's had other women on the side while we were together, or not. I don't know if he has one in Miami and is with her right now. I do think he's slick enough to pull it off, if he wanted to."

Heaving a giant sigh, Charlie shifted his gaze to Bud. "What'd you think, Bud?"

"I think something like that is the last thing Nick would ever do. I don't believe anything in that diary for a New York minute."

Well, Claire did feel a little better that they both believed so steadfastly in Nicholas Black's innocence, and his feelings for her. Maybe she was wrong. Maybe he could explain all this away. *Right, oh, sure,* she thought. She didn't see how he could.

Charlie said, "Are you sure the shirt we found out there belongs to him?"

"Yes, sir," Claire said. "It has his monogram on the right cuff. It's specially made in Hong Kong. I've seen him wear one like it since I woke up. A lot more of them are hanging in his closet."

Charlie uttered a couple of colorful curses, the F-bomb among them, and then he said, "My God, can this look any worse for Nick?"

She didn't think so, but she didn't admit that to Charlie and Bud.

Bud spoke up and entered the fray. "Well, we've got fingerprints all over the murder weapon and the goblets. That could exonerate Nick."

"Or not," she said.

"So what the two of you are saying is that I'm going to have to call Nick and bring him in here for questioning, dadgummit. This is just great, just great."

They didn't say a word.

Charlie picked up the phone. "You got Nick's private number, I take it?"

"Yes, sir." Claire recited it to him, more than interested in hearing Black's explanation for this one.

Charlie punched it in, waited for several seconds, and then said, "Nick, this is Charlie Ramsay. Something's come up and we need to talk to you. Can you come in?"

He paused a few seconds, listening, and then said, "I'd rather get into that once you get here." Again, he listened to what Black was saying, and then looked at her as he said, "No, she's fine. She's sitting right here."

"Okay, he's in the air, and should land in Camdenton in fifteen or twenty minutes. He says he'll get here as soon as he can after that." He sighed again, and then sighed some more. Beside her, Bud sighed. Lots of sighing going on, oh, yeah, you bet.

"Okay, detectives, let's get on down to the interview room and decide how we're going to approach this. Bud, get the evidence bags, and have Shaggy stand by to take Nick's fingerprints. Dammit to hell, this is a pathetic state of affairs. First, Claire languishing in a coma for weeks and now Nick accused of murder. Good God."

Pathetic was a good word, to be sure. Especially for Monica Wheeler lying dead and strangled to death on Buck's autopsy table. She and Bud trailed Charlie down to the interview room and waited. Almost an hour later, somebody rapped on the door. Claire tensed up, and they all looked at each other. Then Bud and Claire leaned against the back wall while Charlie got up and walked to the door, all three of them trying to look noncommittal.

Chapter Eighteen

"Hello, Nick, please, come on in and have a seat," Charlie said, extending his hand.

Nicholas Black took it, shook it, and then looked around the small interview room where an unknown deputy had led him. Claire was standing against the back wall. So was Bud. His major concern had been that she was hurt again, or dead in the line of duty, which was always his biggest fear when she worked a case, and that Charlie was waiting to tell him the bad news in person. Relieved, he looked at her and tried to keep his voice level. "You okay, Claire?"

She nodded and looked away. Bud wouldn't meet his eyes, either. Something was seriously wrong inside this room. They were hiding something from him, but he had a feeling he'd find out soon enough whatever it was. This was their interrogation room. Whatever followed was not going to be good for him. What the hell was going on?

Black took the chair that Charlie pointed out, one facing Bud and Claire. Charlie sat down across from him and laid a manila file on the table.

"So, what's this all about, Charlie? Why am I getting some really ugly vibes all of a sudden?"

Charlie didn't pull any punches. Black knew he wouldn't. It wasn't his style. "We found your private nurse, Monica Wheeler, today. Dead, strangled to death."

Shocked, Black didn't try to hide it, couldn't, even if he wanted to. "What?"

Silence. Too long, too ominous. Nobody seemed to want to answer that or say anything.

"Why am I here?" Black asked, but he knew. He was nobody's fool. They thought he did it, and they had a reason why they thought that.

Charlie reached down and pulled a man's white dress shirt out of a brown paper bag. Black recognized it at once as one of his. It was encased in a clear plastic evidence bag.

"This your shirt, Nick?"

At that point, Black knew exactly what was going down. They had physical evidence that pointed to him. For the first time, he felt a quick tide of anger rise up hard inside his chest, and he didn't bother to hide it. "It looks like mine. The monogram's right there, easy for anyone to see. So I guess it is. What's going on, Charlie? You accusing me of murder? Is that it?"

"What about this? Do you recognize this belt?" Charlie pushed a second evidence bag toward him. This one held a black leather belt.

Black was careful to maintain his calm, but it was difficult. "It looks like one of mine. I can't say for sure that it is. Why? What's going on here?"

Instead of answering, Charlie handed him a stapled sheaf of papers. Black took it and started reading the first page. After two or three pages, he tossed it back across the table to Charlie. He was really furious now and didn't care if they knew it, or not. "This is bullshit, every single word of it, and I think all three of you know it."

Black looked at Claire, who only stared at him without expression. He ascertained at that point that she wasn't sure what to believe. As hard as it was for Black to believe, he was definitely suspect number one, and he had better calm down, collect his wits, and convince them otherwise.

Charlie remained calm, too. "You had better read that through, Nick. It says some very incriminating things about you."

"I assume this is supposed to be Monica's diary?"

"That's right. It says you two were lovers, that you had sex with Monica Wheeler while Claire was comatose. It says you dropped Monica and threatened her life after Claire woke up and you wanted to resume your life with her. She also says in there that you said if she told Claire about your relationship with her that you would kill her."

Black leaned back, crossed his arms, and yes, he had on his poker face now. Then he looked straight at Claire and said calmly, "And every bit of that is a goddamn lie, Claire. It's totally absurd. I hope you don't believe it. And, yeah, by the way, in case you haven't noticed, this isn't in Monica's handwriting. Anybody could have typed this up and left it for you to find."

Claire said nothing. Black forced himself to release his tight muscles and try to relax. Remain unperturbed. He was completely innocent. They couldn't prove otherwise, no matter what they had on him. Charlie was a good interrogator; Black knew that, even when facing off with an old friend. He watched the sheriff clasp his big workman's hands together on the tabletop, and say, "Nick, we found your shirt in the hamper at Monica Wheeler's house. That belt lying right there is the murder weapon. It was cinched around her neck when we found her."

Repulsed and stunned by the revelations, Black frowned and shook his head. "That's impossible. I've never set foot inside her house. I don't even know where it is."

"Where have you been for the last few days, Nick?"

"I've been in Miami."

"Can you prove that?"

"Of course. I attended all the meetings. Spoke at the opening session."

"We'll have to check it out. You understand that, don't you?"

"Check out all you want. I wasn't here. I didn't do it."

Charlie stared straight into Black's eyes. Black didn't blink, either. Their gazes held for several seconds. "We also found latent fingerprints all over the belt and other objects retrieved at the scene. Are you willing to give us your fingerprints for analysis?"

Black did not hesitate. "Absolutely. Hell, I'll take a lie detector test, too, right here, right now, in front of all of you. Bring it on. I did not lay a finger on Monica. I don't care what your evidence says."

Charlie stood up. "Okay, Nick, come with me. Shaggy's waiting. While he's taking your prints, I'll call in the polygraph examiner."

At the doorway, Black turned and looked back at Claire. Their eyes locked for a few seconds, and then she looked away again. So she feels guilty distrusting him, he thought, but in her detective's mind, evidence was evidence. He knew her that well. True to form, she would remain neutral, and along with the loss of her memory, she'd lost any ability to judge whether he had it in him to kill that poor woman, or not. But his guess was she didn't think he could and wouldn't want to think so. But if she thought he'd done it and they could prove it, then he knew she'd go after him until she saw him looking out at her from behind prison bars.

Outside the interrogation room in the deserted hallway, Charlie looked at Black. "This pretty much sucks, Nick. For what it's worth, I don't believe you're guilty of anything."

"You aren't going to find my fingerprints on anything at that murder scene, Charlie. No way in hell."

"Good. This is not something I relish doing. Claire doesn't, either."

"She thinks I'm innocent?"

"She and Bud have considered that Monica might've stolen those items from your place."

"Why?"

"I don't know, Nick. I was hoping you could tell me."

"I never harmed Monica in any way. She was a friend. I'm as shocked by this as you are."

"Well, if you're innocent, we'll know it soon enough."

After that, nothing else was said, and the stilted silence seemed odd and bizarre between two such good friends. They walked to a lab room, and Shaggy took Nick's fingerprints, apologizing to him the whole time. Black was trying hard to remain unruffled, but calling him a murderer did not sit well, not at all. He didn't like it, didn't like these humiliating tests, but more than that, there was Claire. All he could think about was her, now distrusting him, blaming him for a murder, for Christ's sake. Then he was taken into the polygraph examination room and told to wait there. He did so, composing himself, while every muscle in his body was rigid, every nerve on edge. He needed to get back to Claire, reason with her, make her understand, and call every goddamn doctor at the convention in Miami, if he had to. And there was Jose, too, who could alibi him, but that would be the last resort. Allying himself with Jose Rangos would do more harm than good. After what seemed an eternity, the polygraph examiner walked into the room, connected him to the machine, and Black answered all the questions firmly and truthfully.

All in all, the whole process took almost an hour, and then a young female deputy led him back into the interrogation room. Charlie was sitting at the table again; Bud and Claire were standing against the wall where they'd been before. He sat down, and the four of them remained together there in complete and utter silence, awaiting the results of the tests. Wondering what Claire was thinking, Black stared at her the whole time. She studiously avoided his gaze the whole time. What the hell was taking so long? Finally, there came a knock on the door. Everybody tensed. Shaggy entered with a couple of reports in his hand. He looked at Nick with a hangdog, sorry-I-had-to-do-this-man expression, and Black knew then that the news was not good. But how could it not be?

Charlie took his good sweet time reading through both reports and then looked at Black. "You passed your lie detector test with flying colors."

"I told you I didn't do it."

A heavy sigh was Charlie's answer. "But, I'm sorry to say, your fingerprints match the ones on the murder weapon as well as those on the goblet and the knife and fork. Good God, Nick, I hate to say this, but I think you better call your attorney."

"Am I under arrest?"

"I'm afraid I have no choice. But I can call Judge Clarkson and try to get you bond tonight. I might be able to make that happen, if he's available and willing. I can't guarantee it."

"Then call him." Black turned quickly to Claire. "I need to talk to you, Claire. Alone."

Charlie and Bud walked out of the room, and Claire didn't move but she watched him. Black stood up. He didn't take his eyes off her. She had to believe him. "Claire, it's pretty obvious that I've been set up here. There's no way any of my clothes could be in her house unless somebody planted them there. I was not there, I swear to God. I was never there. I never touched that girl while you were unconscious, or any other time. Monica and I were old friends, and that was it. You cannot believe I'd have sex with her while you were lying unconscious in the next room. Whether you remember me, or not, you can't believe I'd do that to you."

Claire stared at him, apparently considering his heartfelt plea, and he had a feeling that she, too, was having trouble believing the ridiculous allegations. Still, she was looking at substantial evidence against him. She wouldn't ignore it until it was proven false.

"No, Black, I don't think you're capable of doing something like this, but I don't know you well enough at the moment to know for sure. Rest assured that I'll do everything in my power to prove your innocence. But until I do, don't call me, don't come around me, don't contact me in any way. For now, we're done. It's over between us."

She walked out and left Black sitting there, staring after her, but he knew that she meant exactly what she'd said. Whether she liked it, or not, whether he liked it or not, they were finished. On the other hand, he sure as hell wasn't ready to accept that little decree. They weren't done, not by a long shot.

Jesse's Girl

Right this minute

Squatting in the thick tangled undergrowth behind Annie's lakeside cabin, Jesse sat motionlessly, never moving a muscle. He listened to the buzzing, croaking, and rustling of nocturnal creatures that permeated the quiet late-night hour. He heard the sounds of crickets and tree frogs, all quite peaceful and normal and unaware of the man crouching among them. Jesse smiled to himself. He was going to take Annie back tonight, take her away from Nicholas Black forever. The time had come, and he was so delighted inside, so happy, that little thrills started expanding inside his stomach and cartwheeling all the way up to his heart. They were going to be together. Tonight. At last.

The first part of his plan was going great. He couldn't be more proud of himself. Everything was falling into place in the most excellent way. Earlier that day, he had concealed himself in the woods across the road from Monica Wheeler's house and waited for the cops to show up. The patrol car had roared up within minutes after Jesse had put in the anonymous call to the sheriff's department, and not too long after that, Annie and her partner swerved into Monica's driveway. He waited for hours until they all left, except for a lone patrol car. Then he trekked back to Miss Rosie's blue Caprice where he'd hidden it in the tree cover and followed Annie back to the sheriff's office. Sometime later, he nearly shouted in triumph when Nicholas Black showed up in his great big chrome-and-black Hummer. The cops had plenty enough evidence to arrest him, and that meant Annie would be coming home alone.

The time was at hand to snatch her and tie her up. And Nicholas Black would be rotting in jail. They might not keep him there long, but it would take time to figure out if his alibi could prove him innocent, if he even had an alibi. Whatever, Jesse would have time to get to Annie. Hell, they'd probably be hundreds of miles away by the time Black was released, no matter how clever his attorneys were.

There was a light on in Annie's house, the one over her kitchen sink. Gripping the Remington rifle he'd stolen from Miss Rosie's house, he crept down closer to the backyard. All was still and deserted, so he stepped quickly around front and climbed onto the front porch. He waited again, listening. Nothing. Nobody around. The alarm system was activated, so he punched in the appropriate numbers, just as he had watched Monica do when Nicholas Black had sent her to pick up some of Annie's personal things, bed pillows and such, to make her feel comfortable when she was in her coma at Cedar Bend. Luckily, he had been able to convince Monica to let him come along. Yes, he couldn't have done this without good old Monica. It was a shame that she had to die, that she was lying on an autopsy table waiting to be cut up, but she probably didn't mind. She seemed to like Annie and him. She would want them to be together with Miss Rosie in a sweet, loving family.

Jesse had the key to the front door as well, had Monica's whole keychain, in fact, just in case he needed her house or car for anything in the future. Her home would be shut down behind police tape for quite some time. It would be a perfect place to hide. The minute he inserted the key, a shrill yapping started up inside the living room. His little friend, Jules Verne. He grinned. He really did love that little dog. He could come with them, if he didn't try to eat Miss Rosie's head.

"Hiya, lil' fella," he whispered, going down on one knee and hugging the dog. Jules Verne stopped barking and wagged his tail. Jesse got out the bacon he had in his pocket and fed it to the tiny dog. He loved on the poodle for a while, and then he made a slow and methodical search of Annie's house. Once he had Annie under his power, he would have to pack a bag for her with all her favorite things because they'd never come back. He would take her far away, but he'd just about decided on the high sierra in Old Mexico. No one could find them there. Or perhaps they'd keep driving, all the way down to Belize. He had seen that little Central American country on the Discovery Channel, and found it to be a beautiful place with lush verdant vegetation and lovely sandy beaches.

Upstairs in Annie's loft, he lay on her bed for a time, waiting for her to return, burying his face in her pillow, inhaling the scent of her shampoo and her skin. Oh, God, he had waited so long for this moment. He almost went to sleep; he was so content there among her things, and was actually dozing, when he heard a car approaching the house. Jumping up, he ran to the window. It was her partner's white Bronco, all right. He heard her get out and slam the door, and then the Bronco crunched the gravel as it turned around and headed back up the road. Then the front door opened amid Jules Verne's barking, and Annie walked into her house. She stopped long enough to reset the alarm, and he tiptoed across the upstairs bedroom and concealed himself behind the long window draperies. He peeked out and watched over the loft railing as she picked up Jules Verne and cuddled him.

"Oh, Jules, what are we gonna do now?" she murmured softly to the dog.

Well, he knew what she was going to do. He fingered the bottle of chloroform in his hand. She wouldn't have a chance in hell. All he had to do was clamp the chloroform-soaked rag over her nose and mouth. She was stronger than Monica, of course, but who wasn't? Monica was a tiny little girl. He would be able to hold Annie down long enough for the drug to take effect. And, then, oh, yeah, she was gonna have quite the adventure, starting as soon as she came up those steps and went to bed. His mouth actually watered at the thought of having her totally under his control again, at being able to lick her skin and squeeze her breasts any time he wanted to. At last, at last, thank God, the time was here at last.

Chapter Nineteen

Totally depressed and demoralized, Claire glanced around her empty house. She missed Black's company, she truly did. Even after all she'd seen and heard that night at the sheriff's office. She shouldn't, but she couldn't help it. She also knew his high-priced, top-notch lawyers would get him out of custody so fast that Charlie's head would spin.

But still, all the accusations, all of Black's betrayals and lies; everything seemed so surreal. She felt lonely to the core, like throwing herself facedown on the bed and grieving for all she'd lost. But she would *not* do that. If Black had seduced Monica, he wasn't worth her misery. And if he had, he wasn't a man she wanted to be with, for damn sure. Just when she had accepted their relationship, that they had been together, all this had to happen. Agitated, she got up, walked to the fridge, and retrieved a can of Cherry Coke. Popping the tab, she leaned against the bar and absently watched Jules run up the steps to the loft bedroom. He was ready for bed, it seemed, but she certainly wasn't. She had lots of thinking to do, and lots of decisions to make.

Down deep inside her heart, she could not bring herself to believe that Nicholas Black would do something as stupid as kill an employee with his own belt and leave it behind for detectives to find. He was way too smart, too savvy, and too versed in forensic psychology to make those kinds of stupid mistakes. If he wanted to commit a murder, even if he'd snapped and gone into a rage, he still wouldn't leave any clues behind for them to uncover, and he would probably find a way to get away with it.

The ugly scenario did smack of a frame-up. Of course, it did, just as Black had said, and a clumsy one at that. All of them, Charlie, Bud, Claire—they all knew something seriously wrong was going on at that crime scene, but who would want to set up Black for murder? It was likely that Black might have enemies. After all, he was a rich and successful doctor and wealthy businessman, not to mention the type of man who attracted any woman with eyes in her head. Jealous husbands, jealous ex-lovers, there were all sorts of possibilities from his past. Sometime, somewhere he might have offended somebody, intentionally or not. But he did pass the polygraph, thank God. That would go a long way to help him prove his innocence, but it wasn't admissible in court.

Blowing out a deep breath, Claire sank onto the couch and dropped her head back on the cushions. She shut her eyes. She had almost let Black back in, almost succumbed to his charm and fallen for his loving attention. She tried to imagine how hard it had been for him to watch her lying there in that coma and then to continue to love her when she didn't remember him as her lover. It would've been frustrating for him, to say the least. He had handled it pretty well, actually. But had she fallen for him all over again? The squeezing pain in her heart told her, yes.

Angry at herself, she got up and tried to shake off thoughts of Black. What she needed was to get a good night's sleep, and then start picking apart the crime scene inch by inch. Whoever had killed Monica Wheeler must have left a clue and must be someone who could access Black's personal belongings. Or, perhaps Monica had just taken them home as Bud had suggested. If Monica was infatuated with him, she might have taken something of his to hold on to in bed at night. How sick and obsessive was that? But then again, Black was something else to behold. He obviously had been charming enough to win her heart before the accident and was damn close to doing it again right now.

Turning on the television, she tried to get interested in something, anything, but the news of Monica Wheeler's murder was all over the news, even down in Springfield on KY3.

"Dammit, anyway," she muttered, then gave up and switched off the news.

Instead, she trudged up the steps to the loft. Jules was lying half in and half out of the flowing window draperies. He wagged his tail and it swished the bottom of the curtains back and forth a bit, but the toy poodle didn't get up and jump on the bed like he usually did.

"You must be pooped out, too, Jules. You're not very friendly tonight. And just when I need a little TLC."

The poodle wagged harder but didn't budge, so Claire sat down on the end of the bed. She untied and kicked off her high-top Nikes. Okay, she'd take a long hot shower, wash her hair, and relax her tight muscles. Maybe even spend some time in the hot tub downstairs. She unbuckled her shoulder holster and laid it on the bedside table while she leaned over and unstrapped her ankle weapon. She laid the .38 beside the Glock. For a minute or two, she just sat there, thinking, trying to figure things out, and wishing things were different. She pulled off her T-shirt and stood up. She felt exhausted—mentally, emotionally, physically. Maybe she wasn't as strong as she thought. Maybe Black and Charlie were right about her needing to take it easy.

A moment later, she stood in the bathroom and stared at herself in the mirror, still trying to figure out who would've wanted Monica Wheeler dead. If she ruled out Black having the affair with Monica, Black didn't have any motive to kill her, not that Claire could see. Neither did anybody else. Monica had really been into Jesse, but she told Claire that he treated her like a queen. They were moving in together, for God's sake. She wondered if Bud had gotten hold of Jesse yet. They found Monica's cell phone on the floor with the spilled groceries, and Bud had called him. Jesse hadn't picked up, and he hadn't returned the call.

Maybe it was Jesse. Maybe they'd had a fight, and he lost it, and strangled her. He was a strange man, probably capable of doing it. But with Black's belt? None of it made sense. But it was a lead to pursue, and why hadn't he called them back? Why wasn't he calling in, looking for Monica, asking them where she was, and what had happened to her? Yes, pursue Jesse's alibi she would, first thing in the morning.

Just as she sat down on the side of the tub, ready to turn on the taps and enjoy a long, hot bath, she heard the unmistakable sound of a powerful motorboat entering her cove. She jumped to her feet, already knowing who it was. She hastily threw her clothes back on, grabbed her weapons, just in case Black wasn't the nice guy everybody thought he was and had come out to strangle her, too.

Once downstairs, she took a moment to strap on both guns, and then threw open the front door. Jules was on her heels now, and once the door stood wide, he lit out toward the dock where Black had maneuvered the Cobalt 360 to berth and was tying up. Claire stood where she was, outside on the porch, and waited for him to charge up to the house and plead his case. Only thing was, he didn't. He climbed back into the boat and disappeared from sight.

Frowning, she decided to walk down there and confront him, wondering what the devil he was doing. Was he luring her down there so he wouldn't leave blood spatter inside the house? She just couldn't believe that, but why was he there? He couldn't stay, of course. She had made it clear that they were not going to see each other again. On the other hand, down deep, she was one happy gal to see him out of jail and tied up at her dock. Technically, she wasn't on his case yet. Charlie had made it fairly obvious that she wasn't ever going to be, either. But going down there to talk to him was not a good idea. If she was smart, she'd go back inside and lock her door, take that leisurely bath, and go to bed. However, she wasn't that smart, she guessed, because she walked down the hill to the lake and out on the dock to his big powerful boat. Black was sitting on the stern seat, a rifle lying across his knees. He had on a black T-shirt and jeans and a frown that you just wouldn't believe. Jules was lying on the dock watching him, also sensing his dangerous mood, no doubt.

"What are you doing here?" Claire demanded, in as unfriendly fashion as she could muster, but she kept her eyes on the high-power, scoped hunting rifle. "And what's with the gun?"

"I am not leaving you out here alone. Somebody wants me out of the picture and went to a lot of trouble to make it happen. That's what all this is about. So I'm going to sit out here and make sure nobody sneaks up on you the way they did Monica."

"I can take care of myself. I'm armed to the hilt. It doesn't look good for you to be here when we're investigating you."

"I don't care. I'm not leaving. I guess you can have me arrested again. You seemed to enjoy that well enough the first time around."

"That's not fair, Black."

"You're in danger out here by yourself, and if you're smart, you'll listen to me."

"How did you get out of custody this fast?"

"Charlie decided not to charge me until he and Bud checked out my alibi. Which is ironclad, by the way, just in case you're interested in whether I killed her, or not."

That felt like a slap in the face, but she could take the hit. She merely said, "I don't think you killed Monica."

"Could've fooled me." Black was so angry that it radiated off him in waves, like heat off a radiator. In the soft moonlight and the distant glow of the dusk-to-dawn light at the end of her dock, his face was carved with deep shadows that made it hard to read his expression. But his voice nearly shook with contained rage.

"I'm a law enforcement officer, Black. I've got to remain unbiased and stay away from you until you're completely cleared. If your alibi pans out, believe me, I'll be the happiest person around."

"Get in the boat and sit down. I want to talk to you."

Hesitating, she decided that they did need to talk it out. She climbed down and took a seat a few feet away from him.

"Now don't get too close. I bite, you know. I also, for no apparent reason, kill innocent young women who're good friends of mine."

Ooh, sarcasm, executed quite well, too. "You need to listen to reason, Black. You're in very deep trouble here. It's gonna be hard for Charlie to ignore all this evidence."

"All this so-called evidence was planted and we all know it. Who planted it—that's what we've got to figure out."

He was right. None of it made a lick of sense. It really didn't. "Okay. I've been thinking about it, too, and I agree with you. But if not you, then who?"

"I think I know, but I'm not sure how I can ever prove it. I've already got my private investigator working on it."

"John Booker?"

"That's right. And he's damn good. He'll come up with something to help me."

"You need to tell us what you suspect so we can go after this guy. He's twisted, if he can do something like that to Monica."

"You just don't know."

Claire was getting a little peeved at this secret speak he was tossing around. "Okay, you give it to me straight, Black. I need to know, especially if you think I'm in danger enough that you're willing to sit out here on guard duty all night."

Black hesitated for several beats, just staring at her. He was still irate; she could see how his fists were clenched. He was ready to erupt; all he needed was a trigger. But who could blame him?

Black finally answered, very low, very tight. "I didn't want to tell you this. I still don't think you're psychologically ready for it, but you need to know the truth. You need to stay with me at Cedar Bend. Your place is too isolated, too vulnerable to intruders. And don't tell me you can take care of yourself, goddammit. You can't always take care of yourself, and it's time that you face that."

She hadn't seen him this furious and antagonistic before, so she didn't argue with him. "Then go ahead and tell me. Otherwise, I'm staying right here. By myself. And you're going home."

Black was veritably clenching his teeth now. She could almost hear them grinding against each other. "Okay, you know that guy who took you off that bridge with him. I think he's still alive and stalking you again."

Stunned by that, Claire said, "You told me he was dead."

"Well, I don't think so anymore. This murder frame-up is exactly something he'd pull. He's been locked up in a hospital for the criminally insane since the last time he went after you, but he's as clever as hell and pathologically obsessed with you. He loves you and thinks you love him."

Mightily taken aback now, she tried to absorb all that. "Who is it?"

"His name is Thomas Landers, but if he is the killer, he's using an alias, you can bet on that. He's good at changing his appearance, too. He's disguised himself as a woman in the past, for God's sake."

"No way."

"Good enough to fool both of us, Claire, and everybody else around here. Including Harve."

"I don't understand."

"Then sit there and listen to me for a change. You're in for quite a ride. I wanted you to remember all this on your own, if you had to remember it at all. I don't know if you can handle some of the stuff you've been through."

"I want to know. I'm telling you I can handle it."

"This sicko lunatic's been in your life since you were a little girl. He has this sick and twisted fantasy that the two of you belong together, and he'll do anything to make it happen. And I mean anything."

"Since I was little? That doesn't seem possible."

Black barked a short laugh, utterly humorless. "It's possible, all right. He just got me accused of murder when I'm totally innocent, didn't he? This guy's a psychopath, driven completely insane from severe childhood abuse. Terrible stuff was done to him. He will not stop until he's got you in his hands, and he'll do anything: commit murder, lie, steal, behead, anything, I tell you, to get you back under his control."

Despite the warm night breeze, a shiver rippled its way down over Claire's bare arms, just at the thought of being stalked by that kind of man, but no awful memories welled up to enlighten her. So she didn't say anything else. She only sat there, silent, trying to digest what he'd said and what she needed to do about it. Trouble was, this time she didn't know what to do.

Black didn't wait for her to respond. This time his tone was calmer, which made his words even more effective. "Claire, listen to me, please. I love you. I'm scared for you. This man is truly psychotic, but criminally brilliant. He's after you right now. I feel in it my gut. If you won't come with me, let me stay here with you. I'm begging you, Claire. You don't remember how dangerous this guy is. If you did, you would know that you need my help. Oh, God, please, Claire, listen to me, just this once, listen to what I'm saying."

Claire sat there and heard him out, pleading from his heart, no question about it. And she was also pretty sure that Black was not a weak man, not fearful, not one to be afraid of anything. He seemed about as strong and self-confident and tough as any man she'd ever known. Yet he was scared for her. And that did scare her.

"Okay. You can stay here, but come inside the house. It's stupid for you to sit out here with mosquitoes eating you up."

They both jumped when Jules suddenly bounded up and raced off toward the house, barking his head off. Black was on his feet in an instant, moving up into the bow and looking up toward the house. Somewhere out in the darkness, Jules yelped and raced straight back to them, as if frightened by something. Claire scooped him off the dock and put him down in the boat with them. Black turned around and faced her, and she could see the seriousness on his face reflected in the dim cockpit lights.

"C'mon, Claire, take Jules and spend the night at Cedar Bend with me. This is not a safe place, even with me standing guard. I'll stay clear of you. I'll move down into one of the bungalows, if you want, and you can have the penthouse. This guy's not going to stop until we get him. You are his life's obsession. His reason for living."

Before Claire could answer that, a shot rang out, shattering the stillness. She saw the flash of a gun muzzle in the nearby trees, about the same time Black tried to duck down, but not fast enough. The slug hit him in the back, and he crumpled like a dropped marionette and fell forward to his knees and then facedown in the bottom of the boat. She took cover behind the cockpit, pulled her Glock, and unloaded six quick slugs at the spot where the shooter had fired his weapon.

Their assailant returned fire almost at once, now closer to them, but she couldn't spot him, couldn't get a bead on where he would be next. In a heartbeat, she had the boat untied and was idling the Cobalt out away from the dock. Once clear, she shoved the controls forward, and the boat nearly stood on end before it surged off toward the entrance to the cove. Once she got out into the open lake channel, she crouched down beside Black.

"How bad is it?"

"Just get us outta here," he rasped out, trying to turn over.

Claire held the wheel with one hand and grabbed Black's Windbreaker out of the storage pocket and pressed down hard on his chest wound. It looked like the bullet had hit his back and exited

somewhere under his clavicle. She tried to steer the boat and get a
towel under his back at the entry wound. He groaned when she tried
to lift him, and then went unconscious and just lay there bleeding.
She stood back up and pushed the boat even harder, jerking out her
cell and calling ahead to Cedar Bend to have an ambulance waiting
at the marina. She had to get him to a doctor. His wound was bad,
oh, God, it was really, really bad.

Jesse's Girl

Right now

Oh, thank God, he'd finally done it! He'd killed that bastard Nicholas
Black! He'd aimed dead square at his heart, and he'd hit him. The
man went down hard. Jesse was almost positive he'd delivered a fatal
bullet. But then, almost at once, Annie let loose on him, several
quick shots. He tried to get down, but not fast enough, because a
bullet slammed into his arm. It felt like somebody had punched him
hard, and he cried out and fell to his knees in the bushes. He scrab-
bled on all fours behind a tree and fired back at her, but he didn't
want to hit her! He didn't want to hurt her! Oh, my God, Annie shot
him. His Annie, his own special friend, his own Annie, whom he
loved more than anybody in the world! How could she have done it?
Didn't she see that Nicholas Black was keeping them apart? Didn't
she understand how that made Jesse feel?

Annie had ducked down out of sight and was most likely calling
the police on him right now. He had to get away! He started at a run
for the hill behind her cabin, protecting his bleeding arm and scram-
bling and clawing his way up through the clinging vines and thick
vegetation to the logging road where he'd left his car. God, he'd been
so close to grabbing her when Black had to show up in that goddamn
boat. He couldn't believe it. Nicholas Black should've been in jail.

And then Annie had run all the way to the dock to see him, as if Black was her one true love, instead of Jesse.

That's when he'd crept out of the house, made his way down the hill near them. He heard them talking, heard almost everything they said, and he'd heard what Black said about him. The burn began then, the red fire of his hatred had gushed forth into his bloodstream, enraging him so much he couldn't bear it. When Nicholas Black stood up in the boat, presenting a perfect target in the dock's light, he lost all control and didn't hesitate; he raised his rifle and shot him without a second thought. And he did hit him. The big man had been knocked forward to the ground. Annie must have thought someone was trying to kill her, that's why she fired back at him. That must be it; she didn't know it was Jesse. Of course, she didn't.

When he finally reached the crest of the hill and the hidden Caprice, he stopped and listened. He could hear the boat's motor moving away, farther and farther, until it faded to a low hum drifting across the water. They weren't chasing him, but he still jumped into his car and headed straight for home. The roads were deserted so late, and he tried to stay calm, driving carefully so a cop wouldn't stop him. His arm was bleeding profusely, and the idea that Annie had done this to him broke his heart. He began to cry, hard, wracking sobs that made it difficult to hang on to the steering wheel. Annie must not love him anymore. To have hurt him so much like this. He wept with grief and despair all the way home, so sad and hurt that she did this to him. How could she? How could she?

Dragging himself into his house, he slumped down on the sofa, too depressed even to get Miss Rosie out of the refrigerator and tell her what had happened. He couldn't face her; he couldn't tell her that his sweet Annie, the girl that he'd been telling her about all this time, had tried to kill him. Finally, he got out his first aid kit and his sharpest sewing needle and a syringe of morphine he'd stolen from Nicholas Black's personal medicine cabinet upstairs at Cedar Bend. He fingered the wound, but the bullet had passed all the way through. He sat down and slid the hypodermic needle into his open wound, then splashed iodine into it. He screamed with agony, but somehow the suffering made him feel better. He stopped crying and carefully threaded his sewing needle. He inserted it into one side of the

deep cut, and then the other, and then pulled it together in a neat
black stitch. He stitched it all the way up, yelling with pain with each
jab, but the sewing calmed him.

Of course, it wasn't Annie who shot him. It was Nicholas Black.
He had gotten off a shot before he died. Annie would never fire on
him. She loved him. She had told him so in that short time before
when he had gotten her under his control. Now that Black was dead,
she would want Jesse again. She would come with him and Miss
Rosie, and they would be a happy family again. She would come
back home, and he would be there, waiting for her. And once she
saw him, saw how much he loved her, she would pack her things and
they would go away together. Forever and ever.

By now, he was feeling much better about everything that had
happened. He got out some hot dogs and put them on a cookie sheet.
Two for him, and one for Miss Rosie. Soon he would be putting
an extra hot dog on for Annie. Maybe even two, if she was really
hungry. And one for Jules Verne, too. He would serve potato chips
and pickles and Ding Dongs for desert. Or maybe, he'd serve Snickers
candy bars for dessert for her first dinner at home with them. She
loved Snickers bars, especially if they were frozen. Monica had told
him so. Poor old Monica, he really missed her. Too bad he needed
to leave her body for the police to find. Otherwise, he could've cut
her head off and let her be Miss Rosie's new daughter. Oh, well, he
guessed he couldn't have every head he wanted.

He fixed Miss Rosie's plate for her, and then he ate hungrily. Now,
it was back to the drawing board. And he just might have to punish
Annie a bit, if she was the one who had shot at him. She had to learn
that she couldn't shoot the people who loved her most. But then
she'd learn what she had to do for them to be together, and they'd be
happy again.

Chapter Twenty

Frantic to get Black to a doctor, Claire shoved the throttle of the powerful Cobalt 360 cruiser to full power and the big boat leapt ahead at even greater speed as it flew across the dark water. So fast, in fact, that they made it all the way to Cedar Bend Lodge in less than ten minutes. She could see the flashing lights of the ambulance well before they got there. As she steered the boat into the deserted marina, and way too fast, too, throwing a wake into the surrounding berths and rocking the boats against their moorings, she could see the two EMTs with a gurney standing next to an open double berth. She cut the engine and nosed her boat into the slot. The bow hit the rubber tires hard, but her rough arrival didn't stop one EMT from leaping into the stern and kneeling quickly at Black's side, while his partner helped Claire secure the boat.

Dropping to her knees beside them, Claire breathlessly filled them in on what had happened, her voice shaking so much she hardly recognized it. "The slug hit him in the back and exited in front. I tried to stanch the bleeding, but he's lost a lot of blood. A lot of blood!"

"Okay, we got him now," the EMT said, his words terse, quickly wrapping a blood pressure cuff around Black's arm while his partner administered some kind of shot. Black's white T-shirt was completely red now, every inch soaked in blood. Quickly cutting it off, they furiously tried to bind up the wounds and stop the heavy flow of blood, long enough to get him to the E.R.

Black was no longer moaning or trying to talk, just lying there as still and white as a dead man. Claire swallowed down burgeoning panic through a throat constricted with dread. Finally, after what seemed like forever, they got Black stabilized and out of the boat and onto the gurney. Claire picked up Jules from where he was cowering in the cockpit, quivering with fear and reaction, and handed him off to one of the marina attendants helping with the boat. Then they were off running with Black's gurney down the pier to the ambulance. She jumped aboard in back with one of the EMTs, just in case Black woke up, but she was so scared she couldn't breathe. What if he didn't wake up? What if he was gone already, before she even got to talk to him? Oh, God, he had to be okay.

Listening to the EMT transmitting Black's vitals and transport condition to the physicians waiting at the Canton County Medical Center, her heartbeat was simply off the charts. She couldn't seem to draw in enough air. Black's blood was all over her clothes, all over her hands. This was so bad, so terribly bad; his wound was catastrophic, very close to his heart. She needed to calm down, use her training and not lose it completely. Okay, the hospital was prepping for immediate emergency surgery, so that was good. They'd go right to work on him. With trembling fingers, she somehow punched in Bud's number, somehow got out what had happened before her voice just died away to nothing. Bud said he'd call Charlie, and that they'd meet her at the emergency room, to hang in there, and then the line went dead.

The E.R. team was already outside and grabbed Black's gurney at the curb and then they were gone, just like that, into surgery, trying to keep him alive on the run. They blocked Claire from following them through the swinging doors of the surgery unit, and she stood there and tried to see through the small, screened window. But they whisked Black out of sight, and she collapsed weakly on her haunches against the wall opposite the door and tried to get hold of her labored breath and thundering heart.

Out of nowhere, she got a glimpse of a dark-tinged memory of arriving at a run at this very hospital, rushing a different gurney into the emergency room. Bud was with her; they were trying to save somebody. And then that vision was gone, poof, and she dropped her face into her palms and willed herself back into self-control. Black had come out to her place to protect her, to warn her that she was in danger, and she hadn't listened, had brushed off his fears. And he had paid the price for that refusal, maybe with his own life. Was it that Thomas Landers freak? Was he hiding there all along watching them?

Claire sat alone for what seemed like months before a nurse came rushing down the corridor. She told Claire that she was a friend of hers, that her name was Chris Dale Cox. Claire didn't recognize her, but Chris said that Black was in critical condition and not out of danger. He was still in surgery, she said, and would be for probably another couple of hours.

Chris hugged Claire then, and Claire found herself clinging to the woman, wanting human touch, wanting somebody to tell her that Black was not going to die. But nobody did. After a little while, Chris took off, and a few minutes later brought Claire a chair and a large Styrofoam cup of hot black coffee. *Oh, God bless you*, Claire thought, as she sat and gulped down the caffeine, still immersed in that paralyzing daze of terror. If he died, he died protecting her. Was he right about this stalker of hers? Was that who shot him? Or was the shooter aiming at her? They were attacked at her house, after all. She found herself praying fervently and then she stood up and paced the long empty hallway, waiting, waiting, interminably waiting.

Bud and Charlie finally arrived through the outside doors at a dead run. Both looked shocked, and scared, which scared Claire. She tried to tell them how it went down, managing somehow to get out the basics while they listened, frowned, and shook their heads.

"Who was the shooter?" Charlie asked Claire quickly. "Did you get a look at him?"

"How the hell did he get past Harve's security gate?" Bud demanded, looking as stunned as Claire felt. But she was getting steadier, now that they were with her and asking pertinent police inquiries. Her training finally kicked in, thank God.

"He must've come down the hill behind my house. It's heavily wooded. Or by water, he could've come in by water. There are lots of places he could've beached a small boat or kayak along the bank. He could've tied up at Harve's old dock, the one on the point with the blinking blue light. It's not far from my house. Neither of us had a clue he was anywhere near. We were out on my dock in Black's boat. When Jules barked and ran into the trees, Black got up and stood in the bow, trying to see what it was." Her voice died, and she felt bile sour the back of her throat. "The shot just came out of the dark, Bud, and got him in the back."

"What the fuck was Nick doing out there?" That was Charlie, getting to the point in his own unique way. "I told him to stay the hell away from you until we straightened out this Wheeler investigation. Shit. What the hell's goin' on here?"

Claire sank down in the chair again, stomach roiling around, her voice shaky. "He came out there to protect me. I went down to the boat and told him to leave, but he wouldn't. He said he was going to sit out there all night."

Bud said, "Protect you from what?"

"He's convinced he's being framed. He thinks somebody wants to get rid of him to get close to me."

"Who?" demanded Charlie.

"Thomas Landers. Do you know who that is?"

When they exchanged shocked looks, there was a short silence. Then Bud said, "They declared Thomas Landers dead, almost a month ago."

"Black says they never found the body."

"No, they didn't," Charlie agreed. "They searched for days while you were lying next to dead in that damn coma."

"Oh, God, I hope to hell that bastard's dead," Bud said, squeezing his hands into fists. Antsy himself now, he paced a couple of steps down the hall and back again.

"Do you recall anything about this Landers guy, Claire?" Charlie said.

"Not much. But I need to. Black was telling me about him when he got hit. He didn't get to finish."

"Do you think the assailant was close enough to overhear what he was saying?"

"He had to be somewhere close, on the bank, yeah, probably in hearing distance, maybe. He shot out of tree cover. I opened up on him as soon as Black fell, but I can't be sure I hit him. It was too dark, and I didn't know where he was. I hope I got him."

"Okay, I'm getting officers out there right now to canvass the

woods around your house. Maybe he's dead or wounded and lying
out there somewhere. Is there anything else you can tell us?"

Claire shook her head. "He was hiding in the dark. I saw the muzzle
flashes and fired straight at them."

Bud was frowning, worried, too, but he put a bracing arm around
Claire's shoulders. "Black's gonna be all right, Morgan. The doctors
here are great. They got me through a real nasty snakebite once upon
a time."

Nodding, she only stared at him, because she wasn't sure at all.
Bud hadn't seen Black's wound, the bullet so very close to his heart.
It might have been too close, or too close to the aorta. But he was
able to talk for a few seconds. If the bullet slammed into his heart,
he would've died almost instantly. And he didn't. That meant he had
a chance to survive.

The surgery ended up lasting over five hours, and then Black was
transferred out of recovery to the intensive care unit. The doctor
came out, a pretty young woman with long brown hair tied back at
her nape, and large and intelligent brown eyes. But her face was set
in very grave lines.

"Are you the officer who brought in the gunshot victim? Dr.
Black?"

"Yes, I'm Claire Morgan. Is he gonna make it?"

"I'm Dr. Katelyn Atwater, and yes, we think right now that he'll
recover, but we can't say that for sure, not yet. The bullet missed his
heart completely. He was extremely lucky because it didn't miss by
much, only a few inches up and to the left. About here." She touched
a finger to a spot under her clavicle and close to her upper arm. "He
must have been moving when the bullet hit because it exited underneath his scapula in the back. It nicked the bone, but I think we got
out all the fragments. And it cracked the humerus in his left arm. It's
a miracle it didn't break it. There's no sign of infection, but he's lost
a great deal of blood and we're rectifying that with blood transfu-
sions. The next few hours will tell us more, but he's a strong, healthy
man. That's certainly in his favor."

Yeah, and the next few hours in the waiting room were horrendous.
Charlie and Bud both remained there with Claire. None of them said
much of anything, just sat there and stared at each other, eaten up

with concern. Both men obviously thought a lot of Nicholas Black. But who had she met who didn't like him? He was a good guy. He had certainly taken good care of her when she was the one in that hospital bed. She hoped she got the chance to repay that kindness.

Not long after dawn sifted its rosy hued light into the wide windows of the deserted waiting room, Dr. Atwater came back out and told them that Black was doing as well as could be expected. She told Claire that she could go into the ICU and see him, but if he was lucid, not to ask him any questions or upset him in any way. Claire jumped at the chance. Once she got inside, she wasn't so sure about the doctor's prognosis. Black looked about as awful as awful could get. He still had a breathing tube in his nose, his eyes were taped shut, and both blood transfusion and IV tubes snaked out of his arms.

Appalled, Claire just stood there and stared down at him. She didn't know what to do. There was nothing she could do. She just had to wait. The ICU nurse brought her a rolling blue vinyl recliner, and Claire blessed all nurses from her heart as she sat down and leaned back her head. All she could hear was the soft murmur of the nurses at their station just outside Black's glassed cubicle and all the little beeps and blips of Black's monitors. The clock on the wall said six o'clock a.m. She stared at it for a long time before she fell into a light and troubled doze.

Claire woke up with a jerk when the surgeon appeared and ordered the breathing tube removed. Black was coming to, but he was nowhere near mental lucidity yet. He was mumbling incoherently, and they'd taken the tape off his eyes, but he never opened them. She heard him mumble something about where he was, and he muttered her name a couple of times, but mostly he was lost in a fitful and heavily sedated sleep.

Claire left the ICU a couple of times that day, once to say goodbye to Bud and Charlie, who were going home to shower and change before they went back to work. The other time, she walked into the women's restroom, splashed water on her face, and stared at her reflection in the mirror. There was still dried blood on her arms and more that had saturated and dried until the front of her shirt was stiff with it. More blood had discolored her blond hair, making it look

darker with strands sticking together in clumps. Black's blood. He
had lost so much blood that it had pooled in a large puddle under
him in the bottom of the boat.

The idea of so much of his blood soaking into her clothes sick-
ened her, and she was glad when Chris Dale Cox came in and hustled
her out and into the shower in the nurses' dressing room. Grateful
for her thoughtfulness, Claire stripped off her shirt and jeans, kicked
off her bloody Nikes, swept back the white curtain, and stepped into
the stall. She let the hot water beat down on her face and body for a
long time. Then she scrubbed Black's blood out of her hair, dried off
with a towel, and slipped on the clean blue scrubs that Chris had left
for her.

After that, Claire walked to the vending machine for more coffee
and tried to clear her head. She was having lots of trouble doing that
and contented herself by dully watching the coffee drip slowly into
yet another Styrofoam cup. Her cell phone went off. She saw it was
Bud and picked up quickly.

"How's Nick?"

"Holding his own, but they're not saying he's out of the woods.
They did take out the breathing tube, and he's semiconscious at
times."

"Well, that sounds like fairly good news. If he survived the surgery,
he'll probably pull out of this okay."

"Yeah, I hope so."

"Are you still at the hospital?"

"Yes. Tell Charlie that I'm staying here until he's out of danger.
At least until then."

"Don't worry about it. Charlie said for you to take some time off.
He's talking to the Ozark P.D. about the possibility of that psycho
Landers getting out of that wreck alive. He's asking them to reopen
the search. Truth is, Claire, this whole thing sounds like that guy. He
was so obsessed with you that he'd do anything to get you, and if it
is him, he won't let up. You need to watch yourself. Don't let him
get close again."

"That's pretty much what Black tried to tell me."

"So, just be careful, okay. Don't be by yourself unless you have
to. This guy is nobody's fool. Even if it isn't him, somebody's

gunning for you. The shooter could've been firing at you and hit Nick instead. Who knows?"

"Okay." It was all so confusing, and she was so tired, so sleep deprived that she wasn't quite grasping things so well anymore.

"We're out at your place now, Claire, trying to find some kind of evidence to ID this guy. Nothing yet, but we couldn't get much done until daybreak. No sign of him yet."

"Okay," she said again. Seems like that was all she could muster up.

"Get some sleep, Claire. It sounds like you need it."

They hung up, and Claire walked back inside Black's ICU cubicle. She did feel better physically. The shower helped. So did the coffee. He was sleeping peacefully now, or heavily sedated, she wasn't sure which. She just stood there and looked down at him, trying to figure out her next move. She had to find out more about this Thomas Landers guy and just why he was so focused on her. Black needed to tell her everything, or maybe she could find some kind of file he kept on this maniac in his private office. He mentioned the private detective, John Booker. Maybe Booker could tell her what was going on. She felt lost in the dark, groping blindly for answers.

The hours seemed to crawl by minute after minute, with Black neither speaking nor moving a muscle. Then that night around eight o'clock, Black regained consciousness. Claire was staring out the window at nothing when he stirred and mumbled her name. She went quickly to him and picked up his hand. He still didn't look so hot. In fact, he looked ashen and only half alive.

"I'm right here," she said, leaning down close where he could recognize her.

Black tried to focus his eyes on her. "You all right?"

Touched, she whispered, "I'm fine. You had us all worried, Black. How do you feel?"

He shut his eyes, and left them closed. "Like a Mack truck ran over me."

"I can believe that. Do you remember what happened?"

"Landers shot me."

"We don't know for sure that it was him."

"It was him," he said, then stated it again more forcefully. "It was him, Claire."

"Don't get excited, Black. You're not well yet."

His eyes found her face. "Stay here with me, Claire. I'm worried about you."

Claire had to laugh at that. "Hey, it's my turn to worry about you. You've been worrying about me way too long."

"Listen to me. You're in danger. Especially since you can't recognize him."

"I know that. I need to know exactly who or what I'm up against. If it's him, and I'm not at all sure it is, yet, then I need to know what he looks like."

"He tried to frame me, but when that didn't work, he decided to shoot me." Black groaned as he tried to shift position. "He wants me out of the picture. He was at your place, Claire. Right there close to us. He shot me because I showed up." He stopped again, as if tired, but then he said, "But he's after you, not me."

Black's voice was hoarse, his words halting, and she watched the numbers on his pulse and blood pressure monitor start to rise. She put her palm on his hot forehead and brushed back his thick black hair. He was fighting a temperature, all right. "Please, Black, just calm down. I'm not going anywhere until I'm sure you're okay. I promise."

"Promise me you won't be alone. I want Bud with you. Or Booker. I'll call Book and he can stay with you."

"Okay, okay, just calm down. You need to concentrate on getting well so we can get you home."

"You need to get me out of here. I wanna go home. Now."

Claire laughed at that one, too. "No way, Black. You're not going anywhere. Think like a doctor, Black. You've got a gunshot wound to the chest. You are in very serious condition."

Black shut his eyes, as if his strength had ebbed away. She stroked his hair some more and watched his pulse slowly return to normal. He dozed, but after a short time, he jerked awake again and lifted his head. He blearily found her at the side of the bed.

"Promise me you won't go back to your house. Stay at Cedar Bend until I get out of here."

His heart rate was increasing again, and the promise was easy for her. Hell, she was ready to promise him anything if he'd calm down. "Okay, I promise. The security at my house is no longer working, that's for sure. I'll stay at Cedar Bend at night when I'm not working with Bud. That satisfy you?"

"Oh, yeah, that satisfies me." He shut his eyes, the drugs taking him out of it again. Eyes still closed, he kept mumbling. "Get up here with me, Claire. . . ."

That request did make her laugh and think that maybe he was getting back to normal faster than they thought he would. She'd hate to think what Dr. Atwater would think if Claire did climb in bed with him. Then Black slept, and she did, too, on the very uncomfortable chair beside his bed. But maybe when he got home, when he was stronger, she could do what he wanted. Maybe that would make both of them feel better.

Chapter Twenty-one

When Claire was absolutely certain Black was well on his road to recovery, she returned with Bud to her house on the lake and found Charlie and a small herd of her fellow Canton County Sheriff's deputies combing her property for any trace evidence left by the shooter. They'd been turning over every leaf and branch for hours now. Others were inside her A-frame house, dusting for fingerprints that would positively ID this Landers guy, and which would prove, once and for all, that he was still alive and well and stalking her with deadly intent.

After donning protective gear, Claire walked inside her living room. She found Shaggy leaning over the kitchen counter, carefully dusting every inch of the sink and faucet for prints. He greeted her soberly for a change. He said, "The shooter was in here, all right. I've got his prints all over the place. And they look like a match to the one on the bullet casing we found down by the lake."

Ever heard of blood running cold? Well, that's what just happened to me. "He was in here? Inside my house?"

"Yep, and I'm willin' to bet he was probably already in here when you got home last night, hidin' somewhere. I found his print on the keypad of the security system, too. He knows your code. It's in perfect working condition. He had to've known it."

"Shit," said Bud. "You're lucky you're not dead or tied up in that deranged psychopath's lair somewhere."

Claire wracked her brain about the night Black had been shot. This crazy guy was in her house with her while she was undressing, getting ready for a bath? And she didn't suspect a thing? Despite her years in law enforcement, she didn't have a single clue, no sixth sense warning her that he was there, hiding and waiting to attack? Oh, God, she had disarmed herself, too, set her weapons aside. What would've happened if Black hadn't shown up when he had? Her jaw hardened.

"Did you find prints anywhere else, Shaggy?"

"Oh, yeah. On the stair railing. Upstairs in your bedroom. On the bedside table. On the bedroom windowsill. In the bathroom. He was all over the place and touchin' a lot of your stuff."

"Good God," Charlie said. "And you had no idea?"

"No. The deadlock was set when I got here. Security was on and working." At that point, Claire stopped abruptly and looked at Charlie. "Jules was here with me last night. He barks at everybody. Why didn't he bark and alert me?"

Bud said, "Jules's gotta know this guy, Claire. Who's been around your dog?"

Charlie's face was red as fire. "Well, that's just great. And that also means he's got access to you, and you don't even know it."

"But I've been spending most my time at Cedar Bend since I woke up. I've only been out here a few times. Black was usually with me. Joe McKay and his little girl were out here once to visit. But nobody else. Nobody that I can think of."

Bud quickly defended McKay. "Joe's not involved. He cares too much about you. It's got to be somebody over at Cedar Bend. Anybody act suspiciously when you were out there?"

"No. I didn't see all that many people there, either. Just Black, and Monica, and once in a while her boyfriend, Jesse. He walks Jules sometimes. Jules knows him. And he's a real weirdo."

"Sounds to me like he's the one."

"But he's crazy about Monica. He seemed so harmless." Claire realized that despite all that, the guy gave her the creeps. "But I don't trust him. We need to check him out."

"Well, I, for one, trust your instincts," Bud said.

"He always tried to be nice enough, but he just acts so bizarre. Monica really liked him."

Charlie said, "What's he look like?"

"About my height, maybe a couple of inches taller. Slim, athletic, white guy. Brown hair, brown eyes, close-cut beard and mustache. I don't know. Just regular looking. He was out at Jeepers with us the other night. As far as anybody else that Jules was used to, I'd say Miki Tudor, Black's assistant, came into the apartment once in a while to bring Black papers to sign, stuff like that, but not very often. There were maids in and out; sometimes room service waiters came up. I can't think of anybody else. Unless Monica gave Jules to other people to walk, and I didn't know about it."

"Well, somebody knows that mutt, and I think this Jesse guy sounds like the most likely," said Charlie. "So I want him checked out. If it's not him, maybe he knows who else handled the dog. Have you gotten hold of him yet, Bud?"

"No, sir. He hasn't picked up. I got the number off Monica Wheeler's cell and left four messages on his voice mail. Said it was extremely urgent for him to get in touch with us."

"Then find out where he lives and go by his place and pick him up. He's involved with our victim and he's worked with Claire's dog. Bring him downtown. I want to question him myself."

"Yes, sir."

"And, Claire, go upstairs and pack your bags. This place is a crime scene. You can stay at Cedar Bend, can't you? You got a problem with that?"

"No. Black wants me to stay out there until he gets out of the hospital."

Charlie nodded. "Good. I hear he's doing a lot better today, thank God. I put in a call myself to Dr. Atwater."

"He's awake enough to badger them about going home. Says he's fully capable of doctoring himself now."

Bud grinned. "Sounds like Nick. But he's hardly in walkin' around shape yet."

"They can't stop him, unfortunately. He's willing to go home by ambulance and says he'll get a private nurse, if he thinks he needs one."

For a good part of that afternoon, Claire stuck around and helped the forensics team check out her house, which she had only just gotten used to and now had the good sense to get the hell out of. She did grab some clothes, most of them, actually, but the thought of some deranged serial killer going through them, touching them and doing God knows what else with them, made her want to run everything through a hot water wash cycle before she ever put them against her skin again.

Around five o'clock, she made sure Buck's team was finished processing her Explorer, and then she got in and backed it out of the driveway. One of the technicians restrung the crime tape after her. People were still going over everything they could find on her property as she drove away. She stopped at Harve's and briefly filled him in on how things were going, and he promised to up his security measures. When she left him, he had his own .45 out and loaded and in his shoulder holster, just in case any deadly psychos came calling. She didn't ask him about his dealings with Thomas Landers, and he didn't volunteer any details. He said he'd know the devil if he ever saw him again. After that, she got the feeling he didn't want to talk about it.

Claire turned out on the highway and headed back to the hospital, where she didn't really expect to find Black. He was probably already gone, whisked away to Cedar Bend Lodge in his own personal and awesome Bell 430 helicopter. Surprisingly, however, he was still there, but had been moved out of the ICU and into their largest private suite. The nurses she talked to added that he was still complaining and bound and determined to go home. She smiled at that, but was eager to see him again.

His door stood slightly ajar, and when Claire pushed it open, Black was propped up in bed, still hooked to all kinds of blinking monitors and tubes. A tall man wearing a camouflage T-shirt and utility pants was standing on the far side of the bed. They were talking together in low tones until Black caught sight of Claire standing in the doorway.

"Claire. Come on in. We want to talk to you."

We? she thought. She moved over to the bed, more than curious about the other guy. "How're you feeling, Black?"

Black picked up her hand and entwined his fingers with hers. "Not good, but not too bad, considering a serial killer shot me."

"I'm glad you're still here at the hospital. Surprised, but glad. You don't need to go anywhere for a few more days."

"I'm doing okay. I'm a doctor; I happen to know exactly how to take care of myself."

"Good, then you won't do anything stupid, will you?" Claire glanced pointedly at Camo Man, who chuckled at her observation, and then wondered why Black hadn't introduced them. He was usually pretty good at being polite and remembering that she didn't remember anything

"And you are?" she finally said, taking the bull by the horns, not shy about introducing herself. She didn't like not knowing by name and reputation who was loitering around Black, since somebody just tried their best to murder him.

The big guy only grinned. He was broad-shouldered and muscular, nice looking in a rugged, outdoorsy, red-flannel-lumberjack kind of way, with close-cropped dark hair, and eyes a slightly darker blue than Black's. He looked like a tough guy, like he knew how to take care of himself and anybody else who made the mistake of getting in his way.

"This is John Booker. My private investigator. I told you about him."

"How do you do," Claire said, polite but suspicious, too. Why? She wasn't quite sure. Just something about him irked her.

John Booker grinned some more, an expression that seemed amused at her expense. What was with this guy?"

"Oh, you know me, Detective Morgan. You don't like me much, either."

Oh, really? "Why don't you tell me why, Booker?"

Black interrupted quickly. "Don't get defensive, Claire. I had him investigate you once. You didn't like it."

Oh, really? "Well, I don't like it now, either."

"Don't worry. You forgave both of us a long time ago."

Claire tried to remember hating the guy, and couldn't, of course. Damn, if she didn't remember everything soon, she was going to give up and start over. New friends, new memories, nothing she had to have to pick and shovel out of her head. Like watching Black get knocked clean off his feet by a rifle blast. She decided to let it drop. The past was the past. Whatever it was.

She turned back to Black. "We found blood in the woods behind my house. I wounded the guy who shot you."

"Well, good for you. Now we can check out his DNA against Thomas Landers's hospital records. They've got a sample at the hospital where we locked him up."

"We got the shooter's fingerprints off the bullet casing. And all over the inside my house, too."

That got Black's attention, all right. "He was inside your house?"

"They have fingerprints. They might be yours, but we're going to check them against the bullet."

"Okay, that'll double the proof. Unless Landers burned his own prints off with a Bic lighter, or something. I wouldn't put it past him."

Well, that was disconcerting, she did have to say. "So you still think it was him?"

"I know it was, and I'm going to prove it to you. I've got Book on it, already."

That was Booker's cue to tell her his role in all this, she supposed. He looked straight at her, eyes unwavering serious. "I've been down on the Finley River checking out where you went off that bridge. His body was never found, but I'm hiking down along the bank looking for places where he could've gotten out. Maybe the Ozark P.D. missed something. They were looking for a dead body. I'm not. I headed back up here as soon as I found out Nick got hit."

"Charlie says they were pretty thorough with that search. He and Bud were both down there helping out, part-time."

Black said, "Not thorough enough, apparently. Booker will be."

He was convinced, all right, and nothing was going to change his mind. However, Claire had to admit things were pointing in that direction. "We've got to consider all possibilities, Black. You know that. So you tell me. Is there anybody else who might want to come after you? Who might want you dead?"

Black didn't answer, his eyes slid down and to the right, and oh, yes, he looked evasive as hell. And she also caught how the two men exchanged a brief but significant glance. What the hell? He was hiding something from her. Now that caught her off guard. "You're not telling me something. What the hell's going on, Black? And don't lie to me."

"Nothing."

"That is absolute bullshit. Give me some credit here."

Black really looked like he wanted to squirm himself under his bed about now. Guilty, even, oh, yes-siree.

"C'mon, Black, I'm not an idiot. Don't play me. I may not remember everything yet, but I remember how to tell if somebody's lying to me."

Booker now appeared as if he wanted to get the hell out of Dodge, too. He just stood there and looked tough as nails. He obviously didn't have a dog in this fight. But he knew the dog, you can bet on that.

Black looked everywhere but at Claire for a while. Gathering his thoughts, huh? Then he did look at her for a long moment. It finally came out, but reluctantly.

"I can't tell you, Claire. So let's just drop it."

"Oh, yeah, right. Like hell I'm going to just drop it. You and Booker here have a big secret concerning somebody trying to kill you. Somehow that piques my interest. Especially since somebody came after you, or me, or us both, with a high-powered rifle that almost put you out of commission for good. So go ahead, Black. Tell me how holding back pertinent information from my police investigation makes sense."

Black listened, looking guilty as hell. Instead of answering her, he turned to Booker. "Keep me posted, man, okay? If you turn up anything, let me know. I'll probably be back at Cedar Bend by tomorrow."

"Oh, no, you won't," said the sturdy, rather matronly-looking nurse just entering the room. "Dr. Atwater said you will be here for several more days, at the very least."

Booker nodded at Claire and gratefully headed for the hills in a rush. Black was no doubt getting his rational explanation in order, or formulating a serious pack of lies, while the nurse took his blood pressure, checked his bandages, clucked around a bit about lying still and not getting worked up by all these visitors, and doctors should full well know that.

When she left the room, Black squeezed Claire's hand again and tried for a pitiful look. It was hard for a big virile man like him to look very pitiful, and he failed miserably, especially now that he had his color and self-confident, bossy manner back. She'd never seen him look pitiful. Even nursing a recent gunshot wound, he looked vital and in charge. "Claire, I can't tell you anything, other than it deals with my military past. That's all. If it's not Thomas Landers wanting to get me out of the picture, then Booker and I will handle our own private investigation about the shooter. It's highly confidential, that's all I can tell you."

"Did I know about any of this before the crash?"

Black did actually squirm this time. She bet he hadn't done that since he was five years old. "It never came up."

"Yeah, I'll bet it didn't."

Claire questioned him further, trying all her police interrogation tricks, short of pulling off his fingernails with pliers. Unfortunately, Black seemed to know all the same techniques. He must've been an ace interrogator in the service. Whatever he was, or had been, she wanted to know the details. Especially if he had some old but newly motivated and seriously armed enemies out gunning for him.

"It's Thomas that you should be thinking about." He stopped, and looked annoyed, which probably did mean he was feeling better. "For God's sake, Claire, trust me, for once. I know it's him. I've dealt with him before. But I guess you're not going to believe me until we get verification from forensics."

"That's usually the way police officers do it. Tell me more about this Landers lunatic."

"He's the typical obsessed stalker. Except he's totally and completely psychotic. On top of that, he's a homicidal maniac who kills at random whenever it occurs to him. No empathy for others, no remorse, no guilt. He almost killed you and Harve and spent some enjoyable moments torturing me with a stun gun."

Well, Black certainly knew how to lay it on the line. No sugar-coating nothin', unh-uh. Claire could only stare at him, envisioning Hannibal Lecter and others of his ilk.

But Black wasn't finished with his horror story and continued relentlessly. "I've been trying to protect you from the nightmare this guy put you through. I don't think you're ready yet, but I can't keep you in the dark anymore. You've got to know what he is and what he's done to you. You are his whole focus in life. I think when he was in the asylum, he planned all this out. How to get you under his control when he got out. That's his life's passion. For God's sake, Claire, this guy cut your name on his chest with a used syringe needle, one that a nurse accidentally dropped on the floor. He carved it in a fellow patient's chest, too, a guy named Bones Fitch, who's a psychopathic killer in his own right. All of this is noted in his medical file. You can read it yourself, if you don't believe me."

Okay, you betcha, one serious, long-lasting, flesh-crawling, chill-producing shudder inched up my spine at that little tidbit of nutty as a fruitcake, she thought. "If you're trying to scare me, you just hit the jackpot."

"I'm trying to make you understand what we're dealing with. When I get back home, I'm going to get out my files and show you some pictures of him and then some photos of his handiwork."

"Gee, I can't wait."

"You better get serious about this, Claire, and fast."

"Okay, I get it. This guy is a freak and he loves me."

"Don't be cavalier, Claire. He's deadly."

"Okay, you're right. I am serious. I'm not taking this lightly, I assure you. You've got my attention. But I'm armed and dangerous, too. I hit the guy in the dark from thirty or forty feet. Next time I'll put him down."

"That's what you said last time."

His words hit home, and she knew she needed to be very, very careful until they got him. "So you have a picture of him?"

"Oh, yeah. Several. All disguised as different people. He's like a chameleon. He is equally adept at presenting himself as male or female, if you can believe that."

"You already told me that. It's hard to believe."

"Everything about him is hard to believe. I won't rest until he's behind bars again, or better yet, dead, a bullet inside his defective brain."

All righty, now, Black was deathly serious, and Claire better be, too, if she wanted to survive this horrific ordeal. First off, though,

Black had to get well, and she had to be extremely cautious, everywhere, all the time, 24/7. Maybe she'd spend the night in the chair beside his bed again, with a loaded Glock on her lap and a finger resting on the trigger. Maybe that would make them both breathe easier. And tomorrow, armed and ready for trouble, she'd interview the staff at Cedar Bend and see if this Thomas Landers guy had worked his disguise magic on them. Most likely that would be in the guise of one Weird Jesse, she had begun to believe. At first, she had doubted that big-time, but stranger things had happened. Usually to her, as it turned out.

Jesse's Girl

Right now

After a flood of misery and tears, Jesse decided to forgive Annie for shooting him. At first, when his arm hurt so badly that he had to put his head on the pillow next to Miss Rosie so she could comfort him, he vowed to cut off Annie's head and dispose of her betraying body. She had shared herself in bed with that devil, Nicholas Black, anyway. If he killed her, she couldn't ever pick up a gun and shoot him again, now could she?

But then, after several good nights' sleep, he stopped feeling angry and began to miss her. Maybe she didn't even know that he was the one shooting at them. He thought again that she must've thought she was in danger, too, and had to return his fire. Poor Annie. Something bad was always happening to her. She was bound to be a little paranoid, and whatnot.

Black was dead, that was the most important thing. He would not be around to steal her away and wine and dine her and spend tons of his money on her. Yes, he was out of the picture now, dead as a doornail. Jesse was pretty sure he'd hit Black true to aim, probably straight through the heart. At least, that's what he was hoping. So now, it was time to go into phase two. Of course, he'd have to devise a new plan to get Annie under his power. Sometimes she didn't realize how much she wanted to be with him. But he really wasn't too worried about that.

At the moment, his major problem was finding Annie a brand-new little toddler to love on. She missed the little boy that died—Zach. She had never gotten over that. Now that Black was dead and unable to steal her away from Jesse, he would just have to get her a new kid. A pretty, little blond-haired boy that she could love, and that they could raise together as their own special love child. They'd name him Zach, too, and Miss Rosie could be his grandmother. It would all be so wonderful, to have a family again, all together, traveling around the country.

As soon as Jesse's arm felt better and his fever was down, he took Miss Rosie's car and headed out to the grocery store. He retrieved a current newspaper out of a sidewalk stand and skimmed the front page for Nicholas Black's obituary. When he didn't find it, he began to worry and drove at once to Cedar Bend Lodge. Nobody tried to stop him. He still had his staff credentials to show around. It was a risk, but one he had to take.

While he was nosing around on the grounds, his St. Louis Cardinals cap pulled down low on his forehead, his big black sunglasses hiding his eyes, he sat down at a table that overlooked the largest pool and drank a Diet Coke. When he heard the low thunder of rotors in the distance, he picked up the binoculars hanging around his neck and focused them on the Cedar Bend helicopter that was sweeping in over the lake. He watched it bank gracefully and then set down out on the point where Nicholas Black had his private helipad. It was pretty far away, so he stood up and walked to a stacked stone wall and watched them through the binoculars as they unloaded a gurney. Damn it, Black had survived. And there was Annie, getting off behind the nurses and other medical personnel.

Cursing, he clenched his fists until his nails bit into his palms. Now he would have to think of another way to kill Black. Unless the frame-up worked and they put him in jail, Black was still around and causing him grief. But it was Annie that he kept his eyes on, his heart trembling with joy and the longing to hold her in his arms, lick her troubles away, and make her his own special friend.

But then he saw the big guy he had met at Jeepers, the one named Joe McKay. His Annie stopped when Joe and the little girl with him walked up to her. The child ran up and put her arms around Annie's knees. Annie quickly picked up the child and hugged her close. Joe McKay stood by, but he wasn't smiling. He was looking after the gurney, and then he was talking to Annie seriously, probably wanting to know Black's condition. What a happy coincidence. Just when he was looking for a new little kid for Annie, he found one that she already liked a lot and who liked her, too. It was perfect. He could just follow Joe and steal the little girl away at the first good opportunity. Once he had her, Annie would probably come to him on her own accord.

God was with him. God wanted them to be together, all three of them, all a big happy family. He smiled, now that things were working out so admirably, and trailed Joe McKay and his and Annie's future child out to the parking lot.

Chapter Twenty-two

As it turned out, Black did have enough sense to stay in the hospital a bit longer. Right off the bat, however, he was back at work, conducting conference calls to his clinics in Europe from his hospital bed and getting around fairly well on his own. His pain was fairly controlled, but he remained weak. Several days later, he was released and Claire boarded the Bell 430 with him and flew home. Joe and Lizzie happened to be there, swimming in Black's private gated pool, and she spoke briefly with them while Black was whisked upstairs on a gurney, much to his dismay. The guy thought he was Superman, no doubt about it.

After explaining all that had happened, Claire bid Joe and Lizzie good-bye and hurried after Black's little medical entourage. Joe and his daughter wanted to come up and say hello to Black, but she quickly explained the situation and told Joe he should let Black get settled and come back in a few days. Black was weaker than he would admit, and the move out of the Canton County Medical Center had been directly against Dr. Atwater's orders. She had wanted him to stay a full week. Black could be stubborn, oh, yes, he could. Claire was finding that out the hard way.

Upstairs, he was already in the hospital bed Claire had just vacated a short time ago, and she decided that they better leave it in place for a while, at the rate the two of them were ending up hurt and/or wounded. It was a good thing Black was a doctor, but he wasn't in the best shape, either. She just hoped he had plenty of painkillers and antibiotics in his personal medicine chest.

In the penthouse hallway, she passed the hospital ambulance team on their way out. One of the nurses waved as they entered the elevator. "Good luck, detective. You're gonna need it. He's one of the worst patients I've ever had to deal with."

But they all laughed, and so did Claire, because it was oh, so true. He was not as patient with himself as he had been with her. But she owed the guy. He treated her like royalty when she was drifting around in those soft ephemeral clouds of nowhere land in that self-same hospital bed. She walked into the guest bedroom/triage center, and Black was already sitting up on the edge of the bed. "I was just about to come looking for you."

"Lie down, Black, relax. I'm right here, at your beck and call."

"I wish that were true." But he did lie back, and by his grimace, she knew his shoulder was not showing him a grand old time.

"Are you in pain?"

"A little."

"Well, you won't be for long. They gave you a shot of morphine before they moved you."

"Yeah, and I told them not to do that, damn it."

"You need to sleep a lot, regain your strength. It'll be better here in your own digs. You'll be able to order your staff around and make them wait on you hand and foot."

"You're staying here, too."

That was not a request. "Black, you are downright grouchy. You know you can't tell me what to do."

His frown was massive, and she watched his pulse rate shoot up. "You're going to get yourself killed, Claire."

"No, I am not. I am going to do my job, just like I do every day. With Bud. And you are going to go to sleep and sleep most of the afternoon. I'll be back later and feed you dinner. Then we can discuss your theory about what's going on. I will listen to every word you say and if I think you're on the right track, we'll go from there. Fair enough?"

"Hell, no."

Actually, he looked like he was getting ready to sulk, certainly not used to this kind of helpless acquiescence, but then he held out his hand to her. She took it and squeezed his fingers. "Just do what you should, Black. Give yourself time to heal. Stay cool. Quit worrying so much."

"I can't help it. You're in danger. And I can't protect you."

"I'm armed. Bud's armed. We will be extra cautious, just for you."

"Where are you going today?"

"We're going down to check out the rest of Miriam Long's listings here at the lake. Her husband says a murder was committed in one of them and that spooked Miriam. Her partner up here, Kay Kramer, doesn't know anything about it. So we're going to have to go down to Springfield and get a key from her previous employer so we can investigate the place. But we'll probably check out the ones here at the lake first. If Landers is holed up inside one of them, we'll find him. Or Jesse, either, as far as that goes."

"Was it one of your cases, this murder the husband's talking about?"

"We don't know yet. We've investigated some on the lake, but we can't think which one it could be. Most of them are listed right here with lake Realtors. It was probably a different jurisdiction."

"Check out the one where Landers held you and Harve captive. It's got to be that one."

"Yeah, we've already decided to go out there. Bud thinks it's the logical place to start, too. But Landers might be too cautious to return to the scene of one of his crimes."

Black nodded. "Promise me you'll be careful if you go there, and take along backup."

"Sure, we do know our jobs, Black. Now cut the chatter and go to sleep."

He did, of course. That hefty a dose of a powerful opiate will do that to a man. Once he was out and resting comfortably, with his newly hired, elderly RN named Violet Kelly sitting beside the bed, Claire waved good-bye to her and tiptoed out of the room. She was not exactly coveting the poor woman's job when he woke up and started trying to take a jog, or something worse. Violet might even have to get out those bed restraints that he used on Claire. But then again, he did have some legitimate and deadly issues to worry about. So did everybody else involved in this case.

Claire took a quick shower in the master bedroom, fixed herself a cup of coffee in the penthouse's fabulous, black granite and stainless-steel kitchen, and waited impatiently for Bud to call and tell her he was downstairs. Sitting on one of the high mahogany and black leather bar stools in the quiet depths of the penthouse, she decided to check out the staff's human resource records. Jesse's involvement was still troubling her. Not to mention his peculiarity. And she wanted to find another address for him so she and Bud could pay him a visit. The one on Monica's laptop hadn't panned out as legitimate. She wanted to check out every single detail of his life, in fact. She wondered if Jesse could possibly be Thomas Landers, so well-disguised and clever that he could fool everybody. Word was that Landers was prone to do such things, and as far as she knew, nobody who had seen him in his other incarnations had laid eyes on him as Jesse. He could very well have been under their noses the entire time. It seemed too far-fetched and incredible, but she was finding nothing in her life was above being far-fetched and incredible.

Peeking in on Black on her way out, she found him sleeping peacefully, Violet reading a Beverly Barton romance novel on her Kindle in the darkened room. His wound was clean and would heal quickly, thank God. He would be okay. That was one concern she could cross off her list of My Ten Most Horrible Things. She was very curious about this Thomas Landers guy, but on the other hand, she was wary as hell to know everything about him. He sounded like he belonged in her nightmares, not in her daily life. He probably had been one of those monsters, but she didn't recognize him. Jesse's face hadn't shown up in her bad dreams, not that she could remember.

Downstairs, she stepped out of the elevator, nodded at the security guard named Isaac, or The Big I, as she liked to think of him. Maybe because he was about six feet, eight inches tall with shoulders almost as wide. He had to have played pro basketball somewhere. She entered the wide lobby resplendent with its black-and-gold, oak-leaf-patterned carpet, shining crystal chandeliers, and beveled, stained-glass front doors. Cedar Bend Lodge was quite the luxury resort, to be sure. She headed across the room to the back hall leading to the business offices. Halfway there, she saw Nancy Gill.

"Hey, Nancy. What are you doing here? Thought you were headed home."

"Yeah, I was, until all that happened with Monica. Isn't it terrible about what happened to her? How's Nick? Is he going to be all right?"

Claire nodded. "He's doing better now. It's going to be a while before he's a hundred percent."

"I just can't believe Monica's gone. I'm glad I didn't have to work that crime scene, but I thought I oughta stick around for the funeral. Nobody's seen or heard from Jesse. Have you seen him?"

"No, I haven't, but I'm gonna find him." Claire didn't tell her that they had a BOLO out on him. His sudden disappearance pointed a damning finger at him. "Tell me, Nancy, how much do you know about Jesse?"

"Not much."

"His last name's Jordan, right?"

"Yeah. Monica didn't seem to know a lot about his past, either, at least not that she told me. She did say that he didn't have many relatives and that he was from somewhere down in the boot-heel part of Missouri, I think she said that. Why all the questions? Is he a suspect?"

"We're checking out everybody she knew and spent time with."

"Well, I was packing up my stuff down at the M.E.'s office, so don't look at me. I don't even know much about Monica's background. She was Nick's friend, first and foremost. I do know she thought the world of Nick."

"Yeah, that's true. I'm on my way to go through Jesse's employment records right now."

"How about we go to the funeral together? The funeral home says some relatives over in Creve Coeur want to hold a memorial service at the First Methodist Church. That's in St. Louis."

"I don't know yet. Depends on how the investigation goes. Has Buck released the body?"

"No. Sheriff Ramsay wants him to hold off on that for a while."

"Good. Gotta go, Nancy. Bud's picking me up in a little bit."

"Okay, see you later. Hey, don't forget. I'd love to get you on that exchange program down my way in N'Orleans. Think about it."

Claire nodded and bid Nancy good-bye. Moments later, she had no trouble getting access to the Human Resource records. Everybody on the premises seemed to know that she had a thing with the C.E.O., except for her. A quick glance through Jesse Jordan's employment file didn't tell her anything she didn't already know. Jesse had listed a P.O. box in downtown Camdenton, but Claire had a feeling it was as phony as the address he'd given to Monica. But they'd check it out.

By the time Claire returned to the busy lobby, Bud was standing there, finding time to flirt with Nancy. The three of them chatted about Jesse for a few more minutes, and then Bud and Claire took off. First thing they did was drive out to the house where Thomas Landers had apparently held Claire and Harve hostage once upon a time. She stared at the two-story farmhouse, but got no frightening visitations of being held there or what went down. Her mind was still being recalcitrant. Weapons drawn, since they weren't stupid and Landers was a seriously deranged serial killer, they checked out the locks on the doors and the windows, but nothing seemed amiss or suspicious. No cars in the detached barn. No sign of life anywhere. No boat belonging to Miriam Long tied up down at the rickety dock below the house, nothing out of the ordinary. The place was deserted. That didn't mean they couldn't get a key from the real estate guy and/or a warrant and check out the inside, which they would get Charlie to request from a judge ASAP.

For the rest of the day, Claire and Bud spent time going down the list of Kramer-Long clients with no luck whatsoever. All the properties seemed to be owned by regular folks who seemed totally innocent. The empty properties looked undisturbed. No broken windows, no jimmied doors or reports of suspicious activities by the neighbors. All in all, the day was pretty much a bust.

They arrived back at Cedar Bend just before seven o'clock that evening. Black called once and reported that he was awake and up and getting around. She told him to get back in bed and go to sleep and quit giving RN Violet grief. He didn't seem to think that was a good idea.

When Bud let Claire out at Black's private entrance, she walked inside, greeted warmly by The Big I, who was sitting in a chair beside the closed doors of Black's penthouse elevator. Black was being careful. While she was waiting, the Two Cedars chef came out through the restaurant's cut-glass doors pushing a food cart with quite a few dishes covered with the kitchen's curlicued, CBL-engraved chrome warming domes. Her name was Retta Dolman, and could she ever cook. She smiled when she saw Claire waiting at the elevator.

"Don't tell me," Claire said to her. "Black's out of bed and hungry."

"He's hungry. I don't know about the other part."

"He's not being a good patient, which is not surprising. He's supposed to eat gruel and drink tea."

"Well, he's ordered a T-bone steak, rare, and the biggest baked potato we had, and several ears of corn on the cob. All your favorites, too. Coconut shrimp, cherry cheesecake, not to mention another bag of those bite-size Snickers bars. I don't see how you stay so thin, eating all that candy we send up."

Claire laughed at that idea. "Don't kid yourself. I'm not the only one eating them. Besides, he's probably just trying to bribe me not to make him do what Dr. Atwater ordered."

"She fussed at him today, too, at least that's the rumor, because he's already back at work. His patients are being taken upstairs to him."

"Fine with me. As long as he takes it easy. We're just damn lucky he's doing as well as he is."

They rode up together, and it didn't take Claire's stomach long to react to the delicious culinary aromas seeping out from underneath the domes on Retta's cart.

Black was not in his hospital bed but stretched out on a long, roomy, black leather couch facing the wall of windows in his living room. He had a pile of tab folders beside him, and he had more color in his face than when she'd left. He was like Claire; working had a positive influence. He had on a pair of pajamas under a black silk robe and a smile, instead of the striped green hospital gown and a great big frown. The new hovering nurse was gone, baby, gone. So Claire walked inside, bracing herself for the brunt of Black's cooped-up, bad-patient crankiness.

Chapter Twenty-three

When Nick saw Claire enter the room, he breathed a quick internal sigh of relief. However, that didn't stop him from showing her his annoyance. "Well, now, it's about time you showed up. I think you enjoy stressing me out."

Claire showed her surprise. "Well, hello to you, too, your lordship. And what the hell are you talking about? I called you not an hour ago and told you I'd be a little late."

"It's after seven o'clock."

Claire wasn't one to put up with anybody's bad mood, so her response didn't surprise him. "I'm going to freshen up and let you calm down. See you later, Retta."

Black certainly didn't want to fight with Claire, not now that she was beginning to believe they were actually in a committed relationship. On the other hand, he was damn annoyed that she worked all day long instead of the agreed-upon hours and was going about her job as if nothing had happened. Landers was out there, just waiting for his chance to jump her, and Claire didn't seem to take it seriously. Watching Retta lay out two place settings of Two Cedars china and crystal on the table in front of him and unload all his favorite foods, he took a deep, bracing breath. He was still so angry inside. Angry that that bastard had shot him, put him down, for God's sake. He should have figured out it was Landers from the beginning. He should have known better when they didn't find the body. It could have been worse. Landers could've gotten Claire again. God help him, the idea of her being alone with that psychopath terrified him.

As Retta lifted the lids and asked him if he needed anything else, he shook his head and thanked her. Claire was not back yet. Probably giving him time to reconsider his mood. It worked. The anger was gone, but fear for her had taken its place. When she finally returned, he decided to drop the subject, at least for the moment.

"I ordered all your favorites," he told her.

"So Retta said. Thanks."

"Hope you're hungry."

"I am starving. But I've got a surprise for you. One I think you'll like."

Black studied her. She was smiling, so it had to be good. Well, that was a change for the better. Nothing had been good for a while. He voiced his fondest wish. "Please tell me you found Landers with a bullet hole in his head."

"No, not that. Sorry, we tried. He isn't cooperating."

Okay, Claire was going for a good mood. Obviously trying to cheer him up and since he couldn't tie her to a chair so she wouldn't put herself in danger, he decided not to spoil her surprise. "Well, hit me with it. I could use some good news."

Claire sat down beside him. "I remembered something about you today."

Now that was good news. Maybe his stint in the hospital triggered her memory. Suddenly, he was hopeful. He turned quickly, but the sudden movement sent a sharp pain slicing into his shoulder. He fingered his bound wound and adjusted the black sling he had to wear, angry all over again that Landers had got him. "What? Tell me?"

Claire laughed. It was good she could; he had missed hearing her laugh and acting happy.

"Well now, Black, it's pretty sexy and concerns the two of us, but that's all I'm going to say."

"No, that's not all you're going to say."

"Okay, we went swimming one night, right, and ended up getting pretty damn friendly."

Now that sounded like a memory worth reliving. And he remembered it only too well. Every night alone in his bed, he remembered it. "Which time?"

Claire laughed. "How many times were there?"

"Lots, you can trust me on that."

Now she was suddenly serious. Her eyes, so large and blue and wary and street smart, they were holding his gaze and he couldn't look away, didn't want to. "I remember kissing you, hard and long and pretty breathlessly, too. I remember how things got pretty hot and heavy between us. You know what, Black? Like I told you before, I think I'd like for something like that to happen again."

Pure relief shot through him, sharp, relieved, and thankful. He reached out with his good arm and pulled her close. She didn't resist and came into his arms, her head against his shoulder. "So you believe me now? You believe we're in love?"

"I think so," she murmured. "Okay, yeah, I guess we are."

This time Claire let him kiss her for as long as he wanted, and he groaned most of the way through it, more from desire than pain. Claire did some moaning herself but finally pulled away.

"Well, now, I must say, shot up or not, you do know how to kiss a woman."

Black felt alive for the first time since he pulled her out of the flooded river, but she got up and walked over to the windows. "Okay, Black, let's get real here, you're gonna hurt yourself. I thought you were hungry."

Frustrated as hell, he leaned back against the cushions and stared at her. "You just do not know."

"Well, get over it, already, you're gonna start bleeding again."

"So?"

"Just keep that thought going. We'll have all the time in the world after you heal up."

Not looking exactly unaffected, either, Claire sat down on the chair across from him, and he couldn't take his eyes off her. She had no idea how she affected him. Or maybe she did. He'd shown her enough times. But she was right. His wound ached down deep, and felt like pins pricking him around the edges of it. He massaged his shoulder some more, vowing he'd get Landers, if it was the last thing he ever did.

"You can sit beside me, Claire. I'm not going to jump you."

"You've done it before."

"I'm a wounded man now."

Claire smiled. "You're just not ready for me yet."

"But you are saying you're ready for me?"

"Truth? I didn't need a memory of skinny-dipping to know I was ready for you."

Now that sounded more like it. He was inordinately pleased, which made the rest of it bearable. "Just come back over here. I'm stronger than you think."

"No way. I've got a killer to catch. You want him, too."

Black sobered instantly. She was right. "Tell me about this case. Everything. Let me help you. Give me something to live for, sitting around alone all day."

"Don't give me that. I know you saw patients today."

As Claire fixed both of them plates piled high with mouthwatering food, she told him about Miriam's husband and all the dead ends they'd run into. He listened intently and took a drink of the Dixie Beer he'd ordered up earlier that day. Right after breakfast, actually. He had needed a drink then. He needed a drink now. Maybe a shot or two of Chivas, if he wanted to get through another night with a throbbing bullet wound, not to mention Claire being so close but untouchable.

"And you found no sign of him out at the house where he held you captive? You're sure."

"No. It looked deserted."

"Did you go inside?"

"No probable cause. You know that as well as I do. We can't just break in without a warrant."

"Booker could."

"Yeah? And then I'd just have to arrest him for breaking and entering, wouldn't I?"

Black still thought it might be worth the risk. He had to call Booker later anyway. "Well, you and Bud need to get inside. This guy isn't going to leave clues outside for the police to find. But once you go inside, you'll know if he's been there recently. For God's sake, get a warrant."

"You think we haven't thought of that? It'll be sticky, though, but it might happen. The circumstances are unusual, and Charlie wants this guy as much as you do."

"Make up something. Just do it, Claire. Tell Charlie you have to go inside."

Black felt his pulse going up, and knew it wasn't a good thing. He was so completely engulfed in anger, it wasn't exactly easy to get a grip on.

Obviously noting his gritted teeth, Claire decided to change the subject. "What about you? Heard from Booker yet?"

"Not yet. He's been down in Ozark. He's looking around the crime scene at the bridge and now he's ready to contact the Ozark police and get clearance to look into the case."

"Does he have to do that?"

"No, but I don't want him to have a run-in with the local cops down there. This is too important."

Black tried not to, but he couldn't help looking at her lips every time she took a bite. Then she chose that moment to lick a crumb off the corner of her mouth. He felt the reaction in his loins. Good God, how long did this have to go on? He had about had it. There was only so much a man could take, for God's sake. He decided to share his feelings. "I can't believe you waited until I was shot up and helpless before you remembered that thing in the water. That's just cruel."

"You're hardly helpless, but I do agree you're in no shape to make love to me."

Black laid his head back on the sofa cushions and groaned. "This is so unfair."

"Just eat. Think about something else. We can progress slowly and romantically. I still don't recall everything about you, you know—if we dated, how it all happened, just that we liked each other a lot. Definitely a lot. Just look at it this way. At least you're not in a coma, Black. That's a plus."

"Yes, that's true. It could be worse, but not much."

They shared a laugh, and then they dug into the food. Claire ate more heartily this time than Black did, but he didn't exactly starve himself. He was finally getting something substantial inside his stomach and that improved his mood considerably. Under the circumstances and as a doctor himself, his prognosis was good. He was determined to get back on his feet, no matter what it took. Claire was out in the cold by herself. That was not going to last long. When Claire took the tray into the kitchen, Black got up and walked around, trying to ignore the pain. The sooner he got all his strength back, the better.

"I was just thinking that we should go on to bed," he said to Claire the minute she got back. "I'm suddenly very tired."

"Yeah, right. No way. You're too weak, whether you admit it, or not. We'll save some of the fun stuff for when you're not bleeding all over the sheets."

"Killjoy."

"If you're good and behave yourself, maybe I'll sleep in the chair beside your bed again."

"Oh, you will do that, trust me."

"You sound very close to lascivious. Look at you, you're practically drooling."

"I'm lascivious and drooling both, believe me. You've been pushing me away for days now. I'm dying. I really am."

Claire got serious, and he kissed any remaining hopes away. "No, you're not dying. And I am so glad about that. If that bullet had been a few inches lower, you would be dead right now."

"You're the one who's in danger. Stay here with me so you'll be safe."

"I am here."

"I mean all the time."

"There's a killer out there. He's struck twice, almost got you, and he'll strike again."

"The rest of us are just means to his end. You are the end, Claire."

"Sit down, Black, take it easy. Getting all riled up is not going to help you get well. I shouldn't've told you that I remembered. I was trying to cheer you up."

"I am cheered up. Just frustrated as hell. And you're not listening to me. You're too stubborn for your own good."

"Okay, I can't say I like what you just said, but since you have that big bullet hole through your shoulder, I'm gonna let it ride. Let's just get down to brass tacks here. Fill me in on this guy, Thomas Landers. Prepare me for what he might do. Give me his M.O."

Sighing, Black gave up. "His M.O. is crazy, murderous, vile, inhuman behavior, all the time, every time."

Claire looked angry, too. He couldn't blame her, and maybe it was the best thing that could happen to her. "I don't like the sound of that, okay, but I don't like the sound of anything since I woke up from that damn coma. Everything I've seen since I came back is all about life and death and blood and gore." She paused, took a deep breath, and tried to calm herself. "I don't like hearing about some psycho hatchet murderer who's coming after me, but I have to. Truth, Black? Hell, I'd much rather snuggle up with you in your big bed with all those black silk sheets you've got in there, just the way you want me to. But that can't happen right now, and so be it. So get it out of your mind, and hit me with the worst you've got and let's get it over with."

Black stared up at Claire. She was right, of course. Sex should be the last thing on his mind right now. She was ready to face her demons, and thank God for it. He was finally getting through to her. "Sit down, Claire. You're going to need to. Believe me when I say this. I do not want to go into all this with you. I dread it, too, but we have to. You have to know what he's capable of."

Claire appeared relieved. "I'm ready. I know it's going to be bad. I've been preparing myself ever since you got shot."

"You'll never be prepared for this kind of stuff."

"Just tell me, already. You're making it worse."

Black sat down and picked up a thick file lying on the couch. "I'm not going to tell you everything right now. I'm going to show you the rest of the crime scene photos and I'm going to tell you some more details. I want you to look at every picture I've got of this guy and memorize them. But I still think you need to let your mind tell you what you're ready for. Your subconscious is letting some things get through now, so maybe it's going to happen. But maybe not. We'll see what else gets triggered."

Claire didn't say a word, just listened. But her expression was steely and determined.

"All right," Black said, dreading this more than she did. "Here's another picture of him. This is the last one taken of Thomas Landers when he was in the mental hospital. He's been locked up there for several years. He broke out just before your accident."

Claire took the photograph he handed over and looked down at it. "He doesn't look like a monster."

"Psychopaths usually don't."

She was right. The man in the picture looked young. He had tan-colored hair cropped very short and large, innocent-looking blue eyes. And he was a murderous maniac.

Claire said, "You know, he does look familiar somehow. He could be Jesse, I think. Maybe. With different hair and eye color and Jesse looks bigger."

Black alerted to the name. "Who's Jesse?"

"Monica's boyfriend. Remember I told you that on the phone when you called me at Jeepers. He used to walk Jules sometimes. He's number one on our suspect list for Monica Wheeler's murder. I picked up his employment records downstairs earlier. Hope you don't mind."

"Oh, my God, this guy works here?"

Brows knitted, Claire examined the picture. "Not anymore. He quit by phone the day Monica died. Nobody's heard from him since. I checked. Do you have more pictures of Landers?"

Black thumbed through the file. "He lived his life as a woman for a while. Right here under our noses. Fooled us, too."

The photo he handed Claire was of Thomas when he impersonated a pretty young blonde, a friend of Claire's. He watched, but she showed no visible signs of a quick or visceral reaction. No sign whatsoever that she'd ever known the woman. She said, "Are you serious? He's a cross-dresser, too?"

"He does whatever he needs to do to get what he wants. He's quite ingenious sometimes."

"And this guy wants me, and only me?"

"He was trying to get away with you when he drove you off that bridge. What more proof do you need?"

Claire stood up and started to pace. "C'mon, Black, stop with all this piecemeal crap. Give me that file and let me read it cover to cover. I'm ready. I need to know everything that's happened concerning him. Give me a break here. If I'm in so much danger, tell me what I need to know."

Black wasn't convinced. But he knew he had to tell her the truth. This was her decision. "I'm afraid you can't handle it. Nobody could handle all the things you've been through."

"I handled it before, didn't I?"

"You did, but it took you a long time to come to terms with it. And you still have nightmares. If you never remember the details, you'll probably have a helluva better life."

"Just give me the damn file. I'll read a little at a time. If some of it brings my memory back, so be it. If it makes my nightmares worse, so be it. That's what we want, isn't it? If a picture of him didn't bring him back, this probably won't, either."

Still, Black hesitated, gripping the file in his hand, but then he handed it over. Tensed and wary, he watched her, afraid of what would come next.

"I'm going to take this back to the bedroom and read it alone. I'll call you if I need you, so go to bed and rest."

Black watched her go, and then laid his head back on the cushion and waited. He wasn't going anywhere. Now that she held it in her hands, it seemed to him like it was a sleeping snake, one that he didn't want her to wake up.

Jesse's Girl

Right now

It wasn't hard to figure out where Joe and his little girl lived. Their names were written in big red letters on their old-fashioned white mailbox: JOE AND LIZZIE MCKAY. They lived in the nearby city of Springfield on an oak-lined street with lots of beautifully restored old Victorian homes. Their house was built on a corner lot, and it looked like Joe was remodeling it himself. A fancy sign in the front yard said FUTURE HOME OF MCKAY HOUSE—SPRINGFIELD'S FINEST BED AND BREAKFAST. Jesse parked around the corner near an empty home, in a position where he could watch them without being seen.

After that, he followed them everywhere they went. When they decided to have dinner in a Chuck E. Cheese restaurant not far off Glenstone Avenue, Jesse went inside, too, and watched the man and his daughter eat pepperoni pizza. He watched the other children, too, looking for a little boy who resembled Annie's dead son. He remembered little Zachary very well. He had seen the child only hours before he died. He was a cute little thing with white-blond hair and big blue eyes like his mama's. Too bad he wasn't around to kidnap. Then Annie would really want to be in Jesse's family.

After Chuck E. Cheese, they went to the Cost Cutter grocery store and then to Walmart, and he followed them, being very careful to keep out of sight. He found right off that Joe McKay maintained a very close tab on his kid, always putting her in his shopping cart or holding her hand or keeping her close. And the dad was big and strong and tough and could definitely best Jesse in any kind of physical fight. But all parents have a moment now and then when they glance the other way or are distracted by somebody or something. The time would come when he could snatch the tiny little girl and get her home with him where she belonged.

After Joe McKay returned home, he put his child to bed. Jesse could see which room it was because the curtains were open, and he could see a Disney princess poster hanging on a pink wall. It was the one from *Beauty and the Beast*, he thought. What was her name? Ariel, maybe? No, her name was Belle. Jesse would have to go back to Walmart and buy some princess toys for Lizzie to play with at his house.

That night he slept in his car, but it didn't do him any good. The next morning, McKay was always near little Lizzie, watching her like a hawk. Why was he so diligent? Most daddies forgot to watch their children, a lot more so than their mommies. After another day spent sitting in his car in the hot summer heat, he decided to come back some other day. He had time before he was ready to snatch the child. And he missed Annie. She was either at Cedar Bend or working with her partner or out trying to find Jesse. He smiled. She would find him, all right, as soon as he had everything in place once more. It wouldn't be long now, thank God. He had been without her far too long—years, in fact. He couldn't wait much longer.

On the way home, he thought about Annie, and Lizzie, and Miss Rosie. Miss Rosie was lonely on her plate, and she often wept and complained bitterly that she wanted someone to talk to. But she didn't have to wait long. The time was almost at hand. Now that Black was hurt and out of commission, Annie would be easier to get to, and until Black's alibis were verified, he still had the murder rap hanging over his head. The cops at the lake weren't too bright, anyway. They'd proved that lots of times.

Happy now, content, he drove back to the lake and parked in the busy Cedar Bend parking lot, where he had a good view of the door Annie used to go up to her lover's penthouse apartment.

Chapter Twenty-four

As it turned out and after shivering through the first ten pages of Black's thick Claire-Morgan-and-her-bogeyman file, Claire decided not to dig too deep into her sordid past, not just yet. Maybe he was right. Maybe she didn't need to know every single detail of what she'd been through. Maybe the gruesome photos would do the trick. So she studied all of them in detail. Or, and despite her bravado, maybe she was pretty much afraid to see what had been done to her. Yep, that sounded more on target.

Desperately, she tried to determine exactly why the picture of Thomas Landers reminded her of Jesse. The two men didn't look exactly identical, but they were similar, especially in the way their faces were shaped. She needed a full body shot of the two, which would make it easier to judge. If Landers was that good at changing his persona, she bet she wouldn't know him even if she had seen him up close and personal. But she was looking for him, nonetheless, and Jesse, too, and wouldn't stop until she found them. She had a couple of bones to pick with one or both of them—shooting Black, first and foremost. The shooter was not going to get away with that, no way in hell.

As far as Black was concerned, and despite his suggestive and seductive talk earlier that evening, he was a mite more under the weather than he admitted and eventually had to give himself a pain shot. That should also put him to sleep, which both relieved and disappointed her. Go figure. She was beginning to remember their relationship, all right, more all the time. Long-past times where they were only talking or walking or laughing, normal couple-in-love things in quick, quick glimpses, but lots of the bedroom parts, too. Still not enough, however, to blithely jump into bed with him as if nothing had happened. Or maybe she would really soon, and gladly so. Was she conflicted, or what?

So she kissed him good night after he had pretty much gone off to that induced-slumber/drugged-out twilight zone and wouldn't try to grab her. Then she sat vigil beside his bed while she held the open file on her lap and felt fear rolling up and down the back of her neck at the mere thought of jabbing a fork in old open wounds she didn't really want to remember. She finally retired to Black's big bed down the hall and slept on his pillow, which smelled enticingly of his expensive yet über-masculine cologne.

Black was wearing her down big-time, but then, who was she kidding? She was falling for him all over again. It wouldn't surprise her, nope. What was there not to like? Black was hot as hot could possibly be, rich, famous, paid her a lot of very special attention, and told her he loved her often and well. Jeez, the longing in those blue eyes of his was enough to make her want to throw in the towel.

Claire was up well before Black awoke the next morning and had showered, dressed in a clean white polo shirt with the Canton County Sheriff's Office logo on the pocket, and jeans, and a new pair of black Nike running shoes that Black had bought for her after she awakened from the coma. In fact, he had ordered them hand delivered with lots of other clothes that she liked and that fit her. *See, what's not to like? This guy has it all down in spades.*

Black was fast asleep when she went into his makeshift hospital room. He looked even better today than yesterday, thankfully not the white as snow, Edward-the-Handsome-Vampire mask anymore, very peaceful and resting comfortably. RN Violet was back on duty and tiptoeing around soundlessly doing her thing, efficiently, too. Just as Monica had done. She tried not to think of how Monica Wheeler had looked the last time she'd seen her. She left Black in the woman's capable hands and met Bud outside the elevator doors where Isaac, the tough-looking-but-Pooh-Bear-the-rest-of-the-time gatekeeper still stood vigil.

"Okay, where to first?" she said to Bud as she climbed aboard his

Bronco, poking on her sunglasses and turning the air conditioner vent straight into her face. Ninety-five degrees will do that to a southern California expatriate.

"Straight over to Springfield to check out Long's previous real estate office and co-workers. Thank God, I'm ready to get outta here for a while."

"Okay."

"How's Nick?"

"He's curled up like a baby and won't get agitated until he wakes up and finds I'm still a police officer."

With a broad grin, Bud glanced over at her. "He's protective of you, all right. You sayin' he wants you to hang it up?"

That idea had not occurred to her. As if Black, or anyone else, would have a say on how she pursued her career. "It's not his decision."

"It used to be."

Claire turned and gave him one surprised look. "You saying he tells me what to do?"

Bud guffawed at that one. "Nobody tells you what to do, Claire. Believe me. But if anybody tried to take you away from all this crap, it'd be him. He's almost as obsessed with you as Landers. But in a good way. Surely, you've noticed."

She had, of course, but she didn't think he would ever demand that she quit the force, at least she hoped not. She changed the subject. "Any results on the DNA found at my place?"

"Not yet, but it shouldn't be long now. Charlie's expediting the test results any time now."

"Let's just catch this guy and wrap this thing up. What'd you say, Bud? It's getting a little too hairy for me to deal with."

"I say amen to that." Bud slowed and stopped at a traffic light on a busy intersection. He blew out some air, then looked over at her. "I missed you, you know. And I'm glad you're back. You act more like the Claire I know every day."

For some reason, his earnestness touched her. "Thanks. I'm recalling things right and left lately. Now if I can just put everything together. Do I act a lot differently than before? Noticeably, I mean?"

"Oh, yeah, you're usually ten times more annoying and hard-headed than this. Not that you're not now, too."

Claire slapped at his arm. "You love me, and you know it."

"You're pretty hard-nosed and bossy, but you're right, I'm lucky to have you as a partner."

She glanced over at him and found that he looked embarrassed, too. Oh, yeah, Bud was an okay dude.

Miriam Long's previous real estate company was a ReMax affiliate. It was located on Campbell Street, and turned out to be a small and nondescript storefront establishment in a small and nondescript strip mall. When they went inside, a small and nondescript but rotund man, Humpty Dumptyish, in fact, shot quickly out of the back office, as if he'd never seen a client before and was highly excitable. He was very short—came to about her chin—and dumpy, kind of egg-shaped, in fact, and totally bald. He also reminded Claire of one of the taller Disney Dwarfs. Doc, maybe, but she didn't remember the others, so who knows? Maybe Droopy or Sneezy? The guy had a little silver hoop in his pierced left ear, one that had a black-and-white yin yang symbol hanging off it. This didn't really go all that well with his short-sleeved, red-yellow-and-green plaid, button-down-collar shirt and red tie and insurance agent Dockers. He had a wide smile, though, a real pleasant one, and he used it with thrilling abandon.

"Hello, friends. How can I help you folks?"

After his door-to-door-salesman-on-speed greeting, he reached out his arm and glad-handed first Claire, then Bud with more enthusiasm than she'd experienced in a great long time. She decided he had to be a fiery country preacher on the weekends. Or the aforementioned sales operative, used cars, maybe.

"We're detectives from Canton County up at the lake," she said, holding up the badge hanging on the chain around her neck. "I'm Claire Morgan, and this is my partner, Bud Davis." Bud flashed the badge hooked to his belt with some masculine flair, eyeing the good-looking secretary sitting beside them. The young girl hadn't gotten a word in edgewise yet, not even hello. Claire had a feeling she was used to it with Friendly Humpty as a boss. She also had a feeling the young girl was finding Bud quite the sexy cop. But, hey, lots of women did. Probably impressed by that big gun of his.

Mr. Friendly Insurance Man's wide hazel eyes went even wider and more impressed. "Are you *the* Claire Morgan?" he asked, apparently awestruck.

Bud barked a short laugh and bumped her with his shoulder. "See, Morgan, I told you that you were gettin' famous."

The man blushed, yes, she was not kidding. Got all flustered, like they were going to cuff him for branding her detective acumen with a wow factor.

He actually stammered a response. "It's just that you've been in the news around here so much, and all that. My God, that last case you were involved in was so, well, so awful. . . ."

"Yes, sir. I know what you mean. And you are?"

"Oh, sorry. My name's Larry, Larry Carter. Glad to meet you both."

"Mr. Carter, we need to ask you a few questions about Miriam Long. She was an employee of yours at one point, was she not?"

"Oh, yes, of course. Dear God, bless her little heart. I cannot believe she's gone. Just when she got married and was so happy living up there at the lake." He glanced at his secretary. "Gina and I plan to attend the funeral. Poor Oliver. He's just devastated."

Claire glanced over at Gina, who was Carter's beauteous, gasp-inducing young secretary, and who was also a bare quarter-inch from coming out of her low-cut purple blouse, a female that Claire assumed Humpty's wife utterly despised and distrusted. Gina nodded, and adopted a suitably sad look at the mention of their deceased former colleague, all the while batting her long, black, false eye-lashes at Bud. Bud looked like he had hit the babe jackpot at the Bellagio.

"Is there somewhere private where we can talk, Mr. Carter?"

"Oh, yes, of course. Please, come back to my office."

Bud and Claire followed him inside. Bud loitered briefly to tell Gina that she smelled really good, heavenly, in fact, but Claire didn't smell anything particularly tantalizing on the girl's person. The whole place smelled like bountiful bottles of sprayed-everywhere Febreze to her. Then they found themselves inside a small, extremely cluttered office. By cluttered, she meant she couldn't see the top of Larry's desk. He gestured to two green chenille-upholstered chairs. Hers had a torn place at the front and a stack of newspapers on the

seat and was the better of the two. She picked up the papers and
placed them on his desk with several other months' worth of papers.
No wonder he'd heard of her. He was well read. Bud had joined them
now, and everyone sat down. Except Larry. He remained standing.
She wondered why. He didn't say. Maybe there was too tall a stack
of papers in his swivel office chair.

"Is anything wrong, Mr. Carter?"

"No, why do you ask that?"

"Well, you're standing up."

"I have a bad back, lumbar slipped disk. You know, a herniated
one. I have to stand up some throughout the day or I'll pay for it
tonight in bed. Then I'd have to sleep propped against the wall."

"I see."

Bud and Claire glanced at each other with we-got-us-an-odd-bird-
here looks.

"Tell us about your relationship with Miriam Long."

"Well, that girl was like a member of my family. My wife, Edith,
and I loved her so much. I worried about her being a single woman
going out to the listings to meet people, and such things. She carried
a stun gun. I made her."

"She carried a stun gun? Are you positive?" Bud jumped on that
with both his polished Italian loafers.

"Oh, yeah, definitely. I bought it for her myself. That's why I was
so surprised that somebody got to her the way they did. And, truthfully, she was a pretty strong woman. She and Gina used to work out
all the time."

Bud took over, so Claire sat back to enjoy the ride. "Can you think
of anybody who might be angry enough to hurt her? Any stalker
types, maybe? She was a nice-looking woman. Ex-boyfriends, jealous
wives, maybe? She was bound to attract the attention of men."

"Yes, she was. A real lovely lady. All that shiny red hair was very
nice, but she only had eyes for her captain. He was her knight in
shining armor. She worshipped him, truly she did."

"No other boyfriends?" Claire asked.

"In the past, maybe, but when she was here, she was always intent
on forging ahead in her career. I was glad she got on up there at Kay
Kramer's office. Kay's a very good Realtor."

"Are you and Ms. Kramer friends?"

"Yes, but not close. We've passed a few listings back and forth now and again. Seen each other at conferences, and such as that."

Claire sighed, wishing they could just get a break already. "You know the victim very well, sir. What's your take on what happened to her?"

"I think it's what I just said. I worried about the same thing when Miriam worked here. I think she was showing a property to somebody, and they attacked her when she wasn't expecting it."

"Do you have a particular client in mind? Anyone she mentioned who creeped her out, anybody like that?"

"No, but she was dealing with a property of mine that rather worried me. But she insisted on checking on it for me because she lived up there close, and I didn't. One you two are very familiar with, I suspect."

Claire perked up. Okay, this was the key. Her guess now was that Miriam Long had worked the house where Claire and Harve had been attacked by Landers and that meant they had definite cause to go inside. She glanced at Bud.

He had the same enlightened expression on his face. He knew, too. His voice was calm, measured. "What property is that, Mr. Carter?"

"Well, it's that house where that Landers guy took you, Detective Morgan, you know that crazy guy who took you captive? Well, after you put him in the nuthouse, I got the property where he held you and that retired L.A. cop captive."

"You are absolutely sure it's the same place," Bud asked. "And Miriam went out there to check it out for you?"

"Yes, sir. Every week or so."

Claire stared at him, thinking about all those gory pictures she had sifted through the night before, especially the one of Harve Lester in a hospital bed and the close-up of that long line of ugly black stitches on her own chest and shoulder, examples of that self-same psycho's handiwork after he got done hacking her with his meat cleaver.

Larry Carter wasn't done. "Yeah, we were as shocked as you to get that listing. That woman he murdered in that house before he got you? Named Suze Eggers? Her estate hired me to sell it when it's out of probate. It's been closed up ever since. Like I said, after Miriam transferred up there, she insisted that she could see to it. She knew it was really inconvenient for me to drive all that distance. She was sweet, like that. Always offering to help other people."

A distinct image welled up inside Claire's head. She was getting more and more flashbacks, especially today, most of them grainy and black-and-white and scary. This time she got a vivid flash of a young woman in a black-and-tan uniform like Isaac's, with short blond hair, spiked up on top with lots of gel.

Claire turned quickly to Bud. "What did Suze Eggers look like, Bud?"

"Five-six, I guess. Short blond hair, really muscular and masculine. She was a security guard at Cedar Bend."

Excitement overwhelmed Claire. It was coming back; she could feel it coming back now, slowly but surely. Thank God, but she couldn't dwell on that right now. This was it; this was the connection between Miriam and Thomas Landers. He had gotten to her in that house.

"Was she showing it to people?" she asked Carter. "Miriam, I mean?"

"I don't think so. But she went out there once in a while and made sure everything was okay. I remember her telling me that it was real creepy to go inside and look around." He hesitated, and looked apologetically at Claire. "She said it was still furnished, nothing much had been touched since you, well, you know. She said it's still got bloodstains in the basement. We can't clean it up for sale, can't touch it, until the court releases it to her heirs. They live up in New Hampshire. I don't know how they got my name. Probably out of the Yellow Pages."

Claire wondered if it was her blood he was describing on that floor, and considering the dire revelations of late, it probably was. But never mind that—she knew in her gut that Landers had been out there recently, and was probably using the place as a home base. More important by far, this info was plenty enough to get a warrant to enter that house.

"Mr. Carter, could you give us permission to legally enter that house?"

"Yes, of course. No problem. I have a key I can give you."

"Thank you. That will be very helpful, sir. Now, the way I understand it, Mr. Carter, is that the house is your listing. Miriam and Kay Kramer don't even have it on their books, right?"

"That's right. But I was gonna give Miriam a big bonus when it sold, just for taking care of it for me."

Bud said, "When was the last time she checked on it?"

Bud and Claire were actually leaning forward in their chairs. More proof that Thomas Landers was the perpetrator. It was strange he'd risk going back there to the scene of past crimes, but after all, he was insane. Nobody could predict his actions.

"Probably before she planned to leave town. She was a very dependable young lady."

Claire nearly held her breath because she knew what Bud was going to ask next. Turned out she was right, too.

"Mr. Carter, did she ever take her boat out there to check on it?"

Larry Carter looked from Claire to Bud and then back to Claire. "Yeah, she always went by water. That property is situated way back in the woods. She said it was a lot quicker to go in by water."

"Did she ever see anybody out there?"

"No, and she would've told me, if she had. Like I said, she thought the place was spooky."

Claire said, "Can you let us take a look at your file on this property?"

"Of course. You can have a copy of the file, if you need it. Gina will run one for you." He called out through the open door and gave the order.

"Thank you, sir. That would be most helpful. One more question, Mr. Carter. Did Miriam Long ever mention a client named Jesse Jordan?"

Larry Carter shook his head. "Not that I recall."

Outside, after thanking Larry and Gina, and with said house key and photocopy in hand, they almost danced a jig on the sidewalk. The new information was definitely pointing to the fact that Thomas Landers was probably in and out of there at will, planning who to bludgeon next, and using his old haunt as his killing field.

"This's major, Claire. I think we got him. He might be out there right now, holed up in the basement, nursing the bullet wound you gave him. He might've even been inside when we checked it out the first time."

"You bet your life, it's major." She pulled out her phone and found she'd missed a call from Charlie. "Charlie called while we were in there. I turned my phone off for the interview."

Bud was checking his cell, too. "Yeah, me, too. I better get back to him. He's gonna be mad as hell that neither of us picked up."

Claire looked up at the threatening gray sky and feared a thunderstorm was brewing. Lightning flashed on cue to verify her observation, and then came the rumbling thunder that lasted a good ten seconds before fading away.

"Sheriff, sorry I missed your call. . . ."

After that, Bud didn't get out another word, just listened intently, his gaze holding Claire's the whole time. After maybe twenty seconds, he said, "Yes, sir," but Charlie kept going. Something was up, all right. Bud didn't say two words more, and finally got a chance to tell the sheriff what they'd found at the very end of the call. More listening, and then he ended the call with another quick "Yes sir."

"Black called Charlie. His investigator, that Booker guy, thinks he's found the place where Landers came out of the river. Charlie's trying to get an expedited warrant from Ozark P.D. and wants us to go down there and pick it up at the station. Then we're supposed to take Booker and serve it."

"It's looking more and more like this guy's alive and well and killing people." Claire shuddered. She couldn't help it. Her scars all seemed to be throbbing with bad memories. Mental, true, psychosomatic, even, but it still got to her.

"Yeah," said Bud. "But we're gonna get him for good this time."

"What about the lake property where he's holed up?"

"He wants us to check it out, too, as soon as we get home."

Claire filled up quickly with a mild kind of dread at the thought of entering a place where she had nearly died in a most gruesome manner. Her gut told her that was where Miriam Long's life had been snuffed out, too. And that's where they'd find the clues they needed to prove Thomas Landers was back in the murder game, if not Landers himself. Hopefully, they would capture him inside that house and have him back in cuffs before the day was done.

"How far is Ozark from here, Bud?"

"About thirty minutes."

They got in the Bronco, and Bud quickly fired the ignition. The engine revved up and lapsed into a steady purr, but he didn't put the vehicle into reverse. He stared straight ahead, and then leaned on the steering wheel, and turned to face her.

"Do you remember anything about Ozark, Claire?"

"Nope. I think I'm glad I don't."

"That's where the bridge is, the one where you went off into the river."

Claire stared at him, but this time no familiar flashes painted her a vivid picture. "I've been getting more flashbacks today than usual, Bud. I think I'm on the verge of remembering everything I've blocked out."

"That's good."

Problem was he didn't look like he thought it was good. He looked wary and like he didn't want to be with her when she got punched in the gut with the ugly truth.

"Let's get going. I've got to face my past someday. It's all coming out soon, I can feel it."

He nodded, backed out, and shifted into drive. Neither of them spoke again. For the next thirty minutes, Claire sat there and stared straight ahead and steeled herself inside for whatever was about to happen. Seemed she was doing a lot of that lately.

Chapter Twenty-five

"There's the Riverside Inn. Too bad they went bottom up. I dug their food."

Claire glanced over at the deserted building that Bud was alluding to. It had a long parking lot with only one silver-gray Ford SUV parked in it. Truthfully, she was more worried about the sudden thudding cadence going on inside her heart, and the bizarre and scary sense of dread that was firing up every nerve ending in her body. She'd been there before, all right, seen that very building. She remembered driving past it, just like now, and each detail came back in a forceful gush of terror. *Oh, God, this was not going to be good.*

When they started over a narrow one-lane bridge just past the old eatery, Bud stopped the car and said, "Okay, here we go. You went into the water right down there on the far side and landed upside-down in the river."

Pulse absolutely racing, Claire stared at it, silent for a moment. "I don't remember it looking like this. I always figured it was a big bridge with iron guardrails and a wide rushing river."

"Nope, this is it. But the river was flooded that night. Water comes up over the bridge sometimes, makes it impassable. Sometimes it takes the bridge out completely."

Claire's mind was going a hundred miles a second, working hard; she could almost feel it straining, straining, please, please, remember what happened in this spot. She nearly jumped out of her skin when someone rapped on her window. She breathed easier when she saw it was John Booker.

"Sorry if I scared you," he said, as she slid down her window.

"I'm jumpy, I guess. First time I've been back here since . . . whatever happened."

"Okay, I parked over there at the Riverside. Why don't you go ahead and cross the bridge, Bud? Park over there on the shoulder."

As Bud drove across to the far side, Claire stared down at the small running stream, still amazed that she had almost perished in that water. Once they parked, they both got out and met Booker in the middle of the old bridge.

"I've been hiking down along the stream bank, down that way." Booker was still wearing all camouflage clothing and clutching a Remington scoped rifle in his right hand. He had a small hatchet and a bottle of water attached to his belt. He must've been an Eagle Scout. Or a Navy Seal. He pointed downstream. "Down there, looking for Thomas Landers's body."

Bud said, "Did you find anything?"

"I found a place where he might've dragged himself out of the water. There's an old farmhouse near that spot that I wanna check out. Nobody appears to live there. It's all closed up and locked. But I found a few drops of blood on the front porch. I've just got a gut feeling. Did you get the warrant?"

"Yeah, we stopped at Ozark P.D. on our way out here," she said, but more thoughts, more crisp images were burgeoning, dying to be set free. Excited, but frightened at the way her mind was jerking her around, she tried to relax and let it happen. Then, it felt like some kind of mental wall quivered dangerously and then partially collapsed like a dam in a storm surge, and memories of that night poured over in a distant roar. Then she felt like she was inside a car with Thomas Landers again. She could see him clearly in the driver's seat, his profile reflected in the dashboard lights, driving recklessly, calling her Annie, telling her he loved her. Her hands were bound and she was terrified about what he was going to do to her. Breathing hard, groaning with reaction, she dropped to her hands and knees on the ground, and let it come.

Worried, Bud said, "What? Hey, Claire? What'sa matter? You okay?"

Claire barely heard him, seeing only the rushing, terrible filmstrip playing at a furious rate inside her head. "We went off right there,

Bud," she got out somehow. "Black was coming at us in the Hummer, and we rammed him. I can almost hear the metal rending, the grinding, and the glass shattering."

"Your memory's coming back, right?" That was Booker, squatting down beside her, his hand resting lightly on her back.

"Yeah, fast and furious, no holds barred."

"Let me call Nick," Booker said, quickly pulling a smart phone out of the utility pocket on his fatigues. "He'll know what to do."

"No!" Claire cried, forcing herself to be calm. "Don't, Booker. There's nothing he can do. I've got to handle this on my own. Just let me do it my way."

Booker didn't punch in the number, but he kept the phone handy, just in case, as if Claire was about to go stark raving mad and he had to order a straitjacket posthaste.

It took a while, but then she stood up, and looked down the road past Bud's car. "I remember where the road is. It's down there, off to the left. That's where he held us. That's where he killed all those people. C'mon, I want to go there."

Oh, God, it was happening, finally. And it was in this quiet, peaceful place with the soothing sound of the babbling stream and dappled sunlight glinting through the leaves and birds singing their happy songs. It was this place. It was being back in the exact spot where she had been so traumatized and knocked unconscious. When she took off running to Bud's car, the two men followed. They all got in. Claire directed Bud to the correct gravel road and felt her fists clenching and unclenching with tension as they jounced down it and came out at an old weathered warehouse sitting on the riverbank.

"This is it. I remember it now. It's all coming back. Everything."

They climbed out, and the two men stood there outside the Bronco, watching her warily.

"I'm going inside."

"Not by yourself." That was Bud.

More terrible memories flooded through her. "I was drugged. Somebody half carried, half dragged me in there."

The front door was ancient and opened in a long horror-movie kind of *creeeeakkk*. She didn't start trembling until she stepped foot inside. Then she was back there on that terrible night, living inside her own flashback, unarmed and very afraid. She could hear the high river rushing outside. Then she relived it, in all its extreme horror and helplessness and hopelessness. She walked slowly to the center of the big room and looked around at the dusty boxes and dirt-crusted windows.

"I was only half-conscious when I came to, Bud. People were talking around me. I was groggy and confused and kept trying to force myself to wake up."

Yes, she'd forced her eyes open, tried to focus, and had a lot of trouble doing it. She was slumped in some kind of lawn chair, but she could make out the other chairs, too, all in a circle. There were people sitting in them, but dark shadows hugged the corners of the room and obliterated their faces. Who were they?

"You sure you're okay, Claire?" It was Booker again, sounding even more concerned this time. "Please, let me call Nick. I gotta call him."

She wasn't so sure that she was all right, as the horror of it barraged her mind. "Oh, my God, he made us shoot each other."

Claire began to shiver and shake all over, and she saw the blood spattering on the walls, heard the deafening *blams* of the gun, felt the nightmare unfold in all its gory horror. Then everything else came at her in one giant, roaring tsunami tidal wave, like a cataclysmic deluge bringing all of her forgotten past along on its crest: her youth, the deaths of so many loved ones that she'd endured, of her darling, adorable little Zachary and how he died in her arms. She fell to her hands and knees again and wept hard, wracking sobs. The shocking revelations were unrelenting, steady, endless, as her mind let her have it all back, everything at once, all the pain and heartbreak and despair. Her life there at the lake came rushing back with it, the way she'd met Black, the way she'd fallen for him, her relationships with Bud and Charlie and Shaggy, all of them.

Bud was kneeling beside her now, his arm around her, hugging her against his chest, trying to comfort her. Booker was on the other side, his hand tightly gripping her shoulder. She let them try to comfort her, heard their concerned voices, while she struggled to gain control of her shattered, out-of-control, ragged emotions. Then with everything she had, all her strength of will, she pulled herself together, wiped her tears away, and just sat there and tried to absorb it all and put things in order, while the two men hovered and watched her suffer. Still, she waited until she was ready, really had a grip on her nerves. It took some time.

After learning all that she'd been, all that she'd been through, she took a deep breath, clasped her trembling hands, and said, "Okay, I got it now. I'm all right. I remember nearly everything, I think. My memory's back. It's a helluva big shock to absorb, that's all. But I'm fine now. I'm fine. I am."

"I still think I better call Nick, fill him in." Booker again. Despite his big, rugged, tough-guy persona, John Booker looked like he was fighting an alien concept, that of feeling helpless. She bet he'd never felt helpless in his life. And he looked ready to crack under the pressure. Yes, she could understand that, too.

Pushing herself back to standing, Claire inhaled deeply, and took another cleansing breath or two. "Look, guys, I am not going to go crazy, if that's what you're thinking. I'm better now. I remember everything I needed to remember. That should help us find Thomas Landers. And it's Jesse. I'm positive it is. I think we've got to find him and find him fast."

Bud said, "You sure you're up to it? Maybe we should take you home. Let you get some rest. You know, sort through things. Let Nick talk all this out with you."

"Look, I lay there unconscious in a coma for almost a month, Bud. I don't think I need any more rest. This's what I've been waiting for. It's just pretty overwhelming stuff to deal with. But I'm okay. Everything's cool."

Both guys looked inordinately relieved. They also looked unconvinced.

Standing in the room where such unspeakable acts of cruelty actually occurred, her breath caught again, and her heart careened like crazy. Truth be told, she did need time to come to terms and she would. But she was home again, home inside her head, home inside her body. She was stronger now, in every way. And she remembered Black at last, every detail about him, and everything he meant to her. That made it all better. It had taken longer than anybody had expected, but it was a good thing. She had made it through in one piece, whole, relatively unscathed except for all those mental scars she now had to learn to bury again.

"Let's get outta here. Somebody should burn this place down." She gritted her teeth as she thought of the people who died right there in front of her horrified eyes.

Back at the bridge, Booker continued to observe her, concerned as all get out. "Are you absolutely certain you feel up to this? Bud and I can handle the warrant alone. You can drive back right now. Bud can ride back with me."

"No, I want to go on. Where's this house you found?"

"It's about three miles downriver, but there's a road into it, too. I found the place when I paddled my kayak along the bank."

"Let's check out the house first, and then we can search the river-bank for the body, if we don't get a lead inside. What'd you think, Bud?"

"Sounds good. Get your car, Booker. We'll follow you."

Twenty minutes later, they drove close behind him, headed down a rutted, overgrown, and very narrow road. The farmhouse was almost a mile down through the woods. When they came out in the clearing, she saw that it was old, more of a bungalow than a ranch-style house, with a front porch and second story, and it had a dilapidated, neglected look that made it seem deserted and condemned. There was an old barn behind the house.

"Do you know who lives here, Booker?

"The deed I found in Ozark says it belongs to a lady named Rosalee Filamount. That's the name I asked Charlie to put on the warrant. Says she and her husband bought it in 1961 and have lived here ever since. According to census records, he died in '82. She's purportedly still alive and living here."

Black was right about him. Booker got things done. And she hadn't liked him at first, but she did now. He was a good investigator. "But nobody's been here to check this out? Not the Ozark P.D.? Nobody in our department?"

"Nope. But I found a trail leading down through these woods to the river, and it ended near a low bank where Landers could've been washed up by the current and pulled himself out. He could've made his way up here, even if he was injured in the crash. There weren't many other homesteads, roads, or animal trails along the riverbed that I could see him taking. Most of the riverfront acres are nearly impenetrable woods."

They knocked at the front and back doors, tried to dislodge window latches, and called out for the owners, but all was closed up tight, and silent as the grave. Bud and Claire stood back and watched Booker climb onto the front porch. Claire took that time to breathe deeply and get used to all her new and awful life experiences. Booker took a tool from his utility pocket and expertly picked the old lock on the front door. It took him about five seconds flat.

"Not bad, Booker. Maybe we need to check your rap sheet for breaking and entering. Might be interesting."

"It's just a knack I picked up somewhere."

"Yeah, right," Claire said. Booker smiled. She found it pleasant enough. It made him look less large and dangerous and threatening.

Inside, they spread out and cleared the house. Weapon out and ready, Claire took the living room and root cellar, Bud went upstairs, and Booker checked out the kitchen and back porch. The place was really old, all right, dated, not kept up to modern times the way it should've been. It felt timeless, as if she were standing in the middle of a rerun of the old *The Dick Van Dyke Show*. Very 1960s, with lots and lots of family pictures sitting around everywhere. There was a very faint scent of perfume hanging in the air, too. Something old-fashioned, that probably had lavender in it. Somehow she thought it might've been called Intimate, maybe, a cologne one of her foster mothers had worn. It absolutely permeated every single room.

She picked up a picture of a man posed with his elbow on a green military jeep. He wore a tan World War II uniform and black-patent brimmed hat. Another one depicted a different guy in Vietnam War fatigues. Children's photos. Babies. Toddlers. The furniture wasn't particularly dusty, though, no cobwebs. Someone had dusted the inside as of late.

"In here," Booker called out from the kitchen about the time Bud descended the steps toward Claire.

Bud and Claire joined him where he stood in front of a small chest freezer in a tiny pantry just off the kitchen. He had already opened the lid, and the light was on. "She's in here."

Almost afraid to look, Claire moved closer and peeked over the side. There was a corpse inside, all right, a headless corpse, which looked to be a small woman, still dressed in a pretty lilac-flowered sundress and wearing white Keds. Frost was thick and white all over the body, and a good two inches of blood was frozen into red ice underneath her.

"Oh, my God, it is Thomas Landers," she got out, but her voice sounded funny, choked up and unnatural.

"He's still alive." Bud's voice was disbelieving.

Claire stared down at the poor old woman. Black was right. He'd been on target, all along. And Claire was in danger. They all were in danger. Anybody who ever encountered Thomas Landers was in danger, past or present. And more important, where was Landers right now and what victim was he stalking with his bloodstained meat cleaver? She clenched her fists to stop her hands from trembling. It was all coming down on her; she had to control her fear. It was harder than she had ever imagined it would be.

After leaving Booker at the river trying to find further evidence of Thomas Landers's trail anywhere in the vicinity of the cabin, they first stopped at the office and filled in Charlie on the situation. Buck and his forensic team were ordered down to the Finley River to work alongside the Ozark Police Department at the crime scene. They hoped Landers had left behind enough fingerprints or DNA to prove his guilt. Which would probably pretty well exonerate Black, too, for the murder of Monica Wheeler. They were now hot on the monster's tracks and getting closer. Even as on edge as she now was, all in all, it had been a damn good day, and she wanted Black to know it, too. She needed to talk to him, let him calm her down a little. And for once, she let herself admit that.

Chapter Twenty-six

Bored to distraction, Nicholas Black sat in the conference room at Cedar Bend Lodge, listening to quarterly reports given by his hotel managers and trying to remain attentive. The potent painkiller he'd injected that morning was wearing off now, and his shoulder ached like the devil. Absently, he slipped off the sling and massaged the sutured wound, uncomfortable, and annoyed at how everybody was droning on for so long. He wanted to get up and get the hell out of there, but he'd put off so many business meetings when Claire was comatose that it was impossible to ignore his business enterprises any longer.

All he thought about anymore was Claire. Today would be difficult for her. He should be with her to soften any ugly memories that she couldn't handle. She was always on his mind, wondering when she would remember. It was like balancing on the edge of a razor blade. The idea that she was back at the crime scene bugged him. It could trigger something he didn't want her to remember. Not first off. What had happened there had been absolutely terrifying. Hell, it could unbalance anyone who lived through it. Shifting in his chair, he picked up a bottle of painkillers, took two, and chased them with a sip of water. He should be there with her. Booker hadn't called him, though, and he was supposed to if anything momentous happened. So, apparently all was well and he just had to get through this blasted meeting.

Still grimacing from the deep ache in his shoulder, he listened with one ear to the guy who was running Black's newly acquired boutique hotel in the New Orleans French Quarter. The house with a private courtyard next to it was also his property and in the process of being restored, all of which happened before Claire was injured. He was thinking of opening a new clinic down there, too, if this nightmare with Thomas Landers ever ended.

Then, as always when he thought of that devil's name, rage rushed through him, swift and hard and virtually uncontrollable. He clamped his jaw, teeth gritted, and stared at the man speaking about Mardi Gras revenues. But he was thinking about that son of a bitch Landers shooting him down like a damned dog. And nobody could tell him it wasn't Landers who did it. Flexing his fingers and then balling his fists, he realized that he longed to kill Thomas Landers, kill him with his bare hands, and watch him die a slow and agonizing death. No doubt it was the way Landers had watched Monica Wheeler die as he strangled her. Black found himself eaten up with a deep-seated thirst for revenge, for everything that murderous psychopath had done to Claire, all the terror and pain he'd caused her since she was a small child. And by God, since nobody else seemed to think Landers was guilty, he'd find him himself. And when he did, there would be no more mental hospitals, no more jail time, and no more trying to rehabilitate the demons telling him to kill anybody associated with Claire Morgan. Booker would track him down, and they would end his murder spree, once and for all. Claire would never have to worry about that lunatic stalking her again.

Absolutely furious inside, seething with the need to take out Landers, he tried to hide it. He didn't do a spectacular job, judging by the concerned looks his employees were shooting surreptitiously at him. Forcing himself to relax, he picked up his pen and doodled on the notebook lying on the table in front of him. Glancing around, he saw that everyone appeared on edge, too, all dressed exceedingly well in their expensive business attire, professionals in every way. They were all good people, too, top-notch at their jobs. He didn't need reports to know that. He didn't hire incompetent people. He trusted every single one of them and they were loyal to him. Problem was, he simply wasn't interested in how his hotels were doing. He just didn't give a damn, anymore. All he wanted was to get finished with all this boring business and make sure Claire got home again and in one piece this time.

Fifteen minutes later, he glanced at his watch for the umpteenth time, the meeting droning on and on. Miki Tudor, his personal assistant, was sitting next to him, taking copious notes of every word said. He should let her print out a copy for him next time and avoid the unbelievable tedium. He started visibly, as did everyone else, when the outside double doors were suddenly flung open. Everybody turned in tandem to look at the interloper, and April Ward, the woman running his South Beach hotel, stopped her commentary in mid-sentence. Claire Morgan stood there on the threshold, her eyes riveted on him.

Shocked that she'd actually barged into his meeting, Black shot to his feet. Claire did not do that, ever. Hell, she never stepped foot in the office wing for any reason. Something had to be terribly wrong.

"Meeting adjourned," he said quickly, never taking his eyes off her. Claire didn't move, didn't speak, didn't smile, just stared at him.

Looking curiously at Claire, his colleagues hastily gathered their papers and briefcases, got up, and hurried outside. Miki Tudor was last to depart, quietly closing the doors behind her.

"I've got good news and bad news, Black. What's your pleasure?"

"Which do you want to start with?"

"Well, I declare, that's a typical shrink-generated response, if I ever heard one. You always answer questions with questions, don't you?"

Black got what she was getting at right off. Her memory had returned, or at least he hoped to God it had. But she was approaching the conversation in a peculiar way, which made him cautious about how to proceed. He decided to play it her way. "You used to accuse me of that."

"Yeah, I sure did."

They were still standing a good distance apart, and Black felt unsure, not certain where she was going with this. He didn't want to do or say the wrong thing, not at this point. "Okay, tell me some good news. Please do."

"It came back, all of it."

Black's heart began to race with hope, but she'd said bad news, too. Truth be told, nothing was very good, not with Thomas Landers still on the prowl.

"You remember everything?" he asked slowly, their gazes still locked.

She nodded. "Everything. All of it."

"Are you all right?"

"I don't know yet. I need you to help me, I think."

Concerned, Black moved toward her. She rarely asked for help, not from him, not from anybody. Apparently, she was not handling the memory recovery as well as she wanted to. "Sit down here and let's talk about it."

Claire sat down on the leather sofa beside the door, and Black sat down beside her. She was clasping her hands tightly together. Not exactly wringing them; Claire Morgan was not the kind of woman to wring her hands. But she was more upset than she was letting on, which was very Claire Morgan. She was having trouble accepting some of it, all right. He picked up the phone on the table beside him and told Miki to tell everybody to take the rest of the day off and go home, no exceptions.

Then he turned, took both of Claire's hands in his, and felt the very slight tremor in them. "Okay, babe, tell me what you're feeling."

Claire looked down. "I don't know. Sorta like I'm in a daze, I guess. A little shaky, nervous inside. It's a lot to absorb."

"How did it come back?"

"Suddenly."

"What did you do?"

"I felt dizzy and sick at first, but I got back in control pretty fast. When all that passed, everything became clear, all of it, every detail of my life. Or at least I think it was all of it." She looked up, her blue eyes full of anguish. "I know how I feel about you. That's the good thing."

"Yeah, a very good thing, thank God." He smiled and squeezed her hands. She didn't smile; she was somber in a way that he had never seen her before. "Talk to me, Claire. It will help you get through this."

Black could tell that was the last thing she wanted to do, but she finally said, "I think I feel a little bit afraid. I don't usually feel that way, Black. It's strange to me. Fear, I mean."

"You have good reason to be afraid of Landers. Anybody in their right mind would be afraid of him. I'm afraid of him. He's psychotic and cruel and amoral."

Claire moistened her lips, and breathed out a heavy sigh. "I want to get him, Black. I have never wanted anything as much as I want to take him down."

"That's a completely normal reaction to what he's done to you and to so many of the people you love. Don't beat yourself up. You are very strong. You can deal with this, too."

"I want to kill him."

Black was a bit startled at that remark, but hell, if anybody could relate, he could. He wasn't sure that what he was about to say was the truth, but he had to say it. "So do I. But we won't. We'll let law enforcement handle it, and they will eventually catch him."

Troubled, Claire looked up at him. "But I'm a cop. I shouldn't be thinking this way."

"You wouldn't be human if you didn't."

"I really, truly want to see him dead."

Black realized that Claire was appalled at her own murderous feelings, legitimate feelings though they were. She'd never voiced this kind of thing to him before. They were in new territory, but they were going in the right direction. But she didn't need to dwell on her desire to kill Thomas Landers, not now. "We'll get him, Claire. It's just a matter of time. And I'll keep you safe until then. Tell me exactly what happened today."

Claire sat back in her chair, pushed her blond hair behind her ears, and stared straight at him. She began to talk, haltingly at first and then quickly, as if a floodgate had opened. He was so relieved at this breakthrough that he barely breathed. For a long time, they sat there together and she told him how and when and where her memory had returned, how she felt then and before the accident. No longer was she pushing him away, burying her tragedies and horrible memories. She was owning them, thank God. Black asked her all the necessary therapy questions, but he pulled her against his chest and held her close as she talked, content that she let him do that—that she knew him again, knew what they meant to each other. She was doing well, and the more she talked, the more the shock of remembering all that happened seemed to recede.

"Welcome back, babe. God, I missed you."

"I am so glad I remember you, so glad, Black."

After a while spent just sitting there together, they got up and left the deserted office wing and walked back to the apartment. Once there, Claire became agitated again, and paced some, back and forth in front of him. Black knew then that she was still holding something back. He wanted to know what it was, but also knew it would come out in time. He could wait on that, but there was something else he didn't want to wait on.

"Come here, Claire."

When she stood in front of him, he pulled her down onto his lap. She came willingly, sliding her arms around his neck, and he let go of all his suppressed needs, kissing her the way he had wanted to kiss her for weeks on end. She responded in kind, just the way she always had, and they lost themselves in touching and kissing, and then somehow they were in the bedroom, smiling as they undressed each other. Black brought her bodily against his naked chest, his good arm around her waist.

She stopped him, palms against his chest, and breathed out, "Are you sure you're up to this? You know, your arm?"

Black only laughed at that. Then his overwhelming need to possess her won out, and he took her down onto the bed with him, seeking all the pleasure he'd been denied, the need that Claire could ignite in him more than any woman ever had. All of it, all came together, and ripped through him, and he thought of nothing else. After that, they were gone to each other, thinking only of feelings and desires and pleasures. Black savored the moment, surrendered completely, and thought of nothing else, just enjoyed having her in his arms again.

A long time later, Black ordered up dinner, but it got cold before they finished yet another round between those soft black satin sheets. It just felt so good. There were no barriers any longer, no doubts, no fears. They were as they had been before she lost her memory, even after having to relive the terrible nightmare that was the reality of her life. She seemed happy now, as happy as he was to have her back. But there was more she hadn't told him, and he was unwilling to force the issue and break the mood. She obviously wanted to hold back as long as possible, because bad things were still happening all around her, even now while they got reacquainted, and would continue to happen until Thomas Landers was out of their lives for good. Unfortunately, this lovely little respite from real life was not going to last long enough, and he knew that, all too well.

"Wow, Black," Claire said, when he brought in the dinner tray from where room service had left it outside the elevator door. She lifted off the engraved silver domes and looked at the feast he'd ordered. "Look at this, would you? Caviar and shrimp cocktail and Dom Pérignon and steak and baked potatoes. Chocolate fudge cake. Oreos. You are going all out on the celebration thing. Are you hungry, or what?"

"You just don't know."

They sat cross-legged across from each other on the rumpled bed, wearing matching white Cedar Bend robes, the large tray between them, and sampled all the culinary goodies. Then Claire casually threw a bombshell square into his lap, as had been her wont in days gone by. "Hey, Black, remember when I told you I had good news and bad news?"

Black stopped eating, afraid to move. "Yeah?"

Claire's tone had a light turn to it now, but she often spoke that way when she was the most uptight. He'd learned that a long time ago and the hard way. So he played along with the kind of banter with which she masked her serious side and waited, on edge, and not sure what to expect.

"Well, since we're finished with round one of saying hello, and you know that I do love you back . . ."

"Who says we're done with round one?"

"You need to know this, Black. Really, you do."

"Okay, shoot."

Bad choice of words, yes, but Claire was waxing serious now. She kept her eyes on his face, intense and guarded and searching all at the same time. Her real life had reared its ugly head, as black and awful as ever. "You were dead-on. It's been Thomas Landers all along. He's the one who shot you. The one who killed Monica and Miriam Long."

Okay, that came as no surprise to Black. He'd told them that all along. "So you found evidence of his guilt? Did Booker turn up something?"

"Yes, that's when I started to remember, standing out there on that bridge with Bud and Booker, and looking down at the water. Oh, and by the way, thanks for pulling me out of the river that night."

"Same back to you for getting me to the hospital so fast. Saving each other's lives is a habit that we need to break, starting now."

"I'd say it's better than the alternative."

They shared a brief smile, but none of it was amusing and all levity was now out the window. They were serious, and they needed to be. She began talking about what happened at the bridge again. Good—the more she spoke about it, the better. He sat and listened without comment.

"I went inside the warehouse where they took me. That's when everything else hit me. Then Booker led us to a house that he'd located downriver." She hesitated. It seemed that every time she hesitated, his muscles tensed up to the consistency of granite. It wasn't any different this time.

"That's where we found the body," she told him, averting her eyes.

Not expecting that, Black tried to hide his alarm. "What body?"

"There was a corpse in a chest freezer in the pantry. We think it was the owner of the house. An elderly lady named Rosalee Fila-mount." She paused, longer this time, the next revelation coming out hard, probably because she did remember everything now, all the terror, all the threats, all the dark things that Thomas Landers had done to her. "She was decapitated."

Black pushed himself up off the bed and took a few agitated strides across the room. He couldn't help it; he had reached his limit with patience and understanding. Thomas Landers was back in the picture, just as he thought, and that meant Claire was in serious peril again. "Oh, God, Claire, and now it all starts up all over again. I knew it was him, I knew it inside my gut. I tried to tell you, and Charlie, too. Thank God I got Booker down there to look around." He stopped in his tracks and stared at her. "Why didn't Book call me? Damn it, I told him to call me the minute he found out anything. He should've called me the minute you started remembering."

Now Claire was the serene one, just sitting there and watching his anger, hands lying palms-up on her knees, relaxed, almost in a yoga pose. Black knew he had to get hold of himself. This was not good for her. He had to stay calm. He fought down his agitation.

Quietly, she said, "I told him not to. I wanted to tell you myself. See your face. And talk it out with you at home, in private."

"Okay, you did the right thing, I guess." But Black's mind was whirling, fully latched on to Landers now, what his next move would be. There was always a next move. Black wanted to get his hands on that bastard so badly that he could taste the bitterness rising in his throat. "So now we've got to go after him. We can't wait. He's so twisted, there's no telling what he'll do next. What innocent victim will die by his hand while we sit around and do nothing."

Claire frowned. "Bring it down a notch, Black. Take a page from your own mental health notebook. Charlie's putting together a task force, and we're meeting at the sheriff's office before light tomorrow morning. You don't need to worry. He's going down this time."

Black did sit down, and faked a composed expression, but his blood ran hot and he knew what he had to do and he hungered to do it. Claire was still talking.

"Bud and I think Miriam Long was murdered at Suze Eggers's house out on the lake. Apparently, it's been empty since the day we caught Landers the last time. He's been holed up out there. Is there now, we're almost positive."

"Thank God. Then we can surprise him."

"That's the plan. Call in the cavalry and surround him in his own lair. There's no way on earth he knows we're this close. Charlie thinks it'll go down better this way, waiting till morning instead of tonight, just in case he tries to flee. He doesn't want to take any chances of losing him in the dark, but he's got officers watching the road in now and water patrol patrolling the end of his cove. We'll get his fingerprints back from Buck's office soon enough, and if they find the murder weapon with him, they can get him on ballistics for your attempted murder, as well as the other murders. All of this dismisses any charges pending against you, of course. We'll get him this time, Black, trust me. I feel better about that now after talking with you. The police will get him, not you."

At that, Black could only stare at her, not that he was surprised. Claire was not one to back down. "Claire, use your head. *You've* got to back off. You're his primary target. He's hurt you already, abducted you twice, hacked you with a meat cleaver, for Christ's sake. You need to keep your distance and stay out of this capture. Finish getting well. Work through your recovered memories. Let Charlie and Bud and the other guys handle it. Think, Claire, think about what you're walking into."

As soon as he vented his frustration on her, he knew his harsh words would seem offensive to her. He didn't care. They'd both been through enough. They weren't going to endure more torture from this man, not if he could stop it. He waited for her to jump on him, tell him that he didn't own her and couldn't tell her what to do. That was par for the course and always had been.

Surprisingly, Claire remained unruffled, didn't retort, or turn icy. She merely gazed at him, sober-faced and resolute. "You better get yourself under control, Black, or you're gonna lose that shrink license you've got. Take a pain pill or two. And just so you know, I am using my head. I'm not going to do anything stupid. I'm not going to kill him in cold blood, even though I hate him and would like to. Believe it or not, I've learned my lesson, and in the worst possible way, as you well know."

Okay, anger didn't work. He'd told her that little platitude himself, and plenty of times. Maybe pleading would do it. "Okay, Claire, I'm calm now, and I'm begging you. Stay here with me where you'll be safe. This guy is a crazed killer, but he's proven himself clever. He'll try to get to you again. He always does. Let the others deal with him."

"Well, he won't get me. Because I won't go off on my own, I swear to God. I'll stay with Bud and the other officers. And would you stop rubbing your shoulder like that? You're going to open up the stitches again, if you already haven't. You've done more today than you should've, a lot more."

Black did stop. In his tracks. He sank down on the bed. God help him, nobody on God's green earth frustrated him more than Claire Morgan did. "He'll get you again, he will," he repeated, but with less discernible emotion, because he had to resign himself that she was going to do this her way. There wasn't much he could do about it. He just shook his head.

Claire crawled over to him, leaned against his back, and put her arms around his neck. "Don't worry, Black. I'll be careful, I promise. Don't you see? We're going to get him this time, put him away for good. I think he's been living and working here at the hotel under the name of Jesse Jordan. I think he killed Miriam Long when she surprised him at Suze Eggers's house. He got rid of Monica, probably when she outlived her usefulness. Jesse is Thomas Landers, all right. That's how he got in here. He's coming after me, true, and if we don't find him at the Eggers place, then that's the only way we can get him is by using his obsession with me."

"Goddamn it, Claire. What the hell's the matter with you? Do you have a death wish—is that why you do these things?"

Claire resorted then to lightness, no doubt hoping to deflect his attention to more pleasurable pursuits. "I hope not. Not after the way you just made love to me. We have all night before the task force comes together, you know. Let's use it wisely."

"Don't try to distract me, Claire! This is too damn serious!"

She only smiled. "I'm ready for round two now. What'd you say? Or are you too tired? Did I hurt you?"

"You're going to get yourself killed—"

Claire stopped his words with her mouth, and he was fully aware that she was done talking about Landers. He knew they should, that he was right in everything he'd just said. He also knew that she didn't want to think about that right now, and she didn't want him to think about it, either. She wanted him to think about how she was opening his robe, her mouth moving over his chest.

"This is not fair. You are not playing fair."

"Shut up, Black. Please," she murmured, untying the robe and pushing it off his shoulders.

"Damn you, Claire," he said tightly, but that's about all he got out for about the next hour or so, except, of course, for some pleasurable sighs and moans. Claire didn't say much, either. She was showing him how she felt about him and in no uncertain terms, and he was enjoying it way too much to start another argument. But he would have to, sooner rather than later.

Chapter Twenty-seven

At four-thirty the next morning, Claire sat beside Bud in the small conference room in the Canton County Sheriff's Office. Black sat on the other side of her. He wasn't supposed to be there, of course, but he was doing so against her wishes, as well the sheriff's orders. Nobody tried to stop him, though, probably because of the try-to-stop-me-and-I'll-kill-you look on his face. Her expression was similar, she had to admit. Most of the area police officers were there, as well as some Springfield P.D. officials, and an FBI SWAT team out of Kansas City, geared up in their black assault attire and ready to roll. Thomas Landers was facing some extremely serious police involvement now.

"Okay, let's get started. This task force is a joint operation, under me and Michael White, the FBI Special Agent-in-Charge out of Springfield. As you know, there has been a series of murders and shootings"— Charlie glanced at Black and Claire, and then continued—"in the lake area. We have now confirmed by both DNA tests and fingerprint analysis that the perpetrator is one Thomas Landers. Our evidence also shows that he was involved in the murders perpetrated in Ozark, Missouri. Three men were killed there and Canton County homicide detective Claire Morgan was abducted and injured in a car accident as Landers fled the scene. As you all know, she was severely hurt but is doing fine and is now back at work."

Everybody looked at Claire and applauded. Her face grew hot. Okay, maybe she was famous. Infamous was probably more like it. Even so, she was highly embarrassed. She just sat there and didn't react, uncomfortable as hell, and not liking the attention, either. Black chose that moment to place his good arm on the back of her chair, just to show everybody that she was his property, she supposed.

At the front of the room, Charlie continued his rundown. "Thomas Landers is still on the loose and extremely dangerous. We believe his object in this killing spree is the same as it was before. This perpetrator has a pathological obsession with Detective Morgan and won't rest until he's got her under his control. He will stay in this area and create havoc as long as she is here. He'll only leave if she does."

"You are not going to be anybody's bait, no way," Black muttered under his breath.

"I am, if it'll bring him down. Whether you like it, or whether Charlie likes it, or not. He's already killed three innocent women, Black."

Black didn't answer that remark, but she knew he understood what had to go down. She would never again feel safe in this world until this guy was dead or captured. So they had to get him. Simple as that.

The FBI profiler had taken the podium and was talking now. "Landers is deadly, but he's also smart. He is a master of disguises and is brazen in his attempts to overpower his targets. He will do anything, and I mean anything, to get to Detective Morgan. The ultimate goal in his delusional mind, and this is according to his psychiatrists at the mental hospital where he was incarcerated, is for him and Detective Morgan to become a family and live happily together. That's why he pursues her time after time, killing anybody who gets in his way."

Claire shivered. She couldn't help it. Black noticed and squeezed her shoulder. At that moment, she was glad he was beside her. She was glad she was heavily armed, too. Black had eventually helped her alleviate her nerves and confusion and urge to kill. Now she was just ready to get Landers in custody and put him away. That was her mantra.

The task force meeting continued, the first objective being to surround the Eggers house and try to take Landers alive. The parameters were discussed. The SWAT team was to go in first with a flash/bang incendiary. If the suspect was not there, then the sheriff had marked off grids to be searched, and a statewide BOLO would be called in. At that time, the news media would be alerted to warn citizens not to open their doors to strangers and to keep an eye on their children. A picture of Jesse Jordan that they'd found on Monica Wheeler's computer was to be circulated as the murder suspect.

The department was to conduct a door-to-door search in the county neighborhoods and question anybody who called in with suspicious behavior. Claire stood when the meeting ended and watched the various detectives, profilers, SWAT team members, Missouri State Highway Patrol, and officers from every other conceivable law enforcement agency, as they filed outside, discussing the case among themselves. Black was still hanging around and not letting her out of his sight. The guy was a basket case of nerves, not the unruffled psychiatrist he usually was, unh-uh. He'd probably go in the ladies' room with her, too.

"Detective Morgan, I want to see you in my office," Charlie called out to her from across the room.

Uh-oh.

At that point, Black was forced to let go of her leash long enough to allow her to follow Charlie into his private domain. But he stood guard outside the door, bless his furious little heart.

"Shut the door, detective, and take a seat," Charlie said without preamble, or any other attempt at social graces.

Double uh-ohs, triple even. She obeyed.

But then he attempted to do friendly. Halfhearted, true, but he tried. "You're looking a lot better. Bud says you've totally regained your memory."

"That's right, sir."

Picking up his black pipe, he spent a few minutes cradling it in his palm, messing with it, as was his usual habit. She resisted fidgeting, as was her usual habit. It was better to sit still and wait and not annoy him into a cursing tirade with all those F-bombs he liked to throw around. She didn't know what he wanted to say to her, but she was pretty damn sure that she wasn't going to like it. Not even a little bit.

"Well, I might as well just get down to it, Claire. You're off this investigation until we get Landers into custody."

Absorbing that, and not in a good way, she felt her temperature rising about, say, a hundred degrees a second. "I'm fine now, sir. I remember everything. I've worked through some of the troubling things with Black. There's no reason for you to desk me."

"There is a reason, deputy, and you know that full well."

The deputy part was his way of reminding Claire that he was her boss, and she was his minion. "I'm fully capable of joining the task force, sir. Please believe me."

"This is about your safety. You are the target of this maniac, and I'm not about to put your life in danger again. You've been hurt enough by this man. It's time to sit back and let us handle it."

"I appreciate that, Sheriff, I do. But to jerk me off the case completely, that's unnecessary. I can help. I'll stay with Bud at all times. I won't go out to Eggers's place."

"No. I want you to go home and stay with Nick. Sit tight until we bring this guy in."

"You've got to be kidding." She set her jaw, angry, oh, yes. "Is Black behind this?"

"Nope, I don't take orders from Nick Black, as you well know. I haven't even talked to Nick since he got shot. How is he, by the way?"

"He's doing fine, but, Sheriff—"

"That's an order, deputy," he interrupted abruptly. "I can see that you're yourself again. You didn't argue with me like this when I brought you back in."

Claire frowned but gave up the fight. She knew Charlie well enough to know he wasn't going to change his mind. The stern and massive grimace darkening his countenance was also taken into account. She learned a long time ago, from personal experience, that one did not ignore the boss when he was this shade of burgundy. She held her tongue, had to, no choice whatsoever. Her subordinate capitulation to absolute authority did not come easily and was not easy to affect. In other words, she almost choked to death on her next response. "Yes, sir."

"Then go get Nick and go home to Cedar Bend where you'll be safe for a change. You're on paid leave of absence until I tell you otherwise."

"Yes, sir."

Once outside, Claire found Bud first and told him the bad news. He didn't seem upset. He seemed more relieved than anything. But not as relieved as Black looked when she told him.

"Well, thank God, for Charlie's good common sense. Especially since you've lost any hold on yours, whatsoever."

"I should be here. I could help." That's what she said, but inside, in the dark corners of her newly restored memory banks, she saw Thomas Landers's face, his crazy, wild-eyed excitement when he had her tied up and helpless in his truck, and in other dark and scary places. She saw him when he was about to slice open Harve with a fillet knife, which acted to set her nerves on edge again, oh, yeah. Swallowing down the fear that rose up inside and numbed her mind, she felt big-time creeped out, to be sure, more than that even. The guy was fearsome, loathsome, completely and utterly bonkers. She'd been in his clutches twice before, and she didn't want to contemplate how awful a third time would be.

Now that Black got his own way, he appeared solicitous and soothing. "You can help from home. Maybe we can figure out where he is, if they don't find him out at Suze's house."

On their way back to the resort, they were stopped twice by road-blocks. Claire flashed her badge, but the Missouri State Highway patrolman thoroughly checked out Black's giant black-and-chrome Hummer anyway. This officer was serious business, especially when he found Black and Claire both armed to the teeth. A second look at her badge and remembering her from the task force meeting mollified his concern.

"Well, I don't know about you, but I'm feeling a whole helluva lot better now," Black said, turning the vehicle into the great, stacked-brown-rock entrance gate at Cedar Bend Lodge.

Probably because John Booker was standing there, checking every car that went in or out of Cedar Bend. He waved Black on, and they drove under the portico that led to Black's private elevator. Claire had to admit that she did a pretty thorough gander around the immediate area before she stepped out of the car, too. It was amazing that one raving psychopath could cause this much fear and uproar. But Thomas Landers was unique and left a trail of corpses behind him that put Jack the Ripper to shame. Ted Bundy, too. As they rode up to the penthouse, Claire wondered where Thomas Landers was and what he was doing. Then she shuddered at the thought and tried not to contemplate it.

Jesse's Girl

Joe McKay was really beginning to get on Jesse's nerves. He was way too good of a daddy. He kept such a close eye on his darling little girl that Jesse couldn't even get near her. No, wait, now she was Jesse's and Annie's little girl, or soon would be. The daddy's constant attention made it hard for Jesse to snatch her, of course, but not impossible. Nothing was ever impossible. Just after nightfall, Jesse parked behind a tall hedge at the rear of an unoccupied mansion down the alley behind McKay's house. He'd parked there lots of times without being noticed. He moved through the shadows to a large bed of crepe myrtles lining McKay's driveway and concealed himself there in the dark where he couldn't be seen from McKay's house or from passersby on the street.

Lucky for Jesse, however, Joe McKay was a creature of habit. Jesse had recognized that about him from the very first day he had followed McKay home. No doubt one of those diehard military types, the kind who kept such rigid schedules. For several nights, Jesse had watched Joe McKay play with the kid after dinner, either in the front room or outside in the backyard. After that, like clockwork, he took the child, Lizzie, upstairs to bed at precisely eight o'clock.

Right now it was eight-thirty, dark and humid with crickets chirping. Lizzie was no doubt fast asleep and dreaming her sweet little princess dreams. McKay would come out the front door any minute now, dressed the same way he dressed every single night. No shirt, black nylon shorts, and black Adidas running shoes. He would take his run, leaving his live-in nanny in charge while he was gone. Jesse had followed him from afar, and traced his route down to the single second. McKay ran exactly three miles, down the length of Walnut Street, then over to Glenstone Avenue and back again. He ran fast, at a nice steady pace, and it didn't take him long. Joe McKay was in very good shape.

Staring down at Miss Rosie's dead husband's gold Timex watch, Jesse gave Joe enough time to reach the busy thoroughfare of

Glenstone. Then, as McKay's neighborhood of old Victorian mansions settled down for the night and residents enjoyed their favorite television shows, Jesse walked quickly up the front sidewalk, past the neat pots of pansies and ivy sitting around the bright red front door. He pressed his forefinger on the doorbell and heard a faint tinkling of chimes inside.

Moments later, McKay's gray-haired nanny opened the door. She looked exactly like somebody's sweet grandma and wore a pink-and-white-striped cotton housecoat that zipped up the front. She looked inquiringly up at Jesse, and he said nothing, just watched her attention move away from his face, down his chest, and to the handgun affixed with a silencer that he held pointed at her chest. Her mouth fell open to scream, but Jesse pulled the trigger way too fast for her to get it out, before she could utter a sound, in fact. The bullet hit her at close range and knocked her backwards a good five feet and onto her back on the red-and-black Persian carpet in the entrance foyer. She was already dead by the time she hit the floor, of course, her faded brown eyes staring at the ceiling, killed instantly by a bullet through her heart.

Quickly shutting the door, Jesse dropped the note addressed to Joe McKay beside the woman's corpse and took the magnificently restored and varnished staircase two steps at a time. He wished he could take the nanny's head and introduce her to Miss Rosie. They'd be such good friends, about the same age and all, but he had very little time. He knew that little Lizzie had a bedroom at the front of the house, the one with the large bay window right over the front room. He had watched through the open curtains when Joe McKay read her to sleep.

When he opened Lizzie's door, she was sitting up in her little white twin bed. The walls were painted pink with lots of Disney princess sequined stuff hanging all over the place. He kept his pistol tucked in his waistband under his T-shirt and out of Lizzie's sight as he walked to the bed and carefully scooped up the child, and her soft pink-and-yellow princess comforter, sheets, pillow, and all.

"Shh, it's all right, little Lizzie. Your daddy wants me to take you to see Claire. He had to go somewhere. It's okay now, just go back to sleep. I've got you. Don't worry now, sweetie. Nobody's going to hurt you, I promise."

Still very drowsy, the child quieted almost at once and rested her head on his shoulder. Pleased that she wasn't going to put up a struggle, he hugged her close. She felt so tiny and warm and smelled like Johnson's Baby Powder. He couldn't wait to lick her. He bet she tasted like sugar, she was so sweet. What a good little girl he'd adopted! She would be just perfect for Annie and him. He took the back stairs and soon found himself in a newly remodeled kitchen. He opened the rear door with his gloved hand and crept across the deserted veranda and across the backyard. More than relieved, he dissolved into the concealing darkness of the oak trees crouching over the narrow alley. Oh, yes, now, at long last, everything was going according to his plans. All he had to do was get Lizzie to the boat and then go get Annie and their wonderful life together could begin anew. He began to weep as he carried away the sleeping child, so warm and small in his arms, pure joy overwhelming every other emotion.

Chapter Twenty-eight

Without doubt, today had seemed the longest day in Claire's entire life, bar none. She'd been striding the length and width of Black's plush digs since she got back from the sheriff's office that morning. She'd called Bud several times since the SWAT team had rushed Suze Eggers's house and found that Thomas Landers was long gone. But they had found a woman's head in the freezer and a bloody meat cleaver and a lot of new blood spatter in the basement, so it was pretty evident he'd been there playing his usual gruesome games. She watched the local news religiously, but there was no trace yet of Thomas Landers or his vehicle.

It was after dinner now, getting late. Black was lounging comfortably on the couch with Jules Verne curled on his lap, watching her walk the floor and fret and worry, his arm held immobile in the black sling again. He was as calm and collected as he'd been ever since Charlie banned her from working the case.

"You might as well relax, Claire. You can't make things happen by sheer force of will. There's a pretty good chance that nothing's going to happen tonight. And if it does, we'll be the first to know. Bud will call you."

Claire paused and stood in front of him. "I know, but I'm going crazy. I should be out there searching with everybody else. I've got to do something. I'm going crazy."

"I can think of a couple of things. Come here and I'll show you."

"Be serious, Black."

"I am serious. We have a lot of time to make up from all those days you drove me insane with your no-touch, no-sir policy."

"He's out there. No telling what he's doing while we sit around here waiting."

Black switched off his reading lamp. "Our hands are tied. It's getting late. Let's go to bed. Maybe we can find a way to help them tomorrow morning."

She nodded, giving up the fight, but then they both jumped when Black's phone chirped. He answered, listened, and then said, "Yeah, Isaac, go ahead. Send him up."

"Bud?" she asked, heart beating faster. Maybe they got him, maybe it was over.

"No. Joe McKay."

"McKay's here at this hour? Something's wrong, or he wouldn't be here."

"Yeah, I know."

A minute later, the elevator pinged open down the hallway. Two seconds later, Joe McKay bounded into the room at a full run. He was dressed for running; his face was grim, his jaw set hard. He was teetering on the edge of panic, no doubt about it.

"He's got Lizzie! Landers took her!"

"Oh, God," Claire got out, but horror gripped her with icy fingers and froze her in place. "How? When?"

"I was out runnin'. He came to the house and shot my house-keeper. She's dead."

"Oh, God," she said again, her mind reeling with the idea of his darling little baby in Landers's hands. What was happening to her? What was he doing to her?

"Did you call the police?" That was Black.

"Not yet. He left this."

Claire snatched the folded piece of typing paper out of his hand. One corner of it was soaked in blood. Black looked over her shoulder as she opened it.

Lizzie's a dead little princess if you contact the police. Find Claire Morgan and we'll make a trade.

"No way are we handing Claire over to this guy," Black said, grabbing the note out of her hand.

Now McKay was doing the pacing, distraught and extremely close to being overcome by sheer terror. She had never seen him that way. He looked at her. "No, Claire's been through enough. I'm gonna find this guy and kill him. But he's gonna suffer first."

"How, McKay? How're you gonna find him? You don't know where he is," she said, swallowing down the lump thickening inside her throat. Just the idea of that sweet little girl being in that monster's hands made her want to scream. Somewhere he was touching her, and God knew what else he was doing to her.

"You've gotta help me find him. I've never seen this guy before. I know there's a BOLO order out on him. Have you heard anything yet?"

"It's Jesse, Joe! The guy you met at Jeepers!"

"That little punk! How do you know?"

"Never mind that—it's him. I know it."

More calm than the other two, Black said to McKay, "We've got to get out an Amber Alert, right now, before he runs with her."

"There's no goddamn time for that, Nick!"

Claire tried to stay focused. Joe was losing it fast. "He wants to set up a meet. He's gonna call us."

"That's what I thought. I figured he'd already called you."

Claire's chest was heaving up and down, her breathing labored. She downed a deep inhalation, trying to keep control. "Oh, God, McKay, this is so bad. Please let me call the sheriff."

Joe grabbed hold of her arm. "Please, Claire, please don't, I'm beggin' you. He'll kill her. He won't bat an eye. He shot Carol in the heart, the bastard. Just left her on the floor bleedin' out."

Better than anyone, Claire knew the horrible things that Thomas Landers was capable of. How many people had he killed in pursuit of her? Ten? Twenty? More?

"This is my fault. He wants me. He'll call, and then I'll exchange myself for Lizzie. Of course, I will. We'll get her back, McKay."

"Oh, no, you won't." Black looked determined.

Claire turned on him and faced his glower. "What choice do we have, Black? Do you really want Lizzie in that psychopath's hands?

At least I'll have a fighting chance. He doesn't want her. He wants me. He's not going to hurt me if I play along with his fantasies."

"No, Claire, Black's right. You can't do that."

"Oh, really, Joe? What do we do then? Nothing?"

"I'm not putting you in his hands. We'll set a trap. He's clever, but the three of us oughta be able to take him down."

They all stood there, staring at each other, helpless, all of them knowing how savage and unpredictable Landers could be. "We don't know what he wants us to do yet," she said at length. "Maybe we can get him, if he gets careless."

Black said, "Let's just settle down and think this through rationally. There's nothing we can do until he calls us."

The next hour was like being trapped in hell. Time crawled like a wounded warrior, and none of them knew how long Landers would make them wait. Claire fought the horrible visions torturing her mind. Little Lizzie, that tiny, sweet little child, was all alone somewhere in the lair of a savage, perverted killer like Landers. God, there was no telling what he was doing to her. McKay was like a man possessed, treading the floor incessantly, fists balled, jaw working, face distorted with pain and worry. But he was also calm, underneath the outward nerves. He wasn't yelling or smashing his fist through the wall. Claire knew him well enough to know that he wouldn't go off half-cocked, thank God. They just needed to get that call.

"Joe, I think we need to bring in Bud and Charlie," she said after another endless hour of waiting. "Put out that Amber Alert. He could be hours away by now."

"Thomas Landers won't leave this area without you, I guarantee it." Black spoke quietly, still more in control than McKay or Claire, but not displaying his usual sangfroid, either. He loved Lizzie, too. He was doing some serious pacing himself.

When the cell phone in Claire's hand started its song, all three of them froze where they stood. The two men rushed quickly to her side. Caller ID said unknown caller, but she knew without asking that Landers was using a throwaway phone. He was too smart not to. She answered and put the phone on speaker.

"This is Claire Morgan."

"Oh, my, why in the world do you keep calling yourself that, sweetheart? You're Annie, you're my beautiful Annie. You know that now, don't you?"

It was Landers's voice, all right, the creepy tonal inflection out of her worst night terrors, the voice she'd heard echoing through the endless dark, deadly dreams, the voice of a homicidal maniac on the loose. How could she not have detected it when he was masquerading as Jesse? Even with her memory loss? She felt her hands begin to tremble so she clenched the phone tighter. *Think about Lizzie, think about Lizzie.*

"Thomas, is that you? I've been waiting for you to call. I miss you."

"Liar, liar, pants on fire."

That was uttered in a childish, high-pitched voice, a singsong cadence. The hair rose up on Claire's arms, and she tried to control the quiver contorting her voice. "I'm not lying. McKay says we can finally be together. Tell me where you are and I'll come to you right now. He wants his little girl back, and I want to be with you."

A very tense, frightening silence ensued, and then Landers said, "What do you take me for, Annie? I'm not that stupid." This time his voice was low and controlled, a man's voice, completely different than before.

Joe's face was blood red, and he looked ready to explode in pure, unadulterated rage, his teeth grinding, his muscles hard as rock. For the first time since she'd met him, Black looked unsure.

Claire spoke quickly. "Tell me what you want me to do, and I'll do it. Anything you say. I'm telling you the truth, Thomas."

"Oh, yes, you sure will. And I've got lots of fun stuff planned out for us. I'm gonna have to punish you first, though, for shooting me. I hope you understand. That wasn't nice at all, Annie."

Black kept shaking his head, mouthing no, warning her off. She said, "I want to speak to Lizzie. Let me speak to her. Is she okay? I miss her."

"She's asleep. You'll just have to trust me on that."

"Don't hurt her, Thomas. Please don't hurt her. She's only a baby."

"I know. I already love her almost as much as I love you. She's real sweet and her skin's so soft. She tastes so good, too, like pink cotton candy, but not as good as you taste. I tasted you when you were asleep, Annie. I licked you all over. I helped you wake up."

Claire watched Black react to that knowledge, but his rage didn't reach the violence of Joe McKay's. Joe jerked backward bodily as if someone had slugged him in the gut. Black grabbed Joe's arm and restrained him from grabbing the phone out of Claire's hands.

"What'd you want me to do?" she asked quickly. The less time Lizzie was with him the better. Now Claire remembered the case that she and Joe had worked on. She knew the child had endured more trauma in her young life than anyone should ever have to. Claire had to get Lizzie away from Landers. She didn't care what it took.

"Listen carefully, my sweet darlin' Annie. Come to the Grand Glaize Bridge. Alone. I can see the bridge right now. If I get even a glimpse of Joe McKay or Nicholas Black or any cops, I'll tie this little princess up nice and tight and drop her in the lake. Tell Joe she'll sink like a rock. You'll never find her again. I *will* do that, Annie, I will most certainly. That's how much you mean to me. So you better do exactly what I say. Come alone and unarmed."

That threat was more than McKay could bear, and he yelled hoarsely at the phone, his face contorted into an unrecognizable mask of fury. "You lay a finger on her, you bastard, and I'll kill you. I'll kill you. I'll kill you with my bare hands!"

At the other end, Thomas only giggled. "Maybe I'll do it right now, daddy-o, since you're being so rude. Her mouth's taped up nice and tight right now. All I have to do is put another strip over her nose, and bye-bye, sweetie pie."

McKay's knees buckled, and he dropped to the ground, working desperately to get control back. Black put his hand on his back, his face rigid with anger.

"Don't do that, Thomas, or I'll never forgive you. I love Lizzie. I don't want you to hurt her. If you do, I don't think I can love you anymore."

Silence for three long beats, while they all held their breath. "I won't hurt Lizzie, if you come alone and do what I say."

"I will, just hurry up and tell me what you want me to do. I can't wait to be with you."

"Meet me there in exactly one half hour, thirty minutes, no more, no less. Park your car in the mall parking lot, and then start walking out to the middle of the bridge. Bring your phone, and I'll call and tell you what to do next once you get there. When we're together and on our way, I'll call Daddy Joe and tell him where his little princess is."

"Wait, Thomas, please, I need more time. I don't think I can make it there that fast. That's on the other side of the lake. I'm at Cedar Bend."

"Well, you better. If you want to see this little cutie pie again."

The line went dead.

"I'm gonna call Charlie, get snipers in place," Claire told them, but she could hear the waver of uncertainty in her own voice. That was so risky; so risky her heart stopped at the mere idea.

"We don't have time for that, and you know it."

"Then I'm going to do what he says. Both of you stay here and wait for me to call. I'll make sure he leaves Lizzie behind."

Black did not budge. "No way in hell, goddamn it. Not even if I have to lock you up."

"You're not going alone." McKay frowned. "He's got to show himself to take you. If I can get there first, I can kill him the first time he gets into my sights. I've got a sniper rifle with a high-power night scope."

Well, that shocked Claire. "You've got what?"

Black turned to McKay. "Can you get to that bridge fast enough to find a high enough angle to take him out? Without being seen?"

"Yeah, and I've got the rifle in my truck. Loaded and ready to go."

Shaking her head, Claire tried to keep up with them.

Black said, "Then go get into position. I'll get a rifle and do the same thing."

"You've got a sniper rifle, too?" Claire said to Black.

"No, but you do."

"It's in my Explorer. At my house."

"Then let's get going. Your cove's on the way to that bridge. We'll take the boat. It'll be faster and give us time to stop there. And you've got to wear your Kevlar vest, anyway, or I'm not letting you walk out on that bridge. C'mon, let's go. Lizzie doesn't have much time."

McKay was already at the elevator, jabbing the button over and over. Once they hit the ground floor, Joe raced to his truck. Black and Claire headed at a run toward the marina and Black's Cobalt 360 cruiser.

Chapter Twenty-nine

High above them, the night sky was beautiful, black velvet deep, sparkling with millions of glittering stars. A full moon glowed among them, bright and white, as if watching over them. Claire wished it was. Black was at the controls, and the boat absolutely flew across the inky dark water, the Cobalt opened up to full throttle. The cool night wind whipped her hair, fluttered her T-shirt as she stood beside him, but her mind wasn't on anything but Thomas Landers and what he was doing to Lizzie. They didn't have proof of life, but Claire didn't think Landers would kill the child, not yet.

God, they had to get to Claire's house and then make it the rest of the way across the water to the bridge by the time limit. If they didn't, Thomas would drown Lizzie. Claire had absolutely no doubt about that. They made better time than she could ever have hoped for. In only minutes, it seemed, the dusk-to-dawn light on Harve's old dock on the point came into view, blinking with the blue signal post that Harve put up to help navigate him home from night fishing.

Her cove was quiet, the water smooth as ebony glass, but she could see the lighted windows of her house, the timer-driven lamps more evidence of Black's pricey security gadgets at work. She couldn't see Harve's house from where they were, but she had called him earlier to make sure he was okay. Harve had been in Thomas Landers's clutches once upon a time, and he took the current threat very seriously. Black maneuvered the boat into the dock, easily and expertly, and Claire jumped out and tied up. Black turned off the motor and scrambled out after her. They ran down the dock and up the incline to the house.

At the front steps, they both skidded to a stop and pulled their weapons. Thomas had taught them some very good lessons in the past, and they took nothing for granted anymore. "Looks quiet enough," she whispered.

"Yeah. But we're still checking it out before we go inside." Black was holding his injured shoulder. It was way too soon; he shouldn't be doing anything like this with the wound only just beginning to heal. But what choice did they have?

"The alarm should be activated."

"Yeah, and it was activated the night he shot me, too. Stay here. I'm going to check out the back."

Claire watched him step stealthily around the side of the house. First, she found out he was capable of sniper shooting, and now he seemed to have his cat burglar skills down pat, too. Black was keeping secrets that he hadn't bothered telling her. But anxious to get going, she stepped up on the porch and checked out the security system. The alarm light was on and blinking; nothing was disturbed on the front porch.

"I told you to wait, dammit," Black muttered, back to her almost at once and with so light a step she barely heard him. He had discarded the sling again. God, she hoped he didn't break open the stitches.

"No time. We gotta get to that bridge."

"Not until we clear this place."

"Okay, let's just do it."

Claire disengaged the code on the alarm and pushed open the door, Glock out and held in front of her. She pointed it around the living room, both hands, finger alongside the trigger, very cautious now. After all, it was Thomas Landers they were dealing with. Black had his weapon out in front of him, holding it with both hands. Claire went to the right. Black went left. There was no one in the house. Nothing was disturbed.

"I'll take upstairs," she told him. "You take the garage. My stuff's in the back of the Explorer. You know where I keep the spare car keys. Go ahead and take the rifle and vest down to the boat. I'll meet you there in a sec."

"Not until you clear the loft."

Claire ran upstairs. The bedside lamp was on. She cleared the bedroom in nothing flat, and then checked out the closet and the bathroom, aware of how fast the minutes were ticking away. "Nobody's up here. I gotta grab a jacket to hide the Kevlar. He'll suspect an ambush if he sees me wearing it."

"Hurry it up!" Black ran to the kitchen and snatched the keys out of the bowl on the granite counter.

Claire jerked a black Windbreaker off a hanger inside the closet, and then turned quickly to high-tail it downstairs, just in time to see Thomas Landers step out from behind the bedroom drapes. He was holding Lizzie tightly against him with his left arm. Her mouth was taped shut, her big blue eyes wide and terrified, the nose of his .45 pistol pressed hard into her cheek.

His whisper was barely audible. "Hello, sweet Annie. I'll kill her. I will. Toss your gun down on the bed."

Claire hesitated. Then she lowered her weapon, but kept it in her hand. Black was still in the garage; she could hear him. She waited for a second, not sure if she could call out to him without getting Lizzie killed.

Thomas read her mind. That bizarre whisper came at her again. "Go ahead, yell for him. I'll shoot her. Right here, right now. Blow her brains clean out. Even if he kills me. I don't wanna live without you."

Claire debated her chances, but then Lizzie made a little frightened moan from deep inside her throat. She waited, unmoving, until she heard the garage door open and go back down. Black was outside now. She raised her weapon again and pointed at Landers's face, but he jammed his pistol deeper into the child's cheek. Lizzie groaned with pain and began to tremble, and Claire knew then that he'd kill the child if she resisted. Even if he died, too, just like he'd said, he'd kill Lizzie first. Claire couldn't do anything to stop him. He was smiling. He knew Claire wouldn't risk it. She lowered the Glock.

"Okay, Annie, take your left hand, forefinger and thumb, and throw the gun onto the bed like I told you."

She obeyed, eyes locked on his.

"Now the one strapped to your ankle."

Unsnapping the holster, she removed the .38 snub nose. He would kill Lizzie, right there, she knew that from experience. But Black was out there; he was armed.

She spoke, striving to buy time, trying to think. If she lingered, Black would come back to get her. But she couldn't let him barge in blindly, or Thomas would kill him. She had to find a way to disarm Thomas. "How'd you know we were coming here? You said to meet you at the bridge."

"I didn't know. Can you believe my luck? I've been hiding out here with the kid to give you time to get to the bridge. I figured nobody would look for me again out here at your house, once the cops got done with the crime scene and locked up the place. But here you are. See, darlin', our love is meant to be. God is blessing us. He brought you straight to me." He kept his tight grip on Lizzie.

To Claire's horror, and while his eyes were focused intently on Claire, he put his tongue on Lizzie's cheek and licked a long wet swath up into her hairline. The child squirmed hysterically against his hold. At that point, Claire wanted to kill him. Not wound, not imprison, but kill him—shoot, stab, bludgeon him—anything that sent him straight to hell.

"Okay, let's go, Annie, my love, and don't even think about yelling for Black. She'll be dead before you get out his name."

"So will you."

"So be it."

Claire decided to beg and thereby pick up a few minutes for Black to realize she was taking too much time. "Thomas, she's just a little girl. Let her go, and I'll walk out of here with you. I swear I will. I won't even try to get away."

"Yeah, just like last time, huh? But I won't hurt her. Or you. But I'll kill that bastard lover of yours out there. I'll shoot him, if you make a peep. And I'll finish the job this time. All I've got to do is wait for him to come back inside looking for you and then I'll shoot him in the head. He'll never know what hit him."

"I said I'd go with you. Just don't hurt anybody else."

"Okay, you first, down the steps, quick before he comes back. And don't try anything."

Lizzie was whining pitiably. Claire's mind raced to come up with a way to warn Black.

"Open the back door. Hurry it up."

Claire did what she was told. Landers followed her outside with Lizzie stiff and terrified in his arms, his weapon still embedded in her cheek.

Outside, he prodded Claire up through the thick stand of trees lining the back of the house and into denser woods choked with bushes and dead leaves. After about five minutes of climbing, she saw the glint of a car's hood in the moonlight filtering through the branches above them. She was not going to get in that car. If she did, they both would end up dead or worse. The trunk was already standing open, the interior light on, and he dropped Lizzie into it. The child grunted as she hit the floor of the trunk.

"Now, get down on your knees, Annie." That was uttered harshly, but then his voice went back to the high, gentle tone. "Sweetheart, I'm so sorry about all this. Hold out your hands. I've got to tape you up and make sure you don't get away. I don't want you to get hurt, please believe me. So don't fight, just trust me."

Thomas was facing Claire, his gun trained on her chest now. She obeyed, and as she waited there on her knees, she took one bracing breath, doubled both her fists, and drove them up underneath his chin as quick and hard as she could. Screaming in agony, he went down under the force of the blow, but he managed to keep his grip on the gun. It went off, barely missing her. Claire ducked, and then grabbed the sobbing child out of the trunk as he writhed around and spit blood where his teeth had cut deep gouges into his lips. He fired at her again, and Claire didn't waste time but ran into the cover of the dark trees, yelling for Black and holding the child tightly against her chest with both arms.

Thrashing through the tangled brush and briars, she couldn't see where she was going in the darkness. She just knew she had to get as far away from Landers as she could and as fast as she could. Thomas fired more shots after her, but she didn't think he really wanted to kill her, so she kept yelling Black's name and running, hoping to God that Thomas couldn't see her trail. Black would've heard the shots and her cries for help in the stillness; he would be on his way up the hill to find them by now, and he wouldn't be a sitting duck like he would've been in the house.

The woods were so thick with undergrowth and clinging vines and great sticky spiderwebs stretched between the trees that it was hard to push through without falling. Claire knew she was making too much noise as she struggled through the deep layers of dead leaves and fallen branches that littered the ground. But she couldn't stop, not yet. Five minutes later, she drew up and leaned her back against a tree trunk, out of his line of vision if he was behind her, panting hard, listening for sounds of his pursuit. She could hear him coming after them then, his footfalls breaking sticks, shuffling through leaves, and cursing wildly. Farther away, she heard Black yelling her name. Oh, God, she couldn't call out to him again. Thomas was right behind them.

Frantic to get Lizzie to safety, Claire took off again and finally burst into a clearing in the woods where the bright moonlight filtered some illumination in the black night. She made better time there, trying to angle down and back around to her house and her weapons, but Lizzie was getting heavy and now she was struggling against Claire's tight grip. Once out of the clearing, she yelled for Black to help him pinpoint their location, and then quickly darted in the other direction so Thomas couldn't get a bead on her. She heard the sharp crack of a gunshot between her and her house. She changed directions again and headed for the old dock out on the point. Harve used to keep a rowboat there, unless he'd gotten rid of it. She hoped to God he hadn't.

Fighting through wild, clinging, endless vegetation, sharp stickers gouging her face and bare arms at every turn, she felt blood running down her cheek. But she was pretty sure she was well ahead of Thomas now. Maybe he'd stopped or given up and was fleeing back to his car, afraid Black was too close. Breathless, chest aching with exertion, she stopped again and crouched down behind a thick tree trunk. She tried to whisper to the child, comfort her, but the gnats and mosquitoes were swarming all over them, and Lizzie was screaming under the tape.

Gulping in air, trying to catch her breath, Claire tried to speak soothingly, tried to calm the child, but she sounded scared and desperate herself. Maybe she could hide Lizzie in the leaves and try to lead Thomas away from her. But she couldn't; she was terrified to leave Lizzie alone. What if Thomas found her, shot her out of anger, or used her as a hostage again? Oh, God, she couldn't leave the traumatized little baby out in the dark woods alone. She couldn't do it.

Claire loosened the tape over Lizzie's mouth and breathed hushed words into her ear. "Please, Lizzie, don't cry. I'm getting you out of here. He's not going to catch us, but you have to be quiet. You can't make a sound, or he'll hear us."

"I scared, I scared," was all Lizzie could say, over and over, but God love her and despite her terror, she was whispering, too.

"I'm gonna take you down to the lake and put you in a boat, baby, okay? I'm gonna hide you there for a while so he can't find you. Promise me that you'll stay there and not say a word. You can't get out, can't get in the water. Okay, do you understand me, Lizzie?"

Lizzie nodded and pressed her face hard against Claire's chest. Then Claire heard the crashing through the brush again, getting closer, and she took off again, clutching the child and hoping Black was closing in on them, wishing she could guide him to her some way. When she finally got to the bottom of the hill and burst out of the trees and onto the beach, she saw the dock's dusk-to-dawn light and blinking blue signal off to her right. Jutting rocks hid her house a good way down the beach. She ran down the rock-strewn bank and out onto the old rickety dock. Harve's rowboat was still in the water, tied to the pilings, and she splashed out into the shallow water and lifted Lizzie up and over the side into the boat. She fumbled at the rope securing it, wanting to push it out in the water, offshore where Thomas couldn't get to it, all the while watching the tree line behind her. Finally, she got the rope to fall free just as Thomas Landers burst out on the beach and ran straight at her.

Frantic to get Lizzie away from him, she pushed the rowboat underneath the dock, hoping to hide it, and then began to swim out away from the shore. She screamed Black's name again, trying to lure Landers away from the boat and give Black her bearings. She still didn't think Thomas would kill her. If he wanted to kill her, he'd had plenty of chances. All of this, everything he did, was to get Claire back under his control. Then she heard Black yell her name, somewhere close by, and she yelled back as loud as she could and then dove beneath the surface as a bullet cut into the water close beside her. Oh, God, she was wrong; he did intend to shoot her. She swam underwater as far as she could, out farther, away from Lizzie and the dock. Toward the direction of Black's voice. Then, finally unable to hold her breath any longer, she shot back up and broke the surface, gasping for air.

But Landers was not following her. He was walking out on the old dock. While she watched, he reached down and pulled the boat out of its hiding place. Then he jerked Lizzie out of the boat and held her out in front of him by the back of her pink nightgown. He put his gun to her head and laughed, the crazed, shrill sound echoing out over the lake. Claire started to swim back toward them, horrified now that he would just kill the little girl and be done with it. Black had no leverage, either, not now that Thomas had Lizzie at his mercy.

She stopped as soon as her feet touched bottom and stood up, ready to plead for their lives. "Please, Thomas, please, I'm right here. I'll go with you."

Thomas was smiling. He was facing her, his features detectable in the bright dusk-to-dawn light. The blue signal blinking on and off beside him gave him a surreal, maniacal look. He looked like the devil—deadly, smiling, evil. Lizzie hung there against him, mute and silent. "Yes, you are going with me, Annie, but not Lizzie here. She's a dead little girl now, and you can blame yourself that I have to blow her sweet little head off."

"Drop the gun, Landers. I've got you dead center." Black's voice, from a good distance down the narrow beach. Claire sagged with relief.

Thomas Landers laughed again, his gun barrel pressed into Lizzie's cheek. "You're not gonna shoot me, not with this gun at dear little Lizzie's head. . . ."

While Claire stood there, waist deep in the water, terrified for Lizzie, she saw a small black hole suddenly open up on Thomas's forehead, and then the sharp report of Black's rifle shattered the still night. Thomas let go of Lizzie and the child fell into the water, and two more holes opened up in the middle of his chest, the double crack of the rifle sounding again. *Blam, blam.* And then Landers went backwards hard, hit the planks of the dock, and didn't move. As Claire struggled desperately through the water to get to Lizzie, she heard Black running hard down the beach and splashing out into the water, grabbing Lizzie out of the water.

Black turned toward Claire, holding the child with his good arm and the rifle in his other hand. Claire half splashed, half waded toward them. Black boosted Lizzie onto the dock and then grabbed Claire and pushed her up beside her. Claire grabbed Lizzie and pulled her close and held her head tightly against her shoulder so she couldn't see Thomas Landers's lifeless corpse lying on the dock behind them. Black's shoulder was bleeding. She could see the red seeping out on his white shirt, but he put down the rifle and pulled them both into his arms.

"It's over," he said, his voice low, tightly controlled. "He's never gonna come after you again, Claire. Never."

Lizzie was crying and pressing herself closer to Black, and Claire buried her face in his bloodstained shirt and collapsed against him, too. It was really over. She didn't have to fear Thomas Landers ever again. She tried to get her mind around it, but couldn't seem to do it for a minute or two.

But then she sat up, "We gotta call McKay. Now. Let him know that Lizzie's safe."

Black got out his phone and punched in the number while she struggled up and shielded Lizzie from Thomas Landers's body. She didn't look at him again as she unbound the child and carried her off the dock. Lizzie clung to her neck with both arms, and Claire hoped she would be able to survive this awful night. Black hung up and took hold of her arm, and they headed back down the beach to her house to wait for Joe McKay.

Epilogue

There was a court hearing the week following their harrowing flight from the murderous and devious Thomas Landers. Black's wound had opened up again, front and back, but Dr. Atwater had done a second surgery to repair the damage. He was sore as hell and in a bad mood, but he was not incapacitated and was hell-bent to deliver his eyewitness testimony against Landers.

As the facts came to light, Black was not charged for the death of Landers or Monica, of course, and the other murders were attributed to Thomas Landers by both DNA and fingerprint evidence gathered at the various crime scenes. Joe McKay had Lizzie back again, safe and sound, but shaken up more than any child should ever have to be. The doctor said it didn't appear that she'd been sexually molested, thank God, and father and daughter were soon headed off to Disney World to take the little girl's mind off the nightmare she'd been through. Black had already had a counseling session with Lizzie, too, just to make sure she was psychologically sound and not suffering delayed trauma from her ordeal. Unfortunately, Claire was the one who seemed to be suffering that kind of thing and was having a lot of trouble believing she was finally free of the monster who had stalked her since she was not much older than Lizzie.

Black decided they deserved one helluva vacation after what they had just endured. Charlie agreed wholeheartedly, and off they went on Black's Learjet to New Orleans and a beautiful old home that he just happened to own in the French Quarter. One that happened to have its own inner courtyard with its own small lap pool and lots of tinkling fountains and red bougainvillea and a giant magnolia tree that shaded it all from the Louisiana sun. They lazed there in that private, quiet sanctuary and swam and talked and made love and he treated her like he loved her the way she now knew that she loved him.

And that's how Claire felt on a night almost ten days after he had put that bullet in Thomas Landers's head in that creepy, blinking blue light. She sat on a long outdoor wicker sofa in the courtyard, surrounded by banana trees, and palmetto trees, and red, spicy-smelling geraniums and those lovely splashing fountains. Wearing his sling again, Black came out of the tall and open French doors with crystal goblets of icy cold champagne in both hands. He pulled up a chair directly in front of her.

"What's this for?"

"We have a lot to celebrate, don't you think?"

"Oh, yes, sir, that we do, thanks to you."

"So you're grateful to me, right?"

"Oh, you bet. Far more than I can ever tell you. You killed the boogie man and set me free."

"Then do something for me, Claire."

Thinking that he was talking about the big, round, canopied bed upstairs in their equally big round bedroom, she said, "Anything you want. Just name it."

Black's handsome face was somber in the candlelight, and Claire knew then that his mind was not in the bedroom. This was serious stuff. Whatever he was about to say, he was not joking around.

She sat up straighter and gave him her undivided attention. Carefully, she placed her goblet on the glass-topped table. "You're scaring me, Black. What's wrong? Are you okay? Is your shoulder okay?"

"Nothing's wrong. I have a proposition to make you."

"Okay, I'm listening. Your propositions are usually pretty good." She smiled. He didn't. Serious as sin, yes, he was.

"Okay, brace yourself, Claire, this is going to be a big one."

So she braced herself for the big one. Was he going to ask her to marry him? She had a distinct feeling he was and fought all the conflicting emotions that shivered alive inside her heart.

"I know how much you love your job," was how he started out, which gave her a big red-lettered, underlined clue about where he was going with his proposition. But also, it was the one place that she didn't want him to go.

Claire sat very still, almost afraid to move now. But she had to ask him. "You want to break up if I don't quit my job, that it?"

Apparently surprised, Black's expression quickly changed to annoyance. "I ought to want to, after that insulting remark. Give me a break, Claire."

Claire was not deterred. "I'm not quitting my job, Black. Please don't ask me to."

"I'm not asking you to."

Okay, now that was a relief. She waited expectantly; nothing else could be that bad.

Black picked up her hand, kissed the back of it, and then the palm, in that completely tender way he did on occasion. The gesture showed her how much he cared about her, more than all the lovely gifts he liked to shower on her.

"Will you just hear me out, Claire? Without walking away or refusing right off the bat?"

"Are you asking me to marry you?" Nope, she was not one to pussyfoot around stuff.

That surprised him, she could tell. His eyes lit up. "No, but if you'll say yes, I'm all for it."

Claire didn't know whether she would, or not. So she said, "What is this, Black? Like I said, you're making me uneasy."

"I want to set you up in your own business as a private investigator, make you the boss. Anywhere you want to live, anything you want is yours. Booker's already on board with this, if you want him to be a part of it. I have contacts all over the country. I can get you all the work you'd ever want or need. You'll be completely in charge, on what cases you take, where you go, who you hire. Bud, too, if you want him. We can offer him any amount of money you want."

Okay, now he had managed to shock the hell out of her. This was the last thing on earth she had ever expected him to say. She was speechless, which wasn't like her at all. "Why? Why do you want to do this for me?"

Black's eyes were intense in the candlelight, blue as a sunlit sea, sober, searching her face, holding her gaze. "Because I'm tired of seeing you get hurt. I sat there for weeks and weeks and watched you linger in that coma, thinking I was going to lose you, that you might never open your eyes again. You can't imagine what that's like, Claire, what that did to me. I felt dead inside. And it's not just that time. It's every time you've been hurt or shot or clubbed in the head by some monster you're after."

Then she saw the pain in his face, and his voice, all so very clearly, pain he didn't try to disguise. She put a gentle palm against his cheek. "I'm sorry, Black. I'm sorry I put you through so much."

Black shook his head. "I'm not worried about me. I'd feel safer if you lived with me, if you worked side by side with Booker, or Bud, or both of them. You wouldn't just handle murders; probably would never have to face a serial killer again. You're a great detective. I would never want to take that away from you. I would never ask you to quit something you love so much. But I want you to do this, Claire. For me, for both of us. You mentioned marriage. I do want to get married someday. Soon. I want to have children with you. I want to have a normal life, where we're happy and you are safe and don't get hurt every other day. I want to give that to you."

Every word he said was true, every word was uttered with honesty and love and respect, and Claire sat there, not sure what to think or what to do. She looked away from him and thought about what it would be like not to be a homicide detective, not to put criminals, cold-blooded killers behind bars, and couldn't really fathom it. It had been her life as long as she could remember. But what he said, that sounded pretty good, too.

So she was as honest as he was. She owed him that. "I don't know what to say right now. You sprang this on me out of the blue. I've got to think it through."

"I'll give you all the time you need. Charlie already said he'd give you a leave of absence, you told me that yourself. For as long as you want and that you always have a place in his department. You could try it down here for a few months, see if you like it, see if we can make it work. Or we can live here in the winter and there in the summer. I have that kind of flexibility. It's up to you."

Claire stared at him, seriously considering what he had proposed.

"I'll think about it, okay. I won't say I won't do it yet. Is that good enough for you?"

Black gave a triumphant grin and pulled her into his arms. "Hell, that's better than I expected. I thought you'd give me a flat no-way. And while you're thinking about it, think about that marriage thing, too. I can get a priest here in half an hour."

Then he was kissing her, pressing her back against the sofa, and she lost control of all thought, like she always did with him. Truth was, she loved this guy, too, as much as he loved her. Their relationship had reached a turning point now, one that he had been thinking about, and now she had to do the same thing. She was just happy the choice wasn't her career or him, as she had often feared it would be. So all she had to do now was decide. But he had given her that time, time to consider what she really wanted out of her life and how much she wanted it. He had given her a very good way to have her cake and eat it, too. Now it was up to her. Right now she had no idea what she wanted, except that she wanted him to keep kissing her and touching her the way he was doing right now. She could think about everything else tomorrow. That's right, tomorrow was another day. Just like Scarlett O'Hara, but this time with a shiny badge and two trusty guns.

Linda Ladd is the bestselling author of over a dozen novels. *Remember Murder* marks her exciting return to the Claire Morgan series. Linda makes her home in Missouri, where she is at work on her next novel featuring Claire Morgan.

Visit her on the web at www.lindaladd.com.

With Every Turn in the Case . . .

After moving from Los Angeles to Lake of the Ozarks, Missouri, homicide detective Claire Morgan has at last adjusted to the peaceful rhythms of rural life. Until a grisly celebrity murder at an ultra-exclusive "wellness" resort shatters a quiet summer morning . . .

With Every Twist of the Mind . . .

One of Dr. Nicholas Black's high-profile clients, a beautiful young soap opera star, has been found dead, taped to a chair at a fully set table . . . submerged in the lake. Back in L.A., Claire investigated the rich, famous, and the deadly—but she never expected the problems of the privileged to follow her to this sleepy small town. Just as she never imagined crossing the line with her prime suspect . . .

With Every Beat of the Heart . . .

Immersed in the case, Claire finds herself drawn to the charismatic doctor, spending more and more time in his company—and in his bed. Now, to catch a killer, Claire will have to enter the darkest recesses of the human mind. But is Black leading her there to help her . . . or luring her ever deeper into a madman's grip?

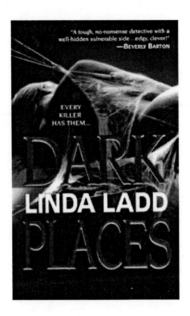

EVERY KILLER HAS THEM...

LINDA LADD

DARK PLACES

Missouri detective Claire Morgan is eager to get back to work after recuperating from injuries sustained on her last job. But the missing persons case that welcomes her home in the dead of winter soon turns more twisted and treacherous than Lake of the Ozarks' icy mountain roads . . .

The man's body is found suspended from a tree overlooking a local school. He is bleeding from the head, still alive—but not for long. Someone wanted Professor Simon Classon to suffer as much as possible before he died, making sure the victim had a perfect view of his colleagues and students on the campus below as he succumbed to the slow-working poison in his veins . . .

Frigid temperatures and punishing snows only make the investigation more difficult. And then the death threats begin—unnerving incidents orchestrated to send Claire a deadly message. Now, as she edges closer to the truth, Claire risks becoming entangled in a maniac's web—and the stuff of her own worst nightmares . . .

Die Young

Hilde Swensen is a beauty pageant queen with a face to die for and a body to kill for. But by the time Detective Claire Morgan finds her in a shower stall—posed like a grotesquely grinning doll— Hilde is anything but pretty. She's the victim of a sick, deranged killer. And she won't be the last . . .

Die Beautiful

Brianna Swenson is the beauty queen's sister—and the girlfriend of Claire's partner, Bud. She tells Claire that Hilde had plenty of enemies, including a creepy stalker, an abusive ex-boyfriend, and a slew of jealous competitors. But what she doesn't say is that they both shared a dark disturbing secret. A secret that refuses to die . . .

Die Smiling

From the after-hours parties of a sinister funeral home to the underworld vendettas of the Miami mob, Claire follows the trail with her lover Nicholas Black, a psychiatrist with secrets of his own. But it's not until she uncovers evidence of unspeakable acts of depravity that Claire realizes she's just become a diabolical killer's next target . . .

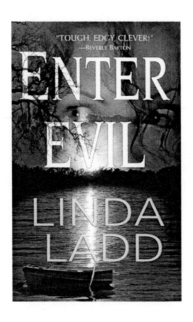

When the Mind . . .

His doctors are the best in the world, his father one of the most
powerful men in the state. But they couldn't stop Mikey from
succumbing to his darkest demons—the ones inside his head.
The ones who told him it was time to end it all.

. . . Plays a Deadly Game . . .

It should have been an open-and-shut case, especially since
detective Claire Morgan's lover, Dr. Nicholas Black, recognized
Mikey as a troubled former patient. Then Claire finds another
body in Mikey's home. Curled inside an oven, charred beyond
recognition, the method of murder mind-boggling . . .

. . . of Murder

Claire's only lead is a beaded bracelet, believed to ward off the
"evil eye," around each victim's wrist. But by the time she
discovers what the dead were afraid of, she's trapped in a mind
game of her own—with a brilliant sadistic killer. And this time,
there's a method to the madness . . .

CPSIA information can be obtained at www.ICGtesting.com
Printed in the USA
LVOW08s1820150114

369567LV00001B/68/P

9 781601 832115